The Spark Girl

Fiona Ford was born in Cornwall and grew up in Bath. As well as having a thirst for books Fiona had a huge interest in history and adored listening to her grandfather talk about his time in the navy during World War Two. Together they spent many a happy afternoon poring over the large collection of photos he had taken travelling the globe, somehow managing to perfectly capture life during wartime. Although Fiona went on to develop a successful career as a journalist, she never forgot her passion for the past. Now, Fiona has combined her love of writing with her love of days gone by in *The Spark Girl*, the first in a series of wartime sagas.

Find out more about Fiona by following her on twitter @fionajourno, or visiting her website www.fionaford.co.uk.

The Spark Girl

FIONA FORD

First published in Great Britain in 2017
by Orion Books,
This paperback edition published in 2017
by Orion Books
an imprint of The Orion Publishing Group Ltd
Carmelite House, 50 Victoria Embankment,
London EC4Y 0DZ

An Hachette UK company

1 3 5 7 9 10 8 6 4 2

A CIP catalogue record for this book is
available from the British Library.

ISBN 978 1 4091 7011 2

Typeset by Input Data Services Ltd, Somerset

Printed and bound in Great Britain by Clays Ltd, St Ives plc

www.orionbooks.co.uk

To Barry and Maureen with love

Acknowledgements

Huge thanks must go to Kate Burke and Diane Banks at Diane Banks Associates for all their help in bringing Kitty to life. Special thanks must also go to Laura Gerrard, my fabulous editor at Orion, whose love and insight into Kitty's story proved invaluable.

I am too young to be an expert on wartime, but would like to thank those at the WRAC Association who answered my questions and helped me understand what life was like for those in the ATS. In particular, Sheila Holley who was patient enough to tell me all about her time as a driver, which I discovered was a time of fear, hard work, fun and friendship in equal measure.

To everyone at the National Archive, Imperial War Museum, ATS Remembered, the Coventry History Centre and the Law Society, a heartfelt thanks to you all for your time in helping me get the detail right.

Camaraderie is at the heart of this book, and to all my wonderful friends and loved ones, thank you for showing me the power and value of true friendship over the years. However, there is one family friend I would particularly like to thank: Diana Barkes. Just as I discovered *The Spark Girl* would be published, Diana found out she had only weeks left to live. Shocked, I did the only thing I could think of and asked if she would allow me to name a character after her in this book. Before she died, she was kind and gracious enough to say yes.

Vibrant, with a wit, generosity of spirit and passion for life that few of us will ever possess, Di was a spark girl in every sense. I would like to express deep thanks to her for inspiring the Di in this book and, Di, I sincerely hope I have done you justice.

Chapter One

April, 1940

The early morning cool air wrapped its chilly breath around Kitty Williams, waking her from a deep fug of sleep. Keen to delay getting up for as long as possible, Kitty fought the chill by cocooning herself in the floral eiderdown. This morning ritual was something Kitty had down to a fine art and she knew without even glancing at the clock by her bedside that there were at least ten minutes before she had to get up for her shift at the car factory.

Lulling herself back into the comfort of sleep, Kitty tried to drown out the noise of her landlady, Mrs Carswell, humming tunelessly in the small kitchen below. Not for the first time, Kitty closed her pale grey eyes and tried to count her blessings. As an orphan without any brothers or sisters, she had struggled to find lodgings when she had left the children's home seven years earlier. Many were put off by her lack of family, or concerned about having a young unwed woman under their roof, but unlike some with rooms for rent, Mrs Carswell had happily welcomed Kitty into her home. Since then Kitty had been grateful to the older woman for taking her in, but there were times, Kitty thought, as she heard the dulcet screech of Mrs C's ear-piercing tones, when she could quite happily live alone. Continuing to clamp her eyelids firmly shut, Kitty was determined to make the most of her time left in bed, and thought about her beloved fiancé, Joe, who was away serving in the Navy.

As she brought his handsome, chiselled face to her mind,

Kitty tried to picture what he would be doing now. Would he be sleeping, eating breakfast with his colleagues or keeping watch, seeing the ship was going where she was meant to go.

Joe's letters, though always filled with longing, were scant on detail. Naturally, he talked about his friends, the terrible food on board his ship, and his occasional bouts of seasickness, but mainly Joe talked about the day war would be over so they could be married. This fight against the Germans was lasting much longer than anyone had expected, and Joe had admitted in his last letter he had been crushed when he realised he wouldn't be back in Coventry in time for New Year.

Kitty smiled at the image of Joe running his hands through his dark hair, scribbling down his thoughts about Navy life. He would know, Kitty thought, how much she needed to see that he still had his spirit. After all, Kitty had known Joe Simmonds since they were nippers when they had clashed heads in the playground. The next day the bruises had been forgotten but a deep friendship had been forged and Kitty knew she and Joe would be together forever. When Joe asked her to marry him last summer, saying yes had felt as natural to her as breathing in and out. He was her soulmate and had been since that childhood accident which had left Joe with a tiny scar on his forehead. Now it had been six months since Joe's conscription and Kitty ached to see his warm smile and feel the weight of his arm around her shoulder as they enjoyed a Saturday night at the pictures. Most of all she just missed him, and it was these precious moments before her alarm went off that allowed her to dream of the day she and Joe would be reunited.

A loud banging coming from the front door cut her daydream short. Lifting her head from the cool pillow and pushing her bobbed light brown hair away from her face, Kitty blinked her eyes open and realised the knocking was becoming more insistent. A quick look at the clock told her it was just after seven. With a sigh, she threw back the bedspread and reached for her thick dressing gown. Pulling open her bedroom door, she heard the sound of Mrs Carswell hurrying along the passage towards the front door, shouting, 'I'm coming, I'm coming.'

As Kitty padded downstairs, she saw it was Hetty, her future mother-in-law, standing on the front step. Quickening her pace, she rushed towards the two women and saw Joe's mother was still in her flannelette nightdress with only a thin green cardigan to keep out the early morning chill. Kitty's heart thudded with fear, as she glanced up at Hetty's face and saw her eyes were red-rimmed and raw, while bags as black as coal hung under her eyes.

Kitty turned to her landlady in the dimly lit hallway, and smiled gratefully as the elderly lady beckoned Joe's mother inside.

'Ta, Mrs C,' Kitty said gently. 'I've got this now.'

'Are you sure, dear? How about I bring you both a cup of tea? You're welcome to use the parlour.' Concern was written across her landlady's face as she opened the door to the room used solely on high days and holidays.

'That'd be lovely, ta, Mrs C,' Kitty said again, as she guided a clearly shaken Hetty towards the small grey settee, dust motes flying through the air.

As Mrs Carswell shuffled out of the room and back along the passage towards the kitchen, Kitty settled herself by Hetty's side and squeezed her arm encouragingly.

'What's happened?' Kitty asked, knees turned towards Hetty's, her head bent low.

'It's, it's . . .' the older woman gasped, struggling to find the words.

Glancing at Hetty, Kitty noticed her hands lay in her lap; knuckles ice-white from clutching a slightly crumpled piece of paper. Looking more closely, Kitty spotted the paper was in fact a telegram, studded with the tell-tale insignia of the War Office and the words, *regret to inform you.*

Kitty's hands flew to her mouth, the reason for Hetty's visit dawning on her. She looked away, her pulse racing as dread coursed through her before she returned her gaze to the telegram and knew her whole world was about to change.

'Joe's dead, isn't he?' Kitty blurted out, her voice shaky.

'Yes,' Hetty sobbed, gripping the telegram more tightly. 'My boy, my beautiful boy is gone.'

'How?' Kitty asked in anguish.

'His troopship was sunk. Those Germans killed my boy.' As Hetty's shoulders rounded with tears, Kitty clasped her freezing cold fingers.

'It's not true,' Kitty said, her voice thick with shock. She felt as though she were watching a film at the pictures. This wasn't her life, it was someone else's. 'Not our Joe, tell me there's been a mistake, Hetty?'

Hetty shook her head in despair, her red-rimmed eyes meeting Kitty's. 'There's no mistake, Kitty, love. I'm sorry.'

As the news sank in, Kitty allowed her head to fall into her lap and she let out a brief tortured wail as she contemplated a future without the man who was her rock. Kitty had never once thought war would drive them apart forever and the thought of never seeing Joe's handsome, smiling face again ripped her to the core.

Kitty had no idea how long she stayed like that, all thoughts of time forgotten as images of Joe throughout the years flooded her mind. They had shared so many memories, had been the centre of one another's worlds, that the idea of a life without Joe was unthinkable. They were meant to be together, everyone said so, what was she supposed to do without him? Kitty had no idea, and the crick in her neck as she remained huddled over her hands told her this wasn't something that could be solved in half an hour.

Gently lifting her face to meet Hetty's gaze, Kitty took a deep breath and shot the older woman a watery smile. She may not have the answers to her own life, but Kitty also knew how much Joe would want her to be strong for his mother and take care of her when she needed it most.

'I'm so sorry, Hetty,' Kitty whispered, reaching for her tea and realising the liquid was now stone cold. Mrs Carswell had padded in silently and, seeing the two women's faces, placed the cups down and retreated. 'I dunno what to say, I only heard

4

from him the other day. He was fine, I don't understand how . . .' Kitty's voice trailed off as the enormity of Hetty's news hit her like a fresh blow once more.

Losing her own parents in a factory fire when she was just eight years old had taught Kitty grief wasn't something you could reason with any more than it was something you could get over. It was something you lived with, but dear God, thought Kitty, had she not seen enough grief in her twenty-one years? How was she supposed to cope with this? As for Hetty, Kitty realised, looking across at Joe's mother still hunched over the telegram, this had to be the worst punishment in the world – for a mother to outlive her son. Joe was her only child and he had been doted on by his family.

Closing her eyes, Kitty cast her mind back to the last time she had seen Joe. Smart and handsome in his Navy uniform, at Coventry train station, about to start his new life in the forces. Before he had left, Kitty had told him she did not want to say goodbye to him like other couples, where the girls wept and clung to their sweethearts. Joe had understood, and been proud as punch when his girl, unlike nearly all the others, had refused to shed a single tear when they had parted. Instead, they had kissed affectionately on the crowded platform, until it was time for him to board and then they had waved each other goodbye, their faces full of smiles and hope.

Leaving the station and walking back to her lodgings, Kitty's stern resolve had failed, and the tears she had stemmed in front of Joe streamed like rivers down her face, soaking the collar of her good coat, once she was safely away from prying eyes.

Now Kitty knew she had to find the same courage again and she sat closer to Hetty on the settee, willing them both to find the strength to cope. They stayed like that for a long time, until Hetty broke the silence with a firmer and stronger tone than the one she had arrived with.

'There's no denying it, lovey, this is a terrible day for us all,' Hetty said, her voice soft and low. 'But I do know our Joe went to fight Hitler and died doing his duty for a country he loved. He was brave and selfless, and we have to try and be the same way as we manage these dark days ahead.'

Kitty nodded, knowing Hetty was right. 'All Joe wanted was for us to have our freedom. He went to war determined, despite the risks, and we've to do the same,' she said, a quiet steel in her voice. 'He won't be forgotten, Hetty. I'll make sure of that.'

'I know he won't, love,' Hetty said in a firm tone. 'I've always felt like a second mother to yer and it's at times like this yer need your family. I want yer to know you'll always be family, Kitty, marriage or no marriage.'

'I feel the same,' Kitty replied fiercely. 'Hitler may have taken Joe, but he won't destroy our love for him. That's what'll give us comfort and the strength to carry on.'

'And work,' Hetty replied, grimly. 'Your job at the car factory making spare parts for all those extra trucks and cars the Army are reliant on will help yer more than yer know, Kitty. And my volunteer work with the Auxiliary Fire Service will help me cope. Joe was the luckiest boy in the world the day he met yer, Kitty Williams. You've more courage in your little finger than half those girls out there. I want yer to stay in touch, Kitty, love. Joe would have wanted that and it'd mean a lot to me as well.'

As Kitty nodded, Hetty managed the hint of a smile, and fumbled in the brown bag behind her on the settee. Pulling out a small package, she pressed it into Kitty's hands. 'Joe wanted yer to have this if summat ever happened to him.'

Kitty looked down at the parcel wrapped in newspaper and pulled at the string. As the fastenings loosened, a sliver of metal glinted in the early morning sunlight and a wristwatch with a stainless steel face fell into her hands. The sight of it brought a lump to Kitty's throat; this was the watch Joe had been given by his parents to mark his twenty-first birthday less than twelve months ago, and he had cherished it. Turning the timepiece over in her hands Kitty realised there was hardly a mark on it. The only trace of damage was a tiny scratch along the side, while the tan leather strap was polished to a high shine. Kitty tucked a stray strand of hair behind her ear and smiled. Typical Joe;

he took such good care of everything and everyone around him that this watch looked as good as new.

'I'll always treasure this,' Kitty said gratefully.

'I know yer will, lovey,' Hetty replied, wearily getting to her feet, already looking a good ten years older than when she had arrived. 'And now I must be off. I've been here long enough, and you've a job to get to. I'll pop round later in the week to talk about the funeral.'

Kitty nodded, still stunned by the news she had just received, and saw it was almost eight. She realised she would be horribly late for work, but that was the least of her worries just now. Seeing Hetty to the door, she hugged her goodbye then hurried upstairs to her room.

Having heard Mrs Carswell go out a few minutes earlier, Kitty knew she had the house to herself so sank onto her bed and fell face down into her pillow. It was only now she could let the tears flow as she wept for the boy who had been her past and her present, but would no longer be her future. She cried for the best friend she could no longer confide in, the boy who always made her pulse race and the fiancé who she had dreamed of finally finding her own happy-ever-after with. She sobbed for the wedding they would never have, the days out at the beach they would never enjoy, the big family Christmases they had dreamed of and finally she broke down for the children and grandchildren they would never have. After Kitty cried herself out, she sat back up on the bed, and looked at the watch she was still clutching. With a sudden shock, she realised it was time to face up to a very different kind of future to the one she had always imagined.

Reaching for the work overalls that lay neatly folded on the wooden chair opposite her bed, Kitty pulled them on and went into the kitchen. Splashing some cold water on her face, she was surprised to bump straight into Mrs Carswell as she turned around.

'I've just been up to the car factory, lovey,' Mrs Carswell explained. 'I've told Mr Phillipson you'll be a little late today.'

'Yer didn't need to do that, Mrs C,' Kitty whispered gratefully. 'I would've had a word with Mr Phillipson when I got in.'

'I wanted to, Kit,' Mrs Carswell told her softly. 'Now, your boss is expecting yer, and the girls'll have a cuppa ready and waiting when yer get there.'

There were sometimes never enough words to express thanks for the little kindnesses people showed, Kitty thought as she squeezed Mrs Carswell's hands appreciatively and made her way to the factory. Arriving at the car plant, Kitty was welcomed by all her workmates, just as her landlady had promised, and together they rallied around, keeping a watchful but distant eye and ensuring there was plenty of tea to help Kitty through the day.

Kitty had expected the day to be nothing short of a nightmare, but it passed quickly. Her work, welding utility truck bonnets and hauling newly made car doors ready for distribution to Army units everywhere, left her physically exhausted, but it helped take her mind away from her grief.

Back home that evening, Kitty was surprised to find a familiar face sitting in the kitchen waiting for her. A tall woman with long blonde hair, pinned in elegant curls, and a smattering of flour across the shoulders of what Kitty knew was her good wool coat, Kitty felt relief thud through her.

'Elsie!' Kitty gasped gratefully, rushing towards her.

'Kit, I'm so sorry, word's been going round the town all day about Joe. I came as soon as I could,' Elsie said softly, getting to her feet and holding her arms wide open for Kitty to fall into. As the two girls embraced, Mrs Carswell set another pot of tea on the table between them and tactfully left them to it.

Breaking apart, Elsie settled Kitty into a chair and poured her a cup then added two sugar lumps, despite the fact it was now rationed.

'For the shock,' Elsie explained, setting the drink down in front of her. Kitty took a sip and grimaced. It was far too sweet for her tastes, but she was too exhausted to complain.

'Has Hetty said anything about the funeral yet?' Elsie asked as she poured herself a cup and settled into the chair opposite.

Kitty shook her head. 'She doesn't know a lot yet. They only got the telegram late last night and it was all she could do to stop herself from coming over straight away. It was George that made her wait until the morning. Said I deserved one more night of peace even if they didn't.'

'Poor Hetty and George. Losing their only child like that, it's a tragedy.' Elsie sighed, as she shook her head in sadness. 'It doesn't seem real, Kit.'

Kitty said nothing, the events of the day beginning to hit her hard. Before war had broken out, she and Elsie had worked together in the town bakery. They would get up at four in the morning ready to start kneading loaves at five, but the gossiping during cigarette breaks more than made up for it. Saturday evenings were spent at Coventry's biggest dance hall, the Crystal, with her beloved Joe, while Elsie and her husband Charlie O'Connor, who was Joe's best friend, made a regular foursome.

Occasionally, Elsie's older brother, Arthur, would join them. He had joined the Navy at the same time as Joe, though they had been stationed with different batteries. Tall, dark and more than a little handsome, with the same olive green eyes and Roman nose as his sister, he had his pick of the girls at home and away but often preferred whirling Kitty and his sister around the dance floor. A fancy mover, with more than a little mischief in his eyes, he would spin them around in a flurry of steps that left them spent, and their sweethearts doubled over with laughter at their shocked and exhausted faces. Kitty smiled at the memory. Life had been so simple then.

'And how are yer managing?' Elsie asked gently, interrupting Kitty's thoughts.

Kitty paused before she spoke. 'I don't think it's properly sunk in yet, Els. I've been going from feeling bereft to angry all day.'

Elsie leaned forward and squeezed Kitty's hands. 'That's natural, lovey. It's going to take a long time to get through this, but me, and the rest of the family, we're here for yer.'

Kitty smiled fondly. Elsie's family had always treated her as one of their own since she had moved into the house next door with her parents, Betty and Sid, when she was just six, and she loved them for it.

'And yer know I'm grateful, but all this . . .' Kitty shrugged her shoulders as she looked helplessly around her before turning to face her friend. 'The truth is, Elsie, I left the bakery to go and work in the factory for Joe. I knew the vehicle factories that were making trucks and cars for our boys were crying out for more help and I got it into me head that welding parts for our boys abroad could help end this war a bit sooner and get my Joe home quicker.'

Elsie smiled wryly at Kitty's confession. 'Well, I didn't think yer left because yer were sick of Eccles cakes! Course yer left to help him, love. There's nothing wrong with that, all of us want to see an end to this war, and we're all doing whatever we can.'

Kitty smiled at Elsie's kindness as she reached into the pocket of her overalls, pulled out the watch Hetty had given her only that morning and set it on the table in front of her friend. Kitty knew she ought to have kept such a treasured keepsake in a safe place, but she had wanted to keep a piece of Joe close to her heart all day long.

'It's gorgeous, Kit,' Elsie exclaimed, turning the timepiece over in her hands and admiring its elegance.

'It was Joe's twenty-first birthday present from his mam and dad last year.' Kitty smiled, watching Elsie admire the watch.

'I remember. They had that little party for him in their front room, didn't they?' Elsie recalled. 'His Auntie Jane was horrified he was being childish, ripping the paper off his presents, because she'd wanted him to save it.'

Kitty pulled a face. 'Like our Joe would be bothered about saving paper! He was a big kid that day. But when he pulled that watch out of the box, he was transformed, Els. There was nothing but joy and gratitude written across his face.'

'He had sworn never to take it off, but then he went into the Navy . . .' Elsie broke off.

Kitty gulped loudly, the emotion of the day suddenly overwhelming her. She reached for the watch where Elsie had left it on the table. As Kitty pressed her nose to it, she breathed in the heady scent of Joe and enjoyed the brief feeling of being transported back to happier times. As she lost herself in the tang of leather, she knew the watch wasn't just a reminder of the childhood sweetheart she had loved and lost. This watch was a reminder to keep fighting until the Jerries were finally defeated. Most importantly, Kitty realised, it was Joe's last message; he wanted her to remember what he stood for and how much he had wanted to join the thousands of other men doing their bit for their country. Kitty set the watch back down. It was time to consider how she could take over where Joe had left off.

Chapter Two

By the time Joe's funeral took place a month later, Kitty felt as though she had been put through an emotional mangle. She was exhausted, her overriding grief for Joe and their lost future together playing over and over in her mind, like a film on a loop. Waking to a suitably rainy morning after a fitful night's sleep, Kitty slipped on her only black dress and examined her reflection in her vanity mirror. She could tell she had lost a lot of weight, even though she had only been a scrap of a thing in the first place. But her face looked as if it had aged a hundred years since losing the love of her life.

Even now there were times when she had to pinch herself that Joe had really gone. After all, there had been no body and, as Kitty lay tossing and turning at night, she would indulge in the possibility that Joe was out there somewhere, lost at sea or in a strange faraway land, trying to find his way back home. But every time Kitty allowed her thoughts to wander in that direction, she had to stop and bring herself firmly back to reality. Joe was gone, nobody on his ship had survived and, as hard as it was to face, Kitty knew she had to accept it.

Since Joe's passing she had taken care to visit Hetty and George each day, calling in on them after work with a simple stew or bottle of stout, just to make sure they were getting something inside them. If she felt overwhelmed with grief, Kitty couldn't begin to imagine how dreadful they were feeling. As their only child, they had worshipped Joe. Kitty knew how scared Hetty had been when Joe was conscripted, but like any mother, she had put a brave face on and told everyone how proud she was. Her performance had been so convincing she had nearly fooled Kitty, but the ghost of a smile she wore like armour whenever Joe's name was mentioned told a different story.

Standing in a packed church beside Hetty and George on the family pew, Kitty saw that wan, ghostly smile appear once more and knew that like Kitty herself, all she would be thinking about was her precious Joe. As the opening bars of 'Jerusalem' sounded, she turned to Hetty, a lump catching in her throat, and saw the older woman's determined gaze towards the front of the church. Kitty knew she had to follow Hetty's lead and opening her mouth, she remembered with a jolt that this was one of the hymns she and Joe had chosen as part of their planned wedding ceremony. The hymn was one they had both adored, and she sang her heart and soul out, wanting Joe to know how much she had loved and cherished him.

The service was mercifully short because there would be no burial. Instead, the vicar invited everyone to say a prayer for the departed. Kneeling onto the hard little cushion, head bent low, Kitty couldn't stop thinking how Joe had been just twenty-one; his life had hardly had time to begin.

'I'll never forget yer, sweetheart,' she whispered as the vicar led the congregation outside into the pouring rain. As well-wishers came to offer their condolences to Hetty and George, Kitty realised she couldn't face any more sympathy today, no matter how well intentioned. Quietly, she slipped off and found Elsie and Arthur, who was on three days' leave from the Navy, sheltering from the rain under a large tree.

'How are yer holding up, love?' Elsie asked through red-rimmed eyes as she saw Kitty approach.

'Bearing up.' Kitty shrugged as she dodged a large raindrop. 'I'll be glad once this wake at Hetty's is over.'

'We all will,' Arthur agreed, brushing a piece of lint off his uniform. 'It's a rotten day, there's no doubt about it, but we'll get through it. Joe wouldn't want us feeling maudlin about it for too long.'

Kitty smiled gratefully at Elsie's brother. He had a way of hitting the nail on the head. She could imagine Joe now, encouraging them all to have a drink to send him on his way, but not to make a performance of his passing. *No showboating*, she could hear him saying.

'You're right.' She laughed quietly. 'He'd say we were going soft if he could see us all now, moping about. He'd tell us he wasn't worth all this fuss.'

'Except he was,' replied Elsie loyally as she stemmed a fresh round of tears with her hanky. 'And yer, Kitty. I've hardly seen yer this past week. I'm worried about yer, it's at times like these yer need your pals.'

Kitty cast her eyes downwards, avoiding Elsie's gaze. As the funeral loomed Joe's loss had become even more real and Kitty did not feel like talking. Instead, she had buried herself in her job and caring for Hetty and George. She opened her mouth ready to explain when Hetty called out to them.

'There y'are, Kit. I wondered where you'd gone.'

'Sorry,' Kitty replied awkwardly. 'I didn't mean to leave yer on your own. I just wanted a quick word with these two,' she finished, gesturing towards the siblings.

'No harm done,' Hetty said, slipping her arm through Kitty's affectionately. 'And anyway, I was glad of an excuse to get away from everyone offering me their condolences for a minute. I know everyone means well,' she smiled guiltily, 'but I felt a bit done-in with it, and I know George can cope. I thought we might walk over to ours together. What d'yer say?'

Kitty nodded as the foursome walked out onto the street towards Hetty's around the corner. As Hetty pushed open the door Kitty saw a spread Joe would have been proud of. Piles of ham and egg sandwiches rested on a large table, while bottles of stout and an urn of tea stood opposite. In the corner Kitty saw a stack of rock and Eccles cakes, which Kitty could tell had been thoughtfully provided by Elsie and the bakery.

'Thanks, love,' Kitty said, squeezing Elsie's hand.

'It was nothing,' Elsie replied quietly.

But Kitty knew it was something. Food had already started being rationed, and she knew Elsie would have had to ask a lot of favours to supply so much food in Joe's honour. The thoughtful yet simple gesture touched Kitty to her core and she hurriedly turned her face from her friend to hide the tears that were threatening to spill down her cheeks. She had no idea what she would do without Elsie, but the past few weeks had taught her she needed to find out.

Summoning up all her courage, Kitty caught Elsie by the elbow.

'Can I have a word?' she asked gently, not waiting for an answer. Guiding her friend out into the passageway, she looked her squarely in the eye. 'I've been doing some thinking.' Kitty gulped.

Elsie eyed her friend with curiosity before she spoke. 'Well that's never a good sign, Kit,' she teased.

'I know what I'm going to do next,' Kitty announced.

'Yer haven't got to do anything, love,' Elsie said gently, as she squeezed Kitty's shoulder.

Kitty shook her head. 'I've got to carry on Joe's fight, Elsie. He wanted to see the back of Hitler once and for all. Now it's my turn to finish what he started. I'm going to join-up meself. I've got an appointment at the recruitment office tomorrow in town.'

'Don't be daft, Kitty. This is just grief talking. You're not serious,' Elsie gasped, visibly shocked.

But Kitty's mouth was set. 'I'm very serious, Els. Me mind's made up. I've thought of nothing else since Joe's passing.'

'But you're doing more than enough, getting cut to ribbons at the vehicle plant, welding bits of Army trucks together,' Elsie pointed out. 'We need people up the factories so our lads have got the equipment they need to keep fighting.'

'It's not enough, Elsie,' Kitty protested. 'I've been reading about how the women's Army needs girls like me who are unmarried and strong to carry out work at home so more of our boys can join-up and fight.'

Kitty met her friend's eyes and instantly knew what Elsie was thinking. That a life in the forces was no picnic, as her husband Charlie was always telling her. He had been called up to serve in the Army shortly after Joe and they had decided to marry before he left rather than wait until he was next on leave.

'Kitty, the Army's hard work,' Elsie insisted, 'and dangerous . . .' Her voice trailing off.

'I know that, Els, but this is important. None of us will ever have a life of our own if Hitler gets his way. Don't yer see?' Kitty implored.

'I do see, Kitty,' Elsie snapped. 'But where's your common sense? Yer might not be fighting on the front lines but if there's a mustard gas attack or worse, who d'yer think Hitler's going to target? Civvies like me or the forces?' she finished before spotting Arthur walking down the passageway towards them. 'Arthur,' she called, beckoning him over. 'Have a word with Kitty, will yer, she's thinking about going in the Army.'

Arthur raised his eyebrows as his sister shoved him forwards towards her friend. 'Tell him, what you've just told me,' she said firmly. 'He'll tell yer how it really is.'

'Er, I'm not sure what I'm meant to be saying to yer, Kit.' Arthur frowned as his sister gave him a firm nudge in the ribs. 'Why are yer thinking of joining-up, like?'

Looking from one sibling to the other, Kitty took a deep breath, before patiently repeating her reasons to Arthur.

'Sounds fair enough to me,' he said, shrugging casually as he turned back to Elsie.

'Have yer gone soft, Arthur Higginson?' she asked, hands on hips. 'It's far too early for Kitty to be thinking about what she wants to do next, never mind joining-up.'

Arthur gave Kitty a sympathetic smile as he addressed his sister. 'I think it's the perfect time for a fresh start. There's nothing to keep her here. Why shouldn't Kitty go off and do more for the war effort in the Army? It's a shame more women don't feel the same way,' he finished.

'Ta, Arthur,' Kitty said gratefully, looking at her friend to gauge her reaction.

Elsie glared at them both reprovingly before finally opening her mouth to speak. 'Yes, ta very much, mouthpiece! Well done, Arthur, if she wasn't set on going before she will be now.'

'Sorry, Elsie, but I'm not going to lie to Kit,' Arthur insisted. 'You're right, the military's hard work and dangerous, but that doesn't mean Kitty shouldn't go. If we all had that attitude, Hitler would have won already.'

Elsie opened and closed her mouth like a goldfish, seemingly struggling with what she wanted to say next. 'Does Hetty know?' she asked eventually, turning back to Kitty.

Kitty shook her head. 'No. I was going to tell her once I'd joined-up,' she admitted.

'And what d'yer think she'll say? She's already lost her son, how d'yer think she'll feel about yer going off to war weeks later?'

'She'll understand,' Kitty reasoned, wrapping her arms around herself protectively.

'Will she?' Elsie said brusquely. 'Because I'm not sure I do.'

'Leave her be, Elsie,' Arthur said. 'Kitty's mind's made up, now let it go.' Turning back to Kitty, he gave her shoulder a quick squeeze. 'I'll walk yer down there tomorrow if yer like? Give yer a bit of support.'

'Yer sure yer don't mind?' Kitty gasped. 'You've only a few hours left before you're off to your next posting, yer don't want to spend it messing about in a recruitment office.'

'I only offered to walk yer down, I'm not joining-up meself,' he teased good-naturedly. 'It's no trouble, I'll call for yer first thing.'

Kitty's mind was reeling. Support could be found in the un-likeliest of places.

'Ta, Arthur, I'd really appreciate that.'

*

The following morning Kitty woke as determined to join-up as she had been the night before. Elsie's reaction had shocked her. She had known her friend wouldn't be pleased, but she had expected her to understand. Kitty had felt so troubled after the funeral that she had taken a sleeping draught as she had not expected to sleep a wink, and therefore she had slumbered straight through the night. After breakfast, true to his word, Arthur called for her and, as she heard Mrs Carswell welcome her friend inside, Kitty stuffed Joe's watch into her pocket for added moral support.

'Morning, soldier,' Arthur called cheerily, as he saw her walking down the stairs. 'Nervous?'

'A bit,' Kitty admitted, as Arthur helped her on with her hat and coat.

'Perfectly natural,' he assured her as he opened the front door and followed her outside.

Together they walked companionably down the road in silence, the sunshine peeping behind the clouds, almost as though the world was encouraging her on, Kitty thought as she looked up at the sky. Despite her nerves, with every step towards the recruitment office Kitty was more and more convinced she was doing the right thing. There was one thing playing on her mind, and turning to Arthur, who was strolling happily beside her, hands in pockets, she couldn't resist asking.

'What's it really like, Arthur?' she ventured. 'Life in the forces, I mean.'

Arthur looked at her curiously. 'Well, as I said yesterday, it's hard work, Kit, but it has its rewards. Yer know you're doing some good with every day yer serve. Yer know you're fighting for freedom and everything else this blessed country of ours stands for.'

'That's what I thought,' Kitty said, nodding. 'I know Elsie thinks it's too soon.'

'She's just worried about yer,' Arthur reasoned. 'She was the same with me when I went. The only difference was that unlike yer, I didn't have a choice.'

'I'm not sure it's a choice for me,' Kitty admitted. 'It feels like summat I have to do. Since Joe died all I've wanted to do is carry on his work, and make something of meself. I don't want him to have given his life for nothing.'

'Yer don't have to explain to me, Kit,' Arthur said, as they reached the small redbrick office at the bottom of the town. 'And that's why you'll make an excellent recruit. Now, knock 'em dead. I'll be waiting here for yer when you're done.'

Walking towards the door, Kitty pulled it open and stepped inside to find a room full of battered filing cabinets and a young woman in a smart khaki uniform behind a small, orderly desk.

Looking around her at the recruitment posters urging women to do their bit for the country, she felt a sense of pride wash over her. Despite Elsie's reservations, she knew she was in the right place and confidently walked towards the young woman.

'I'm here to join-up,' Kitty said, more assertively than she felt.

The woman barely glanced in her direction as she handed her a large form and a black fountain pen. 'Fill this in and hand it back to me when you're done,' she said, gesturing to one of the hard-backed chairs.

Kitty scribbled away as quickly as possible, keen to get on with this next part of her life. Reaching the end, she signed her name, agreeing to serve king and country for the duration of the hostilities, and handed the form to the woman. Sitting back down, Kitty felt pleased to realise that her grief had for a moment been temporarily replaced with hope, and she waited for her name to be called.

Just a few minutes later, a motherly-looking officer wearing a tailored uniform opened a door marked 'Section Leader Gunn'.

'Kathleen Williams,' the woman called, beckoning her into the small corner office. Kitty followed. Clearing her throat, Section Leader Gunn looked through Kitty's application and then trained her eyes on the potential new recruit.

'So, Kathleen, have you left Coventry before?' the woman asked in an accent straight from the Home Counties.

Kitty nodded. 'Yes, to Hunstanton for a day trip to the seaside and I've been to Birmingham once or twice.' Kitty knew she wasn't well-travelled, but did not consider that to be a job requirement.

'You do understand that the demands of the Auxiliary Territorial Services mean you could be posted anywhere for basic training, and that could be far away from Coventry, though not always, of course.'

Kitty nodded once more, showing she understood.

'And you realise you will have to leave your friends and family behind, you may not see them for weeks or even months,' Section Leader Gunn continued.

'I don't have any family, not any more,' Kitty replied sadly.

Section Leader Gunn rested her pen on the scratched wooden desk and put down Kitty's form. 'And is that why you're here?' she asked gently.

Kitty paused. 'It was,' she answered honestly. 'Me fiancé was killed and since then all I've been thinking about is a way to carry on the work he wanted to do. He was so keen to join-up, yer see. And I know that while I still want to do this for Joe, I also want to do it for me 'n'all.'

'Well, then it's my great pleasure to welcome you to the ATS, Kathleen Williams.' Section Leader Gunn beamed, pushing her chair back and getting to her feet. 'You will need to have a medical in the next few days and then if that all goes all right, you will receive call-up papers shortly after. Pay is eleven shillings a week, any questions?'

'No, ma'am,' Kitty replied, astounded it was over so quickly.

'Then I would like to wish you the very best of British,' Section Leader Gunn said, offering her hand to Kitty. Standing up, Kitty shook the smiling officer's hand, then left the office and walked out onto the street to find Arthur waiting for her with a ready smile.

'How did it go?' he said with a warmth to his voice.

'Good, very good in fact,' Kitty said, grinning. 'I've to go for a medical and if I pass that, then I'll be an ATS girl.'

'Piece of cake.' Arthur grinned as they walked back up the road towards the vehicle plant. 'You'll be Volunteer Williams in no time.'

Kitty grinned and hugged herself. She had been unsure what to expect, yet Section Leader Gunn had been very welcoming and forthright, two qualities Kitty always appreciated. All she had to do now was wait.

'So p'raps now you're going to be in the services yourself, I can trouble yer for the odd letter from wherever yer end up so I know how you're getting on,' Arthur said, interrupting her thoughts.

Kitty smiled. The very least she could do was put pen to paper after Arthur had shown her such kindness since Joe's passing.

'I reckon I could do that. Consider me your pen-pal,' Kitty said happily. 'Course, I'll expect the odd one back.'

Arthur gave her a playful nudge in the ribs with his elbow. 'Yer drive a hard bargain, Kitty, but go on then! Pen-pals it is. I'll write yer when I get back.'

'Good to see you're starting as yer mean to go on,' Kitty said affectionately as they reached the factory. 'This is me,' she said, gesturing to the car plant behind her. 'I'd better not dawdle, Mr Phillipson's been ever so good about time off.'

'Understood,' Arthur replied gently as he waved her goodbye. 'Take care of yourself.'

'T'ra, Arthur.' Kitty smiled, mirroring his wave. 'I'll be looking out for your letter.'

*

Just as Arthur had assured her, Kitty passed the medical with flying colours and her call-up papers arrived shortly after, summoning her to report to Leicester's barracks for basic training in just a fortnight's time. Section Leader Gunn had explained to

Kitty that all women in the ATS initially went to a training camp for a month to receive basic instruction in discipline, marching and physical education. But the biggest challenge would be a series of selection tests to determine which trade – cook, storekeeper, driver or orderly – Kitty would be best suited to before being posted elsewhere. Kitty was pleased; she had made her choice and saw no sense in delaying the process. Elsie, to her credit, had been nothing but helpful the moment she saw Kitty had made her mind up. As usual, she had gone out of her way to support her best friend, using any spare money she had to buy her extra chocolate bars to keep Kitty going during her time away.

She had said her goodbyes to Hetty and George who had surprised Kitty with their support. Hetty had understood immediately why Kitty wanted to join-up and had pressed into her hands plenty of writing paper so she had no excuse not to keep in touch. All that was left for Kitty to do was take her belongings over to Elsie's, who had kindly offered to store them for her while she was away.

'Are yer sure your mam and dad don't mind looking after me things?' Kitty asked for the umpteenth time that day.

Elsie rolled her eyes at Kitty's question. 'Don't be daft. With all me brothers gone, they've that much space they don't know what to do with it.' She chuckled, surveying Kitty's boxes, pleased to see there wasn't much. 'There's only Mike, in the front room now Arthur's in the Navy.'

'He seems a nice lad.' Kitty smiled.

Elsie nodded. 'He is. I have to admit I wasn't sure when Mam said we were having a soldier from Brighton billeted with us, but yer have to do what yer can when there's a war on.'

'Too true,' Kitty agreed. 'But he's no bother surely?'

'He's a treasure. And with Charlie gone and our Arthur back at sea, it's nice to have another bloke about the house.'

'Have yer heard much from Arthur since he went back?' Kitty asked as she reached for a box.

'I've had a letter and he seems fine,' Elsie replied. 'But yer know Arthur, he so rarely lets on if summat's troubling him. Just between us, I think Joe's death has knocked him for six. He might have been four years older than him, but they were still the best of pals.'

'I know how that feels,' Kitty admitted.

Elsie smiled sadly and drew her friend in for a hug. They stayed that way for a while until Elsie pulled away and they both wiped the tears from their eyes. 'Now then, I don't want yer missing that train because of me. The Army'll probably court martial me or summat.'

Laughing tearfully, Kitty picked up her battered teal suitcase, carried it down the stairs and said her goodbyes to the landlady who had taken such good care of her.

Thankfully the weather had been kind and it had only taken two trips between them to get all of Kitty's belongings into Elsie's small bedroom. Once everything was neatly stacked in the corner, Kitty realised she had just a few minutes to spare before she had to catch her train.

Sitting down at the Higginsons' oval kitchen table as she had for years, Nora placed a steaming cup of tea in front of her.

'You've time for a few mouthfuls,' Nora said kindly. 'So are yer ready, lovey?'

'As I'll ever be,' Kitty replied as she took a quick sip.

'Don't take on, Kit. I reckon you'll be the best recruit the ATS has ever had,' Elsie said, glancing at her watch again. 'Kit, I don't want to rush yer but I think it's time for yer train. Are yer sure yer don't want us to come with yer?'

Kitty shook her head as she stood up. Checking her watch herself she felt a lurch of fear in the pit of her stomach. It really was time.

'No, ta. I hate goodbyes. I'd just as soon do it here if yer don't mind.'

'Course we don't, yer ninny,' Elsie said, her eyes brimming with tears as she walked around to the other side of the table and squeezed her friend tight.

Standing in the hallway, luggage in one hand, rail ticket in the other, Kitty smiled at the Higginsons' faces for the last time before she opened the front door. Walking quickly, she squared her shoulders, took a deep breath and marched firmly towards the station. It was time to start her new life.

Chapter Three

Kitty stood in front of the vast, grey building in awe as she allowed her eyes to roam over the barracks. The base reminded her of a castle with its Gothic turrets and narrow windows, but the uniformed guards standing authoritatively at the opening gates quickly made her realise a life in the ATS was going to be far from a fairy tale.

As the early evening sun dipped behind the clouds, Kitty drank in her new surroundings. Activity was everywhere with a constant thrum of cars and lorries providing the soundtrack to scores of ATS girls practising fire drills and marches or carrying supplies.

Naturally, Kitty had been unsure what to expect, having never visited an Army barracks before, but since joining-up she had often pictured herself in a khaki uniform and sleeping twenty to a room. The actual barracks, and the work involved, had been unimaginable, but with a sudden jolt, she felt a pang of excitement as she understood she had reached the place where she could honour the love of her life by doing something even greater for the war effort.

Kitty was surrounded by at least fifty other new recruits, who, like her, had been collected from Leicester train station in a large, open-top lorry and whisked back to the barracks. Unlike her, however, most of them appeared to have met on the way up and were chatting to each other, nineteen to the dozen. Steeling herself to make new friends, Kitty was about to open her mouth and introduce herself to the woman next to her when she noticed a smiling woman in uniform had appeared before them.

'Right then, you noisy rabble,' she shouted crisply, making it clear that despite her welcoming face, she was not in the mood to mess about. 'I'm Company Commander Benson and I'm going to divide you into groups.'

Quickly, she reeled off a list and it took Kitty a few minutes to notice Company Commander Benson was only listing surnames. At the sound of her own last name, Kitty picked up her suitcase and nervously smiled at the handful of women she had been asked to join. Wordlessly, they stood together waiting for further instruction from their Section Leader who was scurrying across the yard towards them, brushing crumbs from her khaki jacket.

''Ello, ducks,' she said breathlessly, in a strong Midlands accent as she reached them, tugging her felt cap straight over blonde, curly locks that looked as if they were trying to make a break for it. Kitty liked her immediately, the soft set of her jaw and her crinkly brown eyes making her feel as though this woman was an ally.

'I'm Section Leader Lawton and you'll be under my care for the next four weeks while you're here. I run a tight ship, but I don't believe life should be miserable, especially while you're serving king and country, so I'll encourage yer to enjoy yourselves when you're not on duty. I also know that for most of yer this is the first time you've left home and no doubt you're feeling all at sea, so feel free to come and talk to me if you're feeling down. That said, when you're here, you're here to do a job and I'll expect yer to give it your all. I don't like excuses and I don't take nonsense. If yer give me the run around you'll be for the high jump. D'yer understand, girls?'

Kitty, along with the rest of the new recruits, mumbled a quiet yes, while Section Leader Lawton shook her head.

'Dear, dear, ducks, we don't mumble in the Army,' she chuckled. 'I asked yer all a question, and this time I'd like to hear the answer.'

'Yes!' Kitty and the girls shouted back.

'Much better, ducks,' Section Leader Lawton said, smiling. 'Now if you'll follow me, I'll show yer where you'll be sleeping over the next few weeks.'

As they walked towards the grey building, Section Leader Lawton kept up a running commentary as she gave them a guided tour of the complex.

'This here's the mess where you'll be eating,' she said, gesturing towards a large room on the left, lined with wooden tables and benches. 'Some days are better than others, but Cook does a lovely sausage and mash. Oh, and remember to always take your eating irons with yer, otherwise you'll not get very far.'

'Excuse me,' called a timid voice from the back of the group. 'What are eating irons, Section Leader Lawton?'

'Oh, sorry, ducks,' she said, turning around and stopping so suddenly that Kitty nearly fell on top of her. 'I've been here so long, I forget not everyone knows what I'm on about. Eating irons are knife, fork, spoon and mug. You'll be issued with them at the stores when yer get your uniforms and they'll go with yer wherever you're posted so remember to wash 'em up when you're done with 'em.'

'I'll bet there's a few 'ere who've never washed a pot in their lives,' the girl next to Kitty whispered in a broad West Midlands brogue, a cheeky grin plastered across her freckled face. 'My name's Diana Mills, but everyone calls me Di.'

Kitty smiled as she turned to face the girl beside her. Tall, with an open, honest face, gleaming brown eyes and glossy chestnut hair, she gave off an air of cheeky confidence.

'Kitty Williams,' she replied, briefly shaking Di's hand before Section Leader Lawton turned on her heel and walked them up a flight of stairs, where they passed a large washroom, complete with a long row of washbasins, three toilets and baths.

'Would you look at that bathroom!' one of the recruits gasped. 'Indoor lavvies!'

'We don't say washroom, or even privy in the Army, duck.' Section Leader Lawton chided. 'We call the washroom "ablutions" in the military, if yer please.'

As the girls reached their final destination Section Leader Lawton pushed open a set of double doors then stopped in the middle of a large room filled with twenty narrow single beds. Apart from the steel lockers that stood overhead the room was bare. There were no mirrors, chairs or even blankets, and the small window at the end of the room and stark light bulb overhead gave the room a distinctly bleak air.

'Not exactly the Ritz, is it?' one of the girls loitering near the doors whispered.

'I wouldn't know, duck,' Section Leader Lawton called from the front. 'I've never been, but I do know I've ears like an African elephant so shut your noise and mind what you're saying. Now, how about yer each get yourselves a bed, summat to eat in the canteen and I'll meet yer back here in an hour. Then we'll get yer kitted out in uniforms. See yer later, ducks.'

With that, Section Leader Lawton turned on her heel and marched quickly out of the room, leaving the girls to fight over beds. Kitty, who was no stranger to dorm life, knew the best spot was by the door away from the draught of the single window. She immediately rested her case on the bunk, while everyone else stared helplessly at one another, apart from Di. Quick to spot Kitty going for the bed nearest the door, she took the one opposite.

'You look like you know the ropes.' Di smiled as she hefted her luggage onto the narrow mattress. 'Blimey, you felt these? No wonder they call 'em biscuits, they're 'alf bloomin' baked.'

Kitty smiled at the sight of Di trying to bounce up and down on the bed.

'They don't look comfy, I'll give yer that,' replied Kitty, gingerly sitting on the end and grimacing at the hardness of the thin mattress.

'It's a bally disgrace,' said a voice from the bed next to Kitty. 'How do they expect us to sleep on these?'

Kitty and Di exchanged a smirk as they looked at the girl whose name they had not yet learned, shaking her head in disgust at the thin mattresses on the iron frame.

'I've a jolly good mind to have a word with Chief Controller Gwynne-Vaughan.'

'Oh yes?' Di laughed. 'Know 'er personally, do you?'

'Not me,' the girl said, fishing into her suitcase and pulling out an expensive-looking pair of red pyjamas. 'But Daddy does. Only trouble is Daddy and I aren't talking at the moment so it could prove tricky.'

'That does sound difficult.' Kitty smiled, the devil in her deliberately putting on a fancy voice to tease the posh girl. 'Perhaps your grandfather could help? Or an uncle? I mean you're right, it's an awful bally shame you're stuck in one of those.'

Di rocked with silent laughter at the sight of Kitty, head on one side cocked in faux earnestness.

'It *is* a bally shame,' the girl exclaimed. 'And that's not a bad idea! Uncle Percival does know the Chief Controller too. But then, Uncle P is Daddy's brother so he's probably in cahoots with Daddy over all this blasted business as well.'

The girl sat on the bed, the cogs clearly turning, while Kitty couldn't hold back any longer and roared with laughter. The day had taken its toll and Kitty thought she had gone through just about every emotion possible.

'Are you bally well laughing at me?' the girl asked, hands on hips. 'Because you've no bally right! Don't you know who I am? I'm Mary Holmes-Fotherington. How dare you?'

Kitty glanced up at the girl towering above her. With her curvaceous frame, raven hair, striking green eyes and delicate features, she was clearly a beauty. And now a rather cross one, Kitty realised as she sat up and controlled her laughter. Despite this girl's rather privileged position, Kitty had no desire to make enemies so early on in her new life or upset anyone, come to that.

'I'm sorry,' she said, regaining control of herself. 'I didn't mean to make yer feel bad.' It was true, Kitty realised. Everyone, rich or poor, was struggling to make sense of their new surroundings and it was unfair to laugh at the poor girl.

Mary peered down at Kitty and fixed her with a piercing

stare, before her face broke into a huge grin. 'Only joking!' she exclaimed, swatting Kitty's arm. 'Honestly, your face. I've got three sisters and your leg-pulling is nothing compared to the swine of a time we give one another.'

Sitting back down on her mattress, she leaned towards Kitty conspiratorially. 'So what's your story?' she asked.

'I don't have a story. I wanted to do more for the war,' Kitty explained, realising that her jaw was clenched as she was unable to bring herself to talk about Joe on her first day.

'Tosh! Everyone's got a story,' laughed Mary as she wagged her finger in Kitty's direction and turned to Di. 'And what about you?'

Di, who had by now managed to unpack the entire contents of her suitcase into the locker above her, looked at Mary in amusement.

'I was a Canary Girl in Birmingham till last week. Realised I were taking me life in me 'ands every week packing ammunition so thought I'd get away from 'ome and take me life in me 'ands doing me bit for the country instead.'

Kitty glanced across at Di who was now lolling on her bed, hands tucked casually behind her head. She appeared so relaxed, almost too relaxed, Kitty thought. She had always been able to read people and she had the strongest feeling Di was keeping her cards close to her chest.

Keen to take the glare away from Di, Kitty turned her attention back to Mary. 'So what's your story, Mary?' she asked as she began to unpack her suitcase.

'Oh gosh!' she squealed. 'It's the most frightful gas. Daddy and I had a huge row, so to get back at him, I joined-up.'

'Is that the only reason you're 'ere?' Di asked incredulously, a look of disgust flashing in her large brown eyes.

'Yes, well no, not the whole reason.' Mary sighed. 'Daddy wanted to send me to finishing school in Switzerland, and I thought it the most horrific waste of time, what with there being a war on and all. I said to Daddy that I thought it would be more useful for me to join the services than learn how to walk

properly with a silly old pile of books on my head in the moun-
tains,' she continued, warming to her theme. 'Well, of course,
Daddy went wild. Told me no girl of his would be joining the
forces, and I'd be off to Geneva forthwith. Of course that did it
for me. Nobody tells me what to do, so the next day I went to my
local recruitment office in Chester and joined-up. Daddy went
puce with rage. Threatened to cut off my allowance and all my
trusts but I told him, Daddy, your trust fund isn't going to win
the war against Mr Hitler, and my allowance won't be one bally
bit of good if we're all speaking German in a couple of years.
So I left.'

'Blimey,' marvelled Kitty. 'So where does your father think yer
are?'

'Oh, he knows I'm here. Tried everything to talk me out of
it and even locked me in my room to stop me leaving, but of
course I shimmied down the wall and took off with Driver
before he could do a thing. And here I am.' Clearly exhausted by
her tale, Mary flung herself back on the uncomfortable mattress
and sighed. 'What about you girls? Who are you running from?'

'Nobody,' Di snapped. 'Some of us are 'ere because we want
to be, eh, Kitty?'

'Yes,' agreed Kitty, trying to sound confident. 'And now I
think I want to be in the canteen, because me stomach thinks me
throat's been cut. What d'yer say, girls?'

Nodding their approval, the trio walked to the mess, and
found the place filled with girls in khaki, chattering away about
their days and feasting on minced beef and onion pie. Kitty's
stomach rumbled in anticipation. She had tucked into one of
Elsie's emergency chocolate bars on the train, but it felt like a
lifetime since she had eaten anything proper. Reaching for a tray,
the girls joined the back of the queue before realising that as they
were still to collect their eating irons, the only thing they would
be able to eat were meat paste sandwiches on cardboard-like
grey bread. Disappointed, they ate quickly and returned to their
dorm just in time to meet Section Leader Lawton who marched
them to the stores to collect their uniforms, eating irons, gas

masks along with regulation brushes for hair, clothes, shoe and button.

Once they had been measured, Kitty was pleased to discover that despite her rather rapid weight loss, she was a standard size so would be able to receive everything on the uniform list, unlike some of her colleagues. Those who were too tall, too small or too large were unable to get a full set of clothes and had to wait for items to be specially made. Unsurprisingly, this caused an outcry among some of the new recruits who had not brought enough of their own clothes to last. Once the stores had been exhausted, Section Leader Lawton marched them back across the barracks towards another tin hut where a team of seasoned ATS girls checked each one of the new recruits for head-lice before sending them next door to the medical officer for TB and typhoid jabs.

After their arms were rubbed with iodine and the girls were given a series of pricks with an eye-wateringly large blunt needle, Di, Mary and Kitty returned to their dorm worn out and ready for bed. Already the room was full of hustle and bustle with girls getting changed into winceyette nightgowns or pyjamas, one of the few things that had not been supplied by the Army. The air was alive with nervous anticipation as everyone got ready for bed, all the while babbling about the events of the day.

Di clambered into her bed and thumped her pillow. 'This isn't a bloomin' pillow! It's a sack of spuds!'

'I think a bag of potatoes would be more comfortable,' Mary quipped as she climbed under her army issue blanket and turned to the girl in the bed next to her who was quietly weeping. 'Well, there's no need to cry about it. We're all in the same bally uncomfortable boat,' she said, not altogether unkindly.

'Leave her alone,' Kitty said, eyeing Mary's neighbour with concern. Kitty had not yet had a chance to talk to the girl, but had seen the look of fear she had worn all day. Walking towards her bed, Kitty sat down next to her and pulled a packet of mints from her pocket.

'Fancy one?' Kitty asked, holding the packet in front of the girl's face. With tears pouring down her face, the girl barely glanced at Kitty as she shook her head. Kitty tried again. 'It's hard being away from home, isn't it? The first night's always rough. I'm Kitty, by the way.'

The girl stopped dabbing her eyes with the sodden hanky she was clutching in her hands and turned to face Kitty.

'Peggy,' she whispered. 'And I just want me mum.'

Kitty smiled gently at the girl, who looked as if she was barely out of her teens. Plump and with long, lank, red hair, grey skin and matching eyes, Peggy appeared to be frightened of her own shadow. It was a look Kitty had seen many times before on the faces of the children arriving at the care home. In fact, Kitty had felt that way herself when she spent her first few nights in the home, weeping for her parents. Eventually, Kitty had learnt how to cope and as the months passed and she grew more confident she welcomed the new children to the home as if she were their big sister. Something, Kitty had a feeling, Peggy needed more than anything at this moment.

'First time away then?' she coaxed.

'Never left me mum before,' Peggy replied quietly in her West Country burr. 'Me and me mate Bess thought it'd be a giggle when we joined-up in Bristol. Now it don't seem like such an adventure, 'ere on me own.'

'The two of yer were hoping you'd be kept together then like?' Kitty asked softly.

Peggy sniffed and nodded as more tears welled. 'Bess was the one what led me to the office. We've been friends since we was kiddies so when she said we should do our bit for the war I agreed. But look at them girls,' she said gesturing to the other women in the bunks ready for bed. 'I'm not strong like them.'

As Peggy's frame wracked with a fresh round of sobs, Kitty put her arm around the girl. 'Come on, lovey, there's no need for all this blarting,' she soothed. 'Nobody knows anyone and we're all out of sorts. The beds are rotten, we dunno what we've let ourselves in for, and I expect most of us want to go home. But we're here to muck in together.'

Peggy stopped sniffing and looked at Kitty earnestly. 'D'you reckon?'

Kitty nodded. 'I do. Now, have a mint, get yourself settled in bed and tomorrow everything will seem brighter.'

'Thanks,' Peggy replied, a ghost of a smile playing on her lips as she gratefully took the sweet Kitty offered. As Kitty walked back to her own bed, she caught Di's eye.

'You were very patient with 'er,' Di said, propping herself up on one elbow.

'Not really. I was in a care home for years, it's hard on everyone away from home for the first time.' Kitty shrugged as she threw back her blanket and got into her own bed.

Di's eyes widened in astonishment as she sat bolt upright. 'You never were. You poor love. Why didn't you say?'

'Because I don't want pity,' Kitty said matter-of-factly.

'Whoops, sorry.' Di gasped in embarrassment. 'I shouldn't 'ave stuck me oar in.'

Kitty sighed. She had expected to have to tell her life story when she joined-up, but hoped she would be safe from revealing her heartache during their first night.

'It's fine. Me parents died in a fire when I was eight. I was an only child, no relatives, so I was put in a home until I left school at fourteen and got a job.'

'Golly.' Mary whistled, all ears along with Di. 'How frightful. Were you beaten? Sent up a chimney?'

Kitty shook her head and laughed. 'No, Mary, that's the workhouse. I wasn't Oliver Twist.'

'So what was it like?' Mary persisted.

Kitty was about to open her mouth and beg for mercy, when a loud horn sounded, breaking the relaxed chatter.

'What on earth was that?' Mary gasped in shock, clutching the blankets to her chest.

'Lights out, I think,' Di said, as the bright white light of the bulb abruptly vanished to be replaced by the inky black of the night.

'Night, girls.' Kitty smiled, grateful to be let off the hook.

As softly whispered goodnights gave way to the echo of gentle snores, Kitty lay awake urging sleep to find her, but it was no good. Finally alone with her thoughts for the first time that day, all she could think about was Joe. Whatever would he make of her being in the Army, tossing and turning in the dead of night?

A flash of grief sent a tear rolling down her cheek as she realised her life was moving on without him. He would never see this Army barracks or her uniform or these girls. In fact, they had never even talked about the possibility of her joining-up. She was leaving him behind for an unknown future and the thought terrified her. She had never once imagined a life without Joe in it, even when she was in the children's home, grieving for her lost mum and dad, Joe had been there to help. Now she had to find a new way, and, as the tears silently streamed down her cheeks, her earlier courage started to fail. Could she really cope without him?

Chapter Four

The following morning, the trainees were up by six and stumbling towards the ablutions to ready themselves for breakfast. At some point during the night, Kitty had eventually got to sleep, and, although her pillow was still wet from her tears, she woke feeling pleased at the chance of a fresh start.

As the girls made their way to the canteen for breakfast in the murky half-light of early morning, Kitty encouraged Peggy to join them as they queued for porridge and mugs of tea. Eagerly, the girl agreed, and Kitty was relieved to see her looking a little brighter following her night's sleep.

The only one who looked worse for wear was Mary. With a face like thunder, she complained bitterly to the others, letting them know just how badly she had slept as they sat down to eat.

'I'm writing to Uncle P today,' she growled. 'It's a bally travesty expecting soldiers to sleep on straw mattresses like that, I didn't get a wink.'

'Oh dear,' Peggy sympathised, 'poor you, Mary.'

'Yes, poor old Mary.' Kitty grinned, winking at the other two. 'With all that snoring yer were doing, I'd have thought you'd have managed the odd catnap.'

Mary had the good grace to flush red. 'Well, maybe forty winks,' she admitted.

'Maybe,' Di teased, standing up to wash her eating irons. 'Come on, we've square bashing to get to.'

Peggy looked up at her in confusion. 'What's square bashing when it's at 'ome?'

'Oh, Peggy, it's drill practice!' Mary said in an exasperated tone. 'You know, lots of marching in rotten weather that will probably take most of the day thanks to most of this lot unable to work out their left from their right.'

Getting to her feet, Kitty hid a smirk. She was someone who always struggled with her right and left and she had a feeling that was something she would need to master if she was to get to grips with endless parades.

'It's a shame Section Leader Ducks' not training us,' Di remarked casually.

The other three looked at her quizzically as Di explained. 'You know, Section Leader Lawton, always calling us "duck".'

With that, Di took off their senior officer perfectly, even mimicking her brushing crumbs from her jacket while the girls roared with laughter.

'Yer should be on the stage, Di,' Kitty chuckled, her eyes moist from laughing so hard.

'Section Leader Ducks! You are a card, Di,' Mary exclaimed, slapping the table hard. None of them saw the older woman approaching.

'And yer were all warned I've ears like an African elephant,' Section Leader Lawton snapped as she stood just inches from Di's shoulder.

At the sight of Section Leader Lawton, the colour drained from Di's face.

'I'm sorry, Section Leader Ducks, sorry Lawton, Section Leader Lawton. I didn't mean to offend you,' Di rushed, as she looked at the stern glare fixed across the senior officer's face.

'At ease, Volunteer,' the Section Leader said eventually. 'I'll let it go just this once. But, be warned – if I catch yer taking the mickey out of me like that again you'll be for the high jump, d'yer understand?'

Di nodded furiously. 'It won't 'appen again.'

'It had better not,' Lawton replied. 'But one final thing,

Volunteer, I think Section Leader Duck trips off the tongue a bit easier than Section Leader Ducks, if you're still thinking of giving me a nickname like.' Eyes twinkling, Section Leader Lawton saluted the girls and then left the canteen, relief clearly visible on Kitty, Di, Mary and Peggy's faces.

Drill practice was as awful as Kitty expected, but at least she wasn't the only one struggling to keep up. They spent hours with Company Commander Benson in the warm sunshine, coming to attention, standing at ease and learning to march in step before finally being rewarded with a lunch of mutton stew and a stodgy lump that was supposed to be treacle pudding.

After so much physical exercise, many of the girls were exhausted later that afternoon but there was still plenty to do. With buttons to shine, dorm windows to wash and shoes to polish, Kitty was beginning to realise a life in the Army was a never-ending slog. As she concentrated on getting the buttons of her uniform to glow as brightly as the sun, Section Leader Duck poked her head around the door.

'One final training session today, girls,' she beamed, regarding them all with a friendly twinkle. 'Get yourselves to the gym, quick as a flash, please, and don't forget the gas masks.'

The rain started to fall softly as the recruits piled in behind the older woman and followed her across the concourse. The summer sunshine of earlier was long gone, instead replaced by a dank dreariness that made them shiver. Looking upwards at the sky, Kitty sighed. What did the weather matter when there was so much to be done?

As the girls trooped into the gym, gas masks in hand, they noticed the room was bare apart from wooden benches lining the walls, while all the blackout curtains had been secured. The sound of high-pitched chatter rang across the room as nervous recruits tried to work out why they had been called into the gym.

'Whatever do you think this is all about?' Mary asked, her plummy accent grating against Kitty's ear.

'No idea.' Kitty shrugged. 'I'm sure we'll find out when the powers that be want us to know what's what.'

Sure enough, Company Commander Benson soon entered the room and walked briskly to the centre, clapped her hands and called for everyone's immediate attention.

'Girls, you've had something of a brief introduction to a life in the Army, but it's time for you to understand the very real dangers Hitler brings,' she said, pausing to look around the room. 'I know that most of you have joined-up because you wanted to do more to help end this war, but what you may not realise is that being a member of the armed forces does carry its own risks. We understand the Jerries plan to win this war against us using lethal doses of gas, so it is vitally important you carry your gas mask around with you at all times. Do I make myself clear?'

'Yes, ma'am,' the trainees replied in unison as their superior looked on approvingly.

Clearing her throat, she looked again at the assembled recruits gathered before her and continued. 'You might well be saying yes now, but I want you to understand how dangerous this can be. That's why you're all going to experience just how frightening a gas attack is when you don't have a mask.'

There was a sharp intake of breath as the recruits panicked, realising what the Company Commander was asking them to do. Gas attacks were feared across the country, and for good reason. Although exposure to the poison could cause breathing problems, nausea and blistered skin, there was also a very real possibility of death. Now the recruits were being asked to subject themselves to the poison without protection. Kitty looked around her and saw girls weeping and crying for their mothers with one even screeching about how she was going to die. She turned to her left and spotted Mary's pale face cast downwards, clearly lost for words. Kitty felt a chill before a very real prickle of fear ran down her spine. Were they going to die? Would her efforts to continue Joe's work end right here in this room?

'That's enough, girls,' Section Leader Duck urged them, clapping her hands. 'There's no sense getting hysterical, it'll be over in minutes and nothing's going to happen to yer. Our boys on the front line face worse dangers than this so let's get on with it, shall we?'

The kindly words of the older officer had a calming effect on the girls and on her instruction they formed an orderly line. But as they were led one by one down a set of wooden stairs towards the enclosed room, Kitty noticed how some of the girls' earlier resolve failed at the last minute, with many begging for mercy, much to the disgust of Company Commander Benson.

'Any more nonsense and you'll be placed in the chamber for twenty seconds, not ten,' she roared impatiently. 'Now, gas masks on so you can remove them quickly.'

Nervously, Kitty checked her mask and followed Section Leader Duck down the stairs to the chamber below the gym and stood rigid with terror waiting for her turn. Kitty was sure she couldn't have been there longer than thirty seconds but it felt like an eternity as she watched the recruit before her step timidly into the chamber under the watchful eye of Section Leader Duck. As the door was shut, Kitty heard the ear-piercing sounds of wails and screams as the recruit cried out for help. Kitty gasped in horror – the girl sounded as if she was at death's door. She looked at Section Leader Duck for reassurance. Were they really just going to leave her there? As the senior officer ignored Kitty's gaze, she realised that leaving them in there to suffer, fully expecting to die, was precisely what they were going to do. As the screams continued, Kitty's heart went out to the terrified girl, when seconds later the door reopened and the girl emerged, gasping for breath, and fell onto Section Leader Duck.

'Can't breathe . . . feel sick . . .' she wept as Section Leader Duck calmly patted her back.

'There, there, ducks. It's all over now, yer can stop your carry-on,' she soothed, as she disentangled the girl's arms from around her neck and led her to a nearby chair to catch her breath. 'And you've lived to tell the tale, haven't yer?'

Miserably, the girl nodded before she was sick all over her shoes. As Section Leader Duck managed to get out of the way just in time, she gestured to Kitty that it was her turn. 'Off yer go, Williams,' she grimaced as she looked at the girl's lunch all over the floor. 'Sooner yer get on with it, the sooner it's over.'

'Yes, ma'am,' Kitty replied quietly as she tried to still her quaking nerves and calmly face what was coming to her. As she entered the small, windowless room no bigger than the Higginsons' pantry, Kitty heard the door slam shut. A sharp rap at the door told her it was time to remove her mask and accept her fate. Lifting the respirator from her face, Kitty did her best not to breathe in so she could minimise the effect of the gas, but the bittersweet smell of almonds was making her dizzy and sick. Her throat felt tight, as if it was closing in on itself, and she knew she couldn't breathe even if she wanted to.

Holding onto the wall for support, she closed her eyes and prayed the door would reopen, but no matter how hard she tried she couldn't make out any sounds from outside. As the smell of almonds became overpowering, Kitty's mind became foggy and her thoughts distorted as she tried to remain calm. It was impossible to breathe so Kitty told herself this wasn't forever, just a few seconds, it was just part of the training, but the more she tried to soothe herself the more terrified she felt. She lifted her eyelids, glanced across at the door and realised she could stand it no more. Opening her mouth to scream for help, Kitty realised with fresh horror that her throat had become so tight it was impossible for her to make a sound. Now her skin was starting to feel as if it was on fire and she scratched frantically at the thick Army jacket, wanting nothing more than to rip it from her body and tear her scorched flesh from her limbs. Kitty was sure she had been stuck in here longer than the other recruit and had the chilling feeling Section Leader Duck had forgotten all about her. As panic rose, Kitty realised with a sudden jolt that this really was it. This room was no longer part of a training exercise: it was her coffin and as she fought for any remaining embers of oxygen, she wondered if Joe had known during his final moments that he too was dying. Had he been as scared as she was now or had he simply drowned peacefully, unaware he would never reclaim his life and live out the future he had planned? As she sank to the floor, too weak to stand, time lost all meaning. Kitty felt a sense of peace descend on her as she accepted what she now knew was inevitable.

The sound of a door handle opening roused her. Opening her eyes, she saw Section Leader Duck standing at the door, surrounded by a beacon of light. Is this heaven? Kitty wondered. Run by Section Leader Duck?

'Come on, stop pratting about, Williams, and get to your feet, you're finished,' Section Leader Duck called, hands outstretched, as she helped Kitty up from the floor and out of the room. She breathed in deeply, trying to still the feelings of nausea as she sank into the nearby chair.

'Well then,' Section Leader Duck smiled, as she brushed the hair from Kitty's clammy forehead, 'that wasn't so bad, was it?'

*

Later that night, many of the girls were still shaken from their adventures with their gas masks. Several continued to weep for their mothers, while some were still battling nausea and breathing problems.

After supper, Kitty could bear it no longer and took herself back to her dorm to lie on her bed and scribble a quick note to Arthur and let him know how she was feeling.

15 June 1940

Dear Arthur,

Well here I am, I promised to write to you didn't I? So you can see I'm a woman what keeps my word like. Things are going well so far, it's been a big change for me, life in the Army but on the whole I think I like it. Course it helps, I think, I'm used to sharing dorms with other girls. Some of them, in here, well they haven't stopped crying for their mothers since they arrived. I can't imagine you know much

about that. I expect most of the lads you share with are all
tough as old boots. But for some of these girls it's different.
I've tried to get them to calm down, and remind them why
we're here, but it's not easy.

    Still, there's one girl I've taken under my wing, Peggy,
and she's stopped her tears now and we have a bit of a
laugh. She's a nice girl, good for a natter as is Di. Now, she's
straight talking and reminds me a bit of our Elsie. I like her
a lot and I hope we'll be good mates while I'm here, but
who knows. Everything with Joe has taught me life doesn't
always work out how you think. Then of course there's
Mary. Oh she's a card Arthur, she really is. I dunno what
you'd make of her! Straight out of some fancy posh mansion
with a butler, driver and whatever else. She'd never talk to
me in the real world, but in here, she's full of laughter and
fun. I quite like her, though I never imagined I'd ever meet,
let alone get on with someone like that. That's war for you
though isn't it? Turns your world upside down, or is that just
me? I hope you're all right Arthur. I know you're busy, but
it'd be lovely to hear from you if you've the time.

    Yours fondly,
    Kitty

*

The following day, at lunch, Section Leader Duck said that to
take the sting out of what they had been through, they all could
take the afternoon off. Kitty, along with Mary, Di and Peggy,
decided to walk the mile into the city to get to know the area.
However, driving rain forced them to seek shelter in the nearest tea room. Packed with WAAFs, they had managed to find a
table in the corner and ordered crumpets and gallons of hot tea.
It might be early summer, Kitty thought, but her fingers were
as cold as ice and she wrapped her hands gratefully around the
cup, taking her first sip. Looking across at Mary, who was busy

talking at Di about the letter she was intending to write to her uncle about the beds and now the gas mask training, she had a chance to observe her new friends properly. Mary's face was becoming more animated by the second while Di, Kitty noticed, looked worn out, the sound of Mary's voice going right through her. As for Peg, Kitty thought, she was hanging on the posh girl's every word, clearly believing that at any moment, Mary would arrange for the trainees to be sleeping on four-poster beds with chocolates on the pillow. Kitty opened her mouth, about to change the subject, when Di suddenly sprang into life.

'That's enough,' she snapped, banging the table with such force the teacups rattled against the saucers. 'It's wonderful you're writing to your uncle, but can you stop going on about it, and filling poor Peggy's 'ead with daft ideas. This is the Army, dear, things aren't meant to be nice. Yesterday in the gas chamber should've taught you that. We're at flippin' war!'

'I was only saying,' Mary protested, grumpily folding her arms. 'There's no need to be rude, Di.'

'No, but there's a need to tell you what's what,' Di pointed out, reaching for her tea.

Kitty glanced at Peggy. The poor girl was clearly affected by the row, as her eyes brimmed with tears.

'Come on, belt up, the pair of yer,' Kitty said firmly.

'And what would you bally well know?' Mary snorted, looking at Kitty. 'Nobody tells me when to shut up, and certainly not you.'

Kitty rested her teacup against the saucer and fixed Mary with a steely glare.

'What I know, Mary, is life's too short for rows and falling out,' she said. 'I'll tell yer summat else, 'n'all. Life in the Army without any mates could be long and lonely. Now I know that out in the real world like, me and Di 'ere wouldn't be good enough to lick your boots, but we're not in the real world, Mary, we're in the Army, so stop your whining, and start getting on with it. Otherwise, no matter who your uncle is, you're not going to be very popular.'

Mary looked at Kitty in astonishment. Nobody had ever spoken to her like that before, and certainly not someone like Kitty. She opened her mouth to reply but the sight of Kitty's eyes, narrowed in fury, told Mary that Kitty was a force to be reckoned with.

'Fine. I'm only trying to help,' she said, biting into a crumpet, sending crumbs flying everywhere. 'So what trades are you girls hoping for after we've finished basic training? I want to be a spark girl.'

'Spark girl?' Peggy asked. 'Whassat then?'

Mary looked at her as if she was dense. 'A driver, Peggy! Goodness, don't you know anything? It's the best job in the ATS, and I want it. You get your own uniform, the chance to travel, and we've got selection tests this week, haven't we?'

'I think so,' Di agreed, keen to follow Mary's lead and change the subject. 'As a factory girl, I imagine they'll put me in the stores or summat, I can't imagine I'll be good enough to be a spark girl, I've never driven a car in me life.'

'Me neither,' Kitty admitted. 'Why did yer join-up, Di?'

'I wanted to do me bit,' she said, shrugging.

'Did your parents mind?' Kitty tried again.

Di fiddled with a button on her coat. 'Not really. We're not exactly close.'

Kitty regarded her carefully. There was something Di wasn't telling her, but she respected her privacy. Instead she turned her attention to Peggy who had quietly worked her way through a crumpet and was now helping herself to another.

'Have yer got much in mind yourself, Peg?'

'I'm not too bothered really, Kit. I was a cleaner up me mum's shop back in Bristol, so maybe I'll end up in the stores or as an orderly. Sounds like you've gotta be really posh to be a spark girl.'

'Well, it helps,' replied Mary loftily as she poured fresh tea into everyone's cups. 'And you, Kitty?'

'Well, I've worked in a car factory and a bakery, so heaven knows. I like the idea of being a spark girl, but I don't drive. I just hope they don't put me in a kitchen.' Kitty made a face. 'All I did in the factory was bake bread, and at home, it was a running joke I burned water.'

'Not a natural in the kitchen then?' Di chuckled.

'Yer could say that. My landlady tried to teach me how to boil eggs, but I couldn't even manage that.' Kitty grinned ruefully.

'Oh, but eggs are easy. Couple of minutes in boiling water and they're done,' Mary replied. Kitty and Di looked at each other in amazement.

'How d'you know that?' Di sniffed. 'Thought you'd 'ave had a maid to do summat as basic as that.'

'Oh you'd be amazed,' Mary said, eyes twinkling. 'Our cook taught me. She also taught me how to make a lovely coq au vin.'

'Well I didn't think she'd have taught yer how to make anything normal!' Kitty whistled in disbelief.

'You're a dark 'orse all right.' Di grinned, raising her cup and joining in the salute. Only Peggy left her cup resting on the saucer.

'You all right?' Di asked the younger girl, who was looking at the tablecloth in earnest.

'Yes,' she whispered. 'It's just me mum always made eggs for me tea on Saturday and I've still not got used to going without.'

Mary raised her eyes to the ceiling in exasperation as Kitty shot her a warning glance. 'No, yer won't have eggs on Saturday,' Kitty reasoned. 'But yer might have summat better, did yer think of that?'

Peggy lifted her face from the table and looked at Kitty carefully. 'No I didn't,' she replied as tears filled her eyes. 'But what's better than eggs?'

Kitty winked at Di as she turned to Peggy. 'What's better than eggs? Good grief, lovey, I can see we've our work cut out showing yer what's what.'

*

The following Saturday was the girls' first night off since they had arrived two weeks earlier. Kitty was determined to keep her promise to Peg and show her that life without her mother could be a life worth living. After a supper of Welsh rarebit, Kitty and her three friends walked through the parkland towards the officers' mess.

'Whatever are we doing 'ere?' Peggy asked nervously. 'We're not allowed in 'ere.'

Di shook her head. 'Give over, Peg. We're not alone – look.'

As Di pushed the heavy wooden door open, they were greeted by a rousing chorus of 'The Blackout Stroll'. Walking inside, Kitty could see about fifty recruits singing their hearts out around a stand-up piano, their faces all a picture of joy as they threw themselves into the song.

'What is this?' Peggy hissed.

'Music night,' smiled Kitty. 'Thought we'd ease yer in gently like.'

'Yes, I was all for a night of dancing on our first night off, but Kitty here insisted that might be a bit much for you,' Mary chuckled.

As the song came to a close, the girls walked deeper into the throng and Kitty couldn't help but notice the air was alive with excitement as girls prepared to let their hair down for the first time in weeks.

'Come then, ladies, what next?' a male voice boomed. Kitty recognised it as the chaplin's.

'How about a bit of "They Can't Ration Love"?' one girl suggested to a chorus of groans.

'No, what about "We're Going to Hang out the Washing on the Siegfried Line"?' suggested another.

'No, no, no,' Mary said loudly, clapping her hands to get attention as she pushed her way through the crowd towards the chaplin. 'Let's have "Run Rabbit Run", come on, Vicar, you do know the music, don't you?'

The young vicar looked stunned as Mary reached over him to flick through his sheet music and found the relevant page. 'There you are then, come on, girls.'

Without argument, the vicar struck up the opening notes and Mary belted out the words, her tuneless harmonising the loudest of all the recruits by far. As she clapped her hands in time to the music, encouraging others to do the same, Kitty, Di and even Peg found themselves roaring with laughter at their new friend's bare-faced cheek.

'See, I told yer we'd show yer there was more to life than eggs,' Kitty chuckled as Mary performed an eye-wateringly high leg kick as she shucked off her khaki jacket.

'You did that all right,' Peg giggled, wiping the tears of laughter from her eyes.

It was gone eleven by the time Kitty and the rest of the girls returned to their beds for the night. Sinking her head onto the pillow, Kitty clutched Joe's watch to her chest, as she always did, and was so exhausted after singing herself hoarse that she fell asleep almost immediately. At three in the morning, right on cue, Kitty found herself wide awake again, the grief she had successfully cast aside during the day never failing to find her in the middle of the night where her mind was full of Joe, and the life they had shared together. As she held onto every image and memory, terrified this new life would cause her to forget him, the backdrop of sounds in the dorm room provided the perfect soundtrack to her fears and worries. Kitty had long since learned to find the gentle hum of the pipes from the ablutions next door and the irregular drip of the sink tap comforting. But tonight she heard a new noise, a gentle hiccupping sound from the bed opposite hers.

'Di, are yer awake?' Kitty whispered.

'Yes,' she replied, as quietly as Kitty. 'Fancy a walk?' Kitty looked at the inky black of the room, and was relieved she and Di were nearest the door. They could get safely out into the passage without disturbing anyone.

'All right,' she whispered, reaching for her greatcoat and wrapping it around her.

Together the girls padded across the dorm and out onto the bottom of the steps.

'What's your excuse, then?' Di asked quietly. 'Thought I was the only insomniac in this dorm.'

Kitty let out a low chuckle. 'Sorry, love, I'm awake most nights. I'm lucky if I get a couple of hours. You're quiet though, I'll give yer that, Di, I've not heard hide nor hair from yer before.'

'Likewise, Kit,' Di said in a low voice. 'Thing is, I 'ad a letter off me mam today.'

Kitty sat in quiet wonder. During the time they had been together at training camp, she had noticed Di never seemed to receive letters from her parents. Kitty had chosen not to mention it, sensing it was none of her business, but she could tell the lack of correspondence hurt Di.

'That's a bit out of the blue,' she said carefully. 'Did she have much to say?'

Di snorted with disgust. 'Oh yes, Kit. She had plenty to say to me all right.'

'How d'yer mean?' Kitty asked, puzzled. 'I know you've said you're not close to your family like, but that's no reason to send yer summat horrible through the post.'

'No, it's not.' Di sighed. 'But what I ought to tell you, Kit, is that me mam's always disliked me because she blames me for me twin sister's death.'

'Bless my soul,' Kitty breathed. 'Why ever would she do that?'

Di gave Kitty a sad smile, before looking through the window of the dark sky. 'Our Sarah died when we were small. We'd been out playing in the woods and she fell in the lake. I tried to save 'er and pull 'er out but neither of us could swim, see. She was dead by the time I got 'er to shore. Mam said Sarah's death was down to me. Said it'd been my idea to go mucking about in the woods, that it would never 'ave 'appened if I wasn't so adventurous.'

Kitty raised her eyebrows in disbelief. 'Di, I dunno what to say. That's awful.' She had to admit she was surprised. Although Kitty had not known Di very long, her sense of adventure was just one of the things she had come to admire most about her new friend.

Di nodded, her mouth set in a determined line as she continued. 'Normally I don't take any notice of 'er – our Sarah's death's always made me see 'ow short life is so I've always gone for things full pelt. As for Mam, she's spent the last twenty-odd years 'aving a go at me about summat or other which aside from wanting to muck in with others and 'elp win this war, is one of the reasons I joined up – I wanted to show 'er I could do summat good. That my adventurous spirit could 'elp get rid of those Jerries. But today she wrote and told me that by joining-up I'd broken 'er 'eart. That if I was killed, then I'd be to blame for costing 'er not one daughter, but two.'

Kitty felt a stab of fury towards this woman who had inflicted such misery. Di was so warm, vibrant and full of energy, she deserved a mother who showered her with love. But then, Kitty knew from experience, it was unusual to get what you deserved in life. Instinctively, she reached for Di's hand in the darkness and squeezed it.

'Sounds to me like she doesn't have a heart worth breaking in the first place. And if she can't be proud of yer for your bravery, and commitment to your country, then she's not worthy of being your mam,' Kitty said fiercely as she leaned her head against Di's.

'Remind me not to get on your bad side,' Di whispered in the gloom. 'What about you, then? Why can't you sleep, despite slogging your guts out doing drills all day?'

Kitty lifted her head from Di's shoulder and thought hard. She had always planned to keep Joe's death to herself – he seemed closer that way, she reasoned – but then Di had been so honest, it seemed only right to repay her.

'Me sweetheart was in the Navy and killed a few weeks before I arrived,' she said quietly. 'This country meant the world to him, so that's why I joined up, so I could finish what he started. But it's his memory keeping me awake at night.'

Di shook her head in sympathy and wordlessly wrapped her arm around her friend's trembling shoulders. 'Oh, Kit, I'm sorry.'

Kitty clasped the cool fingers of her friend's hand and before she could stop herself, let out a heart-rending sob. The pressure of keeping her sorrow at bay all day long was too much to bear any longer. And so she found herself telling Di all about Joe, how they had met at school, how they had always loved one another and how they had planned to build a bright and happy future once the war was over. Di listened in supportive silence, and when Kitty had finished, she pulled her friend into her arms for a hug.

'We're a right pair, aren't we?' Di said softly into Kitty's hair.

'Yer could say that.' Kitty sniffed as she stemmed her tears. 'Sorry, lovey, I didn't mean to weep all over yer. Especially when you've your own family troubles to cope with as well.'

'A problem shared is a problem 'alved,' Di said soothingly. 'Your Joe might not be 'ere any longer, but if 'e could see you now, fighting shoulder to shoulder with the rest of us against Mr 'itler, I bet you Joe'd be cheering you on with all 'is might.'

Kitty smiled at the image of Joe shouting from the sidelines, as if her career in the Army was as simple as a game of Saturday football. Di was right, Joe had always been her biggest supporter, and if he were here now, she was sure he would be telling her to get a good night's kip and plough her grief into the rest of her training. It was time to start listening, Kitty realised, as she got to her feet and the two of them walked back to their beds.

*

The day before the end of basic training, Kitty and the rest of the girls were enjoying half an hour to themselves in the mess before supper. As the summer sunlight streamed through the open windows, the scent of freshly cut grass filling the room, Kitty smiled to herself, reached into her knitting bag and carried on with the scarf she was making.

Di looked up from the letter she had just started to write and glanced at Kitty quizzically. 'It's June, Kit, not really the season for scarves, is it?'

Kitty laughed. 'No, not really, but I'm such a rotten knitter, it'll probably take me till winter to finish it.'

'Are you good at anything domestic?' Di teased.

'Cheek!' Kitty giggled, throwing a ball of green wool at Di and narrowly missing her head. 'I'll have yer know I'm very good at sewing. Joe, Arthur and Charlie always used to get me to darn their socks.'

Di raised her eyebrows. 'Really? I 'ope yer got summat in return.'

'Course,' Kitty chuckled as she picked up a dropped stitch. 'Free entry to the dance hall, a fish and chip supper before we went out and a port and lemon.'

'You don't 'alf strike an 'ard bargain,' Di breathed admiringly.

'Funny, that's just what Arthur used to say, when I made him buy me a second drink!' Kitty giggled again, remembering she had received a letter from him that morning. Promising herself she would read it when she would have time to enjoy it, Kitty had stuffed it into her pocket before hurrying out to the quad for daily square-bashing and had forgotten all about it until now. Ripping the envelope open, she scanned the contents excitedly.

20 June 1940

Dear Kitty,

What a treat to hear from you! I got your letter yesterday, and it was a real surprise. Not 'cos I don't think you're a woman of your word, but because I'd wondered if you'd have the time to write. I remember when I did my own basic training I was knackered after the first week, I hardly had time to put pen to paper. Still, I knew Mam'd have my guts for garters if I didn't write, so I think I managed about two lines.

Still, it was nice to hear from you, and I'm glad things are going so well and you've made some friends. I will say, you're wrong about the lads here never crying. Some of them still sob for their mothers and they've been away months now. I don't think it matters whether you're a man or a woman, this war does dreadful things to us, puts us in positions we'd never expect to be in, so it's no wonder a few tears are shed. Course, not me, mind, I'm far too manly to cry like that!

I'd better sign off now, I've not long before I'm due up on deck to start my watch shift, but I will say I'm keeping well and my nose out of trouble. Take care of yourself Kitty, and hope to hear from you soon.

Yours with affection,
Arthur

Stuffing the envelope into her pocket, Kitty ran cheerfully towards the mess. Pushing open the door she saw she was just in time for lunch, where she found everyone discussing one topic – the precious forty-eight hours' leave they would all enjoy once induction was over. Sliding into a seat next to Mary, she was just about to join in, when Section Leader Duck came in, breathless with delight.

'Listen up, ducks,' she called. 'News of your next postings along with your jobs are up on the board outside the mess now. Any problems, yer know where to find me.'

With that, the mess became a hive of activity as the girls clamoured to get through the doors, past Section Leader Duck and out onto the parade ground.

'No running, ducks!' Section Leader Duck shouted as she followed behind the trainees hurtling across the concourse. Rounding the corner, the girls headed straight into the mess, towards the announcements board. Only Kitty held back, slightly nervous now the time had come to leave Leicester. As the crowds cleared, she approached the board and found her own name. *Williams: Northampton: Driver.*

Startled, Kitty looked again. There had to be a mistake. She wasn't a spark girl – although she had assembled hundreds of car parts, she had never been behind a wheel in her life. Confused, she looked around and saw the delighted faces of Mary, Di and Peggy.

'Yer all look happy,' she said, smiling as she pushed her way through the trainees to find them chattering away.

'We are.' Peggy grinned delightedly. 'We're all going to be together.'

Kitty felt a stab of jealousy at the thought of the three of them not having to go to the effort of making new friends. 'That's wonderful,' she said, as generously as she could.

Di eyed her in surprise. 'And why are you looking so glum? I thought you'd be as delighted as we are.'

'Well, course I am, it's just—' Kitty began.

'You do realise we're all in Northampton together, don't you?' Mary said abruptly, cutting her off. 'We're all going to be spark girls.' A flash of surprise crossed Kitty's face.

'You daft apeth. You never checked anyone else's names, did you?' Di scolded.

'I didn't,' Kitty confessed, her face lighting up with joy. 'I was so shocked to find I was a driver, I didn't get further than that.' Never in her wildest dreams had she expected to be so lucky. Spotting Section Leader Duck heading towards them, she waved at the senior officer, catching her attention.

'Are yer pleased with your postings?' she asked, drawing level with Kitty.

'Oh, yes, it's marvellous,' Mary replied. 'I mean I've always had a licence so driving is a natural choice for me.'

'Have yer?' Kitty asked, astounded. 'I always thought yer had a driver to take care of everything.'

'Oh, we do,' Mary explained. 'But Mummy always said how frightfully important it was to be independent so she insisted my older sister Clarissa and I drove everywhere.'

'And me,' Peggy piped up. 'Mother had me doing deliveries so she got me to drive the shop van soon as I passed my test.'

Kitty's mouth gaped open. 'Well, I never did.'

'Well, ducks, the powers-that-be think that's where you're best suited,' Section Leader Duck explained. 'Yer and Mills might not have licences, but you've good co-ordination so the pair of yer will learn how to drive as well as mechanical skills so yer can fix the things when they break down. You'll be our very own spark girls. Now good luck, and don't let me down, ducks.'

As she left the girls to revel in their good news, Di turned to her friends, beaming. 'Well, girls, looks like this isn't ta-ta after all. More like see you in a couple of days,' she said.

Kitty returned her smile. Finding good fortune in the Army was unexpected, but here it was; a new posting with her new friends. For the first time in months things seemed to be looking up and she prayed that this was a sign of better times to come. But as she looked at her pals with fondness, she couldn't shake the strange, uneasy feeling that life was never that simple, and trouble was sure to be just around the corner.

Chapter Five

As the train slid into Coventry station it was all Kitty could do to stop herself jumping excitedly into the crowds of people swarming across the platform

Looking eagerly around her, Kitty realised that the only thing she could make out was the exit, so headed in that direction. But no sooner had she put one foot in front of the other, than a familiar voice rang out through the crowds.

'Kitty Williams! What are yer dawdling for?' a woman shrieked. 'Over here!'

Spinning around, Kitty's face broke into a delighted smile as she came face to face with Elsie. Her long blonde hair pinned up in elegant curls, Elsie looked as glamorous as Loretta Young in her bottle green dress and embroidered black and white cardigan.

'Look at you,' Kitty gasped, pulling her oldest and best friend into her arms. 'Still gorgeous even with a war on.'

'Well, there's no excuse not to look your best, even if the Jerries are trying to give us the run around,' Elsie chuckled as she took a step back to admire her friend. 'How about your khaki uniform, give us a twirl then.'

Smiling, Kitty obliged as a crowd looked curiously on. Elsie admired the ill-fitting khaki jacket and skirt, then threw her head back and laughed. 'Khaki is certainly your colour, lovey. But can't you do something about the length of that skirt? It's almost around your ankles.'

Kitty wasn't at all offended by her friend's comments, and did a little curtsey, much to the amusement of the train porters.

'If yer think the skirt's bad, yer should see me knee-length, army-issue knickers. We don't call 'em passion killers for nothing,' she giggled in hushed tones.

Linking arms, the friends left the station, the air heavy from the midday sun, and walked through the familiar Coventry streets back to the Higginsons' home. Despite the near constant rumble of buses and trams, not to mention the thrum of shoppers, there was a sense of calmness in the air, Kitty thought, as she watched a grocer tidy up a fallen stack of Lux soap boxes in the window.

'So what have yer got to tell me then?' Kitty asked as the pair walked through Broadgate.

'Not much,' Elsie shrugged. 'Things are just the same as when yer left.'

'That can't be true,' Kitty replied.

Elsie paused for a moment. 'All right, not the same, but not a lot's happened. I suppose the big news is that Dad's joined the Home Guard and built us an Anderson shelter in the back garden. It's big enough for eight, so we can take next door as well if needs be.'

'Wherever did yer put it?' Kitty asked, knowing full well the Higginsons' garden wasn't that big.

'Dad dug the rose bed up and put it there,' Elsie replied quietly.

Kitty squeezed her friend's arm in understanding. Ron's rose garden had always been his pride and joy, and he would have been devastated to lose it. Kitty could remember the day she and her parents had moved into the house next door to Elsie's, and how Ron had picked her mother a bunch of roses from his garden to welcome them to the street.

'And what about the bakery?' Kitty pressed, changing the subject. 'Are you at the end of your rope doling out rock cakes?'

Elsie roared with laughter. 'Yer barmpot! I haven't half missed yer, Kitty Williams. Things round here just aren't the same without yer.'

'Well, I'm back now.'

'That yer are,' Elsie smiled. 'And I'm very happy to see yer.'

'Me too.'

As they turned the corner into Elsie's street, Kitty was alarmed when her friend stopped suddenly and turned to face her.

'Before we get inside, there's summat I just want to get off my chest if yer don't mind,' Elsie said, shuffling from foot to foot.

Kitty raised her eyebrows. She knew Elsie well enough to know foot shuffling wasn't a good sign. 'Go on.'

'Well I just want to say that I know I wasn't all that supportive of yer going in the Army and that like, but the truth is, I wasn't just worried about yer going off so sudden after Joe,' Elsie blurted. 'I was being selfish. I didn't want yer to leave me, have adventures of your own. I'm sorry.'

'Oh Elsie,' Kitty breathed, feeling a rush of love for her friend. 'You've nothing to apologise for. Truth be told, I've missed yer summat rotten while I've been away. Yer don't find friendships like ours overnight, yer know.'

Elsie held her gaze. 'I know that well enough, Kitty. But I also want yer to know how proud I am of yer for going off and doing what yer doing, giving back to our country like, well, I know it can't be easy and—'

'It's no different to what your Charlie, your brothers and thousands of others are doing up and down the country,' Kitty replied firmly, waving away the compliment.

'Oh yes it is,' Elsie insisted. 'You're a woman for a start, branching out in a way women haven't done before. And to do it after losing your Joe like that, well – it's a bravery I can only imagine.'

Kitty felt her eyes fill with tears. 'Oh, stop it, yer daft so and so. I'm not brave, I spend me days wishing life was like it used to be, before all this war, when it was the four of us all together . . .'

As her voice trailed off, Kitty looked around her at the street she knew like the back of her hand. The row of terraces stood in pairs, with matching wrought iron gates, sash windows and front doors that were grained and painted black. But now, the evidence of war, and these new uncertain times, was everywhere to see. Almost all the houses in the row, including Elsie's, had their windows taped up with gummed brown paper to prevent glass shards flying inside, in the event of a bomb blast.

'Come on, let's get back,' Elsie said, linking her arm through Kitty's once more. 'It might be a warm sunny day, but I bet yer could murder a cuppa after that journey.'

'Yer not kidding,' Kitty grinned as she walked alongside Elsie towards her front door. 'I'm just delighted tea's not been rationed yet.'

'Hmmm,' Elsie replied, 'I'm sure if Mr Churchill has his way, it'll only be a matter of time.'

Throwing open the door she ushered Kitty into the narrow kitchen while she took off her cardigan and changed into her pink pinny. Kicking off her heavy Oxford brogues, Kitty inhaled the smell of carbolic soap and mutton stew – the scent of home.

'Yer shouldn't have gone to so much trouble,' Kitty admonished.

'I didn't.' Elsie smiled, filling the kettle and setting it on the range. 'Yer know Mam loves the chance to spoil yer and Dad took great pride in supplying the veg.'

'Ron's still spending all his time up the allotment then?' Kitty asked.

'Is the Pope a Catholic?' Elsie said, rolling her eyes good-naturedly. 'Anyway, to be honest, it's not all for yer.'

'Oh?' Kitty quizzed, now tugging off her scratchy khaki jacket and folding it neatly on top of her kitbag.

'Yes, you'll never guess, but I've a surprise.'

'Go on then, what is it? Don't tell me you've cadged extra buns from the bakery?' Kitty chuckled, leaning back against the hard chair just as the kitchen door opened.

'Nothing so exciting, I'm afraid,' a gravelly male voice boomed. 'She only means me.'

'Charlie!' Kitty gasped, rushing to greet her old friend who had appeared at the kitchen doorway. 'Whatever are yer doing here?'

'Much the same as yer, I imagine,' he said, returning Kitty's grin and squeezing her shoulders affectionately. 'I've forty-eight hours' leave before I go overseas and thought it'd be nice to see me wife before I left.'

Kitty looked from Charlie to Elsie and felt the love flow between them as they held each other's gaze.

'He says that now, of course.' Elsie smiled, as the kettle boiled. 'But what he's really here for is Mam's stew.'

Laughing, Charlie walked across the linoleum and wrapped his arms around his wife. 'Well I'd not come back all this way for *your* stew, let's put it that way,' he teased good-naturedly.

'Cheek!' Elsie grinned, leaning upwards to kiss him softly on the cheek. 'I dunno why I put up with yer.'

'Cos nobody else'd have yer, Elsie O'Connor,' Charlie laughed, as he reached behind Elsie for the kettle to pour water into the teapot.

Elsie swatted her husband on the arm. 'Yer twerp,' she laughed. 'Take that back.'

'Now, now, Els, yer wouldn't hit a fella with boiling water in his hands.' Charlie laughed, trying to dodge Elsie's playful swats.

'Flamin' right I would,' Elsie giggled again, as she landed another soft blow on his arm.

Admitting defeat, Charlie put the kettle down and held his hands aloft. 'You're right, I'm sorry,' he said, bending down to kiss his wife.

As Kitty watched the tender scene between Charlie and Elsie, she swallowed a pang of loneliness as she remembered how she and Joe had once been as close. There were days it seemed impossible to believe that she had once found love like that with someone who knew her inside and out. How she ached for those days, when a lifetime with the love of her life was something she had taken for granted rather than treasured.

Stemming the tears that threatened to spill down her cheeks she thought how she would give anything to have just one more kiss with Joe. Looking over at her friends, who were still temporarily lost in their own private world, Kitty hoped they would cherish this moment, in a way she now never could with Joe.

Despite the hard work of the army, Kitty still ached for Joe, missing him every moment of every day. The watch he had left her that still contained traces of his scent was the only physical reminder he had ever existed at all. Like a talisman Kitty clutched it to her chest every night, eventually falling asleep with it firmly in her grasp.

'Kitty, yer in there, girl?' Charlie's voice boomed again. He pulled out a chair opposite Kitty's and helped Elsie set a tray of chocolate cake and tea on the table.

'Oh sorry, Charlie, what were yer saying?' she asked absent-mindedly.

'I was asking if yer were happy, if yer still think joining up was the right thing to do.'

'I do,' she said firmly. 'I love it – I mean, don't get me wrong, it's hard graft – but I love the fact I feel useful, like I'm making a difference and doing summat worthwhile to honour Joe's memory.'

Casting his eyes downward, Charlie glanced uncomfortably at the table. 'I was so sorry to learn about Joe, Kit. When I heard I thought there'd been a mistake.'

Kitty nodded in understanding. 'I couldn't meself. There are days I still can't believe it's happened.'

'I know,' Charlie said quietly. 'We grew up together, he was me best mate, he knew me inside and out, and now he's gone. I didn't even get to go to the funeral and say goodbye ... it still doesn't feel real. I should have been there, paid me respects like.'

'Come on now, Charlie,' said Elsie softly. 'Yer couldn't get leave, yer were fighting for your country. Joe would have understood that better than anyone.'

Charlie said nothing, instead he sipped his tea and smiled weakly at Kitty. 'Still, you're looking well, Kit. Army life clearly suits yer.'

'I could say the same about yer,' Kitty replied, reaching for the tea Charlie had poured for her and taking in his appearance. Dressed in his Army shirt and trousers, his blond hair neatly trimmed and gleaming, he looked like a model soldier.

In fact, Kitty thought, watching Charlie smile fondly at his wife as they held hands, Charlie looked for all the world as if he were the happiest man alive. She was about to say as much, but opening her mouth to speak saw something in his eyes that gave her a jolt of alarm. The warm-hearted grin Charlie was flashing Elsie did not meet his eyes and instead she saw something that looked like a mixture of worry and despair.

Concern gnawed away at her. What on earth could Charlie be worried about? She knew he was going overseas, of course, but so were hundreds of other men in the forces. It couldn't be that; Charlie was one of the bravest men she knew, having been as keen as Joe to join-up before he was called to fight for the country he loved. Taking a piece of cake, Kitty resolved to try and talk to Charlie before he left and find out what was wrong.

'So shall we go up the pictures tonight?' Elsie asked, biting into her day-old cake. '*Bringing up Baby* is on, and I've still not got around to seeing it.'

'That'd be nice,' Kitty smiled as she brushed the crumbs from her shirt onto her plate. 'Are yer coming as well, Charlie?'

Charlie raised his eyebrows. 'A night out with Katharine Hepburn, yer, and me wife? Try and stop me!'

'And Mike.' Elsie smiled, leaning her head onto her husband's shoulder. 'He wants to come along 'n'all.'

'Oh yes, Mike,' Charlie replied, planting a kiss on his wife's forehead. 'I'd forgotten all about him.'

Kitty smiled as she saw the contentment on her best friend's face, but glancing at Charlie, she saw his jaw was clenched as he stroked his wife's hair. Elsie might look as happy as a clam, it was just a shame Charlie didn't appear to feel the same, Kitty thought as she finished her tea and stood up to clear the table.

*

It had been wonderful to return home, even though it had only been for a few hours, Kitty thought as she sat on yet another train, this time Northampton-bound. The three of them, together with Mike, had enjoyed not only a trip to the pictures but a visit to the tearoom, where Mike had insisted on buying them all teacakes. It had been just the break Kitty needed, but now she was raring to go and couldn't wait to get stuck in to her new posting.

As the train pulled up to the platform, Kitty leapt once more into the throng of passengers and walked towards the exit, realising she wasn't the only Army girl reporting for duty. Everywhere she looked, Kitty saw ATS bodies jostling one another on the platform, trying to get to the exit.

Patiently, Kitty joined the throng and swallowed the feelings of frustration she felt as she was pushed and pulled like an old rag doll. Finally she reached the crowded exit, elbowed her way to the front – and was delighted to spot a familiar face.

'Di!' Kitty called, recognising the slender girl with shiny brown hair and striking green eyes. Diana's face broke into a warm smile as she saw Kitty among the crowds. Waving happily, she beckoned Kitty towards her and the two recruits smiled at each other.

'I didn't know you were getting this train 'n'all,' Di exclaimed, adjusting the shoulder strap of her kit bag. 'I'd 'ave saved you a seat if I'd known.'

'No need,' Kitty replied triumphantly. 'Unlike me journey back to Coventry, I managed to get a seat from the very beginning and even finished me book.'

Di nodded approvingly. 'Well done. I found a seat meself, though I had to share with a couple of WAAFs who bored on about the 'ardships of uniform. I felt like getting up and tugging off me passion killers to show 'em what 'ardship was really all about.'

Chuckling, the girls walked towards the Army truck that was waiting to take the recruits back to the barracks. Slinging their kitbags into the back, they clambered in like cattle and positioned themselves among the rest of the girls, squatting on the floor, nodding quiet hellos and pleased-to-meet-yous.

The truck started suddenly and roared off into Northampton centre. As they rounded a corner, Di let out a shriek of annoyance as someone's kitbag flew from the back of the van and straight into the side of her head.

'Ow!' she moaned, shooting the kitbag owner a menacing glare. 'Watch where you put your things.'

'I bet that train journey with the WAAFs is beginning to feel like the Orient Express compared to this,' Kitty shouted above the roar of the engine.

'You're not wrong. I always knew life in the Army wasn't full of glitz but I feel more like a sack of spuds in the back of this glorified grocer's van than an Army volunteer,' Di grumbled, rubbing the sore spot on her head.

Smiling sympathetically at her friend, Kitty craned her neck to see out of the back of the truck and glimpse the sights of Northampton for herself. As they drove past the bustling market square, filled with shoppers making the most of the late evening sunshine, Kitty was delighted to see that the truck passed park upon park. After the grime of Leicester's industrial city centre, it was wonderful to see so many green spaces. Looking up at the cloudless blue sky, she wondered if Northampton might be the start of happier times.

Minutes later, the truck pulled into a large park, and stopped abruptly in the centre. After they were ordered to get out, the recruits lined up alphabetically while the Section Leader who had driven them from the station checked their names off a register. Then they were ordered to march in double quick time to the barracks, half a mile away. Kitty was surprised to see she was surrounded by parkland – it was all she could do not to let her eyes wander as she heeded the Section Leader's 'left, right, left, right', marching down the hill towards their new squadron.

There were some things she couldn't fail to notice, however, such as the beds of vibrant purple heather that surrounded the park, and the huge oak and sycamore trees that stood to attention as naturally as a seasoned brigadier. Kitty took a deep breath and savoured the scent of nature around her. It was sheer bliss and a perfect spot for a driver-training centre. The barracks were a million miles away from those she had been stationed in in Leicester, which had been small, cramped and noisy. Here, the barracks were almost stately and extremely peaceful. Positioned right in the heart of a large part of the park that had been sectioned off for use by the Army, Kitty was surprised at how vast the place was. Row upon row of Nissen huts surrounded a large stone building, while elsewhere the rumble of a convoy of soft-skinned, khaki Tilly trucks thundered up ahead. Kitty felt a pulse of excitement as she realised that in a few days, she too could be driving one of those trucks. As they got closer, Kitty noticed how clean the vehicles were and how each driver sat up straight, focused and determined to drive the truck at a safe but neat distance from the one in front. Ordered to stop outside the large stone building Kitty now knew was the headquarters, they marched inside to receive their billet instructions. Kitty was delighted to discover she and Di were together in the red huts.

Despite the fact it was now evening, it was still very warm and Kitty longed to take off her uniform and wear something lighter. Yet walking down a hill towards a mass of tin buildings, she knew there was no chance of such luxury in the Army. As the girls got closer, Kitty could make out the guard room, closely followed by the officers' mess, a small medical unit, and a canteen. Further down the hill stood the food and equipment stores and a large number of smaller huts. Glancing through the windows as they passed, Diana saw hard-backed chairs and desks and wondered if they were classrooms. Finally, more rows of tin Nissen huts: home.

Each group of huts was co-ordinated by colour and the girls quickly found the red section, arranged around a series of smaller huts Kitty realised were the latrines. Examining the numbers on each hut, they found their billet and Di threw open the white wooden door.

'Can you call Claridge's and tell 'em we've found better

lodgings 'ere?' Di joked, eyeing the twenty-five beds lined along each side of the wall. Kitty's heart sank. The barracks in Leicester had been similar, but here the overpowering smell of damp did little to lift her spirits.

'It's more like an infirmary,' Kitty agreed, noticing just how close they were to one another.

'We'll be lucky if we don't catch lice,' Di said, picking up her kitbag and throwing it onto a bed nearest the door. 'At least this way, the so-and-sos might make a run for it before they find their way onto me scalp. Come on, what are you waiting for? There's nobody 'ere, yet you can have your pick of the beds.'

Kitty looked around the room. This time, each iron bed was separated by a small steel cabinet with a drawer underneath. As for the beds themselves, the by now infamous straw mattresses, or biscuits as they were more commonly known in the Army, looked as thin, narrow and lumpy as they ever had. Turning to the bed opposite Di's, she flung her belongings on it and looked around. Apart from the two small windows lined with standard blackout curtains at the front of the hut on either side of the door, there was no other natural light. Unpacking, Kitty pulled out the few personal items she liked to carry with her. As well as two paperbacks and her writing set, she took out photographs of Elsie and Joe, laying them neatly in the drawer beside her bed. Pulling out Joe's watch, she ran her fingers over the timepiece and she felt a lump form in her throat at how much she still missed him. It had been almost three months since he had died and although she had enjoyed confiding in Elsie about her new life during her two days back home, she had longed to tell Joe. Placing the watch down, Kitty started laying out the items they had been given from the stores. Along with the scratchy Army issue blankets, Kitty had been pleased to pick up two new shirts and another skirt.

Kitty looked across at Di, who had now made her bed and was lying casually across the blankets, looking as though she were on holiday rather than in the Army.

'I shouldn't let our senior officer catch yer like that,' Kitty chuckled. 'We're meant to be having a full inspection later after we've turned out for nit parade.'

'We're on our own,' Di pointed out, raising herself up into a sitting position.

'Yer know what they're like.' Kitty shrugged. 'Let's go and get summat to eat and p'raps we'll bump into Mary and Peggy.'

Grabbing their eating irons, the girls made their way across the grassy field towards the larger catering hut. Inside, Kitty was overwhelmed by the noise as the chatter of what must easily have been over two hundred women rang in her ears. The clatter of forks against plates and the sound of cups of tea being set down in between chatter made Kitty feel instantly at home. Although the canteen was a large Nissen hut, it was a lot bigger than the one she and Di were sleeping in. The windows along the side allowed light to fill the room and the general atmosphere was cheery and bright. Nearly all the large trestle tables were full of diners, Kitty noticed, and she wondered if she and Di would be able to get a seat.

At least there was no queue, she thought thankfully as she held out her plate, and was rewarded with a large portion of cottage pie. Spinning round, she realised her luck really was in as she spotted two girls leaving their seats by one of the windows overlooking the park.

'Could almost be a posh restaurant,' Di noted as she sat down and admired her bird's eye view of the luscious greenery.

'Well it's as close as we'll get anytime soon!' Kitty replied, laughing, and started to wolf down her food. 'So, how was your leave back home like?' Kitty asked between mouthfuls. She had been dying to quiz Di on how things were with her mother as soon as she saw her at the station, but had thought it best to allow her friend a little bit of time to get used to their new surroundings before she asked about her personal life.

'I didn't go 'ome.' Di shrugged. 'I went to stay with me friend Pam in Liverpool instead and we 'ad a whale of a time at the pictures one night, then out to a dance at the church 'all the next.'

Kitty paused mid-forkful. 'What did your mam say?'

'Mam didn't know,' Di said gruffly. 'I 'aven't written to 'er since she sent me that last letter.'

Kitty's heart went out to Di. Although she had been angered by the way her friend had been treated, she had desperately hoped the two would make it up. She knew how hard it was to live without a mother. But then again, Kitty thought, taking another bite of delicious cottage pie, some people were better off without.

Just then, two girls as different as chalk and cheese burst through the heavy-duty doors of the canteen. One had hair as black as a raven, elegantly pinned in a victory roll, and was talking non-stop to a smaller, timid girl with red hair tied in a neat bun.

'And then Daddy said he'd cut me off without a penny if I refused to stay. Well, of course I told him, you can do what you like, Daddy, but if the Jerries bally well win, then you won't have any money to give me an allowance in the first place!' Mary shrieked.

At the sound of the commotion, Kitty stood up and waved excitedly, her hard wooden chair scraping on the stone floor.

'Mary, Peg, over here,' she called.

Catching sight of Kitty and Di, the girls beamed as they hurried over and sat down.

'Jolly lucky we bumped into you,' Mary said cheerily, pulling out her fork and snatching a mouthful of cottage pie from Kitty's plate. 'We didn't expect Northampton squadron to be quite so big, did we, Peg?'

The quieter girl shook her head as Mary carried on. 'I was just saying to Peg, this place is gorgeous, isn't it? Looks more like my pal Henry's pile in Derbyshire than Army barracks, don't you think?'

'I've never met your pal 'enry,' Di replied dryly, pulling her plate firmly out of Mary's reach. 'But this place seems all right so far.'

'Which section are you in?' Mary asked abruptly changing the subject. 'Peg and I have fetched up in blue.'

'We're in red,' Kitty replied, quickly finishing her plateful.

'Oh, dash it all,' Mary grumbled. 'I rather hoped we would be together. How was your leave?'

'Good, ta,' she replied, smiling as she pushed her now empty plate to the side ready to rinse. 'Me mate's husband, Charlie, was back on leave from the Army and it was just like old times.'

'That sounds nice,' Peggy beamed.

'It was,' agreed Kitty. 'But I'm a bit worried about Charlie if I'm honest.'

'What d'you mean?' Di asked.

'Well . . .' Kitty paused. 'He seemed well enough, but there was summat about him that felt off.'

'Didn't you say 'e's a soldier 'n'all?' Di quizzed.

Kitty nodded. 'That's right – he's about to go abroad. But although he was saying all the right things about Army life, I got the impression there was summat troubling him, but for the life of me I couldn't work out what.'

'Well, 'e's probably just worried about going abroad,' Di reasoned.

'That's what I wondered,' Kitty said doubtfully. 'But I'm not so sure. I was hoping to get a chance to speak to him like, but I never got the time.'

'What else could it be?' Di pressed.

'I dunno, I can't put me finger on it, but summat's not right.'

'Sounds to me like you're fretting over nothing.' Di laughed. 'You've enough on your plate 'ere to keep you occupied before you start worrying about others with problems you can't identify.'

'Di's right,' Peggy said. 'Charlie'll be fine.'

'I hope so.' Kitty sighed, smiling gratefully at the younger girl before turning to Mary. 'How was your leave?'

'Good. Though Daddy was, of course, difficult and Mummy kept bursting into tears whenever she saw my uniform,' Mary replied, rolling her eyes. 'It was a crashing bore, to be honest with you. I spent most of my time at my chum Margaret's. She had a little cocktail party in my honour on Saturday evening and I don't mind admitting I got a little bit squiffy.' Mary smiled conspiratorially. 'Poor Jonathan Hatchington-Squires was quite terrified.'

'I bet,' said Kitty, arching an eyebrow. 'Peg? Did yer have a nice time at home?'

'It were all right,' Peggy replied timidly. 'Mother and I did a jigsaw, then I 'elped her with the flowers up the church.'

'Sounds like you need a drink after all that,' Mary said, her eyes twinkling.

'We'll be lucky to get a bitter lemon here,' Kitty said, her eyes not leaving Peggy's face.

Suddenly Mary let out a loud shriek as she pointed to the food area. 'Look, they're serving the last of the cottage pie, Peg. I'd sooner eat Cook's lumpy old porridge than the wretched soggy beans they'll serve up in its place. Come on!'

Quick as a flash, Mary pushed her chair back, gathered Peg by the arm and quickly led her to the back of the queue.

'God help the girls serving the food if there's no pie left by the time Mary gets to the front,' Di quipped.

'I dunno,' Kitty mused, turning her gaze to the queue that was moving quickly. 'Might do her some good not to get her own way all the time.'

'Looks like we're about to find out,' Di chuckled in a low voice, noticing the girl in front of Mary had committed the crime of taking the last piece of pie Mary had clearly earmarked for herself. Looking on in horrified fascination, Di and Kitty couldn't believe their ears as Mary complained at the top of her voice that it was unacceptable for the canteen to have run out of food.

*

Kitty woke early to a cloudless blue sky and a sunny July day filled with promise. Unlike in Leicester, she had mostly slept and, together with the twenty-four other girls in her dorm, had dressed quickly then walked across the grassy parkland for breakfast. This time, she was surprised to see Peggy and Mary were among the first in the queue and happily accepting Cook's offerings of what looked suspiciously to Kitty like lumpy porridge and cold, grey haddock.

By the time she had sat down, Mary and Peg had finished, so Kitty ate what she could, then quickly scraped the rest into a bin by the door, before returning to the wash station to rinse her plate.

As her porridge hit the bin with a heavy thud, Kitty peeked inside and chuckled as she saw she wasn't the only one to have got rid of her breakfast. The bin was nearly overflowing with leftovers, and the stench of fish was overpowering. Thank heavens the tea had been hot, Kitty thought as she hurried back to her hut to prepare for parade. Like most of the ATS girls she had no idea what she would do without a brew. Their days were long and there was such a lot to take in, sometimes the simple act of drinking a cup of tea seemed like the most reassuring thing in the world.

Back at the Nissen hut, everyone was polishing their buttons on jackets and caps or ensuring shoes were buffed to a high shine. As Kitty pulled on her Oxford brogues, she felt pleased she had prepared her uniform the night before. Di had pulled her leg mercilessly for getting out her button stick when they got back but Kitty knew she wouldn't be able to concentrate on a book or knitting when she had things to do. All her working life Kitty had prided herself on being prepared for everything, and felt there was no sense putting off until tomorrow what could be done today.

Watching Di frantically check that her collar was straight, Kitty felt a small sense of satisfaction that she had very little to do. However, she said nothing as the girls marched across the parkland to the parade ground and lined themselves up alphabetically for inspection. With hands clasped firmly behind their backs they waited for their sergeant. Kitty felt a cool breeze around her neck and turned to look up at the sky. A series of dark grey clouds had formed just above them, and she felt sure rain was on its way.

Without warning, she felt the rush of hot breath in her face and drops of saliva spray across her nose. 'Eyes belong forwards not up at the sky!' a voice bellowed.

With a heavy sense of dread, Kitty turned her gaze straight ahead and came face to face with an angry-looking man she had a sneaking suspicion was their sergeant.

'Daydreaming, were we?' he snarled, revealing a perfect set of white teeth. Kitty visibly recoiled at the curled up lips that spat nothing but fury. With his brown-gloved hand tucked around a wooden baton under his arm, he gave off an air of menace. Determined not to show fear, Kitty drew herself up to her full height and quickly checked the stripes on his sleeve, an action that wasn't lost on her sergeant. As she suspected, there were three thick white bands, revealing his full rank.

'Checking who I am, are you, Volunteer?' he snarled again, treating Kitty to a grimace. 'Well let me introduce myself. I'm Sergeant Hopson, and I like to keep a close eye on daydreamers.'

Kitty felt a deep flush creep up her face as she wished desperately the ground would open and swallow her whole. She had only turned her head for a second – how unlucky to be caught out like that. She looked again at the sergeant and felt a sense of unease creep over her. He was a good ten years older than her, Kitty thought, but with his rich brown hair, perfectly shaped oval grey eyes, slim nose and ruddy cheeks, he oozed authority. Despite the plummy voice, Kitty detected the faint whisper of a Midlands accent. She had every confidence he had the ability to make her life hell.

'I'm sorry, sir,' she said in a clear, forthright tone. 'Won't happen again, sir.'

'I should think not,' the sergeant remarked, giving her a cold stare and marching to the front. Kitty breathed a sigh of relief as he took his attention away from her and addressed the squad.

'I am Sergeant Hopson,' he called out, loudly. 'I oversee the driving centre and will be marching you down to the garages to see your cars. You will all be sub-divided into groups, where you will meet your instructors. Any more nonsense and you will all be on latrine duty for the rest of your time here. About turn!'

As they marched down the bank towards the large iron huts where trucks, cars and lorries were parked outside, Kitty couldn't believe her eyes. She thought she had seen a lot of vehicles when she had worked at the factory, but that was nothing compared to what lay before her. Outside one garage, she could see a row of khaki Utility and Lister trucks, their soft-skinned backs clean and sparkling, and bonnets gleaming. Beyond the trucks were at least three dozen cars, Kitty noticed. Squinting her eyes for a better look, she saw a variety of black and khaki Standards and some smart black Humbers. There was a spark girl dressed in overalls either under the chassis of each car or with her head under the bonnet while an instructor stood at the front and shouted orders. Kitty realised with a sudden thrill that the girls were being taught real mechanic's skills. She couldn't wait to get started.

At the motoring school, Sergeant Hopson divided them into classes and Kitty was relieved to discover she, Di, Mary and Peggy were all together. She had half-expected the sergeant to hold her back, but perhaps his bark was worse than his bite, Kitty thought, as the platoon fell in and awaited Sergeant Hopson's instructions.

'As you can see, there's another class going on at the moment, so take an hour's break. We will meet back here at ten sharp and if you're lucky you'll find the NAAFI catering van will have just arrived, meaning those of you who chose to avoid Cook's famous porridge and haddock at breakfast will be able to find a suitable alternative. At ease.'

The girls laughed as Sergeant Hopson dismissed them and they broke off into groups. Kitty turned to Di, Peggy and Mary and smiled, her relief palpable as she re-joined her friends.

'Volunteer Williams,' Sergeant Hopson called. 'Where do you think you're going?'

Kitty froze as the sergeant brushed Di, Peg and Mary aside and stood directly before her. His handsome features contorted into an expression of amusement and disgust.

'The rest of you can go. I only want a word with Volunteer Williams,' Sergeant Hopson snapped, dismissing Di, Mary and Peggy. The girls quickly walked away, but not without shooting concerned glances at their friend.

Kitty wasn't sure what was going on, but knew she wouldn't do herself any favours by showing it. Instead she saluted her sergeant and clasped her hands behind her back.

'Permission to speak, sir?' she said quietly.

'Granted,' he replied.

'To the mobile catering van, sir. You dismissed us for an hour, sir,' Kitty said, remembering the golden rule of not looking her superiors directly in the eye. There was an agonising pause as she waited for Sergeant Hopson to speak.

'Well, you're not dismissed,' he said, in a tone so disarmingly soft, Kitty felt unnerved. Taking a step closer towards her, Sergeant Hopson continued. 'Everyone else may be going to take a break, Volunteer Williams, but you are in need of a lesson in manners.'

Pulling out a black and white badger hair shaving brush from his inside pocket, he held it out to Kitty. Confusion was written all over her face. Her uncertainty only seemed to amuse Sergeant Hopson further as he let out a low chuckle. 'I believe in manners, Volunteer Williams, and I believe you need a little task that will give you plenty of time to reflect on your insubordination,' he said, taking another step closer.

'Now, I want you to take this brush and sweep this car free from dirt. I am going to teach you all about driving using this very vehicle and I want every inch clean and free from debris. Woe betide you, my girl, if I find a speck on it. Perhaps once you've finished, I'll see if you're ready to start learning about cars.'

A wave of horror washed over Kitty as she glanced down at the brush Sergeant Hopson was still holding between forefinger and thumb. He gestured for her to take it and Kitty realised with a sickening sense of horror that her sergeant was serious.

'Well, you'd better get started, Williams, this is going to be a long job,' Sergeant Hopson thundered, as if he could read her mind. 'And, remember, I want every last inch cleaned thoroughly.'

As he dropped the brush at her feet and walked away, Kitty felt angry, hurt tears prick her eyes. She welcomed the chance to do any task, no matter how small, if it benefited the war effort, but she doubted cleaning a car with a shaving brush would help their boys fighting for freedom. Still, Kitty thought, the sooner she got on with the task, the sooner it would be over. With the brush in her hand, Kitty pulled open the car door and let out a gasp of frustration as she saw just how filthy the interior was. Lint, dust, litter and mud caked the footwell, while the dashboard was covered in thick grime. With a heavy heart, Kitty began to sweep the corners, taking great care to remove every speck before moving on. Now, the more she swept the more she thought of Joe and pictured his handsome, smiling face, urging her to be strong. She felt a stab of fresh pain, and her face flushed red with frustration and fury at herself and the sergeant. She could have sworn things were getting easier, but as she opened her eyes and saw the filthy car, Kitty realised hard work was like grief and the only way out of it was through it.

After spending several hours on her feet cleaning, Kitty was finally finished. Her back ached from hunching over the car and her khaki uniform was filthy from the grime she had been knee-deep in almost all day. As for the shaving brush, Kitty had used it so thoroughly it was pleasingly almost out of bristles. Now, as she stood hands on hips in front of the bonnet and surveyed the car, she took a moment to admire her hard work. There was no getting away from it, Kitty had done a good job and she knew it. She had taken great care to follow Sergeant Hopson's instructions to the letter and had made sure every single part of the Humber gleamed inside and out. There was only one thing getting in the way of her satisfaction at a job well done and that was that she had missed a whole day's training. Although she had taken care not to be caught looking at what the rest of her class were up to, she had been unable to avoid the giggles coming from the Nissen hut that doubled as a classroom next door. As part of their mechanical and driver training, Kitty knew they had to learn skills such as map reading and Sergeant Hopson lectured them all on the dos and don'ts of telling north from south before allotting them their cars.

Suddenly the door of the hut flew open and Kitty's classmates tumbled out, their faces alive with smiles as they chattered away about what they had learned. Kitty saw Di, Mary and Peggy and waved triumphantly, beckoning them over.

'By 'eck, Kit! This the same car as this morning?' Di marvelled. 'Looks like it's straight out the factory, it's gleaming.'

'It's fabulous, Kitty,' Mary agreed. 'Very well done indeed. I must say if Hopson had given me a task like that, I'd have run a mile and called Daddy.'

'No surprise there! Oh, watch out, 'opson's coming over,' whispered Di under her breath. At the sight of their sergeant walking towards them the girls fell into a line, arms behind their backs and eyes forward.

'At ease,' Sergeant Hopson said as he strode past before drawing level with Kitty. 'So, Volunteer Williams, shall we take a look at your handiwork?' he said, smirking, before turning to the car, with Kitty trailing anxiously behind. As he ambled around the car, examining every crevice of the Hillman, Kitty held her breath, waiting for the inevitable criticism and punishment. But to her surprise, the sergeant had nothing terrible to say at all.

'Not bad, Volunteer,' he admitted eventually as he turned to face Kitty. 'Had to admit, I wasn't sure how well you'd do, but credit where credit's due. The car is indeed in excellent condition.'

Kitty let out a sigh of relief. 'Thank yer, sir.'

'Now, here's the good news,' Sergeant Hopson continued. 'As you've gone to so much effort, this car's all yours. Almost all of your colleagues have been allotted vehicles but, as you and Volunteer Mills are the only two in this intake that can't drive, you two will share this car for the next few weeks.'

Kitty felt a stab of confusion at her sergeant's attitude. Did the cleanliness of the car have something to do with her change in fortunes? 'Thank yer, sir.'

'I wouldn't thank me just yet. This car might be clean and tidy after you've spent the day working on it, but it's far from reliable,' Sergeant Hopson snapped. 'You and Volunteer Mills will have your mechanical skills put to the test ensuring this thing stays running.'

'Yes, sir,' Kitty said quietly.

'That's what I thought,' Sergeant Hopson said, turning away from the girls and walking back to the classroom before pausing midway. 'Oh and Williams, you'd better make sure you catch up on what you missed by the next class. I don't want to waste time teaching you because you were foolish enough to miss to-day's session.' Without waiting for an answer, Sergeant Hopson returned inside and the girls let out a sigh of relief.

'Oh my God, that man!' hissed Mary. 'He is unbelievable.'

Kitty laid a warning hand on Mary's wrist. 'Just leave it, Mary. It's fine.'

But Mary wouldn't hear of it. 'It's not fine. It's a disgrace. Leaving you two with this vehicle when you don't know the first thing about cars, it's downright dangerous. Do you want me to speak with this chap?'

'No, she don't,' Peggy hissed, despite realising there was a fair amount of truth to what Mary was saying. 'What I 's'pect Kitty wants is for us to leave well alone so we can go up the stores, collect our overalls and help her catch up.'

'It wasn't much, to be honest, Kitty,' Di reassured her. 'Lots of stuff about knowing east from west so you can tell where you're going. Sergeant 'opson took great care to explain 'ow important map reading was for a spark girl now all the road signs have been removed under wartime emergency regulations. It'll take no more than twenty minutes, promise.'

'Ta, girls.' Kitty smiled gratefully as they set off up the hill towards the stores.

An hour later the foursome were in the canteen drinking tea, helping Kitty go over what she had missed. Di had been right, Kitty had been pleased to discover, the girls had covered only the basics that day, and as she poured them all second cups of tea, the others started admiring their khaki overalls.

'Aren't they fancy?' Peggy breathed, holding hers up to the light for a closer look. 'I know it sounds daft but I feel ever so special now my job has its own uniform.'

'It doesn't sound silly at all, Peg,' Di said loyally.

'Yes, it does!' Mary shrieked. 'I've never seen a garment so unflattering in all my life. I can't honestly believe they expect us to wear this thing. The ill-fitting khaki uniform was bad enough, but at least it had a shape. This,' she continued, jabbing her finger at the thick cloth, 'is downright ludicrous.'

'Oh Mary, let it be, will yer,' Kitty spluttered. 'It's been a difficult enough day as it is without listening to yer blathering on about overalls.'

'Well, I was only saying,' Mary pointed out as she took a sip of tea.

'Well I'm only saying 'n'all,' Kitty said warningly, setting her cup on the table and fixing Mary with a piercing glare. 'Honestly, Mary, for all your moaning, I've no idea why you've joined-up. Surely you've been away long enough to get back at your father by now.'

Mary's face darkened as she regarded the table. 'Is that honestly the only reason you lot bally well think I'm here? To upset my father?' she bristled. 'Well let me assure you, that although upsetting Daddy may be a silver lining in this whole episode, I'm here to do my bit. I love my country, and I'm not about to see it ruined by Hitler!'

'Oh Mary, ignore me,' Kitty sighed wearily. 'I'm sorry, it's been a long day; I shouldn't have said anything.'

'Which is why we need summat to look forward to.' Di grinned. 'There's a big dance up the town next month, why don't we go? We can let our 'air down.'

'I dunno about that, Di,' Peg said nervously. 'I've never been dancing. Can't we go up the pictures instead?'

'No,' Di replied, leaning across the table and glancing firmly at her friends. 'We deserve a treat, we worked ourselves to the bone at basic training, and I've a feeling life at Northampton's going to be the same so when an opportunity for a bit of fun turns up we should take it.'

'There's a war on, in case yer hadn't noticed, Di,' Kitty pointed out. 'I'm not sure we should be enjoying ourselves when our loved ones are off fighting.'

'Don't you start,' Di scolded. 'Those dance 'alls are full of service men and women enjoying a bit of time off when they can – why d'you think they let you in 'alf price if you go in your uniform? I know there's a war on, Kit, but that doesn't mean life 'as to be a misery every minute of every day.'

'But I've got two left feet,' Peg protested. 'I'm not sure, Di.'

'Don't talk daft,' Di insisted. 'Why don't we practise a few steps in the mess tonight after we've written letters home?'

Kitty frowned at the idea. 'I'm ever so tired, Di, I'm not sure I'm in the mood.'

'Even more reason then,' Di said eagerly. 'Come on! What d'you say?'

Kitty observed her friend and recognising the determined glimmer in her eye knew there was no point arguing.

'Go on then,' she groaned as she finished her tea and stood up to return to duty.

Following the others back outside, Kitty realised there was a lot more to being a soldier than following orders and learning how to march properly. More often than not, Army life was about doing things you really did not want to.

Chapter Six

It had been three weeks since Kitty had arrived in Northampton and, despite a difficult start, she had thrown herself into her new role as a spark girl with zest. Together with Di, Mary and Peg, she spent her mornings in the classroom learning about mechanics, while afternoons were spent either under the chassis getting covered in grease or learning to drive. All this was peppered with regular exercise sessions, known as PT, designed to keep the girls fit and healthy but in fact only making them groan at the thought of getting hot and sweaty in the blazing summer sun.

Kitty had been delighted to discover she was a natural driver and, from the moment she sat behind the wheel of the Humber, had found she could effortlessly communicate with the car around the barracks as easily as if it were an extension of herself. Di, on the other hand, had not been so lucky and had struggled so much with the basics, she had found it difficult to move the car more than a few feet without stalling.

Life at a real posting was so much more demanding than at basic training, and Kitty couldn't believe how much things had changed. At Leicester, they had enjoyed the odd Saturday night and afternoon off. Here, she was expected to work full days and weekends too, when she and the rest of the girls would be on guard duty until they were relieved in the small hours.

Occasionally, they would be allowed a few hours off, and she and her friends would slip into town to the pictures, for a cuppa at the tearoom, or, with summer in full swing, take a stroll through the park. They would do nothing more than sit on the grass, sneakily remove their khaki jackets and talk about their hopes for the future.

One of the old Nissen huts near the back of the squadron had been turned into a recreation room for the recruits and occasionally one of the senior officers would organise a dance or film for them all to enjoy. Otherwise when the doctor was off-duty he would play the piano and together some of the girls would enjoy a good sing-song until lights out, just as they had in Leicester.

The tiredness Kitty had experienced in Leicester had been a revelation, but in Northampton, there was so much to learn and remember she was usually asleep long before lights out. Now Kitty slept the sleep of the dead, the grief-stricken nights where she woke up thinking of Joe a thing of the past. These days, although Kitty still ached for Joe, she was finding her heartache easier to manage and as a result found thoughts of her fiancé a comfort, helping her cope with the endless slog of army life.

Kitty's role as a spark girl was far more intense than she had expected. Surprisingly, Sergeant Hopson had eventually deemed her fit to drive a vehicle unsupervised and now she was turning her attentions to ambulances, Tilly trucks, tiny little Fiats, known as Bug cars, and three-ton lorries so she could drive in convoy. Likewise, Kitty and her friends would also need to have a solid grasp of vehicle maintenance so if there was a problem out on the road they would be able to fix it. The term 'spark girl' wasn't just an affectionate one for the drivers and mechanics, she had come to realise. It meant you had to have something about you to cope with the endless amount of responsibility the vehicles demanded.

Alongside Di, Peg and Mary, Kitty worked full days at the driver instructor training centre, and after a quick supper in the canteen was usually straight back to the hut to go over all she had learnt that day. Schoolwork had never been Kitty's strong suit – she struggled to commit the information to her brain.

Never mind the fact her back ached from spending most of her afternoons hunched over a car bonnet and her fingernails were as black as the road from all the grease she handled day in day out.

Kitty hated to admit it but she occasionally looked at the other volunteers who had been assigned roles as cooks, or store keepers, with envy. They seemed to have far more time off than the spark girls, and were able to nip into town a couple of times a week for drinks or a visit to the pictures while Kitty and her pals swotted over their mechanics studies.

The one saving grace was that she had to spend far less time with Sergeant Hopson than she expected. Apart from a session in the classroom each morning, where he would teach them everything from navigation skills to the workings of an engine, Kitty had little to do with him and was taught by a handful of other instructors who she found much friendlier and easier to talk to.

Kitty couldn't understand why she still felt so uneasy around him. Since the rebuke in her first week, Hopson had never openly scolded her again, but he seemed eager to make her life difficult in other ways, by giving her extra chores to do after class such as stacking the chairs onto the tables, cleaning the blackboard or washing the cars.

The glint of pleasure in Hopson's eye when he instructed her to stay behind told Kitty he seemed to enjoy disciplining her but she had no idea why. She'd written to Arthur about her worries a week earlier. This morning she was delighted to discover a reply was waiting for her and she had savoured the thought of its content all day, looking forward to devouring the letter over supper before starting work on her books.

15 July 1940

Dear Kitty,

Thanks for your letter, which I received yesterday. I just wanted to write a few lines before we ship out tomorrow to goodness knows where, as I wanted my reply to reach you sooner rather than later.

First of all I'm sorry you're having a bit of grief off your sergeant. If it's any consolation I can't say I'm surprised. When I was at work on the railways a few years back, I had a similar problem and found the best thing to do was take it all with a pinch of salt. The fella, my boss, it was, soon got bored when I didn't react to anything he did and he moved onto some other poor so and so. Course you'd expect better in the Army, but folk are folk, and some are never happier than when they're making others' lives a misery.

It sounds as though you're finding out first-hand that life in the ATS is tough, not just because of all the hard work, but because you have to mix with people who in real life you'd cross the street to avoid! But Kit, you're strong and always have been. You'll get through this with grace, just like you have every other problem you've coped with and I have every confidence this sergeant, whoever he is, will rue the day he ever picked on Kitty Williams.

Anyway, I must be off now, we've a drill to do on the upper deck and it'll be me having problems with my superiors if I don't get a move on.

Keep your chin up, Kit, and write soon,

Yours,
Arthur

Kitty looked down at the paper and smiled. Arthur had always known just how to cheer her up, and this letter had been the tonic she needed. He was right, of course, she had seen bullies like Hopson off a dozen times at the children's home and knew he would eventually get bored and move on to someone else. In the meantime, she would refuse to give him the satisfaction of knowing he had bothered her.

Stuffing the letter back into the envelope, Kitty pushed her chair back and stood up to wash her eating irons. She checked her watch and saw it had gone seven. She would have just three hours to study in the Nissen hut before lights out, which was a pity. They were doing a practical mechanics test tomorrow and Kitty had hoped to get as much revision in as possible, but as ever, Hopson had kept her behind that evening, this time to dust every inch of the classroom.

'You look exhausted, Kitty,' Di called as she walked into the hut.

'I've felt better,' Kitty admitted, sinking onto her bed for just a moment. 'Hopson's quick tidy-up took nearly two hours.'

'You're joking!' Mary exclaimed. 'I thought you would be no more than about ten minutes. I've said it before and I'll say it again, that man is a scoundrel!'

Kitty smiled at her friend's outrage on her behalf and shrugged. 'Afraid not, and I'm miles behind me revision for tomorrow.'

'Oh, don't worry about that – you're a natural, everyone says so,' Mary said, shrugging. 'And tomorrow's our first vehicle maintenance test so they won't make it difficult; it'll be a piece of cake.'

'Maybe,' Kitty grumbled. 'But some of the maths we have to learn as part of our engineering training seems downright unnecessary. I mean, what've fractions got to do with how to change a radiator valve in an ambulance?'

'Search me, love,' Di sighed. 'It's the driving side of things I'm struggling with. Changing a spark plug's easy. P'raps I'm more suited to vehicle maintenance instead of getting behind a wheel.'

'Give over!' Kitty objected. 'It's just because it's new, that's all. You'll get there.'

Reaching for her notepad, Kitty began to read determinedly, but before long felt her eyelids start to droop as the tiredness she had been fighting all day set in. Rousing herself to continue she tried to understand the technique behind double declutching before realising she had read the same paragraph three times over. It was almost a relief when the horn sounded lights out and she could finally give in to the land of nod. Pushing her pad to the floor, she turned over and hoped that tomorrow, luck would be on her side.

*

The sunshine warmed her face and Kitty smiled with pleasure as she strolled through the quad towards the motor centre, ready to start the day. It really was the little things, she thought, walking down the hill – the sound of birdsong in the trees above – that made life worth living, war or no war.

Pushing open the wooden door to the Nissen hut that doubled as their classroom, Kitty took a seat as everyone else gossiped among themselves while they waited for Sergeant Hopson. He arrived shortly after Kitty, striding authoritatively into the noisy classroom and turning abruptly to the students. Sharply clapping his hands for attention, he brought the idle chatter among the recruits to an immediate halt.

'Right then, you lot,' he called, pacing up and down in front of the blackboard. 'This morning you have all got your practical mechanics test. Don't worry, it's nothing to be alarmed about, there's no court martial if you fail.' He smirked, raising an eyebrow at his own joke. 'That said, my standards, as I'm sure you've come to appreciate by now, are high, and I do expect you all to give it your best.'

The girls looked nervously at the sergeant as he continued to deliver his instructions while handing out the test papers. Listening to Hopson explain the right and wrong way to hold a spanner during the test sent a prickle of fear down Kitty's spine. She had tried so hard to be ready for this, and had woken early to cram some last-minute information into her brain in a vain attempt not to let Hopson down. Now, as they filed out to the cars parked outside, dressed in their khaki overalls, all Kitty could do was hope it was enough.

'One final thing before you get started on your papers,' he shouted as a noisy convoy of lorries drove past just yards behind him. 'I want to make things a bit tougher so I'm going to mix up your usual teams. Don't want you getting comfortable, after all this is the Army, not a holiday camp.'

The sergeant read out a list of pairs and Kitty inwardly groaned as she realised she had been teamed with Beryl Mason, a volunteer from Glasgow who was famous for being the teacher's pet. The girl knew nothing about the spirit of working together, and frequently trampled over others to ensure she got what she wanted. Kitty had only known Beryl a few weeks but, so far, had been unable to find one single commendable quality. Beryl was selfish and seemed to think she was better than every other recruit stationed at Northampton.

Yet when it came to talking to their superiors, Beryl knew how to turn on the charm and it went without saying that Sergeant Hopson adored her, often singling Beryl out for her map reading abilities or attention to detail. Watching Mary and Di team up together and Peg pair off with Sarah Goodison, a kindly older lady from Cornwall, Kitty gritted her teeth and smiled warmly as Beryl approached her.

'Hello, love.' She grinned in what she hoped was a friendly fashion. 'Have yer revised?'

'Only a fool would turn up to a test like this unprepared,' replied Beryl pompously. 'Our job is to assist the British Army, and if you can't be bothered to work hard, then you've no right being here at all as far as I'm concerned.'

'Righto,' Kitty said, discreetly rolling her eyes and glancing at the test paper she and Beryl had been given to work through.

She was pleased to discover the test, filled with twenty exercises, looked relatively straightforward, just as Mary had predicted, and there was nothing on the paper that was a surprise.

'So how should we divvy the work up?' Kitty frowned. 'D'yer fancy working together on each question, or would yer rather work on your own?'

'I think it's best we work alone, Kitty,' Beryl said, smirking. 'Your mechanical skills are shocking at best; you'll only muck up my own efforts. I'll take the first ten exercises, you take the second ten and we'll make it clear who did what. I'll not fail because of you.'

Kitty felt her hackles rise as she eyed the recruit with contempt. The girl was only a year or so older than her, yet behaved as though she was a section leader already. Tall and thin with angular cheekbones and narrow lips, Beryl looked as though she had been born with a mean streak.

'Listen,' Kitty said in a low voice thick with anger. 'Yer carry on talking to me like that and we'll have a problem before we even start, d'yer understand? Like it or lump it we're stuck with one another.'

Beryl squared her shoulders and loomed over Kitty, her cheeks as red as her fiery mane.

'Oh aye, we're stuck with each other right enough,' she growled. 'Because when you mess up, you can be the one to explain to Sergeant Hopson it was down to you. I'm not taking the blame for your mistakes.'

'Oh, don't worry, Beryl. I'd no more expect yer to help someone out than I would see yer fly through the air,' Kitty fired back. 'But I suggest we say no more about it, and carry on.'

Turning back to the car, Kitty realised her hands were trembling as she looked down at the test paper. Reaching for the spanner, she rolled her sleeves up and was about to start work on draining the radiator when she heard a voice behind her.

'That's the first sensible thing I've heard you say since you arrived in Northampton, Volunteer Williams.'

Kitty's heart sank as she spun around and came face to face with Sergeant Hopson.

'If only you were as good at mechanics as you are at mouthing off,' he scolded, hands clasped behind his back. 'I don't expect to hear cat-fighting during my sessions, is that clear?'

'Yes, sir,' Kitty said clearly, doing her best to ignore the rest of her platoon who were watching the commotion agog.

'Good. Because Volunteer Mason had every right to express concern about working with you,' he continued. 'Your mechanical skills are second rate and, rather than reassure her you would do your best, you chose to enter into a slanging match.' Sergeant Hopson shook his head and took a step towards Kitty. 'For your insubordination and complete lack of respect towards a colleague, you will be docked a mark from this exam.'

Kitty groaned inwardly. She was failing the test before she had even begun, yet she knew there was no point complaining.

'Understood, sir,' she replied miserably.

Once Sergeant Hopson dismissed her, Kitty turned back to the test in hand. She could kick herself for being so daft, she knew better than to get into a row with the teacher's pet and wasn't sure what had come over her, other than a huge desire to wipe that smirk off Beryl Mason's stuck-up face.

Wordlessly, she worked through the rest of the test, determined to prove Beryl and Hopson wrong. By the time her sergeant sounded the whistle to signal time up, she was pleased to find she had finished the exam with seconds to spare and couldn't help shooting Beryl a look of triumph as she closed the car bonnet.

Anxiously, she watched Sergeant Hopson inspect each team's effort, taking the time to praise each one for a particular task completed well, or pointing out where mistakes had been made and how they could be corrected. By the time he arrived at Beryl and Kitty's car, Kitty was on tenterhooks, eager to know just how well she had performed.

As Sergeant Hopson took his time examining the car, Kitty was sure she had done a good job and hoped finally to hear one word of praise from her superior officer. As the inspection came to an end, Sergeant Hopson rocked backwards and forwards on his heels, and shot both girls a genuine smile.

'Excellent work, I must say,' he said in a friendly tone. 'I know you both divided up the exercises which clearly worked well. Marvellous delegation skills there, Volunteer Mason,' he beamed, turning to a simpering Beryl. 'And Volunteer Williams, I must say you've surprised me. You've shown great skill during the test and I'm pleased to say you've both passed.'

Glancing at her friends standing just behind Hopson, she saw them grin happily as they performed a silent handclap to show Kitty their support.

'However, there is just one thing, Volunteer Williams,' Sergeant Hopson said slowly. 'I'm afraid you exceeded your time changing the oil and, as you know, we have strict regulations surrounding vehicle maintenance.'

Instinctively, Kitty opened her mouth to protest. She was sure she had only taken the allotted two minutes. But remembering she was a soldier, she shut her mouth as quickly as she had opened it and instead listened to her sergeant, not wanting to make things any worse for herself.

'The Army doesn't set these tests for fun, we set them because lives depend on it,' Hopson lectured. 'If you were out in the field and took a long time to change the oil when Jerries were all around, there would be a good chance you could be captured or even killed. As for the precious cargo you would likely be carrying in your vehicle, it could easily fall into enemy hands – and all because you were too slow. I'm afraid that although you have passed the test, Volunteer Williams, I am forced to give you a CB notice for a week. That should give you plenty of time to practice your oil changes. At ease.'

Kitty was shaking with anger. A Confined to Barracks notice meant that not only would she remain firmly on the base for a week, but any free time she did have would be spent helping out in the kitchen peeling potatoes and washing floors as well as cleaning the latrines.

'Oh, what a shame,' Beryl said smugly, as Sergeant Hopson walked back inside the classroom. 'And you were doing so well.'

'Belt up, Beryl,' Kitty growled, as she saw her friends walking towards her, ready to offer their support.

'Yes, do shut up, Beryl,' added Mary as she reached the girls. 'I think we've all heard rather enough out of you for one day. Why don't you get back to your cauldron and start stirring?'

'That's rich coming from you,' Beryl chuckled. 'I'd have thought with your coven it'd be you lot that'd be in need of the big wooden spoon.'

'Oh, leave it, Beryl, you've 'ad your fun, now go and polish your 'alo ready for 'opson to inspect. I know you wouldn't want to let 'im down,' Di snapped, turning her back on the Scot.

Beryl stormed off up the hill in the direction of the NAAFI. Kitty looked at each of her friends gratefully and tried to disguise the hurt she felt. She was sure she had completed each task not only well, but within the allotted time. In fact she had time left, so how was it possible she could have messed up badly enough to earn herself a CB notice?

'D'yer think Hopson's got it in for me?' she asked eventually. 'Because I don't understand why he's always singling me out like this.'

'Oh it's not that,' said Di. 'I expect 'opson's just showing off, that's all.'

'D'yer really think that's all it is?' asked Kitty miserably. 'Because it doesn't feel that way to me.'

Di regarded Kitty quizzically. 'What else could it be?' she asked, her voice softening. 'This probably happens every time he gets a new crop of recruits. You know, picks on one to show 'em all who's boss. It'll pass, trust me.'

Peggy nodded. 'Di's right. You've just been unlucky, he's gone and set his sights on you, but he'll soon get bored and move on.'

Kitty turned over the girls' words in her mind before she spoke. 'I'm being silly,' she admitted. 'Whatever this is, he'll get over it.'

'Of course he will,' Mary said. 'Don't forget this isn't personal, to him you're just some annoying little upstart and he wants his fun. More than likely he's a crashing bore and half his trouble is he's never had a sweetheart.'

'Mare!' Peg gasped, her cheeks reddening with embarrassment. 'You can't talk about a superior officer like that. He'll have your guts for garters.'

'I don't care.' Mary shrugged. 'I'm sure it's perfectly true anyway, though I'm sure the lovely Beryl would be more than happy to offer him a bunk up in the dorm!'

Kitty shuddered at the thought. 'I'm with Peg on this, Mary

'– that's enough. The thought of Hopson getting saucy with Beryl is enough to put me off me dinner for life.'

'You're not wrong there, lovey. Talk about disgusting,' Di agreed, adding in retching noises for effect, much to the amusement of the others.

'Oi, Di! Pack it in, Hopson's coming back,' Kitty whispered, spotting the sergeant striding towards the group and nudging her friend violently in the ribs.

'Still here, are we? I must say you are all keen for more, aren't you?' Hopson chuckled, his smirk almost reaching the tips of his ears. 'Or perhaps you're eager to join Volunteer Williams with a week's CB notice?'

'Oh no, Sergeant Hopson,' babbled Mary. 'We were just offering Kitty the benefit of our mechanical wisdom so she could see where she had gone wrong. After all, you were so good to point out how successful our own oil changes had been.'

Glancing at her friend, Kitty thought she might be sick. She knew Mary was just trying to get them all on the sergeant's good side, but did she really have to be so nauseating? Kitty shuddered. She wasn't sure she could ever be such a crawler, and with a sudden jolt she realised that was perhaps where she had gone wrong all her life.

Still, she thought glancing up at Hopson, Mary's words seemed to have the desired effect, as Kitty noticed his smirk had been replaced with more of a triumphant beam.

'Very good, that's the way,' he said, his voice filled with jollity. 'Now why don't you all disappear for lunch, while I get Volunteer Williams started on the first of her extra CB duties. I'll see you back here at two sharp.'

'Yes, sir,' the others replied briskly as they walked towards the NAAFI, leaving Kitty alone with Sergeant Hopson.

As she looked up at him waiting for her orders Kitty was surprised to notice that she felt more than a little self-conscious. Should she open her mouth and start speaking uninvited or was it better to wait until she was spoken too? She hated this indecision, and was fearful of saying or doing the wrong thing.

But thankfully Hopson saved her the trouble. Once Di, Peg and Mary were out of sight, he cocked his head to one side and regarded her thoughtfully.

'I suspect you're wondering if we've got off on the wrong foot, Volunteer?'

'Er, not really, sir,' Kitty replied evenly, sensing Hopson was trying to provoke her. 'I made a mistake, sir, and I'll do me best to make sure it won't happen again.'

'Yes, you did make a mistake, Volunteer,' he hissed quietly. 'But you're wrong, it will happen again.'

Kitty was confused. Turning to face him, she was about to explain that it really would never happen again when Hopson brought his face so close to hers she could see the wrinkles around his eyes crinkled in amusement.

'I can assure yer, sir, I'm doing me best here,' Kitty replied in what she hoped was an appeasing tone.

'Oh, I know that, Volunteer,' Hopson said, pulling his face from Kitty's. 'But you see girls like you always make mistakes.'

'Girls like me, sir?' Kitty quizzed, unsure what the sergeant meant.

'Yes, girls like you, Williams. Girls who are thoughtless, girls who are ignorant, girls who think that it doesn't matter if you take over two minutes to complete an oil change. I was watching you, Williams, and that's how I know you're slapdash and care-free. You're one of the girls who think they don't have to operate under the same rules as everyone else.'

'Sir,' Kitty interrupted, keen to set the sergeant straight. 'I don't think that. Course I think the rules apply to me.'

'That's enough, Williams!' Hopson snapped. 'Or do you want to scrub another car with a shaving brush as yet another punishment for insubordination?'

Kitty said nothing and gave a quiet shake of her head.

'No, I thought not,' the sergeant mused. 'I've been in the Army a long time, Williams, and I've seen girls like you come and go. I know you better than you know yourself and I can tell you that you will make more mistakes because you will always be thoughtless. The ATS doesn't need girls like you, Williams.'

'But, sir . . .' Kitty tried again. 'I really want to learn. The ATS means everything to me.'

The sergeant looked straight at her before speaking again. 'You may think that, Williams, but frankly I think that the Army means very little to you. Your job here serving your country is probably nothing more than a nice distraction for you from whatever it is that's going on in your little life back home, and you thought joining up would be a bit of a jape. Well let me tell you, Williams, the ATS is not a jape, and I despise girls like you who think that it is.'

With that, Hopson finished and stalked up the hill away from her, leaving Kitty rooted to the spot. As she watched Hopson's retreating back, Kitty drank in the enormity of what he had just said. What did he mean, girls like her? She was not one of those girls that he had described and never had been. Kitty prided herself on her ability to get stuck in, work hard and do her bit. Where this had come from Kitty was unsure, but she had the strangest feeling that she was no longer just some recruit to pick on before moving on to another girl. Hopson appeared to be deliberately targeting her. The question was, why?

She looked at the floor, in despair. How many more battles was she going to have to endure before she could find her own kind of peace? She closed her eyes and brought Joe's handsome face to mind. Just the image of him gave her instant comfort and in that moment she vowed that nobody would stop her finishing what he had started. Sticking her chin out defiantly towards Hopson as he disappeared over the hill, Kitty knew that whatever this wretched war threw at her, she would withstand it all, for Joe.

Chapter Seven

There was no denying it, Kitty thought as she walked into the mess, it had been a long week. Joining the back of the queue for breakfast, she sniffed the air appreciatively and grinned with delight – bacon and eggs, talk about luxury. Although Kitty and the other recruits certainly never starved in the Army, she was well aware just how hard it was to get hold of food since rationing had become stricter. Bacon and eggs was a dish rarely on the menu and she couldn't wait to tuck in.

With a wink, Cook piled her plate high with soft runny egg and bacon leaving Kitty as excited as a child on Christmas morning as she turned towards the body of the dining hall to take a seat. Spotting Di, Mary and Peg, sitting jacketless in the continuing July heat wave, she hurried to join them.

'Blimey, I've never seen yer so chirpy,' Di marvelled affectionately, taking in Kitty's expression.

'Well, this is the best thing that's happened to me all week, if not all month,' Kitty remarked, eagerly slicing into a rasher of crispy bacon. 'Cup of tea and a proper breakfast. What more does a girl need?'

As Kitty took her first mouthful, she savoured the saltiness of the bacon hitting her taste buds. Cook had done them proud, this was better than lumpy porridge any day of the week.

'I rather think Cook's given you a little more than the rest of us.' Mary sniffed, interrupting Kitty's enjoyment. 'I'm not sure that's right. I only had two pieces of bacon, you appear to have three.'

'Oh leave off, Mary,' Di scolded, quickly coming to her friend's defence. 'I doubt that very much. You were probably too quick stuffing your breakfast down your cake hole to appreciate what was on your plate. Besides, even if Kitty has been given extras by Cook, no doubt she's earned 'em after the week she's had.'

'You're not kidding,' Peggy marvelled. 'What time d'you knock off last night, Kit?'

Kitty placed her fork on the side of her plate and tried to remember exactly what time she had finished scrubbing the kitchen and blacking the step of the mess hall. It had been back-breaking after a day huddled over a bonnet of one of the little Fiat cars they had all been instructed to take care of, and there had been times when she had wondered if she would ever sleep again.

'Must have been about two in the morning I think,' she replied, stifling a yawn.

'Goodness me, Kitty,' Mary said admiringly. 'I take it all back. I think you've more than earned that extra piece of bacon. Do tell me that blasted CB notice has finished now. I feel as though you've been dished out a life sentence and I'm serving every day of it with you.'

Kitty chuckled at Mary's obvious fury. The CB notice had certainly taken its toll. What with a day's work driving, then another day's work ensuring the barracks were more than spick and span, to say Kitty was exhausted was an understatement.

'I finished last night,' Kitty said triumphantly through a mouthful of egg. 'Cook said the kitchen had never looked so clean this morning.'

'That explains the bacon,' Mary pointed out.

Di shook her head in exasperation. 'Will you stop going on about flippin' bacon, Mary. You've 'ad your share, and our Kit looks as though she needs building up.' Di sighed and turned to face Kitty, squeezing her arm gently in sympathy. 'You look done in, love, if you don't mind me saying.'

'I don't mind at all.' Kitty smiled as she devoured another

forkful of her breakfast. 'I *am* done in. I'm no stranger to hard work, but I feel about ready for the knacker's yard.'

'It can't really 'ave been that bad, can it, babber?' Peggy asked sympathetically.

'Bad?' Kitty raised her eyebrows. 'Let's put it this way, I always thought us girls were a clean and tidy bunch but after cleaning out those latrines every night, I think it's fair to say some of 'em might need a lesson in personal hygiene. The state of 'em was a disgrace.'

'Ewwww.' Mary wrinkled her nose in disgust. 'Let's not discuss latrines at breakfast, please. Look on the bright side. You'll never have to do it again, as long as you don't get on the wrong side of Hopson of course.'

Kitty roared with laughter. 'Well, if that's the deal, I think I'll be back on CB notice next week and every other week I'm here then. He had a go at me yesterday 'cos I left a smear on the windscreen of a Tilly truck he had me washing after class.'

'He really will get over this eventually,' Mary promised as she sipped her tea thoughtfully. 'No matter what his problem is, this will stop and he'll move onto someone else.'

'I'm not sure about that, and even if he does leave me alone and pick on someone else then it's not fair on them either,' Kitty replied. 'Don't forget he's got the measure of girls like me, whatever that means.'

'It means 'e's a nasty, spiteful little man,' Di fired, banging her tin mug on the table for emphasis.

'Di!' Peggy hissed, clearly alarmed. 'If he hears you, we'll all be for it.'

'Well 'e deserves it,' Di snapped. 'I've no idea why 'e said those awful things, Kitty. If anyone's a true spark girl it's you. You're always busy learning and working 'ard. It's time 'e let up on you.'

'Well I think there's more chance of us having bacon for breakfast tomorrow than there is of him changing his mind about me anytime soon,' Kitty replied quietly, finishing the last of her breakfast and reaching for her cup. 'Let's just forget it.'

'No, let's *not* forget it!' Mary squawked. 'He's no bally right singling you out like this. Do you want me to talk to Uncle P? I could drop him a note and I'll have that slimy little toad out of here before he can tie his shoelaces.'

Kitty smiled kindly at Mary, touched by the gesture. Since she had told her friends just what Hopson had said to her after putting her on CB notice, they had been full of support. 'No, lovey. Thanks for the thought, but a letter to your uncle's not what I need right now.'

'Then what is?' Mary asked, looking at Kitty squarely in the eye.

'I'm not sure. But I do know telling tales won't solve anything,' Kitty said firmly, eating irons in hand. 'And I also know being late won't help either, so if you'll excuse me, ladies, I'm going to wash up and get to the classroom early.'

With that Kitty pushed back her chair and after washing up her things, hurried towards the motor centre. If she was honest, she not only wanted a head start on Hopson, but was also hoping to give the room a final inspection to check nothing had been missed. She had been tasked with clearing the classroom up before starting on the kitchen last night and Kitty would hate to give Hopson any extra fuel to throw at her. This past week had been more than tough and she was in no mood to repeat the experience. She walked in and was dismayed to discover Sergeant Hopson had beaten her to it and was sat at his desk, legs crossed, his face hunched over paperwork. Kitty braced herself for rebuke, sure he would tell her off for being too early, but instead she was surprised to see he looked flustered, his face flushed red, as he caught sight of her.

'Permission to speak, sir?' she said, loitering in the doorway.

'Granted.'

'Sorry if I've interrupted yer, sir. I can come back in a few minutes if that's easier?'

'No, not at all, Volunteer Williams. Nice to see you here early. Take a seat,' he said, offering her a slight smile.

Feeling slightly blindsided by the lack of scolding, Kitty sat at a desk at the back of the room and observed the sergeant. When he wasn't shouting and snarling he had a pleasant way about him, she thought. His eyes were in fact kind and he even looked handsome when he smiled. Was it possible there was another side to Hopson? A kinder, gentler side? Kitty hoped so, but as the others filed in to the classroom, she realised it was unlikely to put in an appearance over the course of the morning.

'Right then you lot,' he shouted above the din of the girls' chatter. 'Today you're all going out on your own, unsupervised. This is a real test of how much you've learned as I'll be asking you to put into practice your map-reading and driving skills. I'll ask each of you to take a variety of routes to a variety of destinations with different rendezvous points along the way. That way I'll know you haven't all sloped off on a jolly if you've an officer to meet, who, mark my words, will inform me if any of you are even a second late to your meeting point. Clear?'

A ripple of excitement went around the room as the girls realised this was their first chance to show just what they could do out on the open road. After the long slog of training they were delighted to put into practice all they had learned and show off their skills, Kitty particularly.

As the girls signalled their approval, Sergeant Hopson looked down at his desk and then at Kitty. 'Now, as Volunteer Williams has shown me just how keen you all are to get going, I thought we would start the morning off with a little impromptu test. Get out your notebooks, everyone, as I'll ask you a series of questions, and the girl with the fewest marks will be staying behind.'

The recruits groaned at the news, only for Sergeant Hopson to shout above the hubbub. 'Quite right, ladies, I think we'll make it the two with the lowest score to stay behind and clean the truck garages. And please, if you have any complaints, do take it up with Volunteer Williams. If she hadn't been quite so prompt this morning I would never have realised how keen you were to show me how well you're doing.'

As Kitty reached for her notepad, she met Di's sympathetic gaze and felt momentarily comforted, before realising that a room full of eyes was shooting daggers at her. Gloomily she tore out a sheet of paper and scribbled her name on the top. She wasn't even sure there was an awful lot of point taking this test, after all, it was more than likely she would be the one staying behind, clearing out the truck garage and whatever else Hopson could dream of to punish her.

Just over an hour later and the ordeal was over. To her surprise, Sergeant Hopson had chosen not to fail her and Kitty was delighted to discover she had scored highly in the test.

'Credit where credit's due, Williams,' Hopson said as he dismissed the class. 'You've done well today, but of course I don't expect you to keep it up. Just remember, I've got my eye on you.'

'Yes, sir,' Kitty replied, before turning on her heel and joining Di, who was waiting for her outside the room.

'I've got my eye on you,' her friend mimicked, screwing up her face into a Hopson-like grimace, causing Kitty to collapse into a fit of giggles.

'Shh, Di! He'll hear yer and then we'll be in trouble.'

'Oh stuff 'im!' Di shrugged as they walked along the corridor and out into the sunshine towards the tiny Bug – they had been assigned for their task. 'I bet 'e was devastated when 'e realised 'ow well you'd done. Still, we'll show 'im, Kit.'

The girls clambered into the car, Kitty behind the wheel, and familiarised themselves with the vehicle. Unlike the Humber they had been training in, the Bug was a lot smaller and lighter and Kitty realised she wouldn't need to accelerate quite so much to pick up speed. That said, with petrol rationed and speed restricted during blackout hours she knew they wouldn't be going over twenty miles per hour once darkness fell, so she and Di would need to make the most of the daylight if they were going to drive over forty miles to Peterborough.

'Come on then, I'll take first shift behind the wheel, yer can do the map-reading,' said Kitty, as she switched the starter motor on and brought the little vehicle to life. 'Can yer see the rendezvous points easily enough with those latitude and longitude co-ordinates Hopson's given yer?'

Di nodded. 'Looks as though our first one is near Wellingborough.'

'Lovely, hope he's picked a nice cafe for a late lunch,' Kitty replied, sliding the car smoothly out onto the road.

'Ooh that'd be nice, Kit, though I've a feeling if 'opson's organised it, it's more likely 'e'll have picked a shack in the middle of nowhere. Remember what 'e said – no jollies,' Di said, stabbing the map with her forefinger for emphasis.

'Like I'd forget,' Kitty remarked, arching an eyebrow.

Once Kitty and Di had left the barracks and were out on their own, they were delighted to discover they made an excellent team. Di was a natural navigator and could quickly assess the best way to reach each rendezvous point along the way, giving Kitty clear and precise instructions, so they were easily in time to meet their supervisors. As for Kitty, she felt a sense of freedom like no other as she steered the vehicle free from supervision. Looking out of the window at the glorious and lush English countryside that unfurled before her, she forgot for a second there was a war on. With trees swaying in the breeze, flowers blooming in the hedgerows and barely a cloud in the sky, everything seemed idyllic. The only clue to the fact they were fighting Hitler were the khaki Army trucks filled with soldiers that thundered along the road.

By the time Kitty and Di reached their final destination in Peterborough over three hours later they were more than ready for a cuppa and something to eat. Thankfully, the officers they were meeting on the outskirts of the city were far more accommodating than Sergeant Hopson and encouraged the girls to pull up a chair and join them for tea and biscuits before they returned to barracks.

Feeling thoroughly rested, the two friends bid their superiors goodbye and returned to the car. Kitty immediately walked towards the driver's door, only for Di to dig gently at her arm.

'Er, wait a minute Kit, it's my turn to drive,' Di said awkwardly.

Kitty paused, her face giving away the briefest of concerns. 'I know, but it'll be dark soon and it's just started to rain, don't yer think I should drive us back? It's our first trip out on our own and I don't want to do anything that'll get us into trouble with Hopson.'

'I know that, Kitty,' Di said patiently, 'but I'm not likely to get any better at driving if you don't let me take a turn. If I get stuck I'll say, I promise.'

Biting her lip, Kitty thought for a moment, before walking around to the passenger side of the car. 'Fair enough. I'll take over the navigation.'

'Thanks, Kitty. And remember you'll need to stick your 'ead out of the window once twilight falls, as I won't be able to see so well.'

Kitty grumbled under her breath. Driving at night was difficult thanks to the blackout restrictions and Kitty sometimes thought it was only due to a wing and a prayer that they made it to their destination. The car's lights had been specially adapted to allow only a small pinprick of light to emerge from the front, while white markings on the road helped the driver make out what was in front of them. Yet the reality meant it was nigh on impossible to see, Kitty thought, which was why she and the rest of the spark girls had been encouraged to poke their heads out of the windows and shout helpful hints about bends and tight corners to the driver. Now it was raining, which always made the task extra tough, and all Kitty could do was hope it would ease off over time.

As they set off, Kitty was relieved to see that Di at least looked calm and confident behind the wheel. It was a good start, she thought, and hopefully if today went well, then Di's driving skills would improve. With only one rendezvous point on the way home, Kitty was confident they would arrive back at their base within plenty of time.

But as darkness fell and the rain became heavy, Kitty noticed Di seemed flustered, causing the little Bug to shudder and jerk. Kitty knew better than to offer to take over, and also knew that Di was right: there was no chance of her skills developing if she only drove in good conditions. Instead, Kitty stuck her head out of the window a bit further and tried to shout out clear instructions from the little she could see up ahead.

'Careful, Di, there's a sharp bend coming up and then we need to take a left according to the map,' she instructed.

'Understood,' Di replied, as she gripped the wheel tightly, her knuckles so ice-white, they were visible in the darkness.

With the junction successfully negotiated, Kitty was relieved to see Di's hands relax a little. 'Nicely done, love,' she said, her voice warm with praise. 'I'm struggling to see a hand in front of me face, so heaven only knows how you're managing.'

'By the skin of me bloomin' teeth,' Di whistled, her body hunched over the wheel, chin practically on the dashboard as she desperately tried to make out each white line on the road to help guide her. 'This rain's coming down like stair-rods, 'ow far away d'you think we are from the barracks?'

Kitty made some rough calculations in her head. 'About an hour. We've no more rendezvous points, which is good, and I think despite this weather, we're making good time.' She braved the rain once more and stuck her head out of the window to peer at the road around her. Kitty remembered this particular bit of road had been difficult to manage on the way up. 'Watch out for a big ditch coming up, Di. It nearly had me off the road earlier so make sure yer take it a bit slow.'

'Well it's not like I can go 'ell for leather even if I want to, Kit,' Di chuckled, loosening her grip on the steering wheel and taking her eyes away from the road to turn to Kitty. 'The limit's twenty, I don't think I can do a lot of damage at that speed.'

Kitty's eyes widened in horror as she saw her friend narrowly avoid a passing Army truck. 'Get your eyes back on the flamin' road, Diana Mills!'

'All right, all right, keep your bloody 'air on,' Di snapped, as she turned her gaze back to the road ahead. Only it was too late. The car skittered left then right in the driving rain, juddering all over the road.

'Christ, Di, get control of the bloody thing!' Kitty roared.

'What d'you think I'm doing? Filing me nails?' Di shouted

back as she struggled to regain control of the vehicle.

Sensing danger, Kitty grabbed hold of the wheel and attempted to pull the car away from the edge of the road, but the tarmac along the quiet country lane was slippery and the wheels on the little car had barely any traction. Despite their best efforts, the Bug slid from the road and plunged headlong into the large, cavernous ditch Kitty had wanted so desperately to avoid. As it tumbled to an abrupt halt, Kitty and Di let go of the dashboard they had been clutching and turned to each other in shock.

'Are you all right, Kit?' Di gasped.

'I think so,' Kitty replied, moving each of her limbs and checking for damage. 'I don't think anything's broken. What about yer?'

'I'm fine,' Di said shakily. 'Bit wobbly, that's all.'

'Me 'n'all, lovey,' Kit replied as she peered out of the window and looked down. 'Well, we're going to have a fine job getting this car out. It must be stuck in at least two inches of mud.'

Di groaned, resting her face on the steering wheel. 'Tell me it's not that bad.'

'Only one way to find out,' Kitty replied grimly, opening the car door and immediately finding herself ankle-deep in mud.

As she suspected, the car was completely stuck with both back wheels seemingly jammed in thick sludge. With a heavy heart, Kitty walked around the car, the mud now up to her calves and the rain trickling down her back. Thankfully, the pinpricks of light from the car allowed her to get a sense of how much trouble they were in. As she ran her hands around the chassis and the bumper, Kitty let out a sigh of relief – the car appeared to be undamaged.

'Is it bad?' Di asked, her face a picture of despair as she stuck her head out of the window.

'Well the good news is the car's all right. The bad news is I've no idea how we're going to get it back on the road,' Kitty replied, wiping the raindrops from her face.

Di flung open her door and joined Kitty. 'Oh Christ! Look at it.'

'Yes, it's a flamin' nightmare,' Kitty agreed. 'D'yer fancy getting back in and flooring that accelerator, seeing if we can't get out of this mud?'

Di shook her head. 'You do it, Kit. I've caused enough damage. I'm sorry, I should never 'ave driven us back.'

Kitty patted her friend's hand comfortingly. 'Don't talk soft. Yer were doing great, till yer stopped looking where yer were going.'

Di smiled sheepishly. 'Well, lesson learned for the future, eh? Always keep your eyes on the road.'

'It'd help,' Kitty teased. 'Now then, in yer go, and I'll see if this car's going to move.'

Di did as instructed, and pressed her foot against the accelerator. 'Anything?' she called.

'Hasn't budged an inch.' Kitty grimaced. 'But on the bright side, the rain's stopped.'

'Every cloud,' Di roared over the nose of the engine as she floored the pedal once more.

'No, stop,' Kitty shouted, as Di covered her in wet mud. 'All you're doing is wedging us further in the sludge.'

'So what d'yer suggest?' asked Di as she got out of the car and joined Kitty.

Pursing her lips, Kitty had to admit she wasn't sure. She was about to say as much when the noise of a car up ahead caught her by surprise. Quickly, she jumped out into the road and waved frantically to the car. Perhaps with an extra pair of hands they might be able to give the car a push. Signalling to the driver for help, she was delighted when the car stopped a few feet ahead, and even more delighted when a familiar face clambered out of the driver's side.

'What the devil are yer doing here?' Kitty called in surprise.

'I could ask you the same thing,' Mary shouted back cheerfully. 'The ditch is no place to spend a Friday night, Kitty. A dance hall's more the thing.'

'We're stuck,' Kitty replied.

'Well any fool can see that,' Mary laughed, before turning

back to the car. 'Come on, Peg, out you get, we're needed.'

Together the two girls walked down the narrow road and Kitty felt a surge of happiness at the sight of her two friends.

'What a bally state!' Mary gasped as she neared the car. 'How on earth did you get into this mess?'

'I was driving,' Di admitted.

'I might have guessed!' Mary sniffed.

'Come on, Mare, there's no sense blaming anyone,' Peggy said, quickly leaping to Di's defence.

'No, no, Mary's got a point. It's my fault. Only trouble is now I've got us into this mess, I'm 'aving trouble getting us out of it.'

'You've tried flooring the accelerator?' asked Mary.

Kitty nodded. 'We have. All I can think of is lifting it.'

'We can't do that,' Di protested. 'We'll break our backs.'

'And if we don't, Hopson'll do it for us. Come on, Di, we've no other choice. At least these Bugs are nice and light,' Kitty pointed out.

'Kitty's right,' Mary agreed, moving towards the front of the car.

'And between four of us we should be able to manage it,' Peg added.

Di sighed. 'Come on then, no time like the present.'

With only the moon to guide them, the four of them trudged through the mud and grabbed the underside of the vehicle. Bending down and bracing herself for the weight, Kitty glanced gratefully at her friends.

'On my count,' she called decisively. 'One, two and three.'

With much huffing and puffing, the girls gasped at the weight of the car, but between them managed to shift it a couple of inches from the ground.

'That's it. Come on, bally well put your backs into it,' wheezed Mary.

'We're hardly baking a cake,' Kitty panted, as the car moved further forward.

'Oooh,' Peg squealed suddenly, 'I just got mud in me eye.'

'Join the club,' Di shouted, who was by now covered in muck.

'Set it down now,' Mary ordered, ignoring the girls' protests. 'It's less muddy here and you should be able to drive straight back onto the road.'

With a thud, the girls set the little car on the edge of the tarmac and breathed a sigh of relief.

'Thanks, girls.' Di smiled. 'I think Kit and I would've been 'ere all night if it weren't for you pair.'

'Think? I'm flamin' sure of it.' Kitty chuckled.

Smiling appreciatively at Mary and Peg, she bit her lip as she regarded each of her friends. Despite the lack of light, she could see their uniforms were caked in mud and would no doubt need a good soak once they got back to their barracks.

'Come on then, take us home, lovey,' she said, turning to Di.

Only Di shook her head. 'I think you should do this, Kit. I don't want to make it any worse.'

'Yer won't,' Kitty reasoned.

'Well it's entirely possible she might,' Mary said, doubtfully, hands on hips.

'Mare,' Peggy hissed. 'Leave her alone, she's had a fright.'

'I'm not saying she hasn't, Peggy dear, but to be honest things are bad enough for poor Kitty as they are, the last thing she needs is to give Hopson another excuse to make her life miserable.'

'She's right,' Di said gently, nudging her friend. 'Go on, Kit.'

'All right,' Kitty agreed reluctantly, walking towards the driver's side.

Getting back inside the car, she turned the starter motor on and was delighted to find the car chirruped into life straight away.

'Well done, Kit,' Peg called, delightedly.

Kitty poked her head out of the window. 'Well done to all of yer, more like. Me 'n' Di would never have shifted this thing on our own.'

'True,' Di agreed. 'Ta, girls. It was lucky we bumped into you when we did.'

'Everyone deserves a bit of luck.' Peggy smiled.

'Exactly. Besides, I knew it was nothing a bit of teamwork wouldn't solve,' Mary said airily as she clapped her hands together. 'Right then, we'd all better get back.'

As Mary and Peg returned to their vehicle, Di hopped in beside Kitty and smiled delightedly. 'I never thought I'd say this, Kit, but thank God for Mary and Peg tonight.'

Kitty chuckled as she drove the car smoothly along the road towards Northampton. 'I know what yer mean. Now let's hope we don't have any more excitement. I'm not sure I can take it.'

Thankfully the rest of the drive back to the barracks passed without incident. With Di back to shouting her precise instructions as she poked her head out of the window, Kitty was able to navigate their Bug safely home and with time to spare as well. Giving one last look around the vehicle in the well-lit garage, she was pleased to see that aside from a bit of mud the car was in perfect working order. After a quick hose down, she and Di changed out of their wet, muddy uniforms and walked across to the mess to get something to eat and drink.

With a steaming cuppa in one hand, and a slice of fruit cake in the other, Kitty sank back into one of the chairs by the window and tried to relax. Di was busy gossiping with one of the other girls in their dorm. This was the first time Kitty had been able to enjoy a few minutes to herself and she was determined to make the most of it. She had received a letter that morning from Elsie and had been dying to read it all day. Pulling the envelope from the pocket of her overalls she ripped it open and greedily devoured her friend's news.

30 July 1940

Dear Kitty,

How are you love? Well, what can I tell you? Especially as everything's much the same here. Well, we've had a very warm few days which has meant Dad's been up the allotment more than usual and this week we've had a lovely crop of runner beans. Mam says Dad's so green-fingered he ought to think about growing some crops on top of the Anderson shelter now food is becoming scarce.

Other than that, we're all fine. The big news is Mam's joined the Women's Institute! I know after all the stick she used to give them, for being only for posh folk, and now she's joined herself! Reckons they're not so stuck up these days, what with there being a war on. As for me, I've been busy up the bakery. Things are difficult with less flour and that, and there's talk of something called a new national loaf, but I don't know all the ins and outs.

Mike's well, he's still with us and likely to be for the foreseeable and all. He says he doesn't mind, he quite likes Coventry and I have to say it's nice having a bit of male company about, what with all my brothers and Charlie gone of course. We went to the pictures the other day to watch Gone with the Wind. Have you seen it, Kit? Mike and I loved it and went for a cuppa in the teahouse afterwards where he pretended to be Rhett Butler! He was ever so funny, got a real knack for voices. If the weather stays nice then he's suggested we go to the seaside next week. I can't remember the last time we went to the sea, Kitty, can you? Must have been that time we went to Hunstanton with Charlie and Joe a couple of years back and had that ice-cream eating contest.

Anyway he says I deserve it, I work so hard, which brings me onto my next bit of news. I don't know how best to say this, so I'll just come out with it. I'm having a baby, Kitty, I'm pregnant! Everyone's over the moon, and Mike's been a treasure, making sure I get my rest. The doctor says the baby's due in November, so he or she will be here for Christmas. I hope you'll be able to come back and see us, if you can – I can't have my nipper growing up without getting to know their Auntie Kitty!

Well love, I think that's all my excitement. How about you? What have you been up to? Arthur told me in his last letter you were having trouble with some higher up fella?

Well, I said to Arthur it won't take long for our Kit to see him off. She's always been a fighter! Anyway, if you've not given him what for yet, let me know and I'll come up and sort him out, I'll not have anyone make your life a misery, and no doubt there's a fair few around here that'd feel the same way.

I saw Hetty and George up the town the other day, they were looking well all things considered and send their love as do I. Take care of yourself, Kitty Williams, you hear me? Life's not the same around here without you, but I'm so proud of all you're doing for us, for your King and for your country. You're a marvel, Kit, and don't let anyone tell you otherwise.

Write soon, all my love,
Els xxx

As Kitty reread the letter, she felt a lump form in her throat and tears prick the back of her eyes. Elsie was pregnant, it was wonderful news and she couldn't be happier for her best friend. Kitty knew that Charlie and a baby was all Elsie had ever wanted and she was delighted her pal's dreams were coming true. Yet there was something about the note that made Kitty feel uneasy. She and Elsie, Kitty mused, as she sipped her tea, were clearly moving forward with their lives but never before had they moved in opposite directions. Kitty wondered with a stab of alarm if her unease was because she was jealous of her friend's happiness. Was that it? Because she too should have been thinking about marriage and babies with Joe, rather than fighting a war and fending off bullies?

She reread the letter once more, trying to pinpoint exactly what it was that bothered her. With a start, Kitty realised it was the fact that Elsie had barely mentioned Charlie in her note and instead talked a lot about Mike. Kitty knew Elsie was missing her husband, but she hoped Mike wasn't taking advantage of a lonely woman, and a lonely pregnant woman at that. She thought back to when she had seen Charlie and Elsie last. Was Mike the reason Charlie looked so worried? Or had it merely been concern about what horrors this war would bring next?

Concerned, Kitty refolded the letter and stuffed it into her pocket. Usually she wrote back to Elsie immediately but this time she wanted to consider her reply. Elsie was right, Kitty thought, life really was changing for them all, she only hoped the changes that lay ahead were all good ones.

Chapter Eight

The next morning it was clear the summer heatwave had passed. Kitty woke to find the skies a murky grey. Dressing quickly she hurried to the mess for breakfast, delighted to find Cook wasn't serving up porridge but was instead offering everyone toast.

Devouring a couple of slices, with a scraping of butter, she, Di, Mary and Peg walked across to the driver training centre where she found Hopson had already arrived and was standing next to an engine positioned on a large table in the centre of the classroom.

As they joined the rest of the recruits, Sergeant Hopson strode around each of them with purpose and told them they had all completed the driving task successfully.

'I can't imagine it's something I'll be saying to you both again, but congratulations Mills and Williams,' Hopson had announced loftily at the beginning of the session. 'You two were the only pairing who made it to each rendezvous point in time.'

'Thank you, sir,' Di replied, saluting the officer.

As for Kitty, she was so surprised Hopson appeared not to have discovered their mishap, she scarcely registered the words of praise that fell from his lips. Instead she stood, open-mouthed in stunned silence, much to the amusement of Sergeant Hopson.

'Cat got your tongue, Williams?' he asked with a sneer.

'No, sir!' Kitty replied quickly, remembering to salute. 'Thank yer sir,'

'Yes, well,' Hopson said, staring at Kitty a fraction longer than was necessary, before moving back to the table. 'Today we're concentrating on the engine and we'll finish with a test as usual. I want you to memorise every element, take it apart then put it back together again.'

As Kitty watched the other girls panic at coping with what she knew they would find a mammoth task, she felt relieved. Her time at the car factory meant she was more familiar than most with the inner workings of an engine, and she was surprised to find she was looking forward to getting stuck in.

'Come on then, girls,' she said cheerily, walking towards the engine. 'Now then, who wants to take notes as we go round?'

The girls were keen to follow Kitty's lead and together they worked as one large team, scribbling down each part, jotting down drawings and dismantling spark plugs and pistons, re-membering where each part was to go. Each recruit was acutely aware this would be their last classroom session and, if all went well, they would soon be receiving details of their new postings as drivers. This final assessment was important, as the last thing anyone wanted to see next to their name was the dreaded letters RTU. A Return to Unit notice meant you were not good enough to work as a driver and would no doubt end up in the stores or worse.

As Kitty worked her spanner to loosen the distributor cap, she realised she had mixed feelings about the prospect of going elsewhere. On the one hand, it would be wonderful to leave the hated Sergeant Hopson behind, but on the other, she couldn't stand the idea of not seeing Di, Mary and Peg each day. They had all become so close, first at basic training and now here at Northampton.

Still, she realised, the cap finally loosening, making friends was not the reason she had joined the Army. She had joined to honour Joe's memory and she would serve wherever her superiors thought her best suited. Besides, it wasn't all doom and gloom. She and the rest of the girls were going to let their hair down at a dance hall later that night. For the first time since arriving at Northampton they had all been given an entire

Saturday night off, and Mary, naturally, had insisted they have a proper night out instead of a quick trip to the pub for half a stout.

Kitty smiled. Against her better judgement she had found herself agreeing to join them all at the Rialto Dance Hall later. Since Joe had died, dancing had been the last thing she wanted to do and if she was honest, she still felt guilty at the idea of enjoying herself. But Elsie's letter had got her thinking. There were no prizes for standing still and just because she tried to make the most of her life, her love for Joe still burned as brightly. She had lain awake most of the night thinking about Elsie and how her life was changing and realised that like her oldest friend it was time to move forward.

Watching Hopson walk towards them, ready to announce time was almost up, she caught sight of Peg struggling to tighten one of the valves. Her heart thudded with fear as she could just imagine Hopson punishing her alone if they failed this task. Now she had decided to go out that night, she was damned if Hopson would take the chance away from her.

'Give it a whack with your spanner, Peg, love,' Kitty hissed at the younger girl who by now was almost purple with effort.

'Eh?' she panted.

'Give it here,' Kit said, shouldering her friend quickly out of the way. With a hasty glance behind her she was relieved to see Hopson had been waylaid by Beryl Mason. As she heard Beryl let out one of her horrible raucous laughs, Kitty banged her spanner sharply on top of Peg's troublesome valve and was gratified when it fell into place immediately.

'Blimey, Kit!' Peggy whistled. 'I'd not want to bump into you down a dark alley.'

'All in a day's work,' she chuckled, returning to her distributor cap. 'But remember, Peg, if in doubt, no matter what, a whack with a spanner usually sorts it.'

As the girls smiled at one another, Kitty felt a sharp tap on her shoulder. Spinning around she came face to face with Hopson and her heart sank as she caught his menacing stare.

'A word, Volunteer Williams,' he said chillingly, beckoning her to the front of the classroom.

Heart heavy, Kitty followed Hopson towards his desk, wondering what he would do next.

'Halt,' Hopson called as Kitty stood to the side of the desk. 'Eyes forward.'

Kitty did as she was told and stared straight ahead, conscious that despite the unexpected coolness of the day her forehead felt clammy with nerves. What on earth could she have done to upset Hopson now?

Feeling a large bead of sweat trickle down her face, Kitty glanced across at Hopson and watched in horror as he produced a fresh shaving brush from his drawer and set it down on his desk. By now you could hear a pin drop in the classroom as the class stopped and stared in agonising silence.

'Little present for you, Williams,' he sneered.

'Excuse me, sir?' Kitty whispered.

Staring at her with a look of disgust, Hopson picked up the brush and pressed it into Kitty's jacket pocket.

'You thought I wouldn't find out about what happened during your driver training exercise, didn't you?' he snarled. 'Well I've got news for you, Williams: nothing gets past me. I know everything that goes on in my unit, and your misdemeanour did not go unnoticed. I hear everything, Williams, everything.'

'Yes, sir,' Kitty whispered, beads of sweat continuing to gathering pace across her forehead.

'If you had only come to me and explained what had happened, I would have understood,' Hopson said slowly, pacing up and down the front of the room. 'All accidents need to be reported, you know that, so we can assess the vehicle for safety, but once again your thoughtlessness shows me you have learned nothing.'

Staring straight ahead at the blackboard, Kitty wanted the ground to swallow her up whole. She should have known Hopson would have discovered the accident and could kick herself for her stupidity.

'Excuse me, sir.' Di's loud call from the back of the room wrenched Kitty from her train of thought. 'But the accident was my fault. If you should be 'aving a go at anyone it should be me.'

Surprised by the interruption, Hopson peered at Di, who was by now walking towards the front of the room to stand next to Kitty.

'Volunteer Mills, you have no right to be up here,' blustered Hopson. 'It is Volunteer Williams at fault, not you. Get back to your seat immediately.'

'But with respect, that's my point, sir,' Di continued, ignoring Hopson's last instruction. 'It's not Kitty – I mean Volunteer Williams – you should be blaming, it's me. I'm the one that ran into the ditch, Kitty was just 'elping me.'

'I see. But you are the weaker driver, are you not?' Hopson enquired, cocking his head to one side as he looked Di up and down.

'Well yes—' Di began, only for Hopson to cut her off.

'And that is also my point, Volunteer Mills. Williams here knew you were the poorer driver yet still let you drive in the dark, showing extremely poor judgement yet again. No, I'm sorry, Mills, whilst I am extremely displeased with you, it's not you who needs to learn from this sorry mess, it's Williams here. Now back to your seat.'

Reluctantly, Di turned on her heel and mouthing 'sorry' at her friend as she passed. Kitty shot her a watery smile in return before glancing back at Hopson. None of this was Di's fault, Kitty thought sadly, in fact Kitty was touched her friend would put herself in the firing line like that, but it was clear from the smirk on Hopson's face her superior couldn't wait for an opportunity to dish out another punishment.

'As I was saying,' Hopson continued, 'you clearly need time to consider how your actions impact on others, Williams. That's why I want you to sweep clean every Tilly truck that was out on convoy last night with the shaving brush I just gave you.'

'But, sir,' Kitty begged despairingly. 'More than ten trucks were out last night.'

'I know that, Williams,' Hopson replied triumphantly, 'but don't worry, I have another brush should you need one.'

Kitty hung her head, knowing full well she was defeated. 'Thank yer, sir,' she replied in a low tone.

'Well off you go then, Williams, those trucks won't clean themselves,' Hopson said, dismissing her. 'The rest of you, back to work.'

*

As dusk began to fall Di kept up a steady stream of excited chatter as she led her friends towards a brick and stucco building in the centre of town. Doing her best to keep pace, Kitty dragged her weary body a few yards behind them, and wished for the hundredth time that evening that she could have just gone straight to bed.

The afternoon spent cleaning had been as hellish as Kitty had imagined, and she had a sneaking suspicion she would still be there now had it not been for her friends, who had insisted on giving her a hand during lunch. Thanks to them, she had not only finished before nightfall, but also earned the grudging respect of Sergeant Hopson by performing a job well done in half the time he was expecting. And so, while every bone in her body ached, Kitty knew she couldn't let her friends down after they had gone to so much trouble. So reluctantly she had agreed to join them.

Spotting a glimmer of light peep from the entrance, Kitty saw Di push open the glass door and stepping inside was instantly transported to a world of wonder. There was no getting away from it, the Rialto was beautiful both inside and out. With its high ceilings and opulent glass chandelier, the red-carpeted foyer of the dance hall was thick with people and the air heavy with anticipation. Kitty forgot her tiredness as she watched men in service uniforms chat with the girls around them and couples walk to and from the dance floor. Together the girls strolled into the hall itself just as the final notes of the band's foxtrot faded out and the dancers returned to their seats for a breather. Finding a rare table close to the dance floor, Kitty and Peg agreed to stand guard while Mary and Di went to the bar for a round of port and lemons. When the girls returned Kitty took a grateful sip and relaxed as she felt the cool liquid slip easily down her throat.

Setting her glass down, she turned to her friends and smiled. 'I just want to say thanks to the lot of yer for today. There's no way I'd be sat here with yer all now if it wasn't for your help. I'm touched.'

'Give over,' Di admonished, waving her hand dismissively. 'You'd 'ave done the same for any of us.'

'Hear, hear,' Mary agreed, raising her glass in salute.

Peg wrapped her hands around her drink and beamed at Kitty. 'Goes without saying, we'd help you out. You're our friend, and been there for us enough times.'

Kitty looked into her glass, clearly embarrassed at so much attention. 'Well, let's just say I appreciate it and I can only hope yer won't have to help me out like that again now driver training's nearly at an end and hopefully my days with Hopson.'

'What choices did you put on your preferred posting forms?' Di asked. 'Did you make sure you put where you didn't want to go at the top of your lists?'

Kitty nodded. 'I decided to take a risk with the old wives' tale, thinking there'd be some truth in it.'

'What old wives' tale?' Peggy asked, a look of panic flashing across her features.

'Yer know, some of the older recruits who'd been about a bit longer, told us in the mess last week that the worst thing yer could do was put down where yer actually wanted to go,' Kitty explained.

'That's right,' added Di. 'Instead you 'ad to put down the place you *didn't* want to go, to make sure you didn't end up there.'

'But why?' Peggy asked, eyes wide with horror.

''Cos it's not a flippin' holiday camp!' Kitty exclaimed. 'If the powers that be get wind of the fact there's summat yer fancy, they'll make sure yer don't get it. I stuck Northampton down as me top choice, thinking at least that way I can say goodbye to Hopson once and for all.'

'You didn't,' Di laughed. 'I put Birmingham – I don't want to be anywhere near me mother.'

'Quite right too,' Mary agreed, taking another sip of her drink. 'I hope I'll end up in France or somewhere like that. I'd love an adventure.'

'I bet you would.' Di nodded wryly. 'I take it you speak fluent French then?'

'*Mais oui*,' chuckled Mary as Di and Kitty shook their heads with laughter at their friend's confidence.

Glancing across at Peggy, Kitty saw her face was still a picture of despair. 'What is it, lovey?'

'I thought that old wives' tale thingy was a joke!' Peggy said mournfully, 'My first choice was Bristol, 'cos I do want to be nearer my mum and my last choice was Edinburgh! If Mother finds out I'm going further north than here, she'll have me guts for garters.'

'None of us are going anywhere yet,' Kitty reasoned.

'Exactly, and anyway, Edinburgh's nice,' Di pointed out.

Peggy remained unconvinced, and Kitty smiled at her again in a bid to chivvy her up. Since she had got to know Peggy over the last three months Kitty was delighted to see she had blossomed. Tonight she had taken a leaf out of Mary and Di's book: they were both done up to the nines for the occasion with smart victory rolls in their hair. While Peggy hadn't gone quite as far she had at least pinned her hair into a neat bun and applied a touch of panstick to her face, and Kitty found herself marvelling at just how much she had changed.

'Well here's to us then, ladies.' Mary smiled, raising her glass and bumping it against the others'. 'We've all done bally well over the last few weeks.'

'We certainly 'ave,' Di sighed, as she reached into her jacket pocket for her cigarettes and lighter. 'Is it what you expected?'

'Driving school?' Mary asked, casually helping herself to one of Di's cigarettes, 'or the Army?'

'All of it,' Di replied.

'I'm not sure,' Mary said. 'I will say I've rather enjoyed driver training.'

'Me too,' admitted Kitty. 'I finally feel I've found summat I'm good at.'

'You're an absolute wonder behind the wheel,' Mary said, blowing a smoke ring through the air.

'And now under the bonnet.' Peggy grinned. 'That trick with the spanner was brilliant earlier. Where d'you learn how to do that?'

'We did it all the time up the car plant.' Kitty laughed, setting her glass on the wooden table. 'If in doubt, us girls'd give summat a whack and whatever it was'd be in, out or off in no time.'

'You want to be careful who you say that to, Kitty Williams, some folk'll get the wrong idea!' Di chuckled.

As the others roared with laughter, Peggy took a delicate first sip of her drink and screwed up her face in disgust. 'Cor, that's evil in a glass that is.'

'Get away,' Kitty laughed, taking a large gulp of her drink. 'Port and lemon's good for yer. Have another sip.'

'I don't think so, Kit, it's not slipping down very easily,' Peggy grimaced.

'Oh, just whack it with a spanner, Peg!' Mary giggled.

The girls burst out laughing once more, happy to have a night off from the hard work life in the army demanded. Tonight was a rare chance to pretend there was no war and that they were just four young women enjoying themselves on a Saturday night.

Peggy pushed the glass to the other side of the table. 'Sorry, girls, but I reckon I'd rather have a lemonade.'

'Can I get that for you?' A young man in an RAF uniform asked, suddenly appearing at Peggy's side.

'Oh no, that's very nice of you but I'm all right, ta.' Peggy blushed, looking anywhere but at the sweet, bespectacled serviceman standing hopefully next to her.

'Well could I trouble you for a dance then, miss?'

A look of horror passed across Peggy's face. 'No, ta,' she said again.

Kitty felt a flash of sympathy for the man. He looked kind, and one dance wouldn't kill Peggy – it would probably do her some good.

'Oh go on,' Kitty coaxed. 'The waltz has just started, and you're always practising your steps in the mess. Go and have a go, it'll make a change from dancing with me or Mary.'

'Yes it will,' agreed Mary, who had cottoned on to what Kitty was trying to do.

As Mary winked at the RAF boy, Kitty saw he too looked as embarrassed as Peggy did. The two were clearly a match made in heaven, she thought.

'I really can't,' Peggy protested again, only for Mary to get to her feet.

'Well I can't see a handsome young man without a partner,' she said, walking towards him. Placing her hand in his, Mary half-guided, half-dragged the poor boy towards the dance floor, leaving Kitty and Di to look on in amusement.

Smiling across at Di, Kitty pushed the drink towards the younger girl. 'Just because I let yer off the hook about a dance, doesn't mean I'm letting yer off the hook about that drink. Now, wash it down, black and brown.'

Peggy looked from Kitty to Di in dismay. 'I can't.'

'Go on. Live a little,' Di encouraged.

The beginnings of a smile played on Peggy's lips. Reaching for the drink, she took a large gulp as Kitty and Di egged her on. With the glass half-empty, Peggy set it down with a triumphant thud and looked at the girls expectantly.

'Blast me, Peggy Collins.' Di whistled. 'You'll get yourself a reputation 'round these parts, if you get through your drinks like that.'

'I pretended it was cough syrup,' Peggy reasoned, 'gulped it in one.'

'Well that's one way, but I wouldn't do that again or you'll get a headache bigger than yer bargained for.' Kitty giggled, turning her gaze back to the dance floor.

Despite the war, the room was flooded with servicemen and women just like Kitty, all dressed smartly in their uniforms.

'I think it's lovely everyone takes such pride in the job they do that they still wear their uniforms out.' Peggy smiled, breaking Kitty's train of thought.

'I think it might have summat to do with the fact we all get in half-price if we wear our uniform rather than any sense of national pride,' Kitty replied gently. 'I mean, that's why us girls are all in our finest khakis.'

Peggy's face fell. 'Oh,' she sighed. 'I thought it was 'cos we were all proud to be spark girls.'

Di stifled a giggle. 'Well, it's that too,' she smiled, patting Peggy's arm comfortingly. 'But the discount's not bad either.'

Watching her friends chatter away, Kitty sat back in her chair and let the tiredness wash over her. Surrounded by couples laughing and giggling as the band struck up the opening chords of 'In the Mood', Kitty felt a sudden lurch in her stomach as the last time she heard this piece of music came rushing back. It had been the night Joe had asked her to marry him last summer. Everything had felt magical.

Closing her eyes, she could see and hear everything as clearly as if she were back there. It had been a balmy Saturday night in August, Kitty recalled, and together with Elsie and Charlie, the four of them had gone to The Crystal. Like The Rialto tonight, the air had been alive with excitement, and Kitty had a strange sense something wasn't quite right as Joe had asked her to wear her best navy polka-dot dress and hadn't let her out of his sight all night.

'Anyone'd think you were terrified I might be snapped up by another fella,' Kitty teased as Joe whirled her around the dance floor.

'More like I want to make the most of my Saturday night with the most beautiful girl in the room,' Joe replied admiringly.

Charlie and Elsie were still on the dance floor as they returned to their table and so Kitty sipped her drink and looked across at the boy she had always adored. Tall, with broad shoulders and piercing blue eyes that were so inviting she wanted to dive right in, Kitty saw a look of nervousness flash across his handsome chiselled features.

'Yer all right, love?' she asked, her voice thick with concern. 'Yer don't seem yourself.'

'I'm fine,' Joe replied unconvincingly, gulping down half his pint of Mackeson's and setting it back on the table with a thud.

Kitty raised her eyebrows as she took in the trickle of amber liquid pooling under his glass. 'Out with it, Joe Simmonds,' she said, sighing heavily.

'You've always been able to tell when summat's on my mind,' Joe said, smiling sheepishly.

'Don't sidestep me; just tell me what yer have to say,' Kitty replied, taking a large gulp of her own drink, somehow sensing she might need some Dutch courage.

Joe didn't reply straight away, leaving Kitty even more un-nerved. Instead he had got to his feet, fixed Kitty with a smile, then reached into his jacket pocket and produced a black ring box. With trembling fingers he opened it and produced a ruby and gold ring.

Kitty's hands flew to her mouth in shock as Joe got down on bended knee. 'I've known yer since we were nippers,' he said earnestly. 'I've seen yer fall out of trees, helped yer with spelling tests and watched yer grimace as yer sipped your first port and lemon. I love yer with all my heart, Kitty Williams; will yer do me the honour of becoming my wife?'

Kitty's heart swelled with so much love, she thought it would burst. This was the boy who had worshipped her when nobody else did. The boy who looked at her with adoration in his eyes, made her heart sing and dreams come true. Tenderly she leaned forward and stroked Joe's cheek.

'It's always been yer, Joe,' she whispered fiercely. 'Nothing would make me happier than to be your wife.'

'Oh Kitty, you're all I've ever wanted. I promise yer won't regret this.' Joe beamed as he slid the ruby onto a delighted Kitty's finger.

Kitty had thrown her arms around an equally ecstatic Joe, as Charlie and Elsie returned to their table, full of congratulations.

That night, as the pair bathed in a glow of joy, the orchestra provided the perfect soundtrack for them to plan their future. Together with their best friends, Joe and Kitty imagined their wedding, their first home, the children they would have and the holidays by the seaside they would all enjoy.

Happiness flooded through her as she remembered how perfect the night was. Breathing deeply, Kitty smiled as the scent of his aftershave flooded her senses, only as she continued to inhale, she noticed it was far muskier than Joe usually wore.

'Williams,' a gravelly voice boomed, causing her eyes to fly open.

Reality hit Kitty like a bucket of icy water, as she realised her perfect life was nothing more than a long-forgotten dream. As if to check, she placed her right hand over her left to twiddle with her engagement ring, but there was nothing there apart from bare flesh. Kitty gasped as she remembered her ring was safely stored at Elsie's, she wasn't in The Crystal, the love of her life hadn't just asked her to marry him. Instead she was in a nightmare as it hit her once again that the man she adored was dead, only to be replaced by a domineering bully of a sergeant who hated her with a passion.

'Sergeant Hopson,' she said, hurriedly getting to her feet like the rest of her friends and saluting her superior.

'So you *are* there, Williams,' he chuckled, motioning for the girls to stand at ease. 'I must say I did wonder. Still, I expect after the day you've had you're exhausted. In fact I'm surprised you're here at all.'

'Sir,' Kitty said quietly.

'Still, no matter,' he replied, his eyes narrowing as he regarded Kitty and her friends with what appeared to be deep suspicion.

As the girls continued to stand to attention, Sergeant Hopson burst out laughing. 'Oh, please sit down, ladies,' he smiled. 'We're not on the parade ground now.'

'Very good sir, thank you, sir,' the girls said, in muted tones.

'So, having a good time?' he asked, resting his drink on the table and slopping some of the amber liquid over the side of the glass.

The girls looked uneasily at each other. None of them knew how to deal with the fact an officer was sitting with them, encouraging them to behave casually. As Kitty had been the one who had suffered the most, she took it upon herself to speak first.

'Lovely evening, thank yer, sir,' she replied, smiling awkwardly. 'Are yer having a good time?'

Hopson smiled, pausing to look at the girls' empty glasses before answering. 'I certainly appear to be having a better time than you ladies. You've almost finished your drinks! Allow me to buy you all another.'

Hopson looked around at them expectantly but the girls, especially Kitty, were rendered speechless. Mary was the first to recover and spoke. 'What a lovely offer, isn't it, girls? Thank you sir,' she said warmly.

'My pleasure,' he said beaming. 'Port and lemons all around, is it?' he asked as the girls nodded and he turned to Kitty. 'Perhaps you could give me a hand at the bar?'

Kitty's stomach knotted with fear. 'Of course, sir,' she smiled as she got up and scuttled after him.

Reaching the bar Kitty felt more than a little self-conscious. Should she open her mouth and start speaking uninvited or was it better to wait until she was spoken to? She hated this indecision, and was fearful of saying or doing the wrong thing. But thankfully Hopson saved her the trouble.

Leaning in towards her after ordering their drinks he offered her a false smile. 'Well, I must say your preferred postings form made interesting reading, Williams,' he said. 'I was quite surprised to learn you wanted to stay in Northampton.'

Kitty's mouth felt dry. She was unsure if it was because she was thirsty or she had no idea where the conversation was going. So she said nothing, and offered her superior officer a tight-lipped smile. He quickly continued, with that same look of hatred Kitty had seen before.

'Well, Williams, I like to think I can make dreams come true, so when we all met to discuss where to send our new recruits I insisted that if you wanted to stay in Northampton then that's where we should send you, or *not* send you, so to speak.'

Kitty stood rooted to the floor in shock. How could this be happening? The older recruits had assured her that you never got your first choice of posting. What had gone so wrong? Kitty met her commanding officer's eyes and saw the flash of triumph there. She knew immediately what had gone wrong. She had inadvertently played right into Hopson's hands, and now he would welcome the chance to continue making her life miserable for as long as he possibly could.

Images of the long months ahead flashed into her mind as she pictured Hopson continually putting her on CB notices, handing her shaving brushes and generally making her life a misery. And worse, this time there would be no Di, Mary or Peggy to help make her cross a little easier to bear. As Kitty reached for her drink from the bar, she wondered how she would ever stand it and looked desperately at the door, wanting nothing more than to run home to Coventry and away from this nightmare.

Hopson's booming voice brought her swiftly back to reality. 'Well cheers, Volunteer Williams.' He smiled, chinking his glass against hers. 'It looks as though you and I are going to have some fun.'

Kitty felt a warm heat grow inside her as she tried to control the anger rising. Counting to ten to steady herself, she was determined to treat this bully just like any other. He won't win, she thought, no matter how hard he tries. Lifting her eyes to meet Hopson's she smiled at him, refusing to give him the satisfaction of knowing how much he had upset her.

'Looks like it, sir,' she grinned. 'I'm looking forward to it and

I appreciate yer telling me early like so I can celebrate the news with my pals.'

'Well, I er . . .' Hopson began, clearly wrong-footed by Kitty's reaction.

'Oh no, don't worry, sir.' She smiled again, reaching for the tray of drinks. 'The girls won't mind you've told me early.'

'Best not, Williams,' Hopson said, his voice not as confident as it had been moments earlier. 'My superiors will haul me over the coals if they thought I'd given you special treatment. Best keep it under your hat for now, if you don't mind.'

Kitty feigned innocence. 'If yer think that's best, sir,' she replied meekly, before threading her way back through the crowds towards her friends.

As Kitty reached the table, with Hopson trailing behind her, she sat down and made a big show of laughing and smiling along with the rest of her friends as her superior officer entertained them with stories of army life. But after half an hour, Kitty could stand the pretence no more and stood up, saying she needed to visit the powder room. Yet crossing the floor, Kitty knew what she really needed was fresh air and, spotting a door near the ladies', headed outside into a small courtyard.

Save for a couple of sweethearts locked in a passionate embrace and a middle-aged man standing by the bins, smoking a cigarette, Kitty had the place to herself. Closing her eyes, she shut out the sound of the music and the laughing couples, and instead breathed deeply, trying to think straight. Not for the first time, she found herself conjuring up images of Joe and wondered what on earth he would say about this latest development. No doubt he would offer to have a man-to-man chat with Hopson, she thought. Joe had never been one for using his fists, not unless he had to, but she had a feeling that even Joe would feel like flattening Hopson after this latest stunt.

Resting her head against the wall, looking up at the stars, she found herself wishing more than anything she could talk to Joe. How she would value his love and support right now.

'Penny for 'em,' said a low, gruff voice, startling Kitty.

Turning her head, she saw the man who had been standing by the bins was now by her side. Unlike most of the men inside the dance hall, he wasn't wearing a uniform, though he wasn't too old to have been called up, Kitty thought, placing him in his late thirties. Dressed in a smart suit and tie, his dark hair, though greying at the temples, was slicked back with pomade. His open face seemed warm as he peered curiously at Kitty.

'Oh, they're not worth that much.' She smiled, seeing the man's eyes were now filled with concern.

'Yer sure?' he replied. 'Yer looked for all the world as though yer were away with the fairies.'

'Doesn't sound like a bad place to be,' Kitty replied. 'Ta, love, but I'm fine.'

'Sure yer don't want to talk? My wife always said I were a good listener,' the man said gently, hand outstretched. 'I'm Billy, by the way, Billy Miles.'

Kitty took his hand and shook it. 'Nice to meet yer. I'm Kathleen, better known as Kitty, Williams.'

'More like Volunteer Williams if the uniform's anything to go by,' Billy noticed, taking a step back and running his eyes over her freshly starched khaki uniform.

'Well spotted,' she said, smoothing her skirt. 'All got to do our bit, haven't we?'

'That we have,' he replied evenly. 'I'm too ill to join up meself. Gammy leg from the last time we fought the Jerries.'

'Oh that's a shame,' Kitty said looking down at the leg Billy had patted. 'What happened?'

'Shrapnel,' he sighed, shaking his head. 'Not a day goes by when I don't wish I were standing shoulder to shoulder with the boys, fighting for our country. But it's not to be, so I do me bit where I can.'

'So what d'yer do?' Kitty asked politely.

'I'm a butcher and I've me work cut out making sure everyone gets their fair share. Heaven help us if folk think someone else has had an ounce more mutton than them.'

'I can imagine,' Kitty said wryly, thinking back to Mary's

reaction to her extra slice of bacon. 'Have yer got help like?'

Billy nodded. 'A young lad, John, helps me out, but he's not a patch on me wife, Bess. She was a wonder with the customers.'

'Oh, is she busy doing war work instead of working with yer like?' Kitty enquired politely.

Billy paused, reaching into his jacket for his cigarettes. 'No such luck.' He smiled wistfully. 'She passed over a few years back now.'

Kitty's gasped. 'Oh, I'm sorry.'

'It's all right.' Billy smiled, offering Kitty a cigarette, then lighting one for himself as she declined. 'She'd been poorly for a long time, it were a blessing really, though I miss her every day.'

'I'm sorry,' Kitty whispered again. 'I lost me fiancé a few months back, I know how it feels.'

'Now *I'm* sorry,' Billy said gently, cocking his head to one side as he inhaled sharply on his cigarette. 'Was he serving?'

'He was in the Navy. Happened a few months ago, but I'd still give anything to just have another hour with him.' Kitty sighed. 'I keep having all these conversations with him in me head, wondering what he'd say about this and that. I miss him so much. Sorry, yer must think I'm barking mad.'

Billy chuckled. 'Not likely. I still talk to our Bess all the time. First few months, after she passed I used to reach for two cups instead of one when I brewed up.'

'When does it get easier?' Kitty asked sadly, resting her head against the cold brick wall.

'It's different for everyone like,' Billy replied quietly, stubbing his cigarette out. 'The important thing is yer keep putting one foot in front of the other. Some days are easier than others and it's that, that'll carry yer through.'

Kitty looked at the man gratefully. She had only popped outside to clear her mind, but talking through her feelings with someone who knew how she felt was the pick-me-up she had needed. Smiling, she squared her shoulders and turned to Billy. 'I'd better be getting back inside, my pals will be worried about me.'

'Nice to meet yer, Kitty.' Billy smiled warmly. 'Feel free to pop into the butchers any time you're in town and say hello if yer fancy a chat like. '

Kitty returned his grin. 'Ta, Billy, I might just do that.'

Chapter Nine

Kitty woke the next morning in a cold sweat, terrified and confused, after a nightmare-filled sleep. Sitting up on the uncomfortable mattress, the rest of the recruits in the hut still fast asleep, she desperately tried to recall what had upset her so much. She knew it was something about Hopson and never leaving Northampton but couldn't for the life of her remember any more than that.

Breathing deeply to try and calm herself, Kitty swung her legs out of bed and onto the cold stone floor. It was just a dream, she told herself, before the truth hit her like a bucket of ice water. She really was staying in Northampton and her commanding officer would continue to make her life hell.

Exhausted, she padded over to the pitcher they kept in the corner of the room and washed her face in freezing water, only to hear the sounds of Di waking.

'You all right?' Di asked, as she yawned and stretched her hands over her head.

'Fine.' Kitty nodded, patting her face dry on the little hand towel she kept near her locker.

'Well if that's fine, I'd 'ate to see what terrible looked like,' Di quipped as she nudged Kitty out of the way to wash her own face. 'You still mulling over what 'opson said?'

'What d'yer think?' Kitty replied drily. 'I thought it was all a bad dream till a minute ago.'

'Ah.' Di paused, clearly trying to think of something positive to say. 'I still think 'e might've been kidding,' she said at last.

Kitty shook her head. 'Nice try, Di, but we both know he wasn't joking.' She moved towards her bed and started to change into her uniform, enjoying the feel of the crisp collar she had starched last night.

After her conversation with Billy, Kitty had returned to the table feeling cheerful about the future, until she saw Hopson, still laughing and joking with her friends. Her good mood disappeared in an instant and with a heavy heart she had sat down, plastering a smile on her face and burying her true feelings, a skill she had learned long ago as a child in care.

It wasn't until the girls left the dance and she had said goodbye to Mary and Peg that Kitty had finally confided in Di, telling her the whole sorry tale.

Naturally Di had been outraged, but she was as convinced last night as she was this morning that Hopson had been pulling her leg.

'We'll find out once and for all later on whether or not 'e was having you on,' Di told her matter-of-factly as she slipped into her uniform ready for drill practice. 'The lists of our new postings will be out later, so put it out of your mind till then.'

'I'll try,' Kitty promised as they walked out of the door towards the mess for breakfast.

Despite the heaviness in her heart, Kitty knew Di was right and she did her best to follow her friend's advice that morning. Working with Mary, she had instead concentrated on learning to repair one of the three-ton trucks they had been assigned to work on before finally driving through the park in convoy.

But when it was time to return for lunch, she found her stomach was turning over with fear as she parked the lorry back in the garage. Walking across to the mess, her feet dragging along the tarmac as she readied herself to discover her fate, she walked inside and saw the notice board was already crowded. Nearing the group she saw girls were squealing with delight or groaning with despair as they discovered whether or not they had been awarded their first choice. Already up ahead was Peggy, Kitty noticed, who was standing on tip toes trying to find her own name on the list. Moving towards her friend, she heard her suddenly squawk and Kitty wasn't sure if the noise meant she was pleased or unhappy.

'Kitty!' Peggy waved. 'I'm going down to Camberley. I'm going to deliver trucks and lorries.'

'That's brilliant, Peg.' Kitty smiled as she pushed her way towards her friend, feeling genuinely delighted for her.

'Well done, Peg.' Mary smiled, clapping her on the back. 'Not so far from your mother.'

'No, and Bess is in Camberley too.' She beamed happily. 'What about you girls?'

'I've not found me name yet,' Di replied, her arms folded huffily. 'There are too many in the way for me to see.'

There was a squeal of delight from Mary, who was now running her finger down the list. 'I'm off to France, oh, how marvellous. Teddy Simpson will be so cross, I told him I'd get across the continent before he did.'

'Mary, that's wonderful.' Kitty beamed, feeling full of delight for her friend.

'It really is,' Mary cried, hugging herself with glee. 'I mean, I knew the fact I spoke fluent French would help, but I was sure those rotters wouldn't send me somewhere I actually wanted to go.'

'Well, it just goes to show,' said Di drily as she found a gap in the crowd and looked for her own name on the sheet of paper. There was a pause as she ran her finger over the list. 'Oh,' she said, her voice deflated. 'I'm staying 'ere.'

Mary's eyes were out on stalks as she jostled her way back through the crowd of girls next to Di, determined to see for herself. 'Don't be ridiculous, there must be some mistake.'

'There's no mistake,' Di replied, pointing to her name for Mary to see. 'It seems I'm to work for the mail service, delivering Army post.'

Peggy's eyes lit up as she took a seat at the nearest table. 'But that's brilliant, Di, I reckon that's right up your street.'

'Which is just as well, considering she'll be delivering the post,' Mary quipped before she turned to find Kitty behind her. 'That's not so bad, Di. You'll be out and about an awful lot, so it won't really matter where you're based.' Mary turned to Kitty. 'And what about you? Time to find out which unlucky straw you've picked.'

Kitty gulped, avoiding meeting her friend's eyes. She knew she could put the moment of truth off no longer. Moving towards the sheet of white paper filled with neatly typed writing, she scanned the list, her heart pounding.

By now Kitty felt so nervous, every word was jumping up and down before her eyes, the letters looking like nothing but a jumble. Eventually she found what she was looking for and her stomach lurched with dismay.

Williams: Northampton, staff driver.

'Well that must be a mistake. You can't be staying here as well,' Mary boomed, leaning over Kitty's shoulder for a better look. 'Hopson hates you; why would he keep you in Northampton?'

'I think that's the point,' Di muttered grimly. 'I'm sorry, Kitty, it seems you were right, 'e wasn't pulling your leg after all.'

'What are you talking about?' Peggy quizzed.

'Oh, 'opson told Kitty he was keeping her back in Northampton last night,' Di explained.

'What? At the dance?' Mary asked incredulously. 'You never said.'

'Well, I was hardly going to break the news while he was sat with us, was I?' Kitty snapped, before smiling apologetically at her friend. 'Sorry, Mary, I'm a bit all over the shop.'

'Not to worry, old thing,' Mary said. 'I'd be bally puce with rage if it were me. Talk about low. The man's nothing more than a coward for this.'

'Oh yes? Anyone I know?' a voice chimed behind them.

'Sergeant Hopson,' Mary said evenly. 'A pleasure as always. We were just discussing our new postings.'

Hands clasped behind his back, Sergeant Hopson strode

towards the group and surveyed the notice board before turning back to the girls.

'Exciting, isn't it?' he beamed. 'I trust you're all pleased.'

'I reckon I'm in clover,' Peg replied happily.

'Over the moon,' Di replied through gritted teeth, refusing to meet his eye.

'It's just what I was hoping for.' Kitty smiled, once again refusing to give Hopson the satisfaction of knowing he had got to her.

Hopson ran his tongue across his teeth and eyed Kitty beadily. 'Good.' He smiled. 'Well I must say I'm delighted you feel that way, Williams. I myself have just found out I will be overseeing the staff drivers so you will still report to me. Isn't that marvellous news?'

Inside, Kitty seethed. Could the day get much worse? 'Marvellous, sir,' she replied in clipped tones.

Back in the Nissen hut, Kitty reached for the special lightweight notepaper and envelopes she kept in the iron cabinet next to her bed. She had just a few minutes to spare before she was to report back for duty, and there was only one person she wanted to talk to – Arthur.

Sinking onto the bed, she took the top off her pen and scribbled furiously, the words tumbling out.

15 August 1940

Dear Arthur,

I wish I could tell you this'll be a nice, happy letter but I'm afraid that's the last thing it's going to be. I'm in a right old mess, and I don't know where to start. I sometimes feel I must be a really wicked person, with all the bad things that keep happening. I'm doing my best to be strong, Arthur, but sometimes it's just so hard.

Today I found out I won't be moving somewhere new, away from my bullying Sergeant. Instead I'm staying put, under his charge. He broke the news to me last night, at a dance would you believe, the first one I'd been to since Joe died. Just goes to show what you get for enjoying yourself, I'm not sure I'll bother again. I don't understand, Arthur, he genuinely seems to hate me, but I've no idea why.

I'm trying so hard to move on, and make a success of things. Everyone else seems to be managing, Elsie's having a baby, my mates here are moving away, all apart from Di, but she's going to be working in a different section, so I don't know how much we'll see each other. I know there's a war on and I shouldn't be feeling sorry for myself, when some poor folk have it ever so much worse than me, but at the moment everything seems so difficult. I'm sorry for bothering you with this, you've your own troubles without me adding to them. I just needed someone to talk to, and well, we've always been able to talk.

I'll sign off now and let you get back to whatever it is you're meant to be doing. I hope you're well, happy and not missing your mam's cooking too much.

> *Yours fondly,*
> *Kitty*

Kitty reread the letter and paused, surprised to find her face wet with tears. She must have needed to let out her feelings more than she realised, she thought, stuffing the paper into the envelope and writing Arthur's name and service number on the front.

With the letter lying sealed by her side, Kitty let out a long slow breath and tried to relax. For months now she felt as though her life was racing rapidly out of control, and that no matter what she did or how hard she tried, things seemed to keep happening to her. Well, perhaps this was the last of it, she thought. Now her fate was sealed, maybe there was a chance life would settle down. At least she knew where she was with Hopson: he made no secret of the fact he disliked her, she thought resignedly.

*

The next morning, Nissen huts across the barracks were a hive of activity with girls everywhere getting ready to leave for their new positions, Peggy and Mary among them. They had collected their rail warrants from Sergeant Hopson, washed their eating irons and were neatly folding clothes into their kitbags, at least Peg was, Kitty observed wryly. Mary was stuffing everything in with the sort of wild abandon that suggested she was off on holiday rather than a long rail and sea crossing across the Channel.

'You're going to 'ave a devil of a job getting them creases out when you reach France, shoving everything in like that,' Di pointed out, as she sat next to Kitty on Mary's bed.

Mary shrugged. 'Oh, you know what they're like in France, they don't care a jot about things like that.'

'I think they might,' Peg pointed out, closing her bag and checking her bedside cabinet to ensure nothing was forgotten.

'What time's your train?' Kitty asked.

'Ten past,' Peggy replied, checking her watch. 'I think you're getting the same one as me, aren't you, Mare?'

'Certainly am.' Mary smiled, closing her kitbag with a flourish. 'Don't suppose there's any chance of a lift to the station, is there?'

Di and Kitty exchanged looks before collapsing into a fit of giggles. They would both miss Mary's cheek.

'Well, I can't,' Di said, getting to her feet and straightening her jacket. 'I've me first mail job over Oxford way in a minute.'

'I'll drive yer,' Kitty offered. 'I'm not needed till lunchtime when I'm taking a bigwig over to Kettering.'

'Ruddy marvellous.' Mary smiled, turning to Peg. 'Hear that, old girl, we'll leave in style rather than rolling around like cattle in one of those bally awful trucks.'

'You sure it's all right?' Peg asked doubtfully. 'I don't want you getting in no trouble.'

Kitty smiled. Peggy was so thoughtful and kind, she would miss her good nature and calm, easy temperament. 'It's fine,' Kitty told her, stepping forward to hug her warmly. 'You worry too much.'

'Where's *my* hug?' Mary demanded.

'Oh come 'ere, you,' Di chuckled, pulling the posh girl into her arms for an embrace. 'I thought you lot didn't do physical affection, you're all too busy with your stiff upper lips.'

'Yes well,' Mary sniffed as she embraced Di warmly, 'perhaps you girls have taught me one or two things about life.'

'Is one of 'em to sometimes think before yer speak?' Kitty grinned as she pulled away from Peg and enveloped Mary in her arms.

'Don't be ridiculous, Kitty,' Mary exclaimed as she warmly returned her squeeze.

An hour later and Kitty had not only dropped the girls off at the station but had also managed to pop into town to buy more notepaper, having used the last of it the day before, writing her letter to Arthur.

With the sun beating down and hardly a cloud in the sky, Kitty decided to make the most of the warm weather. Turning her face towards the sun, she strolled along the high street, nodding polite good mornings to passers-by. Reaching the end of the street, she paused, realising she was right outside the butcher's Billy owned. Taking a step towards the window, she peered inside and saw the shop was full of customers all gossiping amongst themselves as they waited for Billy to serve them. It was a nice shop, Kitty thought as she took in the gleaming white tiles, and sparkling glass counter. Turning her attention back to Billy she saw how effortless he made his job look. He was a natural, she thought, chatting easily with his customers while he carefully sliced meat for his assistant, a lad who couldn't have been more than fifteen, to wrap in brown waxy paper.

He had a way with people, Kitty noticed, as he ripped out a coupon from one woman's buff-coloured ration book and handed it back with a smile. As his gaze moved towards the window, Kitty saw his face light up as he caught sight of her and waved her inside.

'Hello Kitty,' he said easily. 'Nice to see yer again.'

'Well I was just passing,' she said. 'I didn't realise this was your place.'

'Oh yes,' he said, handing over a paper package filled with rabbit to an elderly lady. 'There's a bit extra in there for yer, I've got to get rid of it so that'll see your Bob right for a few days, Mrs Wilkins.'

The woman's face lit up. 'Thanks, Billy, you're a marvel.' She smiled gratefully.

'That was a nice thing to do,' Kitty said as Mrs Wilkins left the shop.

'Well, sometimes I have a bit left over, like when people don't claim all their ration for whatever reason,' Billy explained as he wiped down the surfaces. 'I like to help out where I can like, specially the old girls. Mrs Wilkins is coping with a sick husband and all three of her kiddies away at war. This war's hard on folk.'

Kitty nodded, thinking of Nora back in Coventry, desperately worried about her boys serving, and of course Hetty and George, who had lost their precious child. 'I know what yer mean. I've friends back home in similar situations.'

'And where is home?' Billy asked. 'By the way, have yer time for a cuppa? I was just about to make one for meself like.'

Kitty checked her watch. She wasn't due back at the barracks for another hour yet. 'A quick one,' she replied. 'Ta, Billy.'

Billy nodded and turned to his assistant. 'John, make us two teas, there's a good lad, and when you're done give the back a good scrubbing. I saw some pig's blood out on the step earlier.'

'Yes, Mr Miles,' John replied quietly.

Minutes later she was leaning against the counter, gratefully drinking a cup of tea.

'So yer never said where home is,' Billy said.

'Oh, Coventry.' Kitty smiled, setting her cup down on the glass. 'Born and bred.'

Billy's eyebrows shot up in surprise. 'Get away! Me 'n'all.'

'Never in this world!' Kitty gasped. 'Mind, I thought I recognised a bit of an accent.'

'I know some folk think we've not got an accent . . .'

'. . . but to the trained ear . . .' Kitty giggled. 'So how long yer been up this way then?'

'About ten years now,' Billy replied, wiping his hands on a tea towel. 'After Bess died I needed a fresh start and when a mate of mine told me about this shop up here I decided to pack up. I used to run the butchers over in Dale Street.'

'I remember that.' Kitty smiled. 'Just around the corner from me friend's mother's house in Talbot Street. She always got her meat from yer, said yer sold the best lamb this side of the cathedral.'

'Not Nora Higginson!' Billy exclaimed.

'Yes! D'yer know her?'

Billy chuckled. 'Know 'er? I'm related to 'er. She's me second cousin.'

Now it was Kitty's turn to look amazed. 'Give over, I don't believe it.'

'I swear on our Bess's life,' Billy laughed. 'Our Nora still keeps in touch, told me about yer 'n'all in her last letter. Said there was a girl named Kitty who'd just lost her fiancé and was practically a daughter to her what had joined-up like. Should've realised it was you, but then, I've never been all that good at putting two and two together like.'

'Nora's been like family to me, well all the Higginsons have,' Kitty explained. 'When Joe died, they were the ones that helped me pick up the pieces and cope with what'd happened.'

Billy offered her a warm smile. 'Well our Nora's like that. She were the same when Bess passed. I'd have been lost without her and Ron.'

'They're some of the kindest folk I know.' Kitty smiled. 'How long were yer wed to your Bess if yer don't mind me asking.'

Billy's face softened as he leant against the counter and smiled wistfully. 'Not at all, Kitty love. To be honest, I don't get much chance to talk about her so it's nice to remember her. We were married seven years. I'd just turned twenty-one and had to beg her father to let her marry me as she was only nineteen like.'

'I take it he said yes,' Kitty grinned.

'Not without a fight.' He chuckled at the memory. 'Old Bob Hawkins never liked me, and never liked the idea of me marrying his only girl, but I was determined and so were our Bess. We loved each other as soon as we set eyes on one another and would have wed one way or another. Her dad saw that, so reluctantly gave his blessing. Those years married to Bess were the best of me life, even during the dark days at the end when I nursed her through her illness.'

'Oh Billy,' Kitty sympathised. 'That must've been awful for yer like.'

Billy gave a quick nod of his head and looked away, as though he had been transported back to the last days of life with his wife. 'She had tuberculosis. We tried everything, but it weren't to be and she passed. Course I had help from our families, but in the end, it were just me and our Bess and I wouldn't have had it any other way. I were with her when she died, I held her hand and told her I'd love her forever.'

Kitty's eyes brimmed with tears at the butcher's admission. 'Oh Billy, that's awful, but take comfort from the fact yer were with her when she went. I'd have given me right arm to have held Joe's hand when he passed, just to let him know he were cared for. It breaks me heart to think of him all alone like that.'

At the thought of Joe lying cold on the ocean floor, Kitty shuddered in horror. She had done such a good job of pushing those dark thoughts to the back of her mind these past few months that the image of Joe's lifeless body claimed by the water left her breathless.

Sensing Kitty's despair Billy leaned across the counter and squeezed her arm gently. 'Come on, Kitty, don't take on. Joe's in a better place now and at peace, just like our Bess. It's knowing she's not having to live with this rotten war getting worse by the day that helps me cope with her loss.'

Kitty stemmed the tears from her eyes. 'I know.' She nodded. 'And it's not all bad, the little things in life are the ones that make it bearable these days, like the fact Elsie's having a baby.'

Billy raised his eyebrows in surprise. 'Elsie's pregnant? I didn't know that.'

'I think she's only just found out.' Kitty grinned. 'But isn't it lovely news? Nora will make a wonderful grandma.'

'She will, very caring woman, is our Nora,' Billy agreed. 'She was worried to death over yer when yer joined-up, but never said yer were up this way though.'

'Well she didn't know,' Kitty explained. 'We're not allowed to say where we're posted.'

The butcher nodded. 'Well, I s'pose that makes us family then, Kitty,' he beamed. 'You'll have to pop in for your tea sometime. It's rotten cooking for one.'

Kitty smiled. 'I'd like that, though we don't always get a lot of time off.'

'Whenever yer can, Kitty love.' Billy smiled. 'Our Nora'd skin me alive if she didn't think I was taking care of yer.'

'I'd like that.' Kitty smiled easily, draining her cup dry and setting it on the glass. 'Well, I'll be off now, I don't want to be late.'

'Bye then, Kitty,' Billy said, lifting his hand. 'Don't be a stranger.'

'I won't,' she replied, pulling the door open and waving goodbye.

Walking back to her car, Kitty realised she might have said goodbye to two friends this morning but she felt very much as though she had found another. Was it possible things in Northampton might be looking up? As Kitty slid into the driver's seat and started the Humber, she found herself smiling. She had the strongest feeling that finally, her luck had turned a corner.

Chapter Ten

It had been a month since Peggy and Mary had left for their new postings and in that time life for Kitty had changed dramatically. She had hoped that as Di had also remained in Northampton the two of them would be able to spend as much time together as they had before, but Di's new job with the postal service meant she was often up early and back late, driving across the country. She and Kitty rarely managed more than a few snatched minutes at bedtime.

Kitty meanwhile was tasked with general driving duties all under the watchful eye of Sergeant Hopson. One day she would be picking up an Army officer from the station in the Humber she had now become hugely fond of, another she would be driving lorries containing vital Army equipment as part of a convoy. Only last week, Kitty had sat in the cabin of her three-ton truck, proud as punch as she had driven all the way down to Portsmouth. Despite the fact it was now mid September, the warmth of the late summer sun felt like a luxury. It was almost possible to believe it was just another beautiful summer's day in England without war, Kitty thought as she laid eyes on the shimmering blue sea. However the drive had taken its toll on her – it was the furthest she had ever gone. Despite numerous rendezvous points, she had found it exhausting, particularly when darkness fell, and had been grateful to reach the vicarage she had been billeted at for the night.

The one blessing of being a qualified driver meant that Kitty was able to spend a great deal of time alone, and she found that with only the open road for company she could think clearly. The unexpected arrival of Billy had shown Kitty just how impossible life was to predict. After her parents died and she had gone from care home to care home, she had been grateful to the Higginsons for providing her with a steady and comforting presence. Together with Joe, they had made her feel as though she had a family, and the irony that she had now found another Higginson nearby wasn't lost on her. She smiled, thinking how the family that meant so much continued to look out for her, even though she was miles from home and serving in the army.

Since meeting Billy, she often popped into the butcher's for a chat and a cuppa. Together they discussed life in general and naturally the latest events of the war. But the one thing Kitty enjoyed the most was the way she could talk honestly about her feelings for Joe and her grief with someone who genuinely understood what she was going through. Billy encouraged her not to hide how she felt, or pretend everything was all right when it wasn't. He did not prod or pry, and instead just offered her a place to be herself. At long last Kitty started to feel some of the burden of her loss shift when she was in his company, and she had written to Elsie, Nora and of course Arthur, telling them of her chance encounter with Billy.

Although she had yet to hear from Nora she had been delighted when she received not only a letter from Arthur but also one from Elsie that morning. Now she pulled the Hillman into the train station to drop off a senior officer, saluted him goodbye, then leant against the bonnet of her car, the sunshine warming her face, and took out the letters. She examined each of the envelopes, Elsie's big, looped letters compared to Arthur's neat scrawl were as different as chalk and cheese. She smiled and opened Arthur's first.

Dear Kitty,

I was so happy to hear from you so soon after getting your other letter. I'll admit I was worried when you told me you were staying in Northampton with that sergeant and I had half a mind when I was next on leave to pop down and swing at the bloke. If things get too bad you could always put in for a transfer, but it sounds as though this Billy chap might have helped you turn a corner like. I don't really remember him too well, but then I were only a nipper when he left. I know Mam remembers him, I heard her occasionally say how good his meat was and that Bess, his wife, were a marvel for putting up with him! I never knew what that meant, but it sounds as though he's been good to you, our Kit, and for that I'm grateful.

Your letters, whether happy or sad, always mean the world to me. The days at sea are long, and it's hard to make sense of your place in the world when all you see for days at a time are miles and miles of sea. I know it sounds a bit wet, but I miss my family, messing about with our Elsie and of course seeing your face sat around our kitchen table. You're right, everything's changing, people are moving on and now Elsie's having a nipper! Whoever'd have thought my little sister who used to make mud pies and cut her own fringe with the kitchen scissors, would have a baby of her own? I'm thrilled for her, and myself, 'cos of course it'll be me that'll be the kiddie's favourite uncle. I can't wait to take him to football games and down the road for his first pint! Mind, I expect that you as his aunt will probably try and talk some sense into me.

The lads on board all talk about their sweethearts and the letters they get, some of them from girls in every port I'm sorry to say, but it's your letters that keep me going. They help me realise there's a life out there besides this war, and one day we'll all go back to normal and live our lives again.

All I ever want, Kitty, is for you to find happiness and I'm glad Billy has been able to lessen your load. This war's hard enough as it is without folk going out of their way to make things difficult. Remember me to Billy when you see him, and until your next letter take care of yourself.

Yours affectionately,
Arthur

Kitty grinned as she read the letter once more before folding it back inside her jacket. A letter from Arthur always felt like the best present in the world, closely followed by one from Elsie.

12 September 1940

Dear Kitty,

How are you keeping, love? Well I must say I was astonished to hear you've bumped into one of Mam's relatives. I asked her about it the other day and she were about to say something, only Dad came in covered in mud after yet another day up the allotment and she was distracted, trying to stop him making the place filthy. I think she was probably going to say what I'm about to though, which is I'm pleased you've found someone to confide in. We all need someone to help ease our troubles, especially during these difficult times, and it sounds as if Billy's helping you cope with all that's happened and your new life up there. I don't really remember him if I'm honest, though Mam reckons that's because I were always too lazy to go with her to the butchers – cheek! She did say that I'd remember if I'd met him, as nobody forgot our Billy!

Life here's much the same, Kit. Mike's been a tower of strength to all of us and I think Dad's become quite fond of him and all he's done for us with the boys away. He really is a treasure. He's ever so thoughtful, and often helps out around the house, though Mam's forever telling him off and says that it's her job, but he reckons in this war we all have to muck in together and I suppose he's right. Nothing's ever too much trouble for him and he's always the first to brew up in the morning or last thing at night. Mam says he's got a way of making the tea last that little bit longer, and now we're rationed she hopes he can do the same with a couple of slices of bacon!

As for me, well I'm blooming, Kit, quite honestly. Can you believe I'm almost seven months gone and getting bigger every day! I can't wait till Charlie and you are home and everything's back to normal again. That said, I haven't heard from my husband in weeks. I hope he's just busy Kit and not forgotten me! Feels funny having a baby now, I'm so happy and excited but it seems wrong to be celebrating something so wonderful when there's chaos and devastation all around. The bombs that fell on those poor devils in London are downright disgraceful. I don't know how they're coping with it all – nursing mothers bombed out of their homes. What's the world coming to when defenceless mums and kiddies are attacked like that? It's just not right.

Still, knowing you're out there doing your bit fills me with comfort. You're strong, love, and I know that with you and our Charlie, not to mention all my brothers, we'll win this war eventually. It's just a question of when!

I'd better sign off now, Kitty, Mike's been away for a few days and I want to make him a shepherd's pie to welcome him home like. Don't fret though, I'll do the same for you next time you're back on leave!

Yours with love,
Elsie xxx

Kitty clutched the letter to her chest, feeling a swell of love for her old friend. What she wouldn't give to see Elsie just now, she thought, imagining them having a much-needed cuppa then strolling arm in arm through Owen Owen. They had seen each other every day for years, been with each other through all of life's ups and downs. Now she wasn't around during one of the most important times in Elsie's life and Kitty could scarcely believe it. This was the real tragedy of war, she thought, not just the rationing and the constant fear of what would happen next, but the little things that were destroyed, that they had always taken for granted.

Sighing, Kitty scanned the letter through once more. How she missed Elsie! But at least she was being well taken care of by Mike. Kitty furrowed her eyebrows as she noticed there was still very little mention of Charlie in this letter. She knew he was away, but Kitty just hoped it wasn't a case of 'out of sight, out of mind'. She was tempted to ask Elsie straight out if everything was all right with Charlie in her next letter, or better yet mention something to Arthur about her concerns. Yet Kitty was wary of putting too much in writing: censors read everything and she could just imagine some bright spark in the army making Charlie's life a misery if word got out that there were difficulties in their marriage. Heavens, she knew from first-hand experience how difficult superior officers could be. No, better to wait until she saw Elsie in person Kitty thought, folding the letter back into the envelope and putting it next to Arthur's in her jacket pocket.

Kitty peered at the station clock and saw there were another couple of hours before she was due to report back for work. As it was almost lunchtime, she thought she would stop by the butcher's and see if Billy fancied a cuppa. Since tea had been rationed a month earlier, the drink felt like something of a luxury and as Kitty had attended Pay Parade that morning, she hoped to treat her new friend to a brew at the tearoom on the corner. Clambering back into the car, she drove the short distance from the station into town and pulled in outside the shop, just as Billy was closing for lunch.

At the sight of Kitty, Billy waved welcomingly and opened the door. 'I was just thinking about yer, Kitty, love,' he smiled, ushering her inside.

'Thought I'd pop in and see if yer fancied a brew up the tea-room? My treat.'

'That's very nice of yer, Kitty,' he replied, walking back towards the counter and removing his striped apron.

'Well, with tea rationing we've to manage our supplies. Even us lot in the Amy have been warned we might not be able to brew up as much as we'd like,' Kitty explained.

'Never!' Billy gasped. 'You're working your socks off for king and country. If anyone deserves a cuppa summat hot, it's Army girls.'

'Well, we do what we can.' Kitty shrugged. 'So tea, then?'

'No need, Kitty, I've plenty in,' Billy said firmly. 'Save your money, I'll make one here.'

'Don't be daft,' Kitty protested, as she followed him out to the little kitchenette at the back of the shop. 'You've no need to waste your rations on me.'

Billy said nothing as he switched on the light and filled the kettle with water. The room was no bigger than a cupboard, but Billy had decked it out beautifully, painting it a bright yellow, with a tiny range in one corner next to a little Belfast sink, and two chairs underneath the whitewashed window.

There was a clink of china as Billy pulled two cups down from the shelf above the sink. 'I've plenty of tea. In fact, I'll let yer into a little secret, our Kit. I've a mate of a mate of a mate who's always happy to ensure I've got more than me fair share if yer catch me drift, so you've no need to worry.'

Kitty opened her mouth in surprise. 'What? Black market tea like?'

Billy chuckled and tapped his nose. 'Say nothing!' he said. 'But if you've no objection to some ill-gotten gains I can make yer a brew any time yer like.'

As Billy turned and busied himself making the tea, Kitty tried to digest her new friend's revelation. A sense of unease gnawed away at her. She knew rationing was uncomfortable, but the government had allocated food to everyone for a reason. No matter how well-intentioned, it seemed wrong to take someone

148

else's share. Yet as she watched Billy walk towards her, cup full of the steaming liquid, she bit her lip, knowing she was already going to give into temptation. It was only tea, after all. Where was the harm?

'Get that down yer.' He grinned, handing her the cup. 'What've yer been up to anyway?'

Kitty sipped the hot tea appreciatively. Knowing it was wrong somehow made it taste all the more satisfying. For heaven's sakes, what was wrong with her? 'Just the usual,' she replied.

Billy nodded, aware Kitty couldn't say much about her work. 'That sergeant of yours still giving yer a hard time?'

'He's been on seventy-two hours' leave, so I've had an easy few days,' she admitted, setting her cup on the windowsill and thinking back to the last time she had seen Hopson. It had been when she had returned from Portsmouth and despite several hours on the road, he had insisted Kitty clean her lorry inside and out, along with the other five that had driven down in convoy, before she went to bed. Kitty shuddered at the memory. She had been so tired she had felt like weeping, but knew that would be playing straight into her sergeant's hands. Instead she had done what she always did: rolled up her sleeves and got on with the task in hand.

'Hopefully he'll have moved onto someone else when he gets back and will concentrate on making their lives a misery,' Billy said.

'That's just what Arthur said,' Kitty sighed. 'Speaking of which, he asked me to remember him to yer like.'

'Oh, Nora's eldest, how is he?'

'All right, I think,' Kitty replied. 'Doesn't say a lot, but just hearing from him is enough, least I know he's alive like.'

Billy nodded, understanding only too well how Kitty felt. 'What about the rest of the Higginsons? I've not heard from our Nora for a while. Is she keeping well?'

'As far as I know. I told yer our Elsie's expecting, didn't I?'

Billy nodded once more. 'I still can't get over it. Last time I saw her she was barely out of nappies herself.'

'Well she'll be changing someone else's soon.' Kitty giggled, just as there was a sharp knock at the back door.

Billy's face darkened. 'Flamin' customers. I swear some of 'em can't read. We're closed!' he shouted, only for the loud knocking to continue. 'Excuse me while I deal with whoever this is,' he said gruffly, walking through the kitchenette out into the shop.

Watching his retreating back, Kitty took another sip of illicit tea as she heard him pull open the door.

'What part of closed don't yer understand?' he snapped, before changing his tone. 'Oh sorry, John lad, didn't realise yer were out there.'

'All right, Mr Miles? I've just got those packages you wanted, where shall I put 'em?' a young lad's voice bellowed.

Kitty heard Billy speak again, this time in quieter tones. 'Ta, John. Just leave 'em out the back, will yer, son, now's not the best time.'

'But you said you wanted 'em delivered personally,' the boy protested.

'And I told yer, now wasn't a good time,' Billy replied firmly.

At the sound of the conversation, curiosity got the better of Kitty and she peered around the kitchenette door into the shop, eager to see what was going on. The sight of Billy jostling his assistant dressed in navy overalls roughly into the street surprised her. His jaw was set and his face puce with rage as the boy continued to protest.

'John, I won't tell yer again, if I have to knock yer into the middle of next week to make yer understand now's not a good time, then heaven help me I'll beat yer black and blue. Now clear off!' Billy roared, roughly pushing the boy out onto the street and kicking him deftly on his backside before slamming the door.

Kitty was stunned. She had never seen Billy behave so menacingly before and would never have thought he had it in him. Up until now she had always thought her new friend was quiet and gentle – this dark side was something of a shock and Kitty didn't like what she saw. Hearing Billy's footsteps tap across the tiled floor towards the kitchenette Kitty sat back in her chair and gulped the rest of her tea, clanking the cup noisily on the saucer as Billy reappeared.

'Sorry about that.' He smiled warmly, sitting down, straightening his tie. 'John's sometimes, not too bright.'

Feeling flushed, Kitty nodded, unsure what to say.

'You've finished your tea,' Billy noticed, getting to his feet. 'Shall I make yer another?'

'No thanks, Billy, I'd best be getting back,' Kitty said quickly. 'Thanks for the cuppa though.'

'Yes, of course love.' Billy scratched his head thoughtfully as he took her cup and saucer and set them noisily in the sink. 'Well, don't be a stranger.'

'I won't,' she promised, hurrying out of the shop and onto the street. Walking towards her car, Kitty got into the Humber and started the engine, doing her best to ignore the disturbing feeling gnawing away at her.

Pulling into the barracks she found she still had a good hour before her next job so she walked across to the mess to see what Cook had prepared for lunch. As ever the canteen was bustling with noise and Kitty sniffed the air. It smelled as if Cook's famous Potato Jane was on the menu – heaven. Joining the back of the queue, she jumped out of her skin as she felt a sharp prod in her side. Whipping round in shock she came face to face with a familiar face – Di.

'Whatever are yer doing here?' Kitty grinned gleefully. 'I thought yer were away up north all week?'

Di shook her head as they neared Cook, who ladled them each a portion and handed back their plates. 'Change of plan,' she explained. 'I've got the afternoon off instead as I'm driving over to Oxfordshire in the morning.'

'Well that sounds an easier day,' Kitty remarked, as they made their way through the throng of tables to find a space in the corner by the door.

'So what's up with yer then?' Di asked, coming straight to the point.

'How d'yer mean?' Kitty asked, puzzled, taking a seat opposite her friend.

'I mean you look like you lost tuppence and found a farthing,' Di said bluntly.

Kitty sighed. There was no pulling the wool over Di's eyes. 'I went to see Billy earlier.'

Di's eyes danced with curiosity. 'And? I thought you were in clover now you've found out you're virtually family.'

Unsure what to say next, Kitty paused. Di had been full of support when she had told her about Billy and she wanted Di to like her new friend. However, she felt she needed to talk through the morning's events with someone. Billy's behaviour had seemed so out of character and it had rattled her. Putting down her knife and fork, Kitty quickly told Di what had happened.

'P'raps he was just 'aving a bad day, Kit,' Di said finally. 'I wouldn't worry about it, we've all felt like giving someone a kick from time to time, and no doubt said summat we regret in the 'eat of the moment 'n'all.'

'Maybe,' Kitty said thoughtfully, as she sliced into her potato. 'But his face was so angry, Di, the lad looked terrified, and I have to admit so was I.'

Di chewed her lunch thoughtfully and paused. 'Well, all right then, you've seen 'is bad side, it 'appens. We've all got a temper, Kit, I remember how you 'ad a go at Mary a few months back when she wouldn't stop going on about writing to her uncle.'

'That was completely different and yer know it!' Kitty laughed.

Di shrugged as she chewed a mouthful of her lunch. 'Maybe, but I think you frightened the life out of Mary. All I'm saying is this Billy's been a godsend to you the last few weeks. You've come out of yourself, seemed 'appier and it'd be a shame to see that go because you've seen summat you don't like. Besides, you don't know what else has gone on between 'im and this lad. P'raps John's been in need of a kick up the backside for a while and p'raps 'e 'asn't. All I'm saying is everyone's done and said things they're not proud of, but it'd be rotten if our friends and loved ones judged us solely on that.'

Kitty knew Di was right. So she had seen Billy's temper: nobody was perfect, but something else about the morning still troubled her. 'There's still the tea he's got, I dunno how comfortable I am knowing he's got stuff off the black market like,' she said in hushed tones.

'Give over!' Di roared with laughter. 'There's all sorts out there that's not on the up and up. Mark my words, if folk can get their 'ands on it, they will. Sounds like 'e's got his 'ead screwed on to me. And it's only tea, Kitty, it's not like 'e's offered you a week's worth of bacon and knocked off 'is grandma for it, is it?'

A light bulb felt like it had gone off in Kitty's mind. Di was right, if tea was the worst of Billy's crimes she could live with that. 'You're right,' she muttered. 'P'raps I've blown all this out of proportion.'

'Just a bit.' Di chuckled, devouring the last mouthful of her lunch. 'Look, give 'im the benefit of the doubt. If you see 'im behave like that again, well think on, but until then, treat it as a one-off.'

'I will,' Kitty sighed. 'I'll try and pop in again later in the week.'

'Lovely.' Di grinned again. 'It seems to me 'e's been good for you, Kit. What with 'opson, and me being away more, I think it's nice you've found a kindred spirit. After all, 'e's never been nasty to you, has he?'

Kitty shook her head. 'No, he's been nothing but kind and considerate,' she admitted, thinking of how Billy always listened to her, made sure she had plenty to eat and drink, and even slipped her the odd chocolate bar to keep her going while she was out driving.

'There you are, then.' Di smiled as the pair got to their feet to wash their eating irons. 'Judge as you find.'

'You're right,' Kitty said, squeezing her friend's arm gratefully. 'Ta for listening, Di.'

'Any time, love, it's what I'm 'ere for.'

As the girls walked across the quad, Kitty felt a sense of peace descend over her. So she had seen the very worst in a friend – well, if that was as bad as it got, she could cope. That morning she realised just how fond she had become of Billy, and she savoured the moments they spent together. Di was right, Billy was a kindred spirit and she did not want to lose him. They had become close in the last few weeks and the idea of saying goodbye to him was unbearable. She had spent too much time looking to the past, it was time to look to the future. Kitty realised that she very much wanted Billy to be a part of whatever lay ahead.

Chapter Eleven

In a funny way, Kitty thought, she was relieved to have seen the worst of Billy's behaviour. A childhood in care homes had taught her there was no such thing as a good or bad person, it was all just shades of grey. Sometimes people were nice and sometimes they were horrible, it really was as simple as that.

Aside from Elsie, Kitty found it difficult to confide in many people, but she felt she and Billy had a connection. She had already come to rely on him far more than she could ever have anticipated and Kitty found she looked forward to their regular chats. Yet despite her promises to Di to pop in and see him again, it had been over three weeks since she had last paid Billy a visit and time had marched on. The air had turned cooler, the days had become shorter and the leaves were falling rapidly from the trees, signalling the fact autumn had well and truly arrived.

Guiltily she bit her lip: Kitty had intended to put things right a lot earlier between them, but her driver mechanic duties had kept her busy. Since Hopson had returned from his seventy-two hours' leave he had been more unbearable than ever, sending Kitty out on long distance drives that saw her waking at four in the morning and returning late at night. Kitty was exhausted but – as Di pointed out – it obviously meant Hopson trusted her to do a good job, as no matter how much he might dislike her, he would never dream of instructing her to do something he thought she was incapable of. Every job, no matter how large or small, was vital to the war effort and with the Germans now bombing London each night, every ATS girl knew lives depended on each task they performed.

The war was getting uglier by the second, Kitty thought, as she walked towards the Humber she had been assigned that morning. The news was suddenly full of reports of the devastation the German Luftwaffe was causing across the capital, and even though Northampton was miles away from London, she felt a sense of dread on the streets. Parents held their children a little bit closer, sweethearts cuddled each other a little more tightly and friends squeezed one another's hands and greeted each other like long-lost relatives when they met in tearooms for a gossip. But despite the worry as to what the Germans would do next, Kitty also felt a sense of strength around her as people refused to be intimidated by Hitler's latest assault. Instead she found folk around her clinging to their communities, and heeding ARP wardens' warnings quickly.

Performing the checks she usually made before getting into any car, Kitty saw the Humber was almost out of petrol and filled it up from the cans her unit kept on site. One of the first things the girls had been taught was to always fill their jerrycans as well as their vehicles with fuel and store them in the boot. Although petrol was rationed, priority was given to the military and Kitty remembered only too well the warnings about never allowing your vehicle to run out of petrol.

Walking around to the boot, she threw it open and was relieved to see the previous driver had filled four cans up with fuel. She gave one a little shake and was delighted to see it was almost full. The cans were famous for leaking, spilling petrol onto the floor of the boot and not for the first time Kitty wondered if there wasn't a better solution than these leaky cans to ensure they were always equipped with precious fuel.

With her vital checks complete, Kitty drove out of the barracks and onto the open road. Today she had a rather unusual passenger; she had been tasked with collecting an absconder from Swindon who had run away from a nearby unit a fortnight earlier. Hopson had told her in no uncertain terms that there would be no rendezvous points on the way back and there would be no time for dilly-dallying either, as he put it.

With yet another long drive ahead of her, Kitty pressed her foot on the accelerator and remembered with horror how only last week a German pilot had been shot down, landing in a farmer's field next to the barracks. Everyone had been agog as they rushed to the meadow, with many of the men on the farm shouting they would 'kill the Jerry' that got out.

Kitty had felt a flash of shame when she discovered the pilot had not survived the crash. She knew the Jerries were their enemy but the hatred in people's eyes had shocked her to the core.

Driving through town Kitty passed the butcher's and couldn't help gazing at the shop. She knew it was too early for Billy to have opened up, but the sight of him getting the shop ready for his day's customers tugged at her heart. She couldn't let another day pass without talking to him. If nothing else, Di would never let her hear the end of it. Realising she could spare a few minutes without getting into trouble, Kitty pulled into a space nearby and got out. Reaching the shop, she knocked loudly on the door before she could change her mind.

Billy saw her immediately, and his face broke into a delighted smile as he hurried to let her in. 'Kitty, long time no see.' He beamed, beckoning her inside.

Stepping past him into the shop, Kitty returned his grin, delighted to see he looked just the same as ever. His white overalls still contained traces of dried blood and his navy and white apron was smeared with grease.

'Just thought it had been a while,' she said shyly as Billy shut the door firmly behind them.

'It has,' he agreed, walking back to the counter. 'I was worried I'd upset yer.'

'Oh no, it's nothing like that,' Kitty said quickly, shaking her head, aware she wasn't being honest. 'Hopson's just kept me on a short leash, yer know how it is like.'

'I know that fella's going to get short shrift if he carries on messing yer about like this,' Billy said firmly as he returned to the counter and sliced cleanly through a slab of pork.

Kitty winced as blood spurted across the work surface. There were times she really found it difficult to stomach what Billy did for a living.

'So how've yer been?' she asked, eager to change the subject.

'Same as ever,' he replied, cutting the pork into joints.

Kitty turned away and faced the wall, looking at the many official government posters urging people to register for meat rations. 'Glad to hear it,' she said turning back to him as she heard him put his knife down.

'Time for a cuppa?' he asked, wiping his hands on a teacloth.

She checked her watch. There was plenty of time to reach her destination, so where was the harm? 'Go on then.' She grinned. 'I'm on me way to a job, down south, but I'm gasping for a brew.'

Billy smiled. 'Coming right up. Why don't yer go on through to the kitchenette and make yourself comfortable. I'll be with yer in a minute.'

Taking her usual seat under the window Kitty waited for Billy to arrive and glanced around her. She was pleased to see nothing had changed. The same teacups and saucers lined the tiny shelves and the kettle sat on the range. Running her eyes over to the cupboard where the tea was kept, she noticed the door was wide open. She got up to shut it, only as she got nearer she was surprised to find there were tins and tins of tea, alongside sugar and butter. Kitty craned her neck to get a better look and saw with a start that Billy had enough lining his shelves to feed a family of four ten times over. Where had he got his hands on so many goods that had been rationed out? Everyone else was making do, why did Billy have so much?

That same feeling of discomfort she had experienced the last time she had been at the butcher's gnawed away at her but Kitty did her best to ignore it. When Billy appeared, she plastered on a warm smile and concentrated on how much she had missed her friend.

'So, been to any more dances up The Rialto?' she asked, struggling to think of something to say.

Billy chuckled as he set the kettle on the range to boil and reached for the teacups. 'No, that night I met yer were a one-off. I don't go out much, but a mate of mine persuaded me, so I went to keep him company.'

Kitty felt a flash of surprise. She couldn't imagine Billy sat in on his own every night, he was always full of fun and larger than life. 'I didn't know that. I thought as a single fella, you'd be out all the time.'

The butcher regarded Kitty evenly as he handed her a cup of scalding hot tea. 'That's the thing, Kit, I don't want to be a single man. I want Bess by me side, and I'd do anything to make that happen.'

Guilt surged through Kitty as she took a sip of tea. 'Sorry, Billy, I wasn't thinking.'

'Don't worry about it, Kit, you're right really, I ought to go out more, but me heart's not in it.' Billy shrugged.

Kitty knew only too well what Billy meant. Sometimes it felt like a small victory just to have survived the day, but you kept going, in the hope that one day you would feel normal again. This was just one of the reasons she had missed Billy, she thought: he understood what it was like to live with grief every single day.

'So what's the real reason I've not seen yer about, Kit?' Billy asked, sitting down opposite her. 'And don't give me some old flannel about being busy. You're always busy, it doesn't usually stop yer coming in here.'

Kitty sighed. She might have guessed Billy would never have fallen for that. She weighed up her options. Should she try to think of another reason why she hadn't been to see him or risk telling the truth?

'Thing is, Billy,' she began, 'I saw the way yer talked to that lad, your assistant who came calling and I'd never seen that side of yer before.'

'Oh that!' Billy said, rolling his eyes and waving her concerns away. 'That was only John, he's always a pain in the backside, never listens to a word I say. I never meant to upset yer, but John deserved a good talking to, though p'raps I shouldn't have been quite so forceful.'

Nodding, Kitty realised Di had been right, Billy had just got out of bed the wrong side that morning. But there was something else troubling her as well. Furrowing her brow, Kitty knew she still wasn't comfortable about Billy indulging in extra rationed goods. She had to say something if she wanted their friendship to continue. 'What about all that food you've got in your cupboards?'

Billy's eyes narrowed. 'What food?'

Kitty paused, sensing she had hit a nerve. 'The piles of butter, sugar and tea,' she explained gently, 'I saw them, while yer were still in the shop. I wasn't prying like, the door was wide open, I couldn't help it.'

'And so what if I've extras in, Kitty? What yer got against it?' Billy asked, his voice containing a note of warning.

Kitty shifted uncomfortably in her seat. 'It's not right, Billy, you know that.'

Billy smiled. 'You're telling me yer wouldn't take advantage if yer could?'

'No,' she replied firmly. 'Taking more than your fair share is wrong. There's a war on, we all have to pull together, what with things getting worse by the second. Look at those poor mites in London. By taking food away from the mouths of those fighting for our freedom we run the risk of letting the Jerries win. Food's precious, Billy, our boys need what you've got in your cupboard a lot more than yer or I do.'

Exhausted by her speech, Kitty sank back in the chair, her face red with anger. Pulling together was the only way they were going to win, surely Billy could see that.

'Come on, Kitty, don't be like this,' he coaxed, at the sight of her angry face. 'I'm not doing any harm and I'm happy to pass on a bit extra to others 'n'all, don't take it so seriously.'

Kitty took a deep breath as realisation dawned. The lad Billy had been so cross with must have been delivering illegal rations. A fresh round of fury pulsed through her. How dare he put others' lives at risk like this?

'I'm sorry, Billy,' she said determinedly. 'I don't agree with any of this. Yer might think it's all right, but in my book it's plain wrong. You'll not be seeing me again till yer put this right.'

The moment Kitty had said the words out loud Billy's expression changed from one of warmth to one of fury.

'That's where you're wrong, Kitty Williams,' he said, bending his face towards her, his tone suddenly menacing. 'In fact we'll be seeing a lot more of each other.'

'I don't think so,' she said firmly, getting to her feet, only for Billy to reach out and grab her arm roughly to prevent her leaving.

'Ow,' she said, wincing, freeing herself from Billy's grasp.

'Sit back down, Kitty,' Billy said firmly. 'Yer told me yer had a while yet and I need to explain a few things.'

Something about Billy's expression told Kitty he had something to say she needed to hear. Warily, she returned to her seat opposite the butcher.

Billy eyed her cautiously and took a deep breath. 'The thing is, Kitty love, as yer might already have guessed, I don't just get a bit of tea in off a mate every now and again. I get me hands on things people need nowadays and sell it to 'em at a price they can afford like.'

'How d'yer mean?'

'I mean, I make it me business to help people out. Some folks have trouble going without and I make sure they don't have to.'

Kitty's hands flew to her throat in shock as the reality of Billy's words hit home. 'Yer mean you're a spiv!' she gasped.

Billy roared with laughter. 'I prefer to see meself as performing a public service like. People have needs and I help 'em out like.'

'Public service! That's a joke. The only people spivs help are themselves,' Kitty spat, her face red with fury.

'Now, now, Kitty.' Billy grinned, smoothing an imaginary

crease from his trousers. 'I might make a bit extra like, but this war's hard on folks. If I can relieve that burden, then what's wrong with that?'

Holding up her hands, Kitty got to her feet and backed away. 'I've heard enough, Billy,' she whispered. 'I meant what I said, I think it's best we keep our distance. I don't like this black market carry on.'

'Not so fast,' Billy said in a low voice as he followed her out of the kitchenette and into the shop. 'Yer might not agree with what I'm doing, but you're a good girl and you'd still help a mate out like, wouldn't yer?'

'What are yer on about, Billy?' she asked wearily.

Billy smiled again, only now his eyes were filled with menace. 'Well, we're pals, aren't we, and pals help each other out.'

Kitty froze as he stepped towards her and tucked a stray strand of hair behind her ear. 'See, all that keeps me going since our Bess died is how I can help folk out. Well, when I discovered your Joe had passed, I thought you'd probably get the same comfort I get from offering to help people, so naturally I thought yer might like to join my little set-up.'

A sense of unease washed over Kitty. How could he use his poor wife's name to justify his criminal behaviour? Never mind dragging Joe into it. 'Well you're wrong, I'm not helping,' she snapped.

A vein throbbed ominously at the side of Billy's temple. 'No, Kitty love, I think yer will once you've heard me out.'

Kitty gulped and tried to stay calm. 'I've tried to be nice about this, Billy, but I don't like lying and I don't like hanging about with criminals, so I suggest yer try someone else,' she said firmly, turning around and walking to the door, her heart pounding.

She reached for the door knob but not before Billy caught her arm once more. This time he swung Kitty roughly round to face him and shook her hard.

'I've had enough of this,' he snarled, his calloused hand gripping Kitty's arm so tightly she cried out in pain. 'For weeks now

I've put up with your whining about Joe, your problems with that sergeant and how yer miss them Higginsons. Well allow me to let yer into a little secret. Yer might be too high 'n' mighty to be hanging about with criminals like me, but what about those with loose morals, 'cos yer don't seem to have a problem with that.'

'What are yer on about?' Kitty hissed, as Billy brought his face so close to hers she could smell the kippers he'd had for breakfast.

'I'm on about your best mate Elsie,' he snarled, his arm still gripping Kitty's. 'By all accounts that lad that's billeted with 'em has been keeping her warm at night.'

'Mike?' Kitty gasped. 'Don't talk daft!'

'It's true, Kitty,' Billy replied softly, folding his arms. 'See, Elsie's not as devoted to her poor Charlie who's serving away as yer might think.'

Kitty shook her head in disgust. If this was Billy's idea of a sick joke she had heard enough. 'You're not well in the head, Billy. I suggest yer see a doctor. I'm off.'

Turning on her heel she stalked towards the exit, only for Billy to call out to her in a sing-song voice. 'That baby's not her Charlie's, yer know. It's that lad what's staying with 'em. He's the father.'

'You're lying,' she hissed, turning back to face him. 'Elsie'd never do that to Charlie.'

'Wouldn't she?' Billy shrugged, leaning against the door jamb. 'Yer sure about that?'

'I am. Elsie is as honest as the day is long,' Kitty protested fiercely.

Billy roared with laughter. 'War does funny things to folk, makes 'em lonely. I mean it's common knowledge Elsie's sick to the back teeth of never hearing off her husband like, can't blame her for getting cosy with another fella. Yer forget I've still got friends and family in the town. I know what's what.'

'Give over,' Kitty scoffed. 'If that were true, I'd have heard about it meself by now.'

'I doubt that very much. I mean, folks have gone out of their way to protect yer after all you've been through,' Billy pointed out.

Kitty's heart sank as she remembered the hushed whispers and smiles hurriedly plastered on people's faces as they had seen her approach the last time she was home on leave. Billy was right, people were unable to be themselves with her. Could he be right about this as well? Kitty thought back to the last few letters she had received from her friend. She had talked of nothing but Mike and how wonderful he was. What if there was an element of truth to what Billy was saying? Despair blazed through her. She was sure Elsie was incapable of such a thing, but lately her friend seemed different. Still, Kitty thought, this was nothing to do with Billy.

'Even if it were true, what business is it of yours?' Kitty demanded more confidently than she felt.

'None.' Billy sneered, reaching behind her to turn the closed sign to open. 'Only yer might want to have a think about whether or not you're still refusing to help me, given what I know about your mate.'

Kitty's eyes narrowed. 'What are yer saying?'

'Nothing.' Billy shrugged. 'Just that it'd be a terrible shame if her Charlie got to hear about what she were up to. Yer know what they say, loose lips sink ships, only in this case it'd be loose lips lose marriages.' Billy let out a peal of laughter and shook his head. 'I'd hate for that to happen to poor Elsie, especially with a kiddie on the way and yer could've done summat about it yourself like.'

Kitty gulped and tried to stay calm as she braced herself for the worst. Billy was no friend, he was a monster dressed in a butcher's apron, and she was the hapless victim that had fallen under his spell. Her eyes filled with horror as she returned his gaze and saw the kindness had gone from the brown eyes she had once thought were so warm, and had been replaced with a cool chill.

'What d'yer want?' she said.

Billy smiled, but the grin failed to reach his eyes. 'I just need a bit of help with me extra business . . . I need a driver for the occasional collection and delivery like, nothing much and nothing a spark girl like yer can't handle.'

'A spark girl?' Kitty echoed.

'That's right,' he said, nodding. 'Spark girls can get into all sorts of places without anyone being any the wiser. You'll do perfectly.'

'Please, Billy,' Kitty begged, her mind reeling as she wondered how she could get out of risking her job to keep him quiet. 'There must be some other way. Look, I won't tell anyone what you've been up to but leave me alone.'

The butcher said nothing, then threw his head back and laughed just as a customer pushed the shop door open.

'Someone's in a good mood,' she remarked, walking towards the counter.

'I've just had a bit of good luck, Mrs Fish, this young lady's agreed to give me a hand with summat.' He smiled as he turned back to Kitty. 'Come and see me when you've finished your job tonight like, and we can talk about what it is I want doing, understand?'

Kitty nodded, understanding perfectly what Billy meant and what would happen if she ignored him.

'I'll see yer later,' she said quietly.

'I'll be waiting,' Billy called brightly as she walked out of the shop.

Straightening her cap, Kitty walked towards her car feeling chilled to the core. The friendship she had thought she shared with Billy was nothing more than a sham and despair ebbed away at her as she cursed her own stupidity. She had allowed this man to use the love she felt for Joe and Elsie to his advantage. Kitty knew she was trapped. Tell the police about Billy's crimes, and Elsie's marriage, her reputation – not to mention the future of her child – could suffer. Do what Billy wanted, and Kitty knew she risked her job, her country, her safety as well as the possibility of prison. Dabbling in the black market was more than frowned upon, Kitty knew that. It was downright shameful and the courts were punishing anyone involved with heavy penalties. Getting into the car, Kitty rested her head on the wheel and let the tears of anger and frustration flow. She was in an impossible situation and had no idea which way to turn.

Chapter Twelve

The drive to Swindon was a long one but Kitty found the route offered her the perfect chance for some precious thinking time. As she passed through towns and villages, out into the lush green countryside, she found herself mulling over Billy's threats.

She was fairly sure Billy had only become friends with her because she was a spark girl and she could kick herself for being so stupid. How could she ever have thought she had met someone who genuinely seemed to understand all she had gone through? Life had taught Kitty that when something seemed too perfect it usually was. She could kick herself and wished she had stayed well away from Billy and his shop. It had been the fact that he was related to the Higginsons, the family she loved as if they were her own, that had made her want to stay involved.

They had been nothing but kind and decent since Kitty had known them, and Elsie was as honest as the day was long. Her best friend adored Charlie, and in her heart of hearts Kitty was sure Billy was lying and her friend had remained faithful to her husband. After all, she had known Elsie nearly all her life; the two told each other everything. Kitty thought it was impossible that Elsie would keep something like this a secret. With a jolt Kitty thought back to Charlie's haunted look. What if he had known something was going on between Elsie and Mike? What if that was why he had appeared upset? Kitty shook her head. Her mind was working overtime, putting two and two together and coming up with seventy-five. Billy had to be lying, there was no other logical explanation, yet was refusing him really worth the risk of jeopardising Elsie's future? Even if the rumours were untrue, if Billy's lies got out, they could severely damage Elsie and her reputation, and it was doubtful she or the rest of the Higginsons would ever live down the scandal of an adulterous wife and a child fathered out of wedlock.

Sharply turning the car right into a narrow lane, Kitty realised that what was really making her suspect Billy could be telling the truth was how much he knew. Was it possible Nora had confided in him about what was really going on under her roof? Kitty had not received a letter from Nora in months and wondered if it was because Elsie's mother was afraid of letting something slip. Kitty pursed her lips and gathered her thoughts. She could of course write to Elsie and ask her outright, but the last thing she wanted to do was upset Elsie with vicious rumours, or indeed cause trouble if the letter fell into the wrong hands. She dreaded to think how Nora, Ron or Mike would react if rumours were flying around about Elsie's supposed loose morals. Nora Higginson was a proud woman, with a strict moral code. If she thought folk were even talking about her daughter's baby being fathered by a man other than her husband she would raise merry hell. There was nothing people liked more than gossip, Kitty thought grimly, and so she decided not to mention any of this in her next note to Elsie. It was just too risky. Letters were read by all and sundry these days and you never knew who could be privy to your business. Then of course there was Arthur, Kitty thought. Did he know anything about this? Should she even tell him about the news Billy had shared?

At the thought of Arthur, Kitty smiled. He would no doubt give Billy more than a slap on the wrist if he got wind of what he had said. But then, Kitty thought guiltily, Arthur had done so much for her already, she had no desire to burden him with something so awful, especially when he was so far from home and could do precious little.

In that moment Kitty would give anything to talk to Arthur about what had happened. She pictured them together sipping a cuppa and sharing a teacake as Kitty told him how Billy had turned. Arthur had always been a good listener, and she imagined the set of his jaw as he waited until she had finished before he spoke and helped her work out what to do.

Kitty rubbed her eyes wearily and glanced across at her passenger, Harry, a soldier who like her was stationed in Northampton. He had barely said a word since she picked him up from the barracks in the Wiltshire town, and she was beginning to feel a bit sorry for the lad. He was only a year or so younger than her and had looked close to tears when his superior officers had bundled him into the car and told him to expect court martial when he returned. Kitty had kept trying to make conversation, but the boy wasn't interested, preferring to look out of the car window than chat with his driver.

Glancing at her watch, she realised darkness would fall in a little while and with at least two hours left on the road, Kitty would need Harry's help to navigate the last part of the journey. She tried again.

'Are your family from Swindon, Harry?' she asked over the rumble of the engine.

The lad nodded, his brown hair falling into his large blue eyes. 'My wife's just had a baby.'

'And is that why yer left the barracks like?' she pressed gently.

Harry looked at her, despair written all over his face. 'It's our first, I couldn't miss it. They were shipping me off to God knows where next week, and I wanted to see him, our little lad, before I went, in case of, well . . .' Harry trailed off and turned his gaze down towards his hands.

'In case yer don't come back,' Kitty finished quietly.

'Yes.' Harry nodded again. 'I never knew my dad, he ran off before I was born. I wanted my son to know how much I cared, that I loved him so much I ran away from the Army for him, so I could hold him tight at least once.'

'Would they not just give yer forty-eight-hours' leave?' Kitty asked in amazement.

Harry gave a hollow laugh as he turned back to Kitty and

pushed his mop of brown hair away from his eyes. 'I asked, but my commanding officer said just 'cos my wife'd had a nipper, that was no reason to take me off my duties, especially with a foreign posting in a few weeks.'

'Blimey!' Kitty let out a low whistle. 'And I thought I had it bad in the Army.'

Harry shrugged and looked back out of the window. 'Yeah well, that's the Army, isn't it? It's no picnic as we're always being reminded. There's a war on, in case you'd forgotten.'

Kitty smiled sadly. Harry was right, life in the Army was tough at times and being away from loved ones was the hardest part about it. She looked across at her passenger and wondered if she would have done the same had she been in his position.

'So was it worth it?' she asked softly, the light now fading fast.

The look of pure love that flashed across Harry's face in the half-light told Kitty all she needed to know.

'Without doubt,' he murmured. 'Just to have seen him for a second would've made whatever lies ahead worth it. He's my boy, my family; I'd lay my life down for him. Now, no matter what happens, I'll always have that baby's face in my mind, I'll be able to conjure up those memories whenever I need.'

Kitty nodded and turned back to face the road. Even though she had no parents of her own, she understood more than most the true value of family and how much that meant. As the night sky grew darker, Kitty gripped the steering wheel with grim determination. Her decision was made. She knew what she had to do.

*

By the time Kitty had dropped Harry off at his barracks it was past nine o'clock. She had shaken his hand and wished him good luck before getting back in her car and driving through town towards the butcher's. Kitty knew her ten o'clock curfew was imminent and if she wanted to make it to Billy's and back again without getting into trouble with the dreaded red caps she knew she would have to miss her tea. Kitty's stomach grumbled in annoyance, but in truth she felt too sick to eat anything no matter how hungry she was. Whatever lay ahead of her wasn't going to be easy, but she was going to make Billy a proposal. She had decided on the drive back that she would agree to do one job for him and no more. In the meantime she would request a forty-eight-hour pass back to Coventry, where away from prying eyes, she would be able to ask Elsie outright if there was any truth to the rumours. Once Elsie had confirmed what she already suspected that Billy was lying, Kitty would be able to tell the butcher where to stick his blackmail attempts and she would be free of him forever.

The idea gave Kitty a thrill of satisfaction. She was sick of men like Billy and Hopson pushing her around. This time she was going to show them who was boss. Working outside the law was something that made her deeply uncomfortable, but Kitty knew that when it came to Elsie, or the rest of the Higginsons, she would do anything for them, even this one job if it came to it. As Harry had reminded her, it was family.

Pulling up outside the shop for the second time that day, Kitty's heart beat wildly. She found herself wondering when Billy had turned to crime. Was it something he did while his wife, Bess, was still alive or had he turned to a life filled with wrongdoing afterwards, as a way of coping with his grief? Stepping out of the car, Kitty realised it made no difference. Billy had shown his true colours, and all that mattered now was ensuring she did not end up doing something she would regret for the rest of her life. As her eyes grew accustomed to the gloom she noticed Billy had followed the blackout restrictions. There wasn't so much as a chink of light coming from the shop window but Kitty knew Billy was inside waiting for her.

Sure enough, her hand had barely grazed the front of the door when it was flung open and there was the man himself, ready to greet her with a beaming smile.

'Kitty!' he exclaimed. 'I've been looking forward to seeing yer all day, come in.'

Reluctantly, Kitty followed the butcher inside. She noticed how eerie it was to see dead carcasses swinging from the ceiling in the moonlight and shivered as she followed Billy into the brightly lit kitchenette.

'Can I get yer a cuppa?' he asked. 'Yer must be starving after all that driving today.'

A cup of tea sounded like the best offer she had heard all day but remembering where the drink had come from she shook her head. Besides, she did not want to remain in Billy's company any longer than necessary.

'I'm fine, ta,' she said evenly, turning to face him, her hands in her pockets.

'Well sit down at least, Kit,' he said, ushering her towards a chair.

Kitty shook her head. 'I'd rather stand,' she replied. 'So what's this job yer want doing?'

The beginnings of a smile played on Billy's lips. 'So yer will help me then?'

Kitty felt a flash of annoyance. 'You've not exactly given me a lot of choice, have yer?'

'I s'pose I haven't,' he chuckled, turning to the range to make himself a cup of tea. 'Still, there was always a chance you'd say no. But then I think you're too smart to have done that. I'm glad you've seen sense.'

Kitty said nothing but took a deep breath and willed herself to stay calm. It was just one job, if she could do that then she would be free of Billy Miles for good and she and Elsie would be safe.

'I've a few parcels I want collecting next week, Kitty love,' he explained. 'I want yer to pop 'em on your truck next week and bring 'em to me.'

Kitty couldn't believe her ears. 'Are yer mad? I don't know if I'll even be driving a truck next week, and if I am, my destination might not be anywhere near where your parcels are.'

Billy blew gently on his tea as he waved her concerns away. 'Minor details, Kitty love, and nothing a girl of your capabilities can't sort, I'm sure.'

A wave of panic coursed through Kitty's veins. She had thought he would just want her to collect some money or deliver an extra packet of tea the next time she was passing through town. Even if she was driving one of the Lister trucks next week she couldn't load extra parcels onto it without her superiors knowing. They checked the loads thoroughly, not to mention the petrol that was allocated for each journey. It was impossible, Billy had to understand that.

She opened her mouth to say as much, when Billy stood up and smiled. 'Strikes me, Kitty, that where there's a will there's a way. See, I'm not a complete monster, I know what I'm asking yer to do is risky.' He paused to take a sip of his tea. 'My lads will make sure the parcels are safely secured on your lorry like, so nobody will see what you've got if anyone starts poking about, all I'm asking yer to do is get 'em from A to B like. Easy – a bit like your mate, by all accounts.'

Billy roared with laughter at his own joke. Disgust and despair blazed through Kitty as she realised he really did have a hold over her. So much for hoping to stall him so she could speak to Elsie, this was something she was going to have to do come hell or high water. She felt like sobbing, but knew that wouldn't get her anywhere. All she could do was play along.

'What's in these parcels?' she asked. 'Why can't they just post 'em?'

Billy shook his head in mock despair. 'Now, now, Kitty, I took yer for a girl with half a brain. Yer know as well as I do yer can't go sending anything yer like through the post these days. There's censors and all sorts what are going through our mail with a fine-tooth comb.'

Kitty shrugged defiantly. 'Not my problem,' she said with a bravery she did not feel.

Anger flashed in Billy's eyes and she saw the vein in his temple pulse with fury once more as he rose from his chair and rushed towards her.

'That's where you're wrong,' he snarled, jabbing Kitty sharply in the chest with his forefinger. 'It's *your* problem, because from now on yer work for me, unless of course yer want your precious pal's husband to know her little secret.'

He backed away from her, his face a picture of calm once more. Reaching up to the shelf above him, he pulled a small package wrapped in his butcher's waxy paper and set it onto a plate. 'Now there's no need for us to fall out, Kitty. I'm offering yer the chance of a nice day out like.'

Kitty said nothing, instead she turned away and looked out of the window into the inky black sky. 'When d'yer want this delivery picking up and from where?' she asked flatly.

'I don't know when it'll be just yet but we can be flexible. Like I say, Kit, I'm no monster. Whenever yer can next get yer hands on a truck will be fine, as long as it's in the next few days, of course,' Billy replied, unwrapping the parcel to reveal a bacon sandwich he had obviously made earlier. 'Yer won't be heading too far – Birmingham way – so it shouldn't be too difficult for yer to fetch the delivery when you're passing.'

Kitty turned back to face Billy and watched in amazement as he poured himself another cup of tea and bit hungrily into the sandwich. Watching him stuff rasher after rasher into his mouth, fear exploded in her chest. Billy's heart was clearly as black as the night sky and Kitty suddenly felt terrified of what she was getting involved in.

'All right,' she groaned, closing her eyes and taking a deep breath to try and steady herself. 'Let me know where and when yer need me.'

Billy finished his sandwich. 'Pop in next week, Kit, I'll have more details then,' he said, his mouth full. 'I'll expect yer, mind, don't go thinking yer can walk out of here and never see me again, not unless yer want your mate's secret to be the talk of Coventry of course.'

Kitty fought the urge to scream. How had her life come to this? That she should be involved in something so evil and repulsive beggared belief.

'Of course, Billy,' she replied flatly.

Back at the barracks, it was all Kitty could do not to fling herself face-down on her bed and burst into tears. Instead she sat on the cold stone floor and hugged her body tight, replaying the day's events in her mind. So lost was she in her own thoughts, she never heard Di come in.

'Kitty, you all right?' she asked, crouching in front of her.

Slowly Kitty came to, and with a start looked at her friend, who looked as tired as she felt. With dark grey circles under her eyes and her pale skin ashen, Di looked as though sleep was something she had not seen in weeks.

'I'm fine, Di,' she said reassuringly.

Di reached out and rested her arm on Kitty's shoulder. 'You're shaking, love, you're far from fine.' Pulling a blanket from Kitty's bed, Di wrapped it around her shoulders. 'Want to talk about it?'

Kitty shook her head, aware now that her teeth were chattering with cold. 'Honestly, I'm all right, love. It's been a long day, I'm probably just overtired or summat.'

Di was far from convinced; she had never seen her friend in such a state. Kitty's eyes were glazed, and her fingernails chewed to the quick. More than anything Di wanted to find out what had happened but sensed now was not the best time to ask questions.

'Come on, let's get you into bed,' Di said, helping Kitty to her feet. 'Seems to me you need your rest.'

Like a child, Kitty allowed Di to wrap her overwrought body in the rough, scratchy sheets. As her head sank against the thin pillow, Kitty closed her eyes and immediately fell into a shattered sleep. Throughout the night she dreamed over and over that she was being led into a tiny prison cell, where a jailer laughed in her face before throwing away the key.

Chapter Thirteen

A week into October and the bombs continued to rain down on London, sending shockwaves through the capital and the rest of the country. The newspapers and wireless were full of nothing but reports of the nightly devastation, and the nation had never been more vigilant about keeping to the blackout rules, determined not to give the Jerries an advantage.

Kitty was as worried as everyone else and coped with the developments by throwing herself into driver mechanic duties. Sergeant Hopson no longer had to ask Kitty to clean the extra cars or service the trucks because Kitty did them as a matter of course, much to the astonishment of Hopson and her friends.

'Any particular reason you're showing us all up by doing more work than is good for us?' Di asked good-naturedly one morning. Kitty was flat on her back underneath the chassis of a Tilly truck that had been declared 'fit for the knacker's yard' by one of the recruits the day before, doing her best to resurrect it from the dead.

'How d'yer mean?' Kitty's muffled voice asked.

Di squatted on the floor next to her friend's overall-clad legs and handed her a spanner. 'I mean, you're working all hours, Kit. When us lot 'ave knocked off for the day you're still at the depot, cleaning, repairing, organising bits and bobs in the garages and whatever else wants doing. I could understand it if 'opson had told you to do all this, but as far as I can make out you've volunteered for this lot yourself.'

Kitty crawled out from under the truck and sat up to look at Di, her face covered in grease and her fingernails as black as the road.

'I just want to do me bit, that's all,' she said, shrugging.

'You're doing your own bit and every other spark girl's besides.' Di smiled as she rocked on her haunches. 'Seriously, Kitty, what's wrong? You've not been yourself since you picked up that absconder the other week. Tell your Auntie Di all about it.'

Despite herself, Kitty smiled. Di always knew what to say to make her laugh. 'Nothing,' she replied, sifting through her tools and finding the pliers she needed.

'Don't give me that rubbish.' Di snorted. 'You're barely eating or sleeping and spending every waking moment working. I'm not as green as I am cabbage-looking.'

Kitty remained silent, scared to look at Di for fear of giving herself away. Since that night when she had sobbed herself to sleep, she had been desperate to confide in someone about Billy's threats but she had to keep what was happening to herself. She was terrified of putting pen to paper and writing to Elsie in case she suddenly found herself confessing everything. The deceit, along with the fear of what lay ahead, was crippling her and she struggled to sleep or eat.

Not wanting to make things worse, she had called in to see Billy two days earlier and he had told her the packages were ready to be collected whenever she could get away. Kitty had simply nodded, and said she would let him know when it would be possible, all the while hoping she would be able to delay having to do as Billy asked. She was still waiting to hear whether her request for leave had been approved. Until then Kitty felt the best thing she could do was keep herself busy and her mouth shut.

'Kitty,' Di tried again, her tone gentle. 'Come on out with it, you know you can tell me.'

Lifting her head, Kitty's heart lurched as she saw the worry across Di's face. More than anything, she wanted to tell her everything but instead, Kitty took a deep breath and thought on her feet.

'Adolf's hitting us where it hurts and if I can do me bit by making sure every one of these vehicles is in good nick before they go out on the road, p'raps there's less chance those Jerries'll naffing well win, and we'll be one step closer to winning this flamin' war.'

'Well said!' Hopson boomed, his voice echoing through the garage as he walked towards the pair. 'I never thought I'd hear myself say this, but you might want to think about taking a leaf out of Volunteer Williams' book, Volunteer Mills.'

Kitty and Di scrambled to their feet at the sight of their commanding officer walking towards them. 'Yes sir, very good, sir,' they said in unison, raising their arms in salute.

Hopson smiled, for once his grin reaching his eyes. 'At ease, soldiers.'

Immediately the girls relaxed and looked at Hopson who was now strolling around the truck, looking at it with interest.

'How long have you been working on this Tilly, Williams?' he asked.

'A few hours, sir,' she replied.

'A few hours – but it's only eight in the morning,' Di hissed. 'You've not been 'ere all night?'

Kitty shrugged. 'I couldn't sleep,' she whispered. 'Thought I may as well make meself useful.'

'Excellent attitude,' Hopson boomed again. 'Have you fixed it yet, Williams?'

'I've turned her over, sir, and she starts first time,' Kitty replied. 'I'm just tidying her up now, but she seems good as new.'

Hopson walked around the vehicle, giving it a final inspection. 'Well, well, Williams,' he remarked, raising an eyebrow and patting the bonnet. 'This is a turn-up for the books, isn't it? Perhaps you're not the village idiot I thought you were, which is why I'm afraid I've turned down your request for leave. You've made yourself indispensable.'

Kitty felt a stab of despair in the pit of her stomach. She had placed all her hopes on seeing Elsie, so she could sort this mess out once and for all. Now it was not to be. She opened her mouth, about to plead her case, but caught Hopson's warning gaze. The look of fire in his eyes told her she would only make things worse for herself, and so she closed her mouth and tried to calm the sense of fear coursing through her veins.

'Anyway,' Hopson continued, ignoring Kitty's obvious disappointment. 'If she's up and running you can drive over to Walsall tomorrow. We've some equipment that needs to be delivered to the barracks there, and this truck's perfect for the job. No need for a convoy, it's not that far and there isn't that much.'

Waves of panic washed over Kitty as she took in Hopson's instructions. She was out of excuses: if Billy got wind that she had driven near Birmingham and kept it to herself, then Elsie would be ruined. Kitty knew she would have to go and see him and collect his parcels, or her world and all she held dear would come crashing down around her ears.

'Williams, are you all right?' Hopson quizzed. 'You're as white as a sheet.'

Kitty nodded, remembering to fix her eyes past his shoulder. 'Yes, sir, fine, sir.'

Hopson paused as he narrowed his eyes and glanced at her curiously. 'Seems to me, Williams, that you're a bit peaky and I can't send you out on a journey if you're not feeling well.'

'No, sir,' Kitty replied, her breathing beginning to still as she wondered if Hopson was about to tell her she didn't have to drive to Walsall.

'I always find the best thing when I'm tired is to do some exercise,' Hopson said slowly. 'I know PT keeps you girls busy most afternoons, but I think it's time for you to do a bit extra, Williams, see if we can't keep you fit, healthy and above all else awake.'

'Sir,' Kitty said, her heart sinking with dread at whatever fresh hell her commanding officer was about to throw her way.

'So this afternoon, I'd like you to run three laps of the barracks and then finish with twenty press-ups, is that clear?'

Kitty's eyes widened in shock. 'But a lap of the barracks is three miles, sir.'

'That's right, Williams, good to see your mathematical skills aren't as appalling as your mechanical ones. Is there a problem? We can always make it four laps.'

'No, sir,' Kitty said, shaking her head, 'no problem.'

'Excellent. Looking forward to seeing how you get on,' he finished before walking across the room towards the door. 'And don't forget, nice and early tomorrow, Williams.'

'What a prat,' Di called from behind the Tilly truck she had been inspecting.

'I just don't know what I've done, Di,' Kitty said sadly. 'It doesn't matter what I do, he seems to thrive on making my life a misery.'

Di squeezed her friend's shoulder affectionately. 'Come on, love, don't let 'im see 'e's got you down, it's what bullies like 'im want. Tell you what, I'll run round the barracks with yer, at least it'll be a bit of company.'

Kitty visibly brightened at Di's suggestion. 'Really, yer'd do that for me?'

'Course I would, it's what mates are for.' Di smiled.

*

The rest of the day passed in a blur for Kitty as she worked on trucks, lorries, cars and even ambulances. Like a whirling dervish, she cleaned, polished and repaired, leaving the rest of the spark girls amazed at her solo efforts. Kitty had always believed in the power of hard work and now, the sheer physical challenges of the tasks she had given herself helped her cope with all that lay ahead.

She had gone to see Billy at the shop just before closing to discuss arrangements. This time he had instructed her to arrive at the back door, and every bone in her body protested as she made her way there. As she had expected, the butcher had been smug and full of self-importance as he led her into his kitchenette and told her precisely where to collect the parcels and at what time.

'But I may not be able to get there at that exact time,' Kitty had said, her voice filled with panic.

'You'll find a way to make it work, my girl,' he said sharply. 'And remember, yer tell anyone about this and I'll tell everyone about what your mate's been up to.'

With a jerk of the head he had dismissed her from his shop and Kitty spent the rest of the night working on the truck she would drive tomorrow, checking everything was working. By the time she turned in, she was exhausted, but too overwrought to sleep and spent most of the night tossing and turning. When it was time to get up she already felt as though she had done a day's work and after eating a quick breakfast in the NAAFI, she offered up a silent prayer of thanks Di was nowhere to be seen that morning. The spark girl had left late yesterday afternoon for a job in Northumberland and was billeted away for at least two days. Kitty was such a bundle of nerves, if she had seen her friend there was every chance she would have confessed everything to Di.

Instead, the only person Kitty had spoken to that morning was one of her dorm mates who had picked up a letter from Elsie for her. As her fingers grazed the envelope, Kitty felt a flash of hope the letter might contain news that would mean she no longer had to work for Billy.

25 September 1940

Dear Kitty,

So much has happened since you wrote, I'm not sure where to start. I'm sitting here writing this in the kitchen with the wireless on. The reports are full of the bombs that have dropped in London, and finally it feels like this war's real. Don't get me wrong, it's not as though I thought we were messing about like kiddies in the street, but it suddenly all seems like it's finally happening. I've been worried sick about you and Charlie, though Mike's been on at me to take care of myself and stay off my feet. I know he's right, but it's

181

hard, Kitty. You know what I'm like when I worry, we're the same, us two, aren't we, like a bit of graft to get ourselves stuck into, so this morning I blacked the step, ran sopping wet clothes though the mangle and polished the brasses.

Mam laughed when she found me on all fours, scrubbing brush in hand and said I were nesting, but to be honest I've been out of my mind with worry over what those poor devils in London are going through, I had to do something. After those bombs dropped on the outskirts of Coventry the other week, I joined the WVS. It's not much, and I know the incendiaries Adolf dropped over here a few weeks back were a drop in the ocean compared to what's what in London like, but I want to feel useful, Kit. When I think about how brave you, Charlie, and my brothers are for doing what you're doing, I feel like I'm not pulling my weight.

Mike, bless his heart, told me I were wasting my time. Said Jerry'd no more bomb Coventry properly than pigs'd fly, but you can't be too careful and at least this way I can say to my kiddie when he or she's born, I did something for this war.

I finally heard from Charlie the other day, but I hardly recognised him from the letter he wrote. He was rambling on about how he'd never seen such horrors, and he can't even bring himself to think about coming home when there's so much to be done. There was none of the warmth of his previous letters, Kit, and it felt like it were from a stranger. I'll be honest, his letter rattled me, and I almost wish I hadn't had it. I showed it to Mike, and he told me not to fret, that war changes men, makes them harder so they can cope with all the nastiness they see. But all I know is my Charlie seems like he's deserted me.

Anyway, how are you? Have you made up with that Billy yet? He sounded good for you, Kitty. You need someone looking out for you while this war's on 'cos heaven knows what Jerry's got planned next. Take your comforts where you can. That's why I thank my lucky stars our Mike's been stationed with us, I don't know what I'd have done without him. He's a godsend, Kitty, a real godsend. I almost never want him to leave, but I know one day I'll have to say goodbye, just like I did to you, Charlie and everyone else I love.

Take care of yourself, Kitty Williams, and write to me soon. Mike thinks I'm a sandwich short of a picnic 'cos I keep talking to the little person inside me, and I'm telling him or her all about you. Like me, they can't wait to see your face.

Fondest,
Elsie xxx

Kitty read and reread the letter, desperately searching for something that would give her a clue as to the truth. Yet despite her best efforts she could find nothing that would tell her whether Billy was telling lies. Elsie's note was still full of talk about Mike, and how wonderful he was, whereas Charlie felt like a stranger. Kitty clutched the letter to her chest and breathed deeply. Was Billy right? Was Elsie finding solace elsewhere? Her friend's words had failed to offer the comfort she longed for and with a heavy heart she knew there was no escaping Billy's task.

*

By 4.15 p.m. Kitty had successfully delivered her lorry full of equipment to the barracks in Walsall and was ready to make her detour to Birmingham. The trip had been fairly uneventful, she had been pleased to find, as Kitty had been slightly worried about her extensive repair efforts. Yet the Tilly truck had started first time and as it had been an unseasonably warm, sunny day, it had turned out to be a pleasure to drive. The soldiers at the barracks where she had delivered the equipment had been incredibly helpful, and told her to enjoy a well-earned rest.

Grateful, Kitty had enjoyed a cuppa and a slice of toast in their NAAFI, while the soldiers unloaded the truck. Once they had finished, she had said her goodbyes before giving the Tilly a good check over. She was delighted to see there was still plenty of petrol left in the tank and even more pleased to find the vehicle started first time. Crossing her fingers she hoped that luck remained on her side and her extra journey would go unnoticed by her superiors.

Yet as Kitty started the truck's engine and drove the Tilly smoothly out onto the road she realised she was still a bag of nerves. Her tummy felt as though it were filled with butterflies, all flapping their wings in her stomach, and she knew she wouldn't rest until this awful job was over.

Thankfully the drive to Birmingham took just over an hour, and as Kitty neared the city she checked the address Billy had given her and realised with a start that she was headed to another butcher's in the north of the town. Were all butchers crooks, she wondered grimly as she turned the truck sharply into a narrow lane and out towards a parade of shops. Checking her map once more, she was surprised to find she had arrived already. With minutes to spare, Kitty took a deep breath and tried to steady her jangling nerves.

Once again she glanced at her watch, only instead of checking the time she stroked the watch face. Today she had decided to wear Joe's watch and even though it was miles too big for her narrow wrist, the feel of the metal against her skin gave her the reassurance she desperately needed. A sharp banging on the driver's window brought her swiftly back to reality and she whirled around to find a tall, thin man with blond hair and piercing blue eyes staring at her.

'You Billy's girl?' he asked sharply.

Wordlessly, Kitty nodded and opened the door to step out of the truck cab.

'Pleased to meet yer,' she said, remembering her manners and sticking out her hand.

The man snorted with laughter, ignored her outstretched arm and walked towards the shop. 'Never mind all that, love, let's just get on with it, the packages are in 'ere.'

Stung by his rudeness Kitty followed the butcher, who appeared to be a little older than Billy, reluctantly into the shop. Like Billy's, it was covered from top to bottom in white tiles with a large stainless steel counter at the back of the room. As the man walked through to the back of the shop, she saw this was where the similarities with Billy's store ended. Instead of the kitchenette Billy had fashioned in the back, this man had a dank and dusty storeroom. A cobweb hit Kitty in the face and she did her best to stifle a scream. The only light came from an oil lamp in the corner which showed a room filled with boxes of all sizes, each clearly placed into different sections.

'Over 'ere,' the man said, walking towards a large stack of boxes of varying sizes in the centre of the room.

There were easily about fifty packages, all wrapped in brown paper. They would fill her truck.

'What's in 'em?' Kitty asked as she stepped towards the boxes.

The man glared. 'You always this nosy? Never you mind what's in 'em. Just pick 'em up and put 'em in your truck like a good girl.'

Kitty looked at the man in alarm. 'Billy said there'd be lads here to help like.'

The man drew himself up to his full height and sneered at her. 'Did he now? Did he also tell yer the streets are paved with gold and that it never rains neither? It's just us doing the lifting, girl.'

'But Billy said—' she began, only for the butcher to cut her off.

'I don't care what Billy said,' he snarled. 'I thought Army girls were keen to show the world you're as strong as men.' He laughed meanly. 'Girls in the Army – I've never 'eard the like. More like playing bloody dress-up. Still, time to put your money where your mouth is. You wanted a man's job, 'ere it is. Get these boxes shifted.'

Kitty bristled with rage. How dare this man talk to her like that. More than anything she wanted to tell him what was what, but had a feeling she would be the one that came off worst. Glancing at him again, she realised she had met her fair share of nasty individuals throughout her life, but nothing like this man. Not only did he reek of booze, but he oozed a wickedness that he seemed to thrive on. Knowing there was no choice but to do as he asked, she started to scoop some of the smaller boxes into her arms and followed him out to the truck. The sooner she did it, the sooner she would be out of here and away from him. Thankfully the boxes were not as heavy as she had feared, and within half an hour she and the butcher had loaded them onto her truck.

'Don't dilly-dally with them parcels, girl. Billy's expecting you by nightfall,' he finished, as the last box was placed in the back of the truck. Then he walked inside without giving Kitty a backwards glance.

Kitty shuddered as she watched him lock the door and pre-pare for blackout. With a start she wondered if this was how she should expect to be treated now she was nothing more than a common criminal herself. Rubbing her hands together to warm them up, she fixed the truck's tarpaulin securely in place, all the while expecting a tap on the shoulder from a police officer asking her what she thought she was up to.

With the last of the straps securing the back, she peered up at the sky. It was still fairly clear, and with a bit of luck Kitty hoped there would be at least forty minutes of light left. She wouldn't reach Billy's by nightfall, but hopefully it wouldn't be much later. Getting behind the wheel of the truck, she was grateful when it started first time, and with an anxious glance behind her to check nobody was watching, she pointed the bonnet in the direction of Northampton and hoped to make it back in one piece.

*

By the time darkness began to fall Kitty was just a few short miles from Northampton itself. Slowing her speed down to the required twenty miles per hour, Kitty felt her shoulders relax and the knot in her stomach unfurl as familiar landmarks appeared.

She was almost home, and vowed never to put herself through this torment again. Billy had got one job out of her, but that was the last of it, she thought determinedly, hitting the brakes to allow a rabbit to hop to the other side of the road. As she watched the bunny jump to safety, she smiled. Would any other common criminal stop to let an animal pass?

Pressing her foot on the accelerator Kitty was alarmed to find the truck would no longer start. Anxiously she fired the ignition switch once more, but the truck still wouldn't budge. Knowing she was stuck in the middle of the road, Kitty thought quickly. The petrol tank was still half-full, and she had taken care to refill the oil and water pumps only that morning. It had to be something to do with the engine, but she was sure she had checked everything thoroughly last night.

Lifting the bonnet, Kitty could easily see the problem: the petrol in the carburettor had evaporated, which was why the gauge was still showing the tank as half-full. Thanking her lucky stars she was carrying spare cans of petrol, she hurried to the back to get one, only to find it had leaked all over a few of Billy's parcels. Groaning with despair, she examined the packages in the half-light and saw the damage wasn't as bad as she had initially feared. There were only about five boxes that were damp from the fuel and she was sure that if Billy let them air dry, they would be fine in no time. Besides, she had no time to worry about that now, her first priority had to be getting off the road, and so grabbing two of the emergency cans she quickly refilled the fuel in the carburettor and tried to start the truck once more.

As the vehicle fired into life, Kitty let out a little squeal of delight and carried on down the road towards Billy's shop. Half an hour later she had arrived, and quietly pulling into the back of the butcher's once more as instructed, she waited for the spiv to arrive surrounded in blackness.

Before long there was a gentle tap at the window and Kitty glanced around to find Billy, the whites of his eyes ablaze with fury.

'What time d'yer call this?' he snarled, throwing open the driver door.

'I had trouble with the truck,' Kitty hissed as she stepped out to face him. 'Just be grateful I'm here at all.'

Revenge came quickly. Billy grabbed Kitty by the neck and pinned her up against the driver's door.

'Did yer just say I ought to be grateful?' Billy spluttered. 'It's about time yer learnt some respect, girl. What I say goes, d'yer understand?'

'Please, Billy,' Kitty rasped, the shock of the assault winding her as much as the steely grip to her neck. 'Just let me go.'

With a loud sigh, Billy released her from his grasp and Kitty rubbed her neck as she tried to catch her breath. In that moment she loathed Billy Miles and would do anything to crawl away from his shop never to see him again. But one glance at the menace written across his face told her what might happen if she tried to leave. Instead she gingerly walked around to the back of the truck and helped Billy undo the catches on the canvas to reveal the parcels.

'Give us a hand to bring 'em inside,' he said gruffly.

The events of moments earlier told Kitty it was best not to argue and so she helped Billy load the boxes into the kitchenette. Once they were all inside, Kitty secured the truck and returned to find Billy inspecting them, his face full of anger.

'What the hell happened here?' he asked, gesturing to the petrol-damaged parcels.

'One of the jerrycans leaked in the back,' Kitty replied. 'They're not very well made and sometimes we end up with more petrol in the back than we do in the can.'

'Is that right?' Billy muttered grimly as he surveyed his parcels from the comfort of his chair. 'Well these are no good to me now,' he said, kicking one deftly across the tiled floor.

'They'll be all right once they've dried out, won't they?' Kitty asked nervously as she eyed the pile of boxes.

'Oh yeah, dried out, 'cos everyone's after sugar that smells of motor spirit,' Billy snarled, his eyes narrowing. Slowly he brought his gaze to Kitty. 'Seems to me you'll have to make it up to me.'

Kitty looked at him in horror. 'What d'yer mean?'

'I mean, yer owe me. You've damaged some of me goods.' He smiled mawkishly. 'Debts have to be repaid, Kitty, yer must understand that.'

Billy's threat was implied, but Kitty was under no illusion what he would do if she failed to do as he asked. The altercation by the truck had shown her that the Billy of old – the gentleman who she had believed to be kind and well-intentioned – was gone. Despair flooded through her as she nodded.

'Good,' he said, slapping his hands on his thighs and getting to his feet. 'Then if yer do me another little job and throw in those cans of petrol in the back of the truck we'll call it quits.'

'Yer can't ask me to do that!' Kitty exclaimed.

Billy raised an eyebrow in mock surprise. 'Can't I? That's what it'll take to clear the debt.'

'But I'll get in trouble if I hand over the jerrycans, they know how many I've got like. I have to sign for 'em,' Kitty protested as she instinctively backed away from Billy.

'Well then we'll pour the petrol into some other containers and yer can keep the cans,' Billy said, smiling. 'I'm a fair man, Kitty, and yer can't say fairer than that.'

Kitty thought quickly. If she gave Billy the petrol, there was no telling where it might lead. 'But, they know how much petrol I'm carrying.'

'Do they?' Billy sneered. 'I thought yer said those cans were useless. Always leaking, yer said. Surely they'll think yer just had some very leaky cans?'

Fury rose, but she said nothing. She would not give Billy the satisfaction of knowing he had got to her. She knew of course he was right. Although Kitty was required to account for every drop of petrol, most of the time it was impossible, thanks to less than reliable petrol gauges and jerrycans.

Kitty could barely bring herself to look at the butcher as she walked past him and out into the cool night air. Reaching for the cans, she whirled around to find Billy standing right behind her.

'Give 'em to me then,' he said menacingly in the darkness.

Reluctantly Kitty handed them to him, and waited for him to return. Moments later he was back, and as he gave the cans back she was astonished at just how light they were.

'Are we square now then?' she asked quietly. 'Debt repaid 'n all that.'

'Well there's still this matter of another little job I want doing,' he said, the amber end of his cigarette lighting his face.

Her heart sank. Stupidly, she had hoped he would have forgotten all about that.

'What is it then?' she asked, in a tone more brazen than she felt.

Billy chuckled. 'All in good time, Kitty. Pop in next week and I'll have more details for yer,' he said, dropping the cigarette to the floor and stubbing it out with his foot. 'I always look forward to our chats, I'd be sorry if our little heart-to-hearts over a cuppa stopped.'

Kitty felt sick to her stomach as she gave him a brief nod and watched him go inside. Securing the canvas straps for the final time that day she got back into the truck and fought the tears that were threatening to spill down her face. She knew that if she started crying now she would never stop. Instead, she started the truck and drove back towards the barracks and did her best to compose herself. She would have to explain the fact she had used four jerrycans full of petrol to the duty officer when she returned and was already worried about her face betraying the lies she knew she would have to tell.

As she rounded the corner and saw the dark outline of the barracks rise over the hill, an image of Elsie came unbidden into Kitty's mind. She remembered how Elsie had held her hand when her parents had been killed and Kitty was crying on the step at school. Even though they were barely more than babes in arms, Elsie had stroked her hair and told her she could share her mummy if she wanted to. It was such a touching gesture, Kitty had been moved, despite her young age, and she had promised herself there and then, she would always look out for her best friend.

Driving the truck past the soldier standing guard at the gates of the barracks and along the track into the garage, Kitty knew that whatever Billy asked her to do she would do it for Elsie.

Pulling into the space earmarked for the truck, Kitty checked her watch. It was gone eleven, far later than she had meant to be out and she would now have to sneak quietly into the Nissen hut to avoid waking the other girls. Carefully she jumped to the ground, her feet crunching noisily on the path, when she suddenly saw a pinprick of torchlight and heard someone walking towards her.

'You're late, Williams,' a familiar voice boomed.

Kitty's heart thudded with fear. Sergeant Hopson had expected her back by nightfall, she would need to think on her feet if she were going to explain such a long absence.

'Sorry, sir,' she replied meekly, giving him the standard salute as his hulking frame came into view.

'Where have you been?' he asked, stopping directly in front of her, killing the torchlight as he saw her face.

'The carburettor broke sir,' she replied quickly. 'It took me a while to work out the problem and repair it.'

Sergeant Hopson cocked his head to one side and regarded Kitty in the dark. 'I find that hard to believe, Williams,' he said softly. 'You're one of the best spark girls there is on site, plus you spent most of yesterday working on that truck, you should have known it inside out.'

Kitty gulped, slightly blindsided by the unexpected praise. 'You're right, sir, but I didn't think the carburettor'd be a problem like.'

Sergeant Hopson said nothing, instead he took a step towards Kitty so his face was just inches away. 'You'd better not be lying to me, Williams.'

Instinctively, Kitty recoiled. 'No, sir, course not, sir.'

'Good,' he hissed, 'because if you *are* lying to me, I will find out and I will make sure your life is a misery. I don't tolerate liars, Williams, do you understand?'

'Yes, sir,' Kitty nodded again.

'You'd better,' he snapped again, before turning back to the truck and pulling out his torch.

He switched on the light to a low beam and used it to guide him as he loosened the catches on the tarpaulin covering the Tilly.

'Don't mind if I give this a check over do you, Williams?'

'No, sir,' Kitty whispered, her feet welded to the spot in alarm.

'It wasn't a question,' he snarled.

With the tarpaulin now free, Hopson shone his light into the back. Kitty was unsure what he was looking for but she was grateful the truck was empty following her meeting with Billy.

'It smells of petrol in here, Williams,' Hopson said matter-of-factly. 'Can you tell me why?'

Kitty's face began to feel clammy and her pulse started to race. 'Yes, sir,' she began. 'I needed to use some of the emergency petrol for the carburettor sir.'

Hopson said nothing, merely removed each can and gave it a shake. When he found each one empty, he threw them into the back and fixed his eyes on Kitty.

'You must have needed a lot of petrol to get that carburettor working, Volunteer,' he said.

'Erm, quite a bit, yes, sir,' she said in a voice that was barely more than a whisper.

By now, Kitty felt so afraid her fists were clenched into tight balls and sweat was trickling down her forehead. Blinking rapidly, she surveyed Hopson and prayed he wouldn't ask her any more questions.

'Four cans is an awful lot of fuel to get through, particularly when it's rationed,' Hopson replied, his tone steely and unflinching.

Kitty drew a breath before she spoke. 'I know, sir, a lot of it spilled, sir, that's why it smells so horrible in the back like. Yer know what those cans are like.'

'That the only reason?' he asked sharply.

Kitty nodded. 'Yes, sir.'

Hopson looked back at the cans and then returned his gaze to Kitty. 'So you're telling me that you got through four cans of petrol today because some of it spilled in the back and you used the rest to fix your carburettor?'

Kitty felt the colour drain from her face. 'Yes, sir.'

'And there's nothing else you want to tell me?' he asked, his voice slightly softer now as he took a step towards Kitty. 'Because now is the time.'

The spark girl thought quickly. More than anything she wanted someone to make this whole mess with Billy go away. But looking at Hopson she knew he was no friend. Ever since she had arrived in Northampton he had done nothing but make her life a misery. If she told him the truth, this would make his year, and he would make sure she went straight to jail, of that she was certain.

'No, sir,' she said firmly, her voice sounding more confident than she felt. 'That's what happened. I'm sorry so much petrol was wasted, but those jerrycans are known for being a bit leaky, aren't they?'

Hopson narrowed his eyes and almost seemed to let out a snarl. 'Apparently so,' he hissed. 'Let me tell you something, Williams. I know you're lying, and I'm going to make it my business to find out what you're up to.'

'Sir,' Kitty protested, 'I haven't—'

'Enough.' Hopson raised his hand in front of her face to silence her. 'I don't want to hear any more untruths from your lips. I knew you were trouble the moment you walked in here; nothing's changed. I detest liars like you, and let me tell you this, when I do find out what you're up to, you'll wish you'd never been born, I can promise you.'

With that Hopson turned on his heel and walked back towards

the barracks, his feet crunching noisily against the gravel. Breathless with fear, Kitty crumpled to the floor as Hopson retreated into the night. He was right – she was finished when he found out the truth. Nobody could save her now.

Chapter Fourteen

The German Luftwaffe's nightly bombing campaign across the London skies gathered pace and towards the end of October much of the capital had been hit, including Buckingham Palace. Tales of broken windows, ruined portraits and ruptured water mains filled the newspapers, with many claiming the Germans had gone too far by targeting the royal family and the palace. Thankfully King George and Queen Elizabeth had escaped unharmed, but had endeared themselves to the nation by expressing their solidarity with fellow Londoners.

The bravery of the King and Queen only made Kitty and every other spark girl more determined than ever to do more for the war effort, with many requesting their superior officers give them extra duties to help stop the Jerries.

As for Kitty, she was more than happy working her fingers to the bone, but when she and Di were rewarded with a rare Saturday night off, she had to admit she was glad of the chance to relax for just a couple of hours. Since Billy had made his demands, Hopson had rarely left her alone, accompanying her on jobs or insisting someone else go with her.

The strain of the situation she found herself in had made Kitty hanker for the safety of the mess on her one free night out. She was exhausted and all she wanted to do was reply to Arthur's latest letter and listen to *It's That Man Again* on the wireless. Unsurprisingly, that wasn't what Di had in mind, and her friend refused to take no for an answer.

'We're not spending our only Saturday night off in months in these blinkin' barracks, Kitty,' Di protested as she rinsed her underwear in a bucket of cold water outside their Nissen hut.

Kitty stood beside her washing out her own undergarments and said nothing. The rest of the girls in the huts were all doing the same. It was an unusually warm October morning and the last thing she wanted was everyone's ears flapping, listening to her business. It was hard enough to keep a secret in the Army without going out of your way to broadcast your news like it was something for the wireless, Kitty thought. Besides, her repeated trips out with their commanding officer had caused quite a stir. Heaven only knows what people were thinking, Kitty wondered as she wrung out a pair of soaking wet stockings and hung them over the makeshift line she and Di had erected with a bit of string hung across the door. Half the girls thought she was up to no good and she was sure the other half thought she and Hopson were secret sweethearts. She had caught a pair of girls gossiping about the two of them in the mess the other day and Kitty could have throttled the pair of them with their cheap talk. Instead she had walked past with her head held high, and shot them a glance Arthur had once described as the most terrifying thing he had ever seen. That had shut the pair of them up without Kitty having to utter a word, she thought smugly. But the truth was, her plate felt so full she was exhausted. How could she make her friend understand just how shattered she was?

'Look, Kitty, I know you're tired and I know you're not yourself, summat's troubling you, but we need a night out, lovey,' Di said, trying again and sending cold water splashing everywhere as she tried to convince her friend.

Kitty sighed. She knew Di would be like a dog with a bone until she relented. 'What d'yer have in mind like?'

'Nothing too exciting,' she smiled. 'A trip to the pictures, I'm dying to see *Gone with the Wind*. I reckon the sight of Clark Gable will be enough to put a smile on anyone's face.' Di smiled as she glanced at Kitty. 'Apart from your miserable mug of course.'

'Hey!' Kitty cried, sending a handful of cold water Di's way. 'Don't be so flamin' cheeky!'

'That's more like it!' Di squealed as the cool water splashed her khaki blouse. 'I wondered where the old Kitty'd been 'iding. Come on, what d'you say? It'll be fun.'

'Go on then,' Kitty agreed reluctantly. 'But I don't want to be back late, I've had enough of all these trips with Hopson and just the thought of another outing with him makes me need a lie-down.'

Di scooped her washing into the basket beside her. 'Yes, what's all that about?'

Kitty shrugged her shoulders as she rinsed her final pair of knickers and hung then on the line. 'Summat and nothing. Yer know he's always got it in for me, p'raps this is his way of letting me know I'll never be off the hook like.'

'You sure that all it is?' Di frowned.

Kitty said nothing and instead pretended to concentrate on hanging the last of her knickers out.

'Well?' Di persisted.

'Yes, I'm sure that's all it is,' she said angrily.

Di said nothing for a moment, giving Kitty a few seconds to calm down. 'What about Billy? You made up with 'im now then?' she asked quietly.

At the mention of Billy's name Kitty felt a sense of dread. Di had no idea they had seen one another and Kitty hated the fact the butcher was infecting her night off. She wanted to focus on enjoying herself for once, and the thought of Billy only caused her to feel upset.

'Yes, we've sorted things out,' Kitty said firmly, indicating the subject was closed. 'Everything's fine now.'

Marching back into the hut, Kitty sank onto her bed and took a deep breath to try and calm the heady mix of fear and frustration that had been bubbling inside her for weeks now. She was still desperate to talk to someone, or better yet, have someone make all her problems magically disappear. But Kitty knew real life never worked out that way, not unless you were Mary, she thought ruefully.

She and Di had received letters from their old friend the day before yesterday and in typical Mary fashion she had landed on her feet. Although she had been unable to reveal exactly where she had been posted, she had said that it wasn't that far from Paris and that she and some of the other drivers had been having a whale of a time in the cafes and bars every night as there had been very little driving for them to do.

Kitty smiled at the thought of Mary running amok in France, causing chaos and destruction in her wake. She knew she owed her friend a letter and intended to write to her before she went out that night. But before she contacted Mary, there was someone else she needed to talk to – Arthur. She had received a letter from him yesterday and his note had given Kitty a much-needed lift. Pulling the letter from the drawer next to her bedside, she reread it with affection.

15 October 1940

Dear Kitty,

It's a Monday afternoon and I'm enjoying a quiet hour to myself after keeping watch all night. I must say I'm tired, but I couldn't sleep without writing a few lines to you first. You didn't sound like yourself in your last letter, Kit. I read and reread your note about what you'd been doing, and you seemed a bit flat.

I can only hope it's me reading too much into things as I'd hate to think of you being unhappy. You didn't say much about that sergeant of yours – I hope that means he's eased off a bit and is making some other poor mite's life a misery. If you're still having troubles, I hope you know you can talk to me about anything that's on your mind. Every time I get a letter and see it's from you, I feel a little jolt of happiness. Hearing what you've been up to and what you're doing makes me feel closer to home and you of course. I miss you, our Kit, but you're a good letter writer and cheer a lonely sailor up on a cold winter's evening.

Well, this'll make you chuckle. Yesterday I got a letter off my dad. He's worried I'm glory hunting! Can you imagine such a thing? Says I'm not to go chasing after decorations for my uniform. Instead, I'm to work hard and come home in one piece! Have you ever heard the like? Me? Glory hunting? I've never chased glory in my life, and I wrote and told him just that. He's got nothing to worry about there – while I want to fight Adolf and will take my turn just like any other lad, the last thing I want is glory. All that'll do me when this rotten war's over is the safety of my own home, oh and a quiet pint of mild at the end of the day – still, a lad's entitled to one or two vices. I can hear you and our Elsie chuckling at the idea of me having one or two vices, no doubt you'd both tell me I've more than a couple eh?

I s'pose my dad's worried about me, even though I'm a grown up. And now our Elsie's having a nipper, no doubt she'll be worrying about him or her till the cows come home as well.

I don't know about you Kit, but all I worry about are my loved ones. I worry my family are safe and sound, I worry about my mates who are serving, and most of all I worry about you, Kit. I know you're strong, brave, kind and clever, far cleverer than me or your Joe ever were, but I still fret about you. You mean a lot to me and I know how hard you're working in the Army. You don't deserve half the things that've happened to you, Kitty, and yet you always come back fighting. I don't know how you do it, you're a marvel, but even marvels need someone to worry about them, and I've taken that job on myself, if that's all right by you. I think that's why I'm so pleased to know you've got Billy up there looking after you. You've not mentioned him much in your last few letters. I hope everything's all right

*with him? It makes me feel better knowing there's a decent
fella looking out for you while you're serving.*

*I'll leave it there, Kit, no doubt you've got work to do, and
I'm due back up on deck soon. Already looking forward to
your next letter.*

Yours fondly,
Arthur

Kitty reread the note one more time and smiled. It was so
wonderful to hear from Arthur, even if he had mentioned how
pleased he was she had a friend in Billy. She had no answer for
that – the last thing she could do was tell the truth. Pulling out
the special airmail pad and paper she reserved especially for her
letters overseas, she started to write her reply.

23 October 1940

Dear Arthur

*I got your letter yesterday, and I must say it put a smile on
my face. I'm sitting here with a night off to look forward to,
but I'll do my best not to give into any of me vices! I'll leave
that to you, our Arthur.*

*Whatever is Ron thinking? I keep hearing war does funny
things to folk, but the idea of you glory hunting is as likely
as us being allowed three rashers of bacon in a week! Still,
that's what family are for isn't it? To worry about you. It
was very sweet of you to say all that. If you want to know
the truth, Arthur, I worry about you too. Your letters are
the ones I always look forward to the most, somehow you
always seem to know just what I'm thinking and what I
need to hear, but then you always did have a knack for that
didn't you?*

*I'm doing all right. Actually, that's not true, I'm having
a few problems. Nothing I can talk about now, but just
know I'm doing me best to sort everything out and make*

everything right again. Life in the Army's tough, that's for sure, but let me tell you, my job as a spark girl is the best in the world. Nothing beats getting behind the wheel of a vehicle, whether it's a car or a truck. I love it, Arthur, I've found a funny sort of happiness I never knew existed or expected to find after Joe. But then, that's what's so odd about war isn't it? We're all doing things we never thought we would to survive and see Adolf and his merry men off once and for all.

I hope you're all right, Arthur, and you've some good mates with you out at sea wherever you may be. I don't see Billy so much these days, we're both busy, but I'm lucky to still have my pal Di with me. Saying that, I could curse her for making me go to the pictures with her tonight but I know she means well. Still, it seems like a long time ago we were all enjoying a night up the pictures together doesn't it? Remember when you, me, Joe, Charlie, Elsie, and that girl you were seeing, Irene, I think it was, all got thrown out for making too much noise? Seems like a lifetime ago now. But it's nights out like that I keep in my mind to remind me why we're still fighting. I want us to return to the good old days Arthur, 'cos I believe that in spite of everything that's happened, we've still got some good times ahead.

Now, I best be off, I've to beautify myself with a panstick and some gravy browning Di's sweet-talked Cook into giving her. Don't laugh – the things us girls have to do these days eh? In the meantime, I'll look forward to hearing from you soon.

Yours expectantly,
Kitty

Scanning the note once more, she hoped she had explained Billy's disappearance from her letters enough for Arthur not to press her again. Then she folded the paper carefully and wrote her friend's name and service number on the front of the envelope to post immediately. It was still a wonder to Kitty that the military postal service knew just where a letter was meant to go from those few scant details. Seeing it was almost four o'clock she jumped up from the bed to find Di. If they were lucky, they could get a cuppa at the tearoom in town before the pictures.

'Are you thinking what I'm thinking?' Di asked, appearing at the doorway of the hut.

'Tea in town?' Kitty smiled.

'Thought you'd never ask.' Di grinned as she reached for her khaki jacket and buttoned it to the top. 'Will I do?' she asked, giving a little twirl.

'Yer always do, Di,' Kitty laughed as her friend did a little curtsey.

'Then let's enjoy an evening with Mr Gable and Miss Leigh.' Di grinned, holding the door open for Kitty and waving her through. 'After you, milady!'

Arm in arm the girls headed out of the door and walked the mile or so into town. A blustery wind gathered speed around Kitty's neck and she pulled the stiff collar of her jacket tightly around her to keep out the chill. Walking through the parkland, Kitty glanced around her and noticed the grass was now looking patchy and the trees were bare. How quickly time moves on, she thought as they reached the tearoom and walked inside.

Pushing open the door, the noisy cafe was a hive of activity with service men and women enjoying the chance of some precious time away from war work. As waitresses weaved their way through the crowded tables, delivering tea and crumpets to hungry mouths, Kitty scanned the room for a table. Spotting one near the corner, she was about to pull Di towards it, when the sight of a lone man dressed in civilian clothes, head bent over the paper, stopped her.

Craning her head over the crowds to get a closer look, Kitty's heart thumped wildly, as she prayed the man wasn't who she thought it was. But his head turned slightly towards her as he lifted his paper from the table, and Kitty knew there was no mistake, it was Billy.

'Come on, Di, it's too busy in here, let's just go straight to the pictures,' Kitty hissed, pulling her friend sharply by the sleeve.

'Give over,' Di said, shrugging Kitty's hand loose. 'There's a table in the corner over there.'

As Di turned to walk towards it, Billy glanced up at Kitty and smiled. To an innocent bystander, the act would seem sincere but Kitty knew he was on the warpath. She had successfully managed to avoid the butcher for over a fortnight and knew Billy would want to see her about another job. Panic rose – she couldn't cope with Billy talking to her with Di around, they would have to leave.

'Di, I'm not hungry, let's just go,' she said determinedly, walking swiftly towards the exit.

'All right, all right,' Di grumbled as she hurried to catch up. 'Who's rattled your cage?'

Safely outside, Kitty drew in great lungfuls of air to calm her racing pulse down.

'I'm fine, Di,' she said eventually. 'I just suddenly felt a bit overwhelmed like. Too many people or summat, p'raps we can pop to the pub after the film?'

'If you're sure?' Di quizzed, her face full of concern.

'I'm all right, promise.'

Di nudged her friend playfully in the ribs. 'You're on, but you're buying!'

'Yer never miss a trick, Di Mills,' Kitty chuckled.

Nearing the cinema, the girls bought their tickets and took seats in an empty row near the back of the theatre. Leaning back against the red velvet of the chair, just as the opening credits rolled, Kitty finally felt herself relax. She was looking forward to escaping from her life for a few hours and a trip to the pictures was just what she needed.

An hour into the film and Kitty found herself transported to the Deep South of America, swept up in the romance of Scarlett and Rhett. In fact Kitty was so engrossed, she barely noticed a latecomer walk into the cinema and sit in the velvet chair next to hers.

'This seat taken?' a deep voice whispered in her ear.

Kitty whirled around in shock. 'Billy! What are yer doing here?' she hissed quietly.

The butcher let out a low chuckle. 'Yer ran out of the tearoom that fast, I didn't have a chance to say hello,' he whispered. 'Fortunately, I saw yer pop in the pictures like, thought we could have a little catch-up.'

'You've been spying on me?' Kitty gasped loud enough for Di to turn around and glare at her.

'Sorry, miss, my fault,' Billy whispered again, leaning across Kitty with his hand outstretched towards Di. 'Billy Miles, how d'yer do?'

Di's face broke into a delighted smile. 'Billy! Nice to meet you. I'm Di, I've 'eard a lot about you.'

'Yer 'n'all,' he grinned, shaking Di's hand.

'Funny bumping into you 'ere,' Di whispered.

'Yes, very funny,' Kitty hissed as she shot Billy a pointed stare.

Billy shrugged. 'What can I say. *Gone with the Wind* is one of me favourites.'

'You've seen it before then?' Di asked, ignoring Kitty's obvious discomfort.

'Several times,' he smiled. 'I love a good romance.'

Di laughed. 'Not many fellas that'd admit to that.'

'Well I'm not like most fellas, am I, Kitty?'

Feeling Billy's gaze turn on her once more, she shook her head. 'No, you're definitely not like most fellas, Billy.'

Meeting her eye, Billy grinned, his smile not quite meeting his eyes. 'P'raps we can go for a drink after? My treat?'

'Lovely, ta, Billy,' Di hissed.

'Ta,' Kitty echoed quietly, the feeling of dread growing by the second.

Kitty could barely concentrate on the rest of the film. With Billy by her side, she found it impossible to lose herself in the love story playing out before her. All she could think about was how there was no escape for her and Billy would track her down no matter what. For weeks now she had managed to successfully avoid him, but the fact Billy had walked into the pictures an hour after he had watched her go in was proof he had her just where he wanted her. Biting her lip, Kitty tried not to think about what Billy wanted and what her punishment would be for avoiding him. Although, in fairness, Kitty tried to reason with herself, her commanding officer had been by her side most days. She couldn't have found a moment to meet Billy even if she had wanted to. Whether Billy would see it that way was another matter.

By the time the film was over, Kitty was a nervous wreck. All she wanted to do was go home and go to bed, but she knew there was little chance of that. Instead she would have to be brave, and so with head held high, she followed Billy out of the cinema and into the foyer.

The harsh glare of the lights after spending so long sitting in the dark startled Kitty and she had to blink rapidly to let her eyes adjust to the brightness.

'So girls, where shall we go? Star and Garter on the corner do yer?' Billy asked, rubbing his hands together with glee.

'Suits me,' Di replied. 'Mind you, I don't mind where it is, our Kitty's buying, aren't you, lovey?'

As Di nudged Kitty's elbow, Kitty was suddenly propelled into reality. 'Yes of course,' she began, only for Billy to hold his hand up to silence her.

'Now, now,' he said. 'A lady never pays for a drink in me company.'

'Well, that's all right,' Di said evenly. 'Kitty's no lady!'

As Kitty watched Billy and her friend collapse into fits of laughter at her expense she tried to ignore the knot of fear building in her stomach.

'I can see yer and I are going to get on, Di,' Billy whooped, as he recovered. 'Now shall we?'

Inside the pub, Billy found them a table right by the bar and ordered them both a port and lemon and himself a pint of mild.

'Well this is nice, isn't it?' he grinned, raising his glass in salute.

As the three clinked glasses, Kitty looked around. The word

'nice' did not quite do the pub justice. The blacked-out windows were grimy, the carpet was stained and threadbare while the teak bar was filthy and covered in deep scratches. As for the stench of stale beer, it was overpowering to say the least. Looking around her, Kitty saw most of the customers looked like Billy. At every table sat at least one man in a suit or jacket and trousers, with slicked back hair. If she was feeling kind, Kitty might have thought it was just because it was the fashion, but she had a feeling this place wasn't just somewhere Billy had stumbled across. In fact she rather thought this was where Billy conducted most of his business.

Grimacing, Kitty took a sip of her drink, and let Billy and Di gossip away. Billy had been right: they were getting on like a house on fire, but it was an act Kitty had seen before and it cut no ice with her. Wearily she wondered if Billy was going to all this effort to have even more of a hold over her, or if he was doing it to try and recruit Di. Well, Kitty thought grimly taking another sip of her drink, hell would freeze over before she would let him make a fool out of her friend. She was so lost in thought, she barely saw Di get to her feet to visit the ladies until she was halfway across the room.

'Just us now then, Kitty,' Billy said smoothly.

As he leaned back in his chair and rested his hands behind his head, Kitty suddenly felt very tired. 'What d'yer want, Billy?'

'Bit direct tonight aren't we, Kit?' he replied, offering her a smug smile.

Kitty placed her glass on the table and leaned in towards him. 'You've made your point. You've snuck into a cinema, scared me out of me wits and shown me yer don't forget. Now, what is it yer want, Billy, 'cos I'm fairly sure it's not a cosy night out with me and me pal like.'

'Well, well,' Billy chuckled. 'You're not wrong. Your mate's as interesting as watching paint dry, but as she's easy on the eye I'm not complaining.'

As Billy drained the rest of his glass dry, Kitty shuddered. It beggared belief how she could ever have thought this man was her friend, but she knew there was no use complaining. She would have to do whatever he asked until she could see Elsie in the flesh and ask her outright what was going on. There was too much at stake for both of them if she backed out now.

'Since yer ask, there's summat I need yer to get for me.'

'What is it?' Kitty asked uneasily.

Billy looked at her steadily. 'Petrol. I want yer to start smuggling me petrol from the Army like.'

Kitty gazed at him in horror, unsure whether to laugh or scream. She couldn't start stealing petrol as a matter of course, surely Billy knew just how dangerous that would be.

'Me sergeant knows I'm up to summat already, he's watching me like a hawk every moment of the day. I'm not even allowed to drive anywhere on me own, it's impossible,' she said eventually.

'Nothing's impossible,' he replied. 'I'm not expecting great lorry loads, just a few jerrycans every couple of days.'

'But military petrol's dyed,' Kitty protested. 'When it's in the tank it looks the same but if it's tested it goes a different colour.'

Billy shrugged. 'So? That's for me to worry about. Let's just say there's quite a few folk that are finding their motor spirit coupons aren't going as far as they'd like, they'll do almost anything to get their hands on a bit of petrol.'

Kitty looked across at Billy. His smile had stretched even further across his face, she noticed, as though he knew he had thought of everything.

'I can't do it, Billy,' she said quietly. 'If I'm caught I'll be for more than the high-jump, I'll be arrested and most likely put in prison.'

Suddenly Billy leaned towards her, getting so close she could make out the overpowering aroma of his cologne. 'Well it's simple then, isn't it,' he hissed menacingly. 'Don't get bloody caught. Yer can bring me four cans tomorrow night.'

'But Sundays are fuel-less days,' she replied, remembering how difficult it was to get any kind of petrol from their quartermaster on a Sunday.

Billy sighed, clearly exasperated. 'All right, Monday then, but you'd better make it eight cans if yer don't want me breathing a word to your mate about what you've been up to,' he said, gesturing towards Di who was now making her way towards them.

'Fine,' she hissed with a scowl as Di sat down.

'You two look thick as thieves, what've I missed?' Di asked, taking a sip of her drink.

Kitty turned to Di with a weary look in her eye. 'Nothing worth bothering yer with. Billy were just saying how he's got to be off.'

'So soon?' Di grinned. 'And just as me drink wants refreshing as well.'

Billy got to his feet, and lifted his trilby towards Di. 'Sorry, love, but Kitty's right, I've got to go. The work of a butcher stops for nobody. But it's been a pleasure to meet yer.'

As he walked out of the pub, he waved goodbye to them both, mouthing *Monday* at Kitty.

Kitty took a final sip of her drink and got to her feet. 'Another port is it, Di?'

As her friend nodded, Kitty gathered the glasses and walked towards the bar. Something told her she would be needing more than Dutch courage to get her through the next few days. She realised that what she really needed was a minor miracle.

Chapter Fifteen

As it turned out, it had not been as difficult to smuggle the petrol Billy demanded as Kitty had feared. Since joining Northampton barracks, she had become friendly with Ian, the quartermaster, who looked after their petrol supplies and two days after she had bumped into Billy had asked him to refill her jerrycans. Ian had barely given her request a second glance, and when Kitty asked a further four times that same week for more fuel he didn't so much as raise an eyebrow, much to Kitty's relief.

'If I've said it once, I'll say it again,' he said, filling out the forms for the motor spirit so Kitty could sign for receipt. 'They ought to find a better way of transporting this fuel. These cans are useless, more ends up on the floor than in the tank.'

Kitty smiled in agreement as the autumn rain thudded as loudly as gunfire on top of the garage tin roof. 'I know, it's all such a waste.'

'And no good for you girls either, if you get stuck on a long journey and are out of petrol,' he sighed.

Looking around him to check they were alone, Ian leaned forward across the fuel pump and Kitty had to stifle a giggle. Tall, thin and with hair greying at the temples, Ian had been in the Army since he was a boy and had seen soldiers through the first war against Germany as well as this one. As a result, Kitty knew he had a lot of wisdom, as well as more than enough gossip to entertain the entire barracks. Officially known as Sergeant Smyth, but always Ian to those who knew him, if he did not know about it, then whatever it was, was clearly not worth knowing about. Yet soldiers always knew that whenever they paid a visit to Ian's stores they would walk away with more than the goods they needed and today was obviously no exception, Kitty thought.

'Did you hear about that lorry Volunteer Jones was driving last week that was robbed?' he whispered.

A jolt of alarm pulsed through Kitty as she shook her head. The concern written across Ian's face showed this was far more than idle gossip to her quartermaster.

'She was carrying a load of food from the NAAFI van, delivering it up to barracks in Liverpool,' he explained, lowering his voice. 'She'd barely made it out of the town before she was stopped by a gang of thieves who held her down and nicked everything.'

Kitty stared at him in undisguised shock. 'You're not serious,' she gasped.

'I'm afraid I am, love. You need to keep your wits about you while you're out driving,' Ian muttered grimly as he handed over the first of her four cans. 'You don't know who's out there on the roads.'

'Have they caught whoever did it?' Kitty asked in shock.

Ian shook his head. 'No, it's been going on for a while. The rumour mill's been working overtime, of course, but it's thought there's a gang around here who are routinely robbing vans blind for goods to sell on the black market.'

Kitty let out an involuntary gasp as she took the can from Ian. Was Billy a part of all this? She had assumed he was a small-time spiv, but was he part of a much larger operation? Her blood ran cold at the thought of him involved in something so violent.

'What's happened to Volunteer Jones?' she asked eventually.

'She's been confined to barracks,' Ian muttered as he filled another can.

'But it wasn't her fault,' Kitty protested.

Ian pulled a face. 'That's the Army, love. She should have been taking better care of her cargo, so she's off driving duties for the foreseeable, and considered lucky not to be court martialled.'

Kitty shook her head in disbelief. This was the reality of life in the Army and rules were to be followed, not broken. As Ian handed her the last of her petrol she waved goodbye after assuring him once again she would be careful when she was driving. Throwing the cans into the back of the Standard she was assigned to that day, she saw she had plenty of time to drop the cans off with Billy before collecting her visitor from the station and bringing him back to the barracks.

Her mind churned as she started the engine up and drove smoothly across the parkland towards town. The wind was strong and Kitty had to keep a firm grip of the wheel to ensure the car stayed on the road. Although they had been taught how to manage a vehicle in most conditions, Kitty knew it would be impossible to prepare for every eventuality. With a shudder, she thought of the reports of London bus drivers who had continued to drive through the city as the bombs rained down. She had no idea how they did it. Not only would it be impossible to pass down the roads with all the devastation, she wondered how the passengers held their nerve, never mind the drivers.

Seeing the grey, rain-filled sky, Kitty said a silent prayer that so far the Jerries had kept their attacks on the Midlands to a minimum. She knew that folk back home joked Adolf would never find Coventry as it was in a hollow, but she had been shocked to discover the Luftwaffe had bombed the city's Rex Cinema just weeks earlier, causing waves of devastation. The cinema had been one of her favourite places to go with Joe and she had lost count of the number of times they had gone to the pictures and watched the silver screen come to life. Now it was another casualty of war, just like Joe, Kitty thought sadly.

Once again the newspaper and wireless reports were full of stories of families bombed out of their homes. The poor mites were sleeping on floors or underground in makeshift shelters until they found alternative accommodation. Worse, when they went back to salvage their belongings, they found they had been looted. Only that morning, the paper had been filled with reports of thieves taking the change out of the gas and electric meters while families were left coming to terms with all they had lost. Kitty shook her head in disgust: this war was turning folk into animals, and the sooner it was over the better.

Pulling into a space outside the butcher's, Kitty hesitated as she saw a long line of people queuing outside Billy's shop. She knew he was always busy at lunchtimes but this was absurd, even for him. Getting out of the car, she slammed the door shut and ran past the bustle of women standing in line despite the rain, buff-coloured ration books at the ready.

'Oi, you, no queue jumping,' one old lady shouted at the sight of Kitty.

'Yeah, we've been 'ere hours,' another called as Kitty pushed past them and walked into the store.

Billy was clearly rushed off his feet. Red-faced, he worked behind the counter, weighing cuts of meat and wrapping them in waxy paper, while his assistant John stamped ration books and bid goodbye to customers.

Kitty stood to the side unnoticed as the woman who had accused her of queue jumping reached the front.

'This week's rations please, Billy,' she said, before leaning over the counter, 'and whatever else you've got,' she added quietly, smoothing her floral headscarf with the palms of her hands.

'Coming up, Mrs Shawcross.' Billy smiled, as he reached under the counter and handed her a tin.

Peering at the label, Mrs Shawcross screwed up her face as she examined the package Billy had handed her. 'What's this then?'

'Tinned peaches,' he said proudly. 'Fresh this morning.'

Mrs Shawcross smiled broadly. 'Well, our Derek'll be happy with his Sunday tea this week,' she said, slipping him her ration book, along with some more change. 'For that little extra,' she said in hushed tones.

Kitty watched in amazement as Billy handed tin after tin of peaches to the long queue of women, all of whom handed Billy their ration coupons, along with a little something else.

As Billy caught sight of her, he gave her a curt nod. 'Be with yer as soon as I can, Kitty, yer don't mind waiting?'

Kitty shrugged, it wasn't so much a question but more of an order. Pushing her back into the wall, she stood to the side, well out of the way of the excitable women delighted to be getting something a little extra with their weekly meat ration. Finally the last customer was served, and as she took her tin of peaches she smiled at Kitty.

'Sorry, love, he's all yours now.' The older woman grinned, buttoning up her raincoat.

'Oh that's all right,' Kitty replied quietly, expecting the woman to pass.

'Are you his sweetheart?' she asked in a loud whisper as she leaned towards Kitty.

A feeling of nausea washed over Kitty at the idea of being thought Billy's sweetheart.

'Er no, he's just my friend,' she said quickly, already hating herself for the lie.

The elderly woman regarded her for a moment before squeezing her hand. 'Well that's a shame. He could do with a young thing like you to keep him on the straight and narrow, he works ever so hard.'

Kitty nodded and returned the old lady's smile, hoping the conversation was over, but she had other ideas.

'I keep telling him, he needs to set his cap at someone,' the woman continued, 'but he won't listen.'

'Yer talking about me again, Mrs Davenport,' Billy said, appearing from the back of the shop and drying his hands on a tea towel.

The woman whirled around and gasped at the sight of Billy. 'You startled me,' she said. 'I was only saying to this young friend of yours you need someone to take care of you.'

'Oh I do all right, don't I, Kitty?' Billy said, walking towards the women.

Kitty nodded once more, the feeling of revulsion growing stronger in her stomach.

'I'm sure you do, Billy,' the older lady continued. 'But you should have someone special in your life. What's wrong with this young lady?' she demanded, hands on hips, her black felt hat cocked towards Kitty.

Billy chuckled as he wiped his hands on a tea towel. 'Our Kitty's far too good for me, Mrs Davenport.'

Too true, thought Kitty as she smiled at Mrs Davenport who was now tugging at the sleeve of her khaki jacket.

'D'you know,' she continued, 'Billy's been driving up and down to London visiting some of the sick and injured that were bombed out of their homes. He's ever such a good boy.'

Kitty glanced at Billy and saw a look of unease flash across his face before he composed himself. 'Really?' she quizzed. Something about the old lady's story felt off.

'Oh yes,' she continued, clearly warming to her theme. 'Billy was asked by one of the hospitals if he would go down and help out with the kiddies, weren't you, Billy?'

'Now, now, Mrs Davenport—' he began, only for the old lady to cut him off.

'You're too modest,' Mrs Davenport insisted as she turned back to Kitty. 'One of his friends, who works up one of the hospitals asked him to help with supplies and his lordship here was only too happy to. I tell you, love,' Mrs Davenport leaned into Kitty once more, 'he's a good 'un, he'll make someone a lovely husband one day.'

'I'm sure he will,' Kitty said evenly, wanting nothing more than for this woman to leave so she could do the same.

'Well, I must be off,' the elderly lady said finally, walking towards the door. 'Lovely to see you, Billy.'

Pulling the door towards her, Mrs Davenport, followed by John, left the shop, and Billy immediately marched over and turned the open sign to closed.

'What have yer got for me?' he asked brusquely as he pulled the blinds down and walked past Kitty into the kitchenette.

'Four cans of petrol like yer asked for,' Kitty replied, following him into the little room and hauling the containers she had smuggled into bags out onto the middle of the floor.

'Good,' he replied. 'I need another four the day after tomorrow.'

'I can't do that,' Kitty protested. 'People will get suspicious.'

Billy shrugged as he stood with his back to her and filled the kettle with water before setting it on the range. 'I keep saying this to yer, Kitty, but yer don't seem to understand. It's not my problem. Now are yer deaf or just simple? I need four more cans sharpish. How yer get 'em isn't my concern.'

As the kettle began to boil, Kitty felt a flash of anger. 'And if I don't?'

'Yer know what,' he said in a low voice. 'I'll make sure your mate's husband knows all about what she's been up to.'

'Are yer really going to London?' she asked, changing the subject. 'It's a long way to go.'

Billy paused as he added a drop of milk to his tea. Kitty noticed he no longer offered her anything, which was fine – she wanted to spend as little time with the butcher as possible.

'Just doing me bit for the war effort like. I mean me gammy leg's already prevented me from signing up, much to me great shame and disappointment.' Billy smirked. 'If I can help those in need, then I'm more than happy to lend a hand.'

Kitty narrowed her eyes. She had never seen Billy limp, and suddenly wondered if that too was all an act, along with his sudden concern for the families who were suffering in London. Did Billy have an ulterior motive?

'What's going on?' she asked. 'What are yer really doing in London?'

Billy rested his cup on the side and folded his arms over his stained overalls. 'Never yer mind my business, girl. Just get on with getting me that petrol.'

'Yer know yer can't sell it, don't yer,' she replied sharply. 'If anyone's caught with it they'll go to prison. It's coloured, I've told yer, it's not like normal fuel.'

Billy said nothing. Instead he looked out of the window and shuffled from foot to foot. He looked on edge, Kitty thought, like a cat on a hot tin roof, which was unusual for Billy. Suddenly the truth dawned on her and she gasped. He wasn't selling the petrol, he was using it himself to drive down to London. But if he was driving to London to help people injured in the blitz, he would be able to apply for extra motor spirit coupons. The government had an additional allowance for those who could prove they were really in need.

'Why don't yer just ask for more coupons?' she blurted. 'If yer told the authorities like, what yer were doing, yer wouldn't need to steal petrol off me.'

Billy glared at her as he leaned against the sink. 'What makes yer think I need the petrol for meself?'

Kitty shrugged. 'It's obvious, isn't it? Yer know as well as I do you'll get in trouble the moment yer start flogging that fuel. Stands to reason yer need it for yourself. But if you're really helping people, Billy, then neither one of us need thieve like this.'

As Kitty trailed off she glanced at the brown tiled floor and heard how desperate she sounded. Yet all the way here she had been thinking of a way to get out of doing more work for Billy. If she could convince him to go to the authorities for extra fuel he would surely have no more use for her. She looked up at Billy only to see he was still staring determinedly out of the window.

'Billy,' she tried again. 'Did yer hear me?'

Suddenly Billy came to life, and brought his gaze back to Kitty. 'I heard yer. And like I said before, it's none of your business why I need that fuel.'

She shook her head in frustration. Why wouldn't he see reason? Kitty turned her gaze to the small shelf above the canister of tea and suddenly saw a sparkling gold carriage clock that she had never seen before. With its delicate face complete with Roman numerals etched in black, it shone like a sun from Billy's dusty shelf.

'That's new. Where did that come from?' she asked, gesturing.

'None of your business,' Billy snarled.

Kitty jumped at the rebuke. 'I was only asking.'

'Well don't,' he hissed, taking a step towards the clock and touching it protectively. 'If yer must know, a mate of mine gave it to me.'

She peered closely at the clock, and leaned over, about to touch it when Billy slapped her hand away. 'I told yer to mind your own.'

Shocked, she pulled her hand away, but not before she saw a shiny gold signet ring on Billy's little finger. She had never seen him wear jewellery before.

'And what about that?' she asked, pointing to his left hand.

Billy looked at Kitty with utter contempt as he grabbed her roughly by the shoulders, his cruel eyes looming large.

'How many times,' he hissed, his face so close to Kitty's she could feel the heat of his breath. 'Yer do what I tell yer, and no more bleeding questions, girl.'

As he shook her free, Kitty took a step back and tried to steady her breathing. Glancing across at Billy, she saw his jaw was clenched and his eyes mutinous. Like a bolt from the blue, the pieces of the jigsaw slotted together in Kitty's mind as she realised what the butcher was really doing in London and she gasped with shock at the villain standing before her.

'You're looting in London, aren't yer?' she blurted. 'That's where that new clock's come from, and that ring you're wearing. You've been going through other people's stuff and taking it as your own. Have yer no shame?'

'Don't talk to me about shame, girl,' Billy snapped. 'It's your mate Elsie that wants to think about that.'

Kitty shook her head, her whole body trembling with shock. 'Oh no, don't yer bring Elsie into this. We're talking about your disgusting behaviour. Thieving things off poor, innocent folk that are suffering is downright wicked, Billy Miles.'

'There's a bleeding war on in case yer hadn't noticed, Kitty,' Billy spat. 'Times are hard for folk – finders keepers and all that.'

Kitty's eyes grew as big as saucers as she stared at Billy in disbelief. 'That clock and ring, and whatever else you've taken, belong to people, Billy,' she cried. 'People that've lost their homes, their loved ones and Christ knows what else. How could yer rob anyone at a time like that? We should be coming together, not making money while people lie dying.'

As she stopped, Kitty thought she might be sick with the pain of it all. She pictured families returning to the site of where their homes had once stood in the cold daylight only to be surrounded by bricks and rubble. She imagined them looking for their own treasured things, the precious mementoes of loved ones they may have lost, only to find they had vanished, just another casualty of war. Instinctively Kitty thought of Joe's watch and the comfort it had never ceased to give her since losing him. At the thought of someone like Billy stealing the most precious item she owned, her eyes blazed with anger. Enough was enough.

'I'm finished,' she said, her eyes flashing with rage. 'I never want to see or speak to yer again and I don't give a monkey's about the consequences.'

With that she turned on her heel and marched towards the door.

'Brave words,' he called after her.

Kitty said nothing, just continued walking towards the door. Hand outstretched, she reached for the handle, only to feel Billy grab her collar roughly from behind. In a flash, he threw her against the wall and she let out a squeal of pain as her cheek collided with the cool tiles.

'Don't give a monkey's about the consequences, eh?' he growled, his hand firmly around Kitty's neck in a vice-like grip. 'Yer bloody well will, girl. What d'yer think you're going to do, tell tales on me to the police? That'll be rich, won't it, think they'll believe yer? Some silly little girl who's playing at soldiers, or me, a fine upstanding pillar of the community who helps sick kiddies what have been bombed out of their homes like.'

The pain of Billy's grip against her throat meant she was firmly squashed against the wall and could barely move her head to speak. 'I don't care,' she said, her voice defiant.

'Don't yer?' he seethed, bringing his face around to meet Kitty's. 'Don't yer care about your mate and her reputation? I mean how would she feel if yer let her down as well as her husband? Strikes me he's already got wind of her situation like, after all, didn't she tell yer in his last letter she felt as if she were reading summat from a stranger rather than Charlie.'

'How d'yer know that?' Kitty croaked, the pain now so bad she wondered if she would ever move her neck again. 'That's private.'

Billy chuckled. 'Yer should know by now, Kitty love, I know everything. And I also know your mate's been up to no good. Now, if yer don't want her reputation in tatters, I suggest yer do as I say.'

Kitty's blood was boiling. How did Billy know how Elsie had felt about Charlie's latest letter? She knew she had said nothing. Could it have been Nora? Had she got in touch with Billy and told her how worried she was about her daughter? Was that why Nora was still keeping her distance? Her mind was spinning, but she knew she had to keep calm, for Elsie's sake as much as her own.

'Now, now, Kitty, I'm a reasonable man,' Billy continued in a sinister tone as he squeezed his grip even tighter. 'I understand that all this extra work is hard on yer, so I'll make yer a deal. After you've got me another few cans of petrol this week say, I'll only ask yer to do one more job for me, then we're even.'

'What d'yer mean?' Kitty rasped. By now she was in agony and felt as though there was a very real chance she might black out.

'I mean what I've just said. Do what I've asked, and I'll never darken your door again,' he snapped, releasing his grip.

Kitty ricocheted back from the wall and staggered to her feet. Regaining her balance, she rolled her head painfully from side to side to ease the pain in her neck muscles before she caught sight of Billy.

He was lolling against the counter, his mouth twisted into a spiteful grin. Kitty would give all the tea in China to wipe that smirk off his face and be free of him once and for all. But could she trust him? Kitty almost wanted to laugh. What choice did she have? He obviously knew far more about Elsie than she had first realised, and despite what she had just said about not caring about the consequences, while she knew that was true for herself, it wasn't true for Elsie. She already knew she would lay her life down for her best friend, and if doing these last few errands for Billy Miles would keep her safe, well there was no choice.

'What's this last job?' she asked sullenly.

A laugh escaped Billy's mouth. 'I'm not telling yer that, girl, you'll go running off to the authorities. No, no, no, I'll give yer the word. In the meantime, yer just get me a few more cans of petrol otherwise yer know what'll happen.'

Billy was clear with his meaning, and as Kitty rubbed the back of her neck, she knew exactly how he would make her pay if she did not do as he said. She caught a glimmer of steel out of the corner of her eye and saw Billy was now standing against the counter, sharpening a large butcher's blade.

'Boning knife, this,' he said, running the blade over and over a wet granite stone. 'Cuts through meat bones like butter, and as for flesh, well, it makes mincemeat out of the toughest of hides.'

Throwing back his head and roaring with laughter at his own joke, Kitty shivered with fear at the thought of what Billy might do next. Ignoring the slivers of pain that sliced through her neck, she scurried across the shop floor. Wincing, she pulled open the door, fleeing for the safety of her car. As she started the engine, she drove away as fast as she could, the image of Billy's knife carved firmly in her mind.

Chapter Sixteen

The blitz continued to rage across the country and as October rolled into November it was all anybody could talk about. The Luftwaffe had now turned their attentions to the south-west of the country, targeting Bristol in a devastating attack Hitler later claimed had destroyed the port city.

In truth, the bombings were nowhere near as bad as the Germans had claimed, and the city was in fact still very much alive. Yet like the rest of the country, Kitty felt nothing but anger towards the Jerries and the destruction they were so hell-bent on causing. Every time she picked up a paper, the scenes of devastation across the country she loved shocked her to the core. With every word she read she longed to do more to defeat the Axis powers – and Billy Miles too, while she was at it.

Since delivering the last cans of petrol, thankfully undetected, Kitty had been on tenterhooks for almost a fortnight, waiting for a message or signal from Billy demanding his final task. She wanted to get it over and done with, and the not-knowing part was making her a nervous wreck. The increase in attacks from the skies meant Kitty had a renewed vigour for the work she had pledged to carry out in Joe's memory, but knowing Billy could come knocking at any moment meant she was struggling to focus. Just last week she had forgotten to change the oil in one of the Tilly trucks Sergeant Hopson had needed, and more recently she had left the barracks on a long drive to Birmingham without any cans of petrol in the back.

Kitty prided herself on her ability to work hard, but since becoming involved with Billy she knew she had not been herself. She knew she ought to feel relieved the next and final job would mean the end of her relationship with the criminal, but something told her Billy was not a man of his word and that this wouldn't necessarily be the last thing she ever did for him. She had met people like Billy before and knew they would keep squeezing you dry for as long as they possibly could.

Which was why Kitty was hoping that her latest request for leave would not be turned down. She longed to talk to Elsie properly, and knew that if she could find out the truth from her friend in person she would no longer be held to ransom by Billy. That afternoon Kitty was driving Sergeant Hopson to Kettering and she was hoping to talk to him in private about how much she needed time off. Taking a deep breath, she ran the sponge of hot soapy water over the Humber one more time, ensuring every speck of dirt had vanished. She wanted to get off to a good start with Hopson, and knew a clean car would help her cause.

As the wind gathered speed and the grey skies threatened rain, Kitty stood back to examine the vehicle that had once looked fit for the scrapheap and smiled at how far she had come since that fateful day. She knew Hopson had been expecting her to give up when he made her clean the car inside and out, but Kitty had never given up on anything in her life, and she wasn't about to start now. She would find a way to defeat Billy no matter what.

Running a dry cloth over the bonnet, Kitty spotted Di. She was driving her Lister truck towards her and Kitty raised her free hand to wave hello.

'All right, love?' Di called, as she slowed the vehicle and wound down the window. 'That car's gleaming.'

Kitty stood back to admire the car from Di's vantage point. 'D'yer think? It's for Hopson, so it needs to be.'

Di paused, the engine ticking over. 'I'd give it another going over then in that case, Kit. Tell you what, I'll get you a tea over at the NAAFI van as a reward.'

Kitty beamed gratefully at her friend. 'That'd be nice, ta, love. I'll see yer in ten minutes.'

'Better make it twenty,' Di called cheekily, as she sped off towards the garage.

In fact it was a full hour before Kitty had finished cleaning and polishing the car to within an inch of its life and was ready to meet Di. As promised, her friend had bought her a cup of tea which was perched precariously on the brick wall next to her. With her legs swinging backwards and forwards, her hair wrapped in an old silk scarf, and dressed in her khaki overalls, Di looked happy and carefree as she sipped her tea. Watching her, Kitty felt a fleeting stab of jealousy. She would give anything to feel that happy for just five minutes, but she kept those thoughts to herself as she took a seat next to her and reached for the drink, which was still surprisingly hot.

'I only just got it,' Di explained as Kitty looked at the drink in surprise. 'I knew you'd be a lot longer, and nobody likes a cold brew.'

Kitty nodded appreciatively as she took a grateful sip of the warm brown liquid. Despite the rationing, she was thankful to the powers that be that she and the rest of her friends had never noticed any change to the amount of tea they could drink, which on a long day or night out driving, could be a godsend.

'No post to deliver today?' Kitty asked.

'Just on me lunch break,' Di explained as she bit into a cheese and tomato sandwich. 'I've got to deliver a package over Oxfordshire way later on.'

Kitty nodded again and looked at Di thoughtfully. 'Don't yer worry though, with all those packages in the back, summat might happen like?'

'Summat like what?' Di quizzed through a mouthful of bread.

'Yer know, like those thieves that held up that van a few weeks back.'

'Oh that,' Di shrugged. 'What are you going to do, Kit, live your life in fear? Not bloody likely, Adolf'd be well pleased about that, wouldn't 'e?'

'But what d'yer think, Di, if they came for your packages?' Kitty pressed.

Di put down her sandwich and looked towards the sky, clearly deep in thought before she eventually spoke. 'Way I see it is this. Chances are those greedy thieves are going to get their 'ands on whatever it is you've got anyway, and if you start arguing with 'em, well, there's every chance you'll pay with your life. Let 'em get on with it, then you can get your revenge later whilst you're still 'ere to tell the tale.'

Despite the seriousness of the subject, Kitty couldn't help smiling. 'You've got it all worked out, haven't yer?'

Di returned Kitty's grin. 'Dunno about that, but I do know I'm not likely to be able to fight off a gang of determined thieves single-handed. As far as I'm concerned, you do what you can to survive and fight another day.'

Wrapping her hands around the cup, Kitty found the warmth comforting against the icy November frost and nodded her agreement. Arthur had said much the same thing in the letter she had received from him that morning after she had told him the details of the robbery, a fact she found herself sharing with Di as she brushed the crumbs of her sandwich from her overalls.

'Well go on then, what else did 'e say?' Di asked.

Kitty reddened. Arthur's letters had felt like a kind of talisman lately, and she wasn't sure she wanted to share them with anyone else.

'Oh go on,' Di wheedled. 'You know I rarely get letters, and certainly not off me nearest and dearest, least you can do is entertain me. Especially when they've got the good sense to agree with me.'

'Still nothing off your mam then?' Kitty asked, neatly side-stepping Di's pleas.

'Not a word,' Di said, shrugging. 'But then I didn't expect anything. She's always been a very 'arsh and unforgiving woman 'as Maud Mills, and me dad's so under her thumb I don't expect to 'ear from 'im anytime soon either. That and he barely knows one end of a pen from the other.'

Kitty squeezed her friend's arm affectionately. Despite Di's brave face, she knew she was hurting. 'I'm sorry.'

'Don't be,' Di replied matter-of-factly. 'I'm not. They only ever made me feel bad about meself; this way I'm free. Anyway, you can stop trying to change the subject. I want to 'ear what Arthur's got to say.'

Rolling her eyes heavenwards Kitty reached into the pocket of her overalls and pulled out the letter. Sometimes it was easier to give in to Di, she thought, as she began to read.

1 November 1940

Dearest Kitty,

It was lovely to get your last letter, though I'll admit you didn't sound yourself. In fact, I don't know whether to feel worried for you or chuffed at your courage. Fancy, robbers holding drivers hostage while they raid their vans. Still, very little surprises me in this war. It seems folk'll stop at nothing to get what they want and live to tell the tale. I think they call it survival instinct or something, but Kit, don't be a hero if something like that happens to you. Let the rotten sods take what they want and make sure you keep yourself safe.

Mind you, our Kit, any thief'd be a fool to think of taking you on. You've a tongue so sharp at times I'm surprised you've not cut yourself, but then that's just one of the things I miss about you.

As Kitty got to that part, she paused, not sure whether to go on. Lately she had found an intimacy developing between her and Arthur through their letters. When she was writing to him, or she was reading Arthur's words it felt natural, but now, saying them aloud to Di, it felt wrong somehow.

'Well go on then,' Di coaxed. 'For 'eavens sakes don't stop there, we're just getting to the good bit.'

'Di!' Kitty protested, only for her friend to nudge her gently in the ribs.

'I'm teasing, you daft apeth.'

Kitty hesitated before she began reading again.

It feels like a long time since I've seen you, and there are times I fret I'll forget what you look like.

Anyway, things have been quiet here for a few days and I hope you don't judge me if I say I don't mind it staying that way for a time or two. We had a bit of a difficult time of it a few weeks back, and I'll admit I was a bit scared, Kit. Still, as I write this I can tell we're in for a beautiful day. I can see from the deck the early morning mist is clearing and a fiery red sun is breaking through the sky. Being away from home has given me a real appreciation for the smaller things in life, and no matter what Adolf thinks, there are some things he'll never take away from us no matter what. When I look at the rise and fall of the sun and moon, it gives me comfort because I know that no matter where I am in the world, my mam, dad, our Elsie and all my brothers will all be looking at the same sun and moon, as will you, our Kitty. So next time you're feeling unsure about the world and how this war's going to change our lives, look up at the moon or watch the sun rise or set and know I'm right by your side, Kitty, wishing you well and wanting only the very best for you. Even though we're so very far apart, we're both fighting the same war. When I think of it like that, you don't seem so very far away and I can always bring your lovely face to mind.

Yours affectionately,
Arthur

As Kitty finished reading she could hardly bring herself to look at Di, who had tears in her eyes. 'Oh Kitty,' she breathed. 'What a sweetheart, I didn't realise the two of you 'ad got so close.'

Kitty felt the hairs on the back of her neck stand on end. 'What d'yer mean by that?' she asked sharply.

'Nothing,' Di said softly. 'Just the lad's obviously sweet on you.'

'No he isn't,' Kitty snapped, stuffing the letter back into her pocket. 'He's just me mate and looking out for me, that's all.'

Di cocked her head to one side and regarded her friend with affection. 'Come on, Kitty,' she said gently. 'You can see it's more than that can't you? It's good for you, this Arthur sounds like a decent lad.'

Kitty screwed her eyes tight and tried to shut Di out. Each word she delivered felt like a fresh blow on Joe's memory. How could her friend possibly think there was anything more than friendship between her and Arthur? They had practically grown up together, and he had always felt like a big brother, something Kitty had been thankful for over the years. When she and Joe had announced their engagement, it had been Arthur who had kissed her cheek and offered to walk her up the aisle when the time came. The ball of fury in her stomach as she thought of how it had been less than a year since Joe had passed, and to suggest there was anything untoward developing between them both was an insult to her, Arthur and to Joe.

Opening her mouth, about to say as much, Di squeezed her hand to stop her and smiled. 'I'm sorry, Kit, I've let me mouth run away with me as usual. It was wrong of me to suggest there was anything going on between you and Arthur. Ignore me, I've got the devil about me today.'

Kitty let out a shaky sigh of relief and returned her friend's smile. 'You're all right, Di. I know yer didn't mean anything by it. It's just it's too soon for me to even think of someone else, yer know, after Joe . . .' She trailed off as Di squeezed her hand once more.

'I know, Kitty, you don't need to say anything else. You're lucky to have someone like Arthur in your life, and for me to make out 'e was more than a friend wasn't fair. I didn't think.'

Kitty drained the tea from her cup. She knew Di had no intention of making her feel bad, and there was no sense in making a mountain out of a molehill, no matter how much her comments had hurt.

'Don't say another word, Di, let's talk about summat else,' Kitty said firmly.

'Fair enough,' Di replied. 'Did I tell you we got a letter from our Peg this morning?'

'No!' Kitty's eyes widened in surprise and delight. 'We haven't heard from her since she left. How is she?'

'Fine, by all accounts,' Di said, fishing into her pocket and pulling out a letter. Clearing her throat, she began to read.

7 November 1940

Dear Di and Kitty,

I hope you're all well. It seems like ever such a long time ago since we were together and I miss you. So much has happened since I left you, I don't know where to start. Well, my mother always reckons the beginning is the very best place, so I s'pose I ought to start by telling you I've moved on twice since I last saw you. I know I'm not allowed to say where, but let's just say my mother weren't too happy when she realised how far away from her I am now. Still, one thing I've learned in the Army is things can change at the drop of a hat, so I've told her not to worry too much, as I could be ten minutes from home in a week or two.

I tell you with all these new postings I've been up and down the country on the trains. Cor blimey, it makes me glad I'm a driver. The other day the train I was on stopped in sidings for six hours to let military trains pass through. I was squashed like a sardine, desperate for air. But I had a shock when I finally made it to my new barracks, they wanted me to start driving ambulances! Well, I didn't know what to make of it, but I think the powers that be realised blood makes me feel a bit sick, so I was put back on general driving duties and had to lead a convoy of trucks the next day and find all the rendezvous points on my own. I was terrified, girls, but I made it! You'd have been so proud of me if you'd seen me, sat up the front taking charge. A million miles away from my first night, eh Kitty, when you caught me weeping for my mum. I found myself doing much the same thing on my first night here. There was one young girl letting out gushing great sobs for her mother and father, and I remembered how kind you were to me, Kitty. I comforted her, and even though I didn't have any mints to offer her, I told her I had once been like her, but that a very good friend had told me I would soon settle in, and how right you were.

I never thought I'd say this but I love my life in the Army. I feel as though I've found what I'm meant to be doing in life. Does that make sense or sound a bit daft? I know I've still ever such a lot to learn, but doing good, helping people all for this wonderful country of ours is what I feel like I was born for. I know, I know, can you imagine if Mary heard me now? She'd be crying with laughter I'll bet. Still, in her own way I know she feels much the same as we all do.

Other than that, I've been to one mess dance and even managed to enjoy a port and lemon. This time I sipped it, and was glad it didn't taste quite so much like the poison I was sure it was the last time I tried.

That's all my news for now. I hope things are working out well for you both, and Kitty I hope a certain someone isn't still making your life a misery. I know we have to suffer in the Army, but nobody should have to endure all that you have.

I'll sign off now, no doubt you're both as busy as me, but I hope we'll see each other again, girls, but until then.

Your friend forever,
Peggy

As Di finished reading, Kitty found she had tears in her eyes, and a huge grin plastered across her face.

'She's come a long way, our girl, hasn't she?' Kitty smiled.

'To John O'Groats and back by the sounds of things,' Di chuckled as she put the letter back into the envelope. 'She's really grown up.'

'I knew she would,' Kitty sniffed. 'She's a good girl, our Peg, and tough as old boots.'

'About time too.' Di grinned. 'She'll be defeating the Jerries single-handed the way she's going. Speaking of which,' she said, glancing at her watch, 'if I want to see Adolf off I'd better get going, this package won't deliver itself.'

Kitty yawned and stretched her arms overhead as she roused herself for an afternoon with Sergeant Hopson. 'I'd better be off meself. Hopson'll go spare if I'm late. I'll see yer later.'

Getting to her feet, she waved goodbye to Di and wandered down the hill, past the groups of recruits all gathered outside the NAAFI van drinking tea and gossiping, towards the garage to meet her superior officer. She was grateful Hopson had not been as hard on her in recent weeks, but still dreaded having to spend any time at all in his company. Although Hopson no longer routinely made Kitty's life a misery with extra tasks, he still talked to her as though she were nothing more than a piece of dirt he'd had the misfortune to step in, while girls like Beryl Mason continued to be celebrated.

Reaching the car, Kitty's heart sank as she saw Hopson had beaten her to it and was standing by the passenger door, tapping his foot impatiently.

'You're late, Williams,' he sneered at the sight of Kitty. 'Been nattering away with your friends, I suppose, as though you hadn't a care in the world.'

'Sir,' Kitty said, greeting the sergeant with the customary salute. 'Sorry I'm late sir.'

Hopson's eyes narrowed. 'At ease, Williams. I'd like to get to Kettering tonight not next week. Let's get on with it, shall we.'

As Kitty lowered her arm, she opened the door for her officer as she had been trained to do and waited until he had clambered into the back seat. Once her passenger was settled, she walked around to the driver's side and started the engine.

Driving through the gates of the barracks, past the guards and out onto the road, she was determined to make sure she got Hopson there on time for her own sake as much as his.

Peering into her rear-view mirror to check the road behind her, she caught sight of Sergeant Hopson gazing intently out of the window. His brow was furrowed and his nostrils slightly flared. She turned her gaze back to the road. What was it about Hopson that made him so angry all the time? she wondered. He couldn't be more than ten or twelve years older than her, yet he seemed to carry the weight of the world on his shoulders. Or perhaps it was just when he was in her company, Kitty thought as she indicated left and turned onto a bumpy country lane.

'For Christ's sake, Williams,' Hopson snapped as the car rattled over the uneven surface. 'Can't you drive more smoothly?'

'I'm doing me best sir,' Kitty replied evenly. Glancing into the mirror she saw Hopson's nostrils flare once more, his cold eyes alight with fury. 'I suppose that's the problem, isn't it, Williams, your best is just never good enough,' he seethed. 'I don't want to hear another peep out of you until we arrive, do you hear?'

Kitty said nothing, instead she turned her attention back to the road in front of her and kept her mouth shut for the rest of the journey. Even though Hopson's rudeness was hard to bear, she preferred silence to the personal criticism she usually endured whenever she was in his company.

With nothing to do but concentrate on the road, Kitty let her own thoughts drift and found herself thinking about Elsie and Arthur. She wondered what they were doing now. Would Elsie be putting her feet up with a cup of tea? She smiled, knowing how unlikely it would be that her friend would ever sit down for a rest. Chances were she would be working her fingers to the bone with the WVS, determined to do all she could to help the war effort before the baby arrived. As for Arthur, Kitty thought, she hoped he was still safe wherever he was in the world. Though she had kept her feelings from Di, Arthur's letters had become a real lifeline, especially over the past few difficult weeks. Even though Arthur knew nothing of Billy's blackmail, just knowing he was there to talk to whenever she needed, was comfort enough.

Pulling smoothly into the driveway, she got out of the car and walked around to the other side to open the door for her passenger. Peering at his face, Kitty saw that he still appeared to be lost in thought.

'Sir,' Kitty said gently, trying to rouse her sergeant. 'Sir, we're here.'

Sergeant Hopson blinked his eyes rapidly and came to. 'Thank you, Williams,' he said quietly, getting out of the car. 'Why don't you get yourself a cup of tea in the mess and I shall come and find you once I'm finished.'

'Yes sir, very good, sir,' she replied, standing to attention as Hopson walked away.

The rest of the afternoon passed quickly as Kitty made good use of her time in the mess by drinking cup after cup of tea. She had intended to amuse herself by going for a walk around the barracks, but the moment she had made it inside, the heavens had opened and so Kitty had settled herself by the warm log fire and pulled out the new Agatha Christie paperback she had bought from Woolworths earlier that morning. She rarely got the chance to read, as she was either too busy or too tired, and to spend a couple of hours with her favourite author was a luxury she had not expected. In fact she was so engrossed in the plot, she barely noticed her sergeant hovering beside her a couple of hours later.

'Not disturbing you, am I, Williams?' he asked, stopping directly in front of her, surprised to see Kitty bent over her book.

Startled by the sound of her sergeant's voice, she jumped to her feet so quickly the book dropped out of her hands to the floor as she saluted her superior officer.

'No, sir,' she said in a forthright tone.

'Then let's go, Williams,' he replied, picking up the book and handing it to her before walking briskly towards the exit.

Kitty followed him as fast as she could, but her legs and feet no longer felt like her own. She had been so engrossed in her book she was feeling a bit groggy from a combination of too much reading and the warmth of the fire and simply walking in a straight line felt like a challenge. As they made their way outside, she saw it was pitch black and still pouring with rain.

As the cold droplets splashed onto her face and slid down her neck, soaking her khaki uniform, she gasped in shock, the icy cold waking her from the fugue she had found herself in just moments earlier.

'Are you a keen reader, Williams?' Hobson asked as she navigated the roundabout at the bottom of the road and drove them smoothly out of the barracks.

'When I get the chance, sir, it's summat I've always enjoyed since I was a child,' Kitty replied, glancing down at the speedometer to check she wasn't going over the 20 mph limit. The last thing she wanted was to get in trouble with the police or Army officials with her superior officer in the car.

'Did you have a happy childhood, Williams?' Hopson asked moments later as the road unravelled ahead of them.

Kitty glanced at her sergeant in the mirror in astonishment. He had never asked her anything about her life outside the Army.

'I asked you a question, Williams,' Hopson repeated when Kitty did not answer.

'Sorry, sir,' she said quickly, returning her gaze to the road. 'Yes, sir, I suppose I did.'

Hopson lifted an eyebrow. 'You suppose you did? Didn't you have a mother and father who loved you? Weren't you blessed with a warm and loving family home?'

Kitty nodded quickly. It was true that up until the point she became an orphan, she had felt very loved by her parents. 'Yes, sir.'

'Well then it strikes me that you must have had a very happy childhood. But then that's the trouble with you, Williams, you don't know how lucky you are. Now I, on the other hand, wasn't blessed like you, Williams. My childhood was deeply unhappy, I didn't have a loving mother and father like you did. No brothers, sisters, aunts or uncles. I had nobody. That's why the Army means so much to me now – over the years it's become the family I never had.'

Kitty was puzzled. Why was Hopson telling her this? Naturally, she was sorry he had not seemed to have much of a childhood, but what business was it of hers? Unsure what to say, Kitty kept her eyes on the road as the rain lashed against the windscreen.

'That's why I care so much about the people in it, you see, Williams,' Hopson continued, his voice flinty and unyielding. 'I don't like to see girls in the Army who don't really want to be here, or see it as a little hobby until they get bored or married. The Army saved me, Williams, and that's why I think it deserves only the very best soldiers it can recruit.'

'Yes, sir,' Kitty replied, still unsure as to where this was leading.

'I don't like liars, Williams, I don't like cheats and I don't like criminals, or those who think the war is an opportunity to make money for themselves. Do you understand me?' Hopson continued without waiting for Kitty to reply.

Kitty felt an uncomfortable heat rise within her. Was it possible Hopson knew she had been helping Billy? She looked up at her rear-view mirror once more and despite the inky black sky, she could see a flash of anger in the whites of her sergeant's eyes.

'The Army has no place for soldiers who think like that, Williams, and yet I know some of them have the audacity to serve in my Army, in my unit no less,' he said angrily, his gaze never leaving the window. 'They should be stamped out and thrown in prison for the rest of their lives. There's simply no excuse for that kind of behaviour.'

'Yes, sir,' Kitty gulped nervously.

As she slowed the car to turn right, her mind worked overtime as she tried to figure out what Hopson was getting at.

'It makes me sick, to tell you the truth, Williams. These soldiers, these disgusting, filthy soldiers that have had every opportunity in life given to them and for what? To profit from the Army, to profit from my family, to profit from those that are casualties of war. I tell you, it's not on, Williams.'

Kitty gripped the steering wheel so tightly her knuckles turned ice-white. He had to know about Billy, that must be what all this was about. This was the moment she had dreaded, the moment she had fretted over. The possibility that her guilty secret would be discovered before she had the chance to put things right with Elsie.

Kitty opened her mouth to say something, but nothing would come out. She tried again, but her mouth was like sandpaper. What could she possibly say that would make this all right? She felt glad of the dark, that Hopson couldn't see the guilt she was sure must be written across her face.

'Did you know I was brought up in a series of care homes?' Hopson blurted suddenly. 'I was passed from pillar to post like an unwanted Christmas gift.'

Kitty felt a rush of surprise. Hopson had grown up without any parents just like her. What were the chances? She tried to make out his expression in the rear-view mirror but it was too dark to see anything. Kitty said nothing; she knew he would continue if he wanted.

It wasn't long before Hopson started to speak again. This time his tone was softer. 'A childhood like that changes you, Williams. It hardens you to the nastiness in this world and for that I was grateful. I had seen the devastation the Germans tried to inflict on this great country of ours in 1914 and I knew that the moment I was old enough I wanted to serve my country. I dragged myself up, educated myself, taught myself to speak properly so I would never be seen as the poor wounded little boy whose mummy didn't love him. I joined up as soon as I could and found a camaraderie I had never experienced before. The Army became a family to me, Williams, and I found the men and later the women I served with were loyal not just to their country but to each other.'

A lump had formed in Kitty's throat and she nodded, unsure what to say.

'The Army gave me something my birth family couldn't. I wouldn't expect you to understand anything like that, Williams, not with you having a loving family,' he said bitterly. 'But for those of us who call the Army home, it's sickening when you see soldiers with no respect for the service.'

'Yes, sir,' Kitty said meekly, wishing for all the world she could think of some way of steering the sergeant onto another subject.

'That all you've got to say, Williams?' he said. 'There are soldiers serving with you that you can't rely on, that are only out for themselves. Doesn't it make you sick?' Hopson paused. 'Why am I wasting my breath? You had the perfect childhood. You have no idea of what it means to come from nothing and see something you care about ruined from within.'

Kitty felt a rush of anger build deep within her. She knew she was at fault by helping Billy, but to suggest she did not care about the Army was a step too far. She wasn't waiting for permission to speak any more, and in that moment no longer cared about the consequences either.

'Actually, Sergeant Hopson, I also grew up in a care home,' Kitty said with a steely determination in her voice. 'My parents died when I was eight, and I too was passed from pillar to post. I know what it means to find family among people who aren't related to yer, and I also know you'd do anything for them, because they mean the world.'

As Kitty finished her speech she felt a weight on her shoulders lift. She was sick and tired of men like Hopson and Billy pushing her around, misjudging her and thinking she was some kind of fool.

'That true, Williams? I saw no mention of it in your file,' Hopson asked in an even tone.

Kitty shrugged. 'It's true,' she said. 'Nobody in the Army asked if me parents were still alive, just who they were.'

Hopson sat back in his seat, as Kitty swung the car into the barracks. 'I had no idea,' he said eventually.

'It's not summat I like to talk about,' she said, switching off the engine. 'I'm sure that's summat yer can understand.'

Without waiting for a reply, Kitty got out of the car and opened the door for her officer. As Hopson stepped out, his eyes met hers and they stared at each other as the rain continued to thud against the ground.

Eventually Sergeant Hopson broke the silence. 'I do understand, Williams,' he said quietly. 'I wish it was something I had known about you before.'

With that he turned away from Kitty and walked towards the mess. Kitty watched him go, not noticing the rain trickling down the back of her collar, her mind a whirlwind. She had sensed something in his eyes, she was sure of it. Was it acceptance? Forgiveness? Or had it been sorrow? And if so, would Hopson finally start treating her like any other recruit? Kitty shivered with delight at the prospect as she realised that she wanted nothing more than to call the Army home, just like her sergeant.

Chapter Seventeen

As usual, the shrill sound of Kitty's alarm clock woke her from the deepest of sleeps. Coming to, she struggled to make sense of her surroundings. She had been having one of those dreams where everything seems so real. Together with Joe, Elsie and Charlie, they had been sat around the Higginsons' kitchen table one Saturday night, drinking tea and playing cards for buttons. As ever she and Elsie had gossiped the night away, leaving the boys to put the world to rights, and Arthur had of course had them in stitches when he joined them midway through the evening with tales of his day at work on the railways.

Blinking her eyes open and rousing herself to sit upright on the uncomfortable biscuits, she felt a rush of sadness at the harsh reality of her life now. She wasn't at home in Coventry, Elsie and Arthur felt a million miles away and Joe was gone. They would never again know a Saturday night like the one she had dreamed of, and there was still a huge Joe-shaped hole in her life that would never be filled.

Despite the hardness of the mattress, all Kitty wanted to do was go back to sleep and shut out the world, but she knew that was impossible. Their daily morning drill awaited her and then she had to drive a visiting company commander to the railway station. That was life in the Army, Kitty thought as she swung her legs out of the warmth of her blankets and onto the cool floor. It was never about what you wanted, it was about doing what was right for your unit and your country.

Glancing around, she saw the Nissen hut was a hive of activity with the rest of the girls getting ready for the day ahead. Spotting Di yawn, stretch and grimace as she clambered out of bed, Kitty couldn't help but smile. Her friend hated mornings as much as she did, and was still to master the art of square bashing, despite her very best efforts.

It wasn't long before Kitty and the rest of her dorm mates were standing in the quad, with their Regimental Sergeant Major bellowing instructions. The chilly November morning had definitely woken Kitty up and she did her best not to shiver, despite the hail that had started to fall as she marched, right, left, right, left.

As Kitty put one foot in front of the other, her mind wandered as it often did when she was marching and she found herself thinking about Sergeant Hopson. Since revealing a few days earlier that she too had been raised largely in a care home, a funny kind of peace had developed between them. Although Hopson was certainly not going out of his way to be friendly, Kitty had noticed he was far less abrupt with her and she hoped it would continue. Obviously, Kitty would have preferred not to have told him about her upbringing, but she was pleased she had found the courage to speak up if it meant a thawing in their relationship. Kitty had never looked for special treatment in her life; she knew there were others out there who had experienced tougher times than her, but at the same time it was nice to feel she was finally being treated like every other recruit, which was all she had ever wanted.

Drill practice came to an end shortly before seven. She filed into the mess and queued for her breakfast of porridge before taking a seat next to Di at their usual table by the window.

'Haven't seen yer the past couple of days, yer been billeted somewhere?' Kitty asked as she sank her spoon into Cook's lumpy oatmeal.

Di nodded. 'Been over Cromer way, letter after letter to deliver. You been all right?'

'Fine,' Kitty said taking a bite of her breakfast. 'Same as usual over here.'

'Well there's a lot to be said for boredom when there's a war on, Kit, you take your thrills where you can find 'em,' Di replied. 'Which reminds me, I bumped into your mate Billy last night when I was in town dropping off me final parcel.'

At the mention of the butcher's name, Kitty paled. The butcher had left her alone for several weeks now, and although she knew it was silly, she had secretly hoped he was leaving her to get on with her life.

'What did he say?' Kitty asked, trying to keep her voice steady.

'Not much,' Di said. 'Said we should all go out to the pictures some time again, that 'e 'adn't enjoyed 'imself like that for a long time.'

'Oh,' Kitty said warily.

'Mmmm,' Di continued, scooping a spoonful of porridge quickly into her mouth. 'I told 'im we would, I have to say 'e's a real character, a proper charmer, I can see why you like 'im.'

Kitty said nothing, just rested the spoon in her porridge and tried to calm her racing pulse. The last thing she wanted was for Di to get close to Billy. What if Di found out what she was up to? Or worse, he dragged Di into his criminal activities by blackmailing her. Just the thought of him causing any more damage to her loved ones made Kitty feel sick. In that moment she couldn't run away from it any longer, she had to put a stop to this once and for all so Billy was out of their lives for good. Pushing her chair back so it scraped noisily across the parquet floor, Kitty gathered her eating irons.

'You off already?' Di asked in surprise.

'Yes.' Kitty nodded, her appetite having rapidly disappeared. 'Got an errand to run in town I'd forgotten about. I've time if I hurry there now.'

'But you've not finished your breakfast,' Di protested, laying a hand on Kitty's arm to stop her. 'And I've summat for you, wait a minute.'

Quickly Di patted her pockets before she found what she was

after. Pulling a scrap of paper from her trousers she handed it to Kitty.

'What's this?' she asked cautiously, taking the paper from her friend and gingerly holding it between forefinger and thumb.

'Note from Billy.' Di smiled between mouthfuls of breakfast. 'Don't worry, I 'aven't read it but in short Billy wants to see you.'

Unfolding the note, Kitty's heart thumped wildly and her hands shook as she realised this was the nod she had been waiting for.

13 November 1940

Dear Kitty,

If you could pop over to the butcher's tomorrow at about six, that little favour we discussed a while back wants doing. You don't need anything special, just bring yourself and a van, and perhaps park it round the back. I'm really looking forward to seeing you.

Yours,
Billy

As Kitty read and reread the note her mind went into overdrive. What could he possibly want with her at six o'clock? The last thing she wanted was to get involved in anything else that was illegal – or even violent – thinking of the Army van and the volunteer that had recently been held up.

'Everything all right?' Di asked, shovelling the last of her porridge into her mouth and getting to her feet.

Glancing up from the paper, Kitty smiled absent-mindedly at her friend. 'Oh, yes, fine, ta, Di.'

'What's 'e want then?' she asked, as she and Kitty washed their eating irons.

'He just wants me to give him a lift to see a friend of his who's got some supplies for those down in London. I said I'd see if I could get me hands on one of the Tilly trucks,' Kitty said, thinking on her feet.

Di screwed up her face in amusement. 'London? What's he been doing down there?'

'Oh, helping those poor folks that have been bombed out of their homes in the blitz,' Kitty said sheepishly, hating herself for the lie.

'Never in this world!' Di exclaimed in astonishment. 'Well good on 'im. I knew 'e was a decent lad. D'you want me to 'elp you tonight? Seeing as it's for a good cause 'n'all. I shouldn't be too long today as I'm only up Corby way.'

A feeling of horror surged through Kitty. 'No!' she cried, and everyone around her in the mess turned to stare at the outburst. 'I mean, no, that's fine, it won't take long, and besides, I'll only be driving him around the corner, there's nothing for yer to do,' she said in a more even tone.

'All right,' Di shrugged. 'Just an idea, but if you change your mind, just let me know.'

'Course,' Kitty nodded, 'and ta for the offer like, I appreciate it.'

'Anytime, love.' Di smiled as they walked out into the cool fresh air of the quad. 'And now, if you'll excuse me, I've got to get on the road. T'ra.'

'T'ra,' Kitty called as she watched her friend walk down the bank towards the garages, her eating irons thrust into her bag.

Looking at her watch Kitty saw it had now gone eight. Just over ten hours to go before she would be free of Billy for good. Looking up at the sky Kitty saw the tiniest hint of sunshine trying to break through the clouds. Perhaps it was an omen, she thought. A sign the day would go well. But until then, there was still plenty of work to get on with, and Kitty knew her first task would involve rubber gloves, a bucket of hot soapy water and a chamois leather.

*

At half-past five Kitty had finished for the day. She had made several trips to the station and back and cleaned the car so thoroughly Sergeant Hopson had commented he could see his own reflection in the bonnet. It was rare praise, and Kitty could only assume it had come about from her revelation the previous week. His comment only added to the gratitude she felt that this would be her final task for Billy. Once this was all over she would be free to get on with her life in the Army, and dedicate herself entirely to continuing Joe's work, all without Elsie's reputation in tatters.

At the thought of her friend, Kitty felt a surge of longing for Elsie. It had been a miserable few weeks, and knowing there could finally be an end in sight made her miss her friend all the more. How she wanted to talk to Elsie and tell her everything. And soon, she vowed, she would be able to do just that. Earlier that day Kitty had heard that her request for leave had been approved. Sadly, permission had not been granted until December, but glancing more closely at the dates she had been afforded, Kitty was thrilled to discover she was one of the lucky ones who had been given a prized forty-eight-hour pass at Christmas. It was a wonderful surprise and by that time Elsie would have given birth to her baby – the perfect Christmas gift.

Kitty smiled at the thought of all that lay ahead. After the year she and her loved ones had endured, she thought they all deserved some good news, and a baby was certainly the ideal way to celebrate new beginnings. But first, Kitty sighed as she walked towards the fleet of Tilly trucks parked outside, there was something she had to take care of.

With half an hour to get to Billy's Kitty knew it was time for her to find the vehicle he had requested and make her way into town. It wasn't unusual for drivers to take vehicles out without permission for an evening, and although it wasn't exactly allowed, Ian frequently turned a blind eye, saying the girls ought to find a bit of happiness when and where they could.

Opening the door of the first truck in the row, Kitty peered inside and was pleased to see it was clean and tidy. Though how long it would stay like that after she had finished doing whatever Billy had planned she wasn't sure. Hoisting herself into the driver's seat, she was just about to start the engine when Sergeant Hopson appeared.

As he walked towards her, his face stern in the fading light, Kitty's heart pounded, gripped by a sudden fear he knew what she was up to. Winding down her window as he stopped outside the driver's side, Kitty tried to stay calm.

'Williams, thought you had finished for the day,' he said evenly.

'Yes, sir!' she nodded. 'I've an errand to run, helping out a friend.'

Sergeant Hopson stood with his hands behind his back and cocked his head to one side. 'A friend, eh? And you're using military vehicles for non-military business?'

Kitty coloured. Just because their quartermaster turned a blind eye, did not mean Hopson would.

'Well, sir, he's been helping out the sick and injured in London like, and he's got some supplies he needs help fetching for his next trip down there, so I offered to help . . .'

As her voice trailed off, Kitty gazed back down at the dashboard of the truck, sure Hopson was going to pull her out of her seat by her collar and court martial her there and then.

'Well that sounds a very nice thing to do,' he said in a sincere tone that Kitty had never heard him use before. 'Don't let me keep you.'

With that, he stood out of the way and tapped the truck on its side as if to wish Kitty a safe trip. Startled, she started the engine, and drove quickly out of the barracks. Although she had driven along this stretch countless times before, this time felt different. Despite Hopson's apparent blessing, she half expected him to come chasing after her, but every glance in her rear-view mirror told her she was alone on the open road.

She made it to Billy's with just a few minutes to spare, and parked in the back as instructed. Shivering despite the warmth of her greatcoat, she got out of the car and rapped lightly on the door. It was flung open almost immediately by John, who wordlessly beckoned her inside the tiny kitchenette.

Billy was hunched over one of the hard-backed chairs, apparently checking things off a list. As he saw Kitty enter, he straightened up and grunted.

'Good to see you're on time,' he said, pushing what looked like overalls off one of the chairs. 'Here, have a seat while I finish sorting out this bit of paperwork.'

Kitty said nothing, just sat down and looked at the handful of garments Billy had moved. On closer inspection they looked more like ARP uniforms than overalls.

'What d'yer need these for?' she asked, holding the garments aloft.

'Never yer mind,' Billy replied sharply as he tapped the side of his nose and snatched the overalls from her grasp. 'Nothing for yer to worry about.'

'So what *do* I need to worry about?' Kitty asked sullenly.

'Driving, Kitty,' Billy replied. 'That's what yer need to worry about tonight.'

'Driving where?' she asked, a note of caution creeping into her voice.

'You're asking a lot of questions tonight, girl,' Billy tutted. 'I never realised yer were such a nosy bleedin' mare. All will be revealed. Now you've space in your truck for me and John, haven't yer?'

'John?' Kitty asked, puzzled. 'Why is John coming?'

'Because he's going to help. Can't have yer doing the heavy lifting, can I?'

Kitty felt frustration grow as she leaned forwards and clasped her hands together. 'Billy, will yer please just tell me what's going on?'

Out of the corner of her eye, Kitty saw John exchange a look with Billy.

'Fine,' the butcher replied. 'I've a delivery to pick up, and I need yer to drive us there.'

'Where?' Kitty asked again, her voice more forceful this time.

'Coventry,' John replied flatly.

Kitty was shocked. Surely Billy had to be joking? She glanced first at John, and then at Billy, but their faces told her they were deadly serious.

'I've not been back for years, Kitty,' Billy explained. 'And John here can't find his way down the end of the street, never mind to Coventry. Yer know the place like the back of your hand. With all these blackouts, we'll need yer to guide us.'

'We can't get to Coventry in a night,' she gasped. 'It's too far. And not only that but I've to be back by eleven or I'll be in trouble. I might not be on duty tonight but that doesn't mean I can roll in when I feel like it.'

'Which is why we'd better get a move on now,' Billy said firmly. 'Sooner we get there, the sooner we get back. It shouldn't take long, especially if yer put your foot down where yer can.'

Kitty shook her head; she knew there was little point in arguing. Billy had already got the whole thing worked out, and 'no' wasn't a word he was used to hearing. Wordlessly she followed him out of the kitchenette and stepped into the truck, the cold night air already wrapping its chilly breath around her. Slamming the door shut behind her as Billy and John got in the back, Kitty gripped the wheel and tried to steady her nerves. Coventry was easily a good couple of hours each way . . . she could only hope whatever Billy had planned would not take all night. Peering through the windscreen and up at the night sky, she saw the inky blackness was illuminated by a brilliant full moon. It was possible, Kitty hoped, that her journey home might not be as bad as she feared.

Chapter Eighteen

After over two hours on the road, Kitty had begun to calm down. She felt a lot less shaky and her eyes had acclimatised to the dark country lanes she was navigating. Despite never having driven to Coventry before, she had a good feeling they were going in the right direction thanks to the map she had consulted before they left and felt confident they would reach the city shortly before eight o'clock. If luck was on her side, she thought, as she gazed up at the moonlit sky flooding the road ahead.

Kitty couldn't help sneaking glances overhead: she had never seen a full moon like it before. It was so powerful and bright, almost as if the night sky was shining a torch just for her. She could see the road almost as clearly as if it were daylight and with a jolt she wondered if this was Joe's doing. Was he looking out for her, making sure this one final job for Billy was a success? She certainly hoped so. Driving to her hometown had been the last thing she had expected Billy to ask of her, and although she had been filled with horror when he had ordered it, now, in a funny way she was glad. He could have asked her to drive him to London to help loot the houses of those that had been bombed out, and she knew she would never have had the stomach for that, which would have meant heaven knows what for her friend.

She shuddered at the thought, thankful the end was nearly in sight for both her and Elsie, and hopefully with it the chance of a bright new future for them both. Elsie was just weeks from giving birth, and Kitty had the chance to throw her weight behind her country and finish what she had started in Joe's name without any more distractions.

Kitty glanced into her rear-view mirror at the outlines of Billy and John, perched on the benches that ran along the side of the truck. They sat in silence, each apparently lost in thought. Neither one had attempted to make conversation during the journey and apart from the occasional instruction from Billy to turn left or right he had remained unusually silent. Kitty had been grateful, the last thing she wanted was to have to make small talk with a man she loathed, but with Coventry just a few miles away she needed more information.

'Whereabouts up town d'yer want to go?' she called.

'Not far from the cathedral,' Billy replied. 'I'll let yer know where when we're nearer.'

Rounding the corner and driving up a gently steeped hill, Kitty began to recognise her surroundings and felt a sudden rush of affection for the town she had grown up in. It had always looked after her. Even when things had gone wrong, as they so often had during her life, Kitty knew that wherever she was in the world, Coventry would always be the place she called home.

As Kitty reached the top of the hill, she was surprised to see the night sky had changed colour. The welcoming white moonlight had been replaced with a surreal but warm, rich red colour that lit up the whole sky. It was a shocking and vivid sight and as Kitty drove down the hill towards Coventry itself, she gasped as she heard a low whine and saw what looked like dancing fairy lights fall from the sky.

'Is that what I think it is?' she exclaimed, craning her head over the steering wheel to peer through the windshield for a better look.

Billy clambered off his bench and peered over Kitty's shoulder. 'Bugger me!' he whistled. 'The Jerries are only bombing Coventry. I never thought I'd see the day.'

'But why?' Kitty said. 'We're not London, we've nothing for 'em here.'

The butcher chuckled. 'Are yer kidding, Kitty? Coventry's like clover for the Germans. All those factories here that are making supplies for the Army. No, this place'll have been on the map for a while for 'em to bomb, I'm only surprised they didn't do it sooner.'

'D'yer think this is revenge for what happened in Munich the other week?' she asked.

'Probably,' Billy said, shrugging. 'Hitler won't have been too happy we ruined his speech like that by dropping bombs on the town. This'll be payback.'

Kitty thought back to the factory she had worked in making parts for trucks. It felt like a lifetime ago. Could the Jerries really be destroying the city? She stared above her in disbelief – the sky was a fiery shade of orange, and the lights that had looked so pretty now appeared threatening as they dropped with force to the ground.

She wound down her window, and shrieked at the noise outside. The whine of the aircraft overhead was deafening, but the scream of the bombs as they fell from the Luftwaffe's planes like raindrops sent waves of terror coursing through her veins. Of course she had been trained to prepare for bomb attacks, but to be in the midst of one was something else. She opened her mouth to speak, but the words wouldn't come out. She was too scared to do anything but keep driving, unable to tear her eyes from the skies above.

'Bloody hell, Kitty, watch out!' Billy roared, bringing her focus back to the road.

With a start Kitty saw she had nearly veered into a ditch, and quickly righted the steering wheel. This had been the last thing she had expected and she couldn't stop fretting over her loved ones. Just how bad was this raid? Were the Jerries targeting the entire city or just the factories? Had Elsie, Ron and Nora managed to get to safety in time? She knew they had the Anderson shelter at the bottom of the garden, and hoped they had sought refuge there, or at least made it to one of the public shelters in the town.

Common sense as well as her training told Kitty that was what she, Billy and John ought to do. But the part of her that adored her country as well as her loved ones wanted to keep driving and do what she could to help.

'Shall I turn around and go back or d'yer think we should carry on and offer our help to the emergency services?' she blurted to the men in the back.

There was a pause, and then Billy suddenly let out a low chuckle and turned to John who by now was also roaring with laughter.

'Did yer hear that, John?' Billy chuckled. 'She thinks we can help some of those poor sods. Half of 'em are probably fried to death by now if London's anything to go by.'

Kitty's eyes narrowed with fury. 'There's no need for that, Billy. Try showing a bit of respect.'

There was silence as Kitty drove on. She saw now they were on the outskirts of the town and it was clear the Germans had launched a major assault, with the devastation plain to see. Entire streets were ablaze as people ran screaming from their homes, seeking safety. She saw mothers, ducking their heads, holding children close, as their worst nightmare unfurled and they dodged the windows, bricks and rubble that flew through the air. Even though Kitty's window was closed, she could feel the heat of the fires through the lorry door and nearing the centre knew it would be impossible to keep driving. It looked like hell on earth, and she realised they were lucky they had not been hit. Kitty thought quickly. They would be no good to anyone injured and the truck was a moving, flammable target. There was nothing for it – Billy would have to arrange his delivery another time. Quickly but calmly, she looked for somewhere safe to park the vehicle but knew there was little point. Chances were the truck would be devastated regardless of where she left it, but if she could get a little closer to the town centre and find Elsie she would be happier.

At the sound of rustling in the back, Kitty slowed the truck to peer behind her. What she saw caused her to gasp in shock:

Billy and John shedding their clothes and changing into the ARP uniforms Kitty had seen earlier.

'What the hell d'yer think you're playing at?' she exclaimed, slamming her foot on the brake so quickly the men fell to the floor.

'For crying out loud, Kitty,' Billy said through gritted teeth. 'I thought yer were meant to be good at driving as yer do it professionally like.'

'I am, when I'm not trying to work out what a pair of common criminals like the two of yer are doing in the back of me truck,' she snarled.

Billy and John exchanged looks before Billy spoke. 'We're getting changed, love, what's it look like?'

'I can see you're getting changed, Billy, I'm not blind,' she said. 'I'm wondering why you're getting changed into uniforms when all hell's breaking loose outside and we're at risk of losing our lives.'

The butcher smiled as he sat back on the bench of the truck and did up the top button of his ARP jacket. 'Because, Kitty love, there's been a change of plan. I no longer need yer to help me sort out me delivery. But there's summat else yer can do as your last job instead.'

Kitty raised her eyebrows in surprise. Surely Billy no longer expected to collect his parcel, whatever it may be. There was every chance that his supplier or his premises were non-existent. Apart from turning back, finding shelter or helping others, what else was there for them to do?

'We're going to salvage some items, Kitty,' Billy continued, as if reading her mind. 'Help make sure things don't get damaged for the folk round here like.'

'How d'yer mean?' she asked, puzzled.

'Well,' Billy said slowly. 'We can make sure folk in bombed-out shops and homes don't lose their valuables. Instead yer, me and John like can keep hold of 'em, store 'em in your van and drive 'em back to me shop to keep 'em safe like, just until they're ready to be reunited with their owners.'

Kitty looked at the butcher in total disbelief. Did he really think she had been born yesterday? She glanced at him and John and suddenly the penny dropped as she recalled Billy's new gold carriage clock and the signet ring. 'Yer want to go looting again don't yer?' she said, aghast. 'In your home town of all places. It's how you've been doing it in London, isn't it, by wearing those uniforms?' she continued, her voice full of contempt. 'A couple of fellas dressed in everyday clothes helping themselves to goods would raise eyebrows, but nobody'd question a couple of fellas in ARP uniforms making off with all sorts. I've read about swines like the pair of yer, it's disgusting.'

'So what?' he snarled, leaning forward and meeting her gaze with defiance. 'Yer owe me, Kitty Williams, so yer can stop arguing and questioning me morals, get out and lend a hand.' He let out a low chuckle as he sank back into his seat. 'Besides, in that uniform you'll be helping us out, you've certainly come dressed for the part.'

Any fear Kitty had felt for Billy disappeared in an instant and it took every ounce of self-restraint not to slap the smirk off his smug face. She knew she could take no more. Outside there were people dying and she was wasting time arguing with a pair of revolting animals like these two.

'Get out!' she screamed with a force she had no idea she possessed. 'The pair of yer, out of my truck now. I don't care what yer do to me, I don't care if yer think I still owe yer one last job, Billy Miles, all this,' she snapped, raising her palms heavenwards, 'is over, I'm not doing anything else for yer ever again. Yer disgust me.'

Billy's eyes were ablaze with fury, and the orange glow from the fires that continued to rage outside made his face appear even more menacing. As fast as a whippet, he leaned back and raised his fist as if to punch Kitty, but the ATS girl was too quick and ducked, causing the butcher to plough his knuckles hard into the back of the tough driver's seat.

As she raised her head, she saw Billy gasp in shock, his features contoured in agony. Kitty seized her chance to get away.

Opening the door, the continuous wail of air raid sirens screaming at her like banshees, she jumped from the truck and raced down the deserted street. At the sight of the burning shops and buildings, a scream caught in her throat. The orange flames were devouring the very lifeblood of the city, and overhead the Luftwaffe showed no sign of slowing their assault as the constant whir of their engines screeched in her ears. Aware of the danger she faced, Kitty kept her head bent low to shield her face from the flying debris and hurried towards her destination.

There was no time to think of Billy. She no longer cared what he did to her, all she wanted now was to get to Elsie's and check everyone was safe. Then she would offer to help the emergency services in any way she could. As she ran, the cry of the Luftwaffe became louder than ever. Raising her head she saw several bombs fall through the air, the whine by now unmistakable. Her heart was in her mouth as Kitty saw they were heading in her direction. She did the only thing she could think of and, closing her eyes, hurled herself into the roadside, covering her head with her hands. A split second later, she heard the thwack and roar of the incendiaries hitting the ground just inches from her feet. Opening her eyes, Kitty realised she had got out of the way just in time. Where she had been standing, a fire raged, and she knew she had narrowly escaped being killed. With legs as unsteady as a newborn lamb, she got to her feet and hurried along Trinity Street.

Despite the cold night, Kitty was roasting thanks to what appeared to be a real firework display complete with the soundtrack of roars, hisses, bangs and explosions ricocheting through the streets. The scene was unreal: everywhere completely ablaze, including the newly built Owen Owen. Cars lined every inch of the roads as firemen operated the pump jets as quickly as they could to gain control of the gathering inferno. Despite the fact their hoses had been damaged by shrapnel and were spurting jets of water like geysers, the firemen worked tirelessly and they were not alone. As Kitty glanced around her she saw what she assumed were genuine ARP wardens helping carry the sick and injured to safety. Chillingly, the wounded, the dead, and various body parts littered the streets, all seemingly blasted to kingdom come. With a shudder Kitty saw rescuers try to free those who were trapped under rubble, their screams haunting as they begged for their lives.

There was so much noise, her senses struggled to take everything in, but seeing a mother screaming as she carried her little boy in her arms took Kitty's breath away. The little boy had clearly had both his legs blasted clean off by an incendiary and was wailing in pain.

'Help,' the mother screamed, her clothes torn to shreds and her face streaked with dirt and tears, 'someone help my Ian.'

Kitty flew at her. 'What can I do?' she begged as a police officer reached her at the same time.

'I've got this, miss, I can take 'em in me car up the hospital,' he said as the mother continued to wail. 'Get yourself to a shelter now. We've no telling when the Jerries'll let up.'

Reluctantly Kitty turned away. Never in her life had she seen such devastation and she hoped she never would again. She vowed to return and help the moment she knew Elsie and her family were safe from the blasts and with a lump in her throat hurried down the street. Rounding the corner, hoping to find salvation in the medieval cathedral, she stopped suddenly and gaped open-mouthed at the sight before her. The city's beloved cathedral was in flames – the Jerries had decimated it.

Kitty stood rooted to the spot in disbelief as she watched teams of volunteers hastily gather ladders and work furiously with buckets of sand and water to put out the inferno raging across the roof and through the chapels below. The sound of the water hissing as it turned to steam roared in Kitty's ears and the thick plumes of black smoke streaming from the blaze were overwhelming, causing Kitty and every other passer-by to gasp for air. Covering her mouth with her forearm, she watched in despair as members of the clergy ran through the cluster of buildings, dodging the flames and fallen incendiaries, desperately trying to salvage candlesticks, crosses and religious icons that were priceless to the community.

It was heart-breaking to see something Kitty had always valued destroyed in just one moment and she couldn't stand to witness the scene any longer. Heart heavy, she pushed through the throng of volunteers that had gathered in place of the fire brigade, who were busy putting out fires across the rest of the city. She hurried towards Talbot Street, hoping against hope the Higginsons were safe.

As she turned left, her eyes stinging from the smoke and grime, she ran headlong into an ARP warden who gripped her roughly by the shoulders. 'Where are yer going, girl? Yer should be in a shelter, not running around the streets, it's not safe,' he said, his face full of concern.

'I know.' Kitty nodded. 'I'm going to a friend's now, Talbot Street. They've a shelter.'

The warden raised his eyebrows in surprise. 'Talbot Street? I hate to break it to yer, love, but the street's in ruins. A bomb hit not so long ago and destroyed six houses, leaving a dirty great crater in the middle of the road. You're best off seeking shelter elsewhere, I can take yer if yer like.'

Panic rose as Kitty took in the warden's words and shrugged herself free, mumbling her thanks. There was no time to waste as she hurtled towards the street she had been born in, determined to find out what had happened to her loved ones. Moments later she arrived, sweating and out of breath, as wave after wave of planes continued to roar overhead. Standing in the middle of the street she saw the scene was every bit as bad as the warden had said. Trembling, Kitty had to shield her eyes from the glare of the burning houses and flying debris as she walked further down the street towards the Higginsons', dodging the huge crater that had ripped the asphalt in two. By the time she arrived at their house she felt faint with fear. The Higginsons had been hit. The roof had been ripped from its beams, a chunk of ceiling had fallen onto what was left of the kitchen table, while the windows and doors were long gone. With a start Kitty realised she could peer directly into Nora's good front room and see out into the kitchen beyond.

Horrified, Kitty walked gingerly through the house, taking care not to tread on broken glass and picking up ornaments that had fallen to the floor. Stepping through the wreckage, Kitty saw a frame containing a photo of Nora's children had smashed to smithereens, the image inside scratched and disfigured. Carefully, Kitty put what was left of it out of harm's way on the mantel and prayed that wouldn't be the last photograph Nora would have of her children together.

Making her way through the kitchen and out into the back, the sight of the garden caused her to sink to her knees in shock. A bomb had demolished a row of houses behind the Higginsons' and rubble from the blast covered their back yard. The outside toilet had only one wall standing, and the shelter itself was engulfed in so many bricks it was a struggle to even make it out.

But there, lit up by the orange sky, was a flash of something shiny Kitty knew had to be the roof of the shelter. Her body galvanised into action and she raced towards the pile of rubble.

'Hello,' she called frantically, picking her way through bricks and iron to try and find the door. 'Can yer hear me? Elsie? Ron? Nora? It's me, Kitty. Are yer all right in there?'

She called again, this time bellowing with all her might to make herself heard. 'Elsie! Are yer in there?' she screamed, flinging brick after brick behind her to try to find the door. After what felt like an eternity, she heard the sound of voices below and her heart raced with joy. 'I'm going to dig yer out,' she shouted. 'Hang on.'

Surrounded by the crackle of burning wood and the stench of cooked meat, she worked quickly, scooping more and more bricks out of the way, scratching her hands and nails and ripping her uniform in the process.

But Kitty couldn't care less about any of it, and eventually made a small hole in the rubble and was able to peer inside the dark cavern. But despite the glare from the blaze she struggled to see anything more than a cluster of figures huddled together.

'Kitty, love?' Nora called shakily.

'I'm here,' she replied with relief. 'Are yer all right? Who's in there with yer?'

'It's me, Arthur and Elsie, Kit.'

'Arthur,' Kitty gasped in surprise. 'I didn't know he was back.' Somehow just knowing he was down there with them made her feel better.

Nora spoke again. 'Are yer on your own, Kitty, or have yer got people with yer like?'

'It's just me,' she said, wiping the sweat from her brow. 'Can I get yer anything?'

'We're all right, Kitty.' Arthur spoke now. 'But we're trapped with all this rubble. The blast from behind sent the door flying and there's a bit of damage.'

'But you're all right?' Kitty persisted.

This time there was a pause before Arthur replied. 'Dad's out somewhere and Elsie, well, Mam seems to think Elsie's gone into labour.'

Kitty's whole body shook, and she thought she might be sick.

'Kitty,' Arthur's voice came again. 'Don't panic. She'll be all right. But can yer get us help? Can yer get us out of here?'

Kitty did not need asking twice. 'Course.'

She flung herself at the bricks, tears streaming down her face and hands trembling as she worked determinedly to save her family. Like a whirling dervish Kitty cleared as much of the bomb damage from the shelter as she could. But the harder she worked the more rubble and debris seemed to fall. She felt as if she were losing the battle, and with hands cut to ribbons, she stopped for a moment to take stock.

Glancing at the heap of bricks, a sense of despair washed over her. She would never clear this single-handedly and in the meantime, her loved ones were trapped below. She needed help, but the near constant clanging of the fire engines, coupled with the roar of the planes overhead told her every volunteer in the city would be working on the devastation in the centre for a good few hours yet.

Looking up at the glare of the Luftwaffe, Kitty realised the

Nazis had no intention of giving up until her city was devastated. Well, Kitty thought determinedly, she had no intention of giving up either. No Jerry was taking her family from her, they had taken enough already.

With renewed vigour, Kitty continued to fling the stones in handfuls. She was determined to free her family from the wreckage. With a start, she suddenly thought of Hetty and George and prayed they were safe and well. Leaning forward to reach for a large brick, she lost her footing and fell in a heap to the ground, landing awkwardly. Wincing, she tried to get to her feet, when suddenly she felt a firm pair of hands on her shoulders.

'You're all right, I've got you,' a gruff voice said, hoisting Kitty to her feet.

Slowly Kitty turned to face the person who had come to her rescue, and gasped in surprise. Her knight in shining armour was none other than Sergeant Peter Hopson.

Chapter Nineteen

Like Kitty, Sergeant Hopson's face was smeared in dust and grime, while a series of gashes across his hands and neck were peppered with stripes of rust coloured blood. His uniform was ripped at the shoulders and knees, while his hat was nowhere to be seen, meaning his usually neatly coiffed hair was black with soot and hung messily in his eyes.

'What are yer doing here?' Kitty asked warily.

'I'm here for you,' he replied solemnly. 'I followed you from the barracks. I knew you were up to something and wanted to find out what.'

Kitty's heart sank. Hopson had warned her months ago that he wouldn't rest until he uncovered her crimes and now here he was. What a fool she was to think they had called a truce. Her cheeks burned at the shame of being caught out in front of the people she loved most in the world. That they would hear the dressing-down she would endure was punishment enough, but if her villainous behaviour got in the way of her saving Elsie and her baby's life then surely that was a punishment too far.

'I'm sorry, Sergeant Hopson, sir,' she said, wriggling free of his grasp and saluting her superior as the drone of the Luftwaffe roared overhead. 'I know I deserve to have the book thrown at me for everything I've done, but please,' she begged, gesturing towards the shelter below her, 'my friends are trapped and I need to help them.'

Hopson took a cautious step towards Kitty and gave her the

briefest of smiles. 'Let me help,' he said gently, moving past her towards the mouth of the shelter.

Working quickly, he started clearing the piles of rubble. His hands were large, Kitty noticed, and he was able to clear much of the detritus more quickly than she had alone.

'Well don't just stand there,' Hopson ordered, turning to face Kitty, 'put your back into it.'

As Kitty kneeled down beside him, she noticed there was a hint of warmth in his eyes as they worked together. With the full beam of the moonlight overhead to guide them, they quickly and efficiently worked out a system where Hopson sorted the larger bricks into piles and Kitty worked with the smaller ones. They made a good team, Kitty realised, and not for the first time she found herself wishing things could have been easier between them from the moment they first met.

She still had no idea why he had singled her out in the way he had, and now he had come all this way to find and punish her, Kitty knew any hope she might have had of a successful career in the Army was shattered. The only place she was heading for now was prison.

Realising the situation could hardly get any worse, Kitty knew she had nothing to lose from trying to uncover the truth, and opened her mouth to speak before she could change her mind.

'Why did yer always have it in for me like?' she asked.

Startled, Hopson looked at Kitty sharply before returning to the bricks he was moving.

'I mean, I know I've proved yer were right now 'n all that,' Kitty continued, in a tone far braver than she felt. 'But what did I do? All I wanted was to do me best, be a good soldier and do right by king and country, but yer seemed to hate me guts, from the moment yer met me. Yer never wanted to give me a chance.'

Lifting himself from his haunches, Hopson stood up and threw the bricks he was holding across the garden. 'You're right, Kitty, I did make your life hell and you deserve an apology. I never should have done that,' he said softly.

Kitty gazed up at him in shock. The last thing she expected

was to hear Hopson apologise. With a start, she realised this was the second time he had admitted he was wrong in as many weeks.

'The truth is I don't quite know how to say this,' he admitted. 'You've no doubt had a lot of shocks tonight, starting with the fact that Billy Miles wasn't just a spiv, but a filthy looter who dresses up in ARP uniforms.'

'I, er . . .' Kitty began, opening and closing her mouth like a goldfish as she trailed off.

'I know you've been working for Billy for months now. I've been keeping an eye on you for the last few weeks,' Hopson told her gently. 'I also saw you were in way over your head. I should have stepped in to help you sooner and I didn't.'

'How did yer know about Billy?' Kitty asked miserably.

'Everyone knows about Billy Miles, Kitty,' Hopson replied matter-of-factly. 'He's the town spiv and always up to no good. He's spent years getting my soldiers to try and work on the side for him and feather his own filthy pockets. Some he's black-mailed, some needed no convincing at all. That's who I was talking about in the car that day – I thought these soldiers were men I could rely on but they betrayed me. When I saw him talking to you at the dance, I knew he'd set his sights on making you his next victim.'

'I thought he was my friend,' Kitty explained sadly. 'He told me all about his dead wife, and how he wanted to go to war but couldn't because he was too sick. When I found out he was a second cousin of Nora's I felt like I'd found family when I needed it most.'

'He was the last thing you needed, Kitty, he's always been a slippery little toad and has managed to wriggle his way out of trouble with the police in the past. Not only has he spent years selling stolen goods, but lately he and his gang of thugs have taken to looting bombed-out houses as well as holding up army trucks and stealing whatever's inside. I've wanted Billy Miles to pay for a long time. Then, when I saw him getting involved with you, rather than stop it I saw an opportunity to expose him for the toerag he really is. I contacted some friends of mine at the police who also knew of Billy's activities and were aware of some of his associates. We were able to piece it all together, then simply watch and wait to see how things played out with you.'

Kitty's eyes widened at all Hopson had said. So her suspicions had been right, Billy was not only a known criminal but he had also been responsible for the truck robberies. Would he stop at nothing to get what he wanted?

'So yer knew all about him and said nothing?' she said finally.

'Please try to understand, Kitty, he was trouble for the town and for my soldiers. Scum like him deserve to be locked up and the key thrown away. I said nothing because I thought you could help gather the evidence the police needed to put him in prison or worse. It's common knowledge he lied about being too sick to join up, that his wife didn't die, she left him because he cheated on her and abused her.'

Kitty thought she might be sick. 'His wife didn't die?'

Sergeant Hopson shook his head gravely. 'No, Kitty, it was just another lie, I'm afraid. He knew all about you before you even met. It was no coincidence you bumped into each other at the Rialto like that. Billy had planned all along to get you to work for him.'

Kitty hung her head low. She had suspected as much, but to discover she had been deliberately tricked, that this man had preyed on her grief and lied to her about a dead wife so she would trust him was despicable.

'But why me?'

'Because it's not easy getting people in the Army to work for you,' Sergeant Hopson explained moving another pile of rocks away from the shelter. 'And Billy has always liked soldiers. Not only can they steal things more easily, they have greater access to petrol, food and other goods, not to mention transport. When he heard you were going to be a driver in Northampton he thought he'd died and gone to heaven.'

'But how did he know?' Kitty asked, her voice teeming with anguish.

'The Higginsons' lodger, Mike. He had worked under Billy for years, and told him what you were up to. Billy was over the moon, but what he didn't bank on was your loyalty to the Higginsons, and downright disgust at his activities. He thought he could sway you with cash or the promise of extra food when you needed it, like he did with everyone else. By the time he realised you were unwilling to play ball, he knew he needed another plan so he got Mike to take Elsie under his wing so he'd have something to blackmail you with,' Hopson explained.

Kitty shook her head in disbelief. She had always known Elsie would never cheat on Charlie, that her love for him was too strong. If only she had found the courage to tell Billy to leave her alone right from the beginning. She felt foolish for not trusting her instincts and allowing herself to get sucked into something so horrific.

Sergeant Hopson stopped moving bricks for a moment reached out and clasped her hand. Kitty jumped at the kindness of the gesture, the comfort of a simple human touch was something she had been longing for all night.

'Don't feel bad, Kitty,' he said tenderly. 'Billy's had years of practice at manipulating people. He ordered Mike to hide Charlie's letters to Elsie so she would think he didn't care and confide in him instead. He guessed Elsie would tell you everything and this way there was a chance you might think Elsie had been seeing Mike behind his back and wonder if the baby was his instead. He needed you to at least wonder if he was right in order for his plan to work.'

'How could he?' Kitty said, her voice shaking with rage. 'I don't know how he sleeps at night.' Consumed with anger, she returned to shifting the debris, hurling bricks rapidly across the garden.

'That's why I wanted to catch him,' Sergeant Hopson said, ducking out of the way as Kitty sent a particularly large stone flying just past his ear. 'This was the only way I could see.'

'Nora should have told me,' she said, ignoring her sergeant and flinging more rocks in his direction. 'If she had written to me and said Billy was her second cousin and a bad 'un, then I would never have had anything to do with him.'

'Actually, she did write and tell you, but Nora never received a reply. She assumed you didn't want to hear the truth, that you had become too fond of Billy and didn't believe her.'

Kitty stopped what she was doing and turned to stare at Sergeant Hopson in disbelief.

'What are yer on about? I've not heard a word from Nora since I got to Northampton.'

'I can assure you she wrote to you, Kitty,' Hopson insisted, as he continued flinging rocks and pebbles away from the Anderson shelter. 'She was desperate to warn you and keep you safe. When you didn't reply she wrote to me instead and told me how worried she was about you, that you had lost your fiancé, had joined the Army and now had the misfortune to have met her second cousin.'

Kitty could scarcely catch her breath as she tried to make sense of what Hopson had told her.

'So why didn't I get the letter Nora sent to me?' she asked uneasily.

Hopson's face looked grave. 'It saddens me to say that I imagine Billy has someone working for him in the postroom and had your letter from Nora intercepted. He would have known she would write and tell you the truth and he couldn't risk it, so no doubt someone in his pocket, and unfortunately someone under my command, would have examined every piece of your mail.'

'That can't be true, can it?' Kitty said, aghast, already knowing in her heart that this was exactly what had happened. 'But Billy told me Nora had written to him and explained who I was,' she said, her mind whirring.

'I doubt that very much,' Hopson said. 'Nora said she and the rest of the family had always despised him and I assured her I would take care of it, that it would be better if she kept all of this to herself for now. The truth was I wanted to catch Billy Miles out once and for all and I believed this was the best chance of doing that.'

'That wasn't the only reason though, was it?' Kitty said defiantly.

'I'm sorry?' Now it was Sergeant Hopson's turn to look puzzled.

'Well, I expect yer thought yer could get one over on me 'n'all. After all, yer know what girls like me are like, don't yer,' she snarled. 'Well you've got what yer wanted. Yer followed me, found me, caught me up to no good and now I'll be for it.'

Apart from the sound of a bomb hissing through the air, there was a brief silence between them before Sergeant Hopson looked down at Kitty and smiled at her. 'You won't be for it, Kitty. Billy is the one that will be getting in trouble. I came down here with some colleagues, and they have apprehended Billy.'

'How d'yer mean like?' Kitty asked, as the wail of the sirens continued to pierce the dark night.

'He and his apprentice were caught red-handed, impersonating ARP wardens, looting shops and homes that were bombed out,' Sergeant Hopson explained. 'Now they can examine the certificate he's got excusing him from active service, as well as search his home and business for any signs of wrongdoing.'

'Well it won't take 'em long,' she snorted. 'His place is riddled with stolen goods, it makes yer sick.'

'I'm sure.' Sergeant Hopson nodded. 'But just so you understand, Kitty, you will be seen as an innocent party in all this. You were manipulated and blackmailed by Billy Miles. If you tell the police all that you will only strengthen the case against him and face no charges yourself, I will see to that.'

Pausing for breath, Kitty looked up from the rubble and saw her sergeant's face in the moonlight. The beam highlighted his features and Kitty saw he was smiling at her almost benevolently. She felt wrong-footed. This whole night had been filled with shocks and surprises, she had no idea what to feel, let alone say. It was shocking, Kitty realised, that someone would take something so personal like the love and grief she felt at losing her sweetheart and turn it into a weapon with which to hurt her. She hoped the police did more than lock him away, Kitty hoped

Billy Miles would hang for his crimes, he deserved nothing less. But there was something still troubling her, and that was why her superior officer, who disliked her so intently, was now going out of his way to help her.

'Why have yer gone to so much trouble for me like?' she blurted. 'I mean, yer hate me. You've never made any secret of the fact.'

Avoiding Kitty's gaze, Sergeant Hopson bent down and started shifting more rubble. They had managed to clear a lot of the debris covering the entrance and with luck, would be able to free the Higginsons in a few minutes.

'I don't hate you, Kitty,' he said quietly. 'I mean not any more. You're right, I did, and when I learned Billy had tricked you into working with him I hoped you would fall. When I told Nora I would look out for you I meant it. What I didn't tell her was that I was hoping to get you into as much trouble as Billy.'

Kitty could scarcely believe her ears. She had fretted she had been going mad over the past few months, imagining Hopson was deliberately targeting her. But she had been right – Hopson had wanted her to suffer.

'But why?' she asked finally. 'Why have yer made my life so difficult for the last few months? Why did yer follow me tonight, if it wasn't to get me in as much bother as Billy?'

Hopson stepped towards her, the moonlight revealing his eyes filled with sorrow. 'Believe it or not, I didn't follow you tonight to get you into trouble, Kitty.'

Kitty stopped throwing bricks for a moment and looked at her superior officer. 'Then why?'

He ran his hands over his face and shook his head, regarding her warily. 'Because, I'm your brother,' he said softly.

Chapter Twenty

Hands covered in dirt, Kitty paused for a moment from clearing debris and stood frozen to the spot in shock. Part of her thought this had to be some kind of joke, an elaborate stunt Peter Hopson thought would be funny to torment her with. Yet as buildings continued to collapse all around them, Kitty could see from his eyes he wasn't lying.

'But you can't be,' she replied eventually, 'I'm an only child, me mam always said she and me dad weren't blessed with another kiddie.'

Sergeant Hopson inhaled sharply and pinched the bridge of his nose. The silence between them seemed to stretch on for a lifetime before he spoke.

'I'm afraid I am, Kitty,' he said sombrely. 'Betty, our mother, gave me away when I was a baby. She was only eighteen and as an unwed mother couldn't possibly have raised me alone, so she got rid of me.'

A bomb hissed and sang, hitting a neighbouring street as Kitty's mind raced. Her mother had never said a word about her having a sibling, but then again, she supposed, as Kitty had been only small when her parents were killed, there perhaps had not been the time. But surely someone else would have known?

'I was raised in a series of care homes, like you,' he explained, his tone gentle. 'And then when I was eighteen I discovered my mother's identity and came looking for her in this very street.'

Peter gestured sharply to the rubble behind him, which had once been Kitty's childhood home.

'What did she say?' Kitty whispered, as she glanced at the mound that had once meant so much.

There was a pause as the Luftwaffe roared overhead and Peter looked briefly at the ground once more. 'She told me she wanted nothing to do with me. That her husband didn't know she had been with another man before him and that she couldn't help me, but wished me well.'

The pain of the meeting was etched clearly across Peter's face as he grimaced at the memory. 'And then I saw you come to the door,' he continued in a low voice. 'Clinging to your mother's legs, she picked you up and held you tight, then shut the door in my face. I hated you in that moment, I hated you because you had received my mother's love when I hadn't. I wondered what it was about you that made you more lovable than me. It was a memory that stayed with me for years. Every time I closed my eyes I saw your face and the look of love she had in her eyes for you, that by rights should have been me . . .'

Peter trailed off and Kitty saw his jaw was clenched in anger, the hatred in his eyes burning as brightly as the fires that surrounded them. Kitty hung her head in sorrow as the image of the woman she knew to be her mother crumbled into dust. Turning her back to Peter, she leaned over the rubble covering the shelter and started to clear the rubbish once more.

'I know,' she said wistfully. 'I remember.'

There was no denying how much she wanted Peter to be lying, and a part of her was angry with him for trying to soil the memory of the mother she had loved and cherished all these years. Yet, Kitty also knew Peter was telling the truth. She remembered a young man coming to the door shortly before her parents were killed. Kitty had been in the kitchen at the time, but had heard her mother sound agitated as she answered the door. Kitty had been curious – her mother never usually had a cross word for anyone. Kitty walked down the hall and had seen a young man standing in the doorway.

She recalled looking back up at her mother and seeing her jaw clenched and her eyes darting nervously from side to side as if she were checking who was watching. She was anxious, Kitty had thought at the time, and clearly couldn't wait to get rid of whoever the man was. Kitty had felt worried for her mother, and so she had hugged her legs before she was lifted into her arms for a cuddle. She remembered the floral scent of the perfume her mother used to wear and how she had felt her heart pound wildly against her chest. She remembered how she had turned to the man in the doorway, wondering who he was, and then the flash of anger in the man's eyes as Betty shut the door on him.

Afterwards Betty had gone straight to bed where she had spent most of the afternoon. By the time her father returned home, it was as though the incident had never happened and her mother had plastered a smile on her face and fixed her father's tea as usual. But at bedtime as Betty tucked her in and kissed her goodnight, she had asked Kitty to keep their afternoon visitor to herself, saying that her father disliked it when men called on the house when she was alone. Kitty had of course agreed, and thought no more of it. Especially when her parents were killed just two weeks later and she had other things to worry about.

Peter bent down next to Kitty to help. 'I had no idea what had happened to Betty and Sid until you told me a couple of weeks ago,' he admitted. 'I had always pictured you living this charmed life where your mother loved you, and I had been shunned with no thought or care. When I discovered you were one of my recruits at the driving centre, I couldn't believe my luck. Finally, I had my chance of revenge on the little girl who had stolen my mother's love. I wanted to make you pay.'

'Yer did that all right,' Kitty said, her voice filled with sadness.

'I'm sorry,' Peter said, his eyes teeming with sincerity. 'I imagined I knew just what you were like. Spoilt, privileged and feckless, with no real interest in your country or ending this war. I thought I'd send you back crying to your mother in days.'

Kitty looked up at the skies and saw the Luftwaffe had renewed their assault on the city. The drone of their engines providing a relentless soundtrack to the pain and horror surrounding them. She knew the Jerries wanted nothing more than to wipe out the city, and she smiled at the thought of Peter Hopson trying much the same thing with her over the past months. She had to admit that there had been times where she would have liked nothing more than to cry on her mother's shoulder.

'Then I saw you at work – nobody worked harder than you, Kitty,' Peter continued. 'Nobody put more dedication into learning than you. You wanted to serve, to learn, to be the best you could be, and I came to admire you. No matter what punishment I threw at you, you got on with it and never complained. Then when I saw you with Billy Miles at the dance, I realised he had set his eyes on you as his next victim, so I watched from afar. I saw you smuggle petrol for him, I knew you were sneaking into town to see him before jobs and I caught the look of worry that seemed permanently etched into your eyes. I knew he was making your life a misery and a part of me, a horrible vindictive part of me, was glad, so glad I nearly shopped you myself to the police.'

'Yer were going to shop me?' she shouted in disbelief, the sounds of the aircraft getting louder by the second.

Peter nodded. 'At first. You getting in trouble with the police was far greater revenge than I could ever have imagined. But then you told me how you were also raised in a care home and it made me reconsider my opinion of you. I realised you weren't to blame for Betty's actions, that she was just a young girl who didn't know any better and had got herself into a bad situation. You weren't responsible.'

'Were yer ever going to tell me?' Kitty wailed.

'Eventually,' Peter shouted, as the Luftwaffe roared overhead. 'Not tonight, not like this, but eventually, when the time seemed right.'

Kitty nodded. Tonight had been life-changing in so many ways, and much as she wanted to find out more about this new half-brother and what that meant, she knew this wasn't the time. She had a job to do – she had to save her friend.

Peering inside the shelter, she realised they had almost cleared the rubble. Scooping down to remove the remaining handfuls of debris, the sound of an ear-piercing scream rose above the din of the aircraft swooping mercilessly overhead.

'Is Elsie all right?' Kitty asked frantically, shining her torch onto the figures inside.

'We're fine, Kitty love,' Arthur called, his strong voice ringing out into the darkness. 'Elsie's little lad's just come a bit early that's all.'

The sound of a baby's first cries caused Kitty to gasp with shock and delight. Peering into the shelter properly, she saw her best friend lying flat on the small bench with Nora crouching over her, placing something small and wriggly on her chest.

'Oh my God,' Kitty breathed, tears welling in her eyes as she took in the scene. 'Elsie, you've got a son.'

Kitty's eyes got used to the torchlight and she saw Elsie and her baby surrounded by Nora and Arthur. Nora was busy pushing the hair away from her eyes, and Arthur was clasping his sister's hand and murmuring something Kitty couldn't make out.

Kitty's heart swelled with love. To think she had witnessed the birth of her best friend's baby. Well, maybe some good would come out of this awful night after all. Catching Arthur's eye, she beamed at him.

'Thank heavens yer were here,' she smiled. 'You're an uncle, Arthur, can yer believe it?'

But Arthur's face remained grave. Instinctively Kitty knew something was wrong and a jolt of fear exploded in her chest.

'What is it?' she asked hurriedly. 'What's happened?'

Arthur looked first at Kitty before nodding a hello at Peter. Shaking his head, he let go of Elsie's hand, stepped towards the mouth of the shelter and leaned in close to Kitty.

The sight of him up close took Kitty's breath away. Arthur looked like he had not seen sleep in weeks. His skin was pale, and his clothes hung limply from his frame. Life in the Navy looked as though it was taking its toll. But it was the worry and sadness in his eyes that made Kitty's knees buckle as she realised he had something awful to tell her.

'Elsie's lost a lot of blood,' he whispered. 'When the door fell on her, not only did it cause her to go into early labour, but I'm guessing it caused her to bleed internally as well. Me and Mam got the baby out as quick as we could like, but Kitty, I think yer should prepare yourself.'

'For what?' Kitty whispered, dreading the answer.

'For the worst,' he said falteringly. 'It doesn't look good, Kit. I don't know if she's going to survive. With all the devastation out there tonight, even if we can get her to hospital in one piece, I don't know if they'll have the blood she needs. I'm concentrating on keeping her stable for now, but other than keep my fingers crossed . . .' Arthur's voice trailed off. Kitty felt the steely resolve she had relied upon throughout her life rise to the surface. Her friend had been there during some of the toughest moments of her life and it was time to repay the favour.

'Wait here for me,' she said, turning to Peter and taking Arthur's hand to step inside the shelter.

'Kitty, you can't go in there,' Peter hissed. 'You could disturb unexploded incendiaries and cause more damage. There's no-where to run inside a shelter.'

'I don't care,' she said defiantly, 'Elsie needs me.'

Taking a cautious step inside, Kitty made her way through the debris and exchanged a sad smile with Nora, who clasped her hand and led her silently towards Elsie and her baby.

On the surface, Kitty thought this was the perfect happy ending. Elsie was lying on the makeshift bed, her beautiful baby nestled to her chest. Elsie's face may have been streaked with dirt and tears but Kitty thought she had never looked more beautiful and at peace. She was smiling down at her baby, as though it were just the two of them in the room, and Kitty's heart lurched with joy. Her friend would be a wonderful mother: she was bursting with so much love, her little boy would never want for cuddles. It was a role Elsie had been made for, Kitty realised, and she was thrilled for her friend. Yet as Kitty cast her gaze down to the floor below, it was all she could do not to gasp in horror. Beneath Elsie seeped a dark, treacly liquid, flooding the floor. Kitty had never seen so much blood in her life, and she knew then Elsie was unlikely to survive.

Stepping towards her, Kitty bent down to her friend and stifled a heart-wrenching sob. Elsie's green eyes were filled with a heady mix of joy and sadness, and Kitty guessed her best friend had realised she was not long for this world.

'Yer don't half pick your times, Elsie O'Connor!' Kitty admonished as she blinked back her tears. 'Fancy having your baby down a shelter! You'll be the talk of Talbot Street.'

Elsie smiled back at her, though Kitty could tell it cost her a great deal of effort to do so. 'Well, I knew you'd need a bomb under yer to get yer back here!' she teased, her voice weak and rasping.

'Yer didn't have to go this far, Els,' Kitty replied. 'Yer know I'm always here for yer.'

Elsie nodded sadly, wincing in pain at the slightest movement. 'I know, Kit, yer and me have been friends for that long, I don't know how I'd have managed without yer half the time.'

'You'll never have to find out, Els,' Kitty whispered, gently squeezing her friend's hand. 'I'm going nowhere.'

There was the longest of pauses as Elsie's eyes bored straight into Kitty's, with an intensity she had never seen before.

'But I'm going somewhere, Kitty love,' Elsie croaked, her voice weakening by the second. 'And I'm going to need someone to keep an eye on this little one. Make sure he's not led astray by his uncle over there.'

Elsie gestured with her eyes towards Arthur, who was standing by the door, his arms folded and head hung low. A lump gathered in Kitty's throat.

'Don't talk rubbish, yer hear me, Elsie O'Connor?' Kitty growled. 'You're going to live and see your little boy grow up to be a fine young man. You're the best mother this lad could wish for. Don't yer dare give up on me now.'

A tear escaped the corner of Elsie's eye and slid down her face.

She struggled to open her mouth, the energy seeping from her as quickly as the blood gushing to the floor. 'Kitty, we both know me time's come,' she croaked. 'That's why I need yer to do what I can't. I want yer to look out for little Joe here, make sure he's well-loved and wants for nothing . . .'

Kitty gasped in surprise as she looked from Elsie to the baby, resting contentedly on his mother's chest. 'Joe? You're calling him Joe?'

'What else could I call him?' Elsie said, her breath now agonisingly shallow. 'I know you'll help me mam out with him when yer can, and love him as much as yer did your own Joe.'

Kitty stared down at the baby, snoozing peacefully against Elsie. Snuggled in a patchwork blanket Nora kept in the shelter, his little chest rose and fell in a way that showed he had no idea these were his last few precious moments with his mother.

'Yer know I will, Els,' Kitty promised, her voice shaky.

Still holding Elsie's hand, Kitty leaned over her friend's face and planted a gentle kiss on her forehead. Then she rested her own head next to Elsie's so they were cheek to cheek. Elsie's eyelids flickered and as Kitty locked eyes with her she felt the love flood between them. They had shared a lifetime together and Kitty knew the love that had always ebbed and flowed between them would continue to live on through baby Joe. She squeezed Elsie's fingers tightly and as she loosened her grip, Kitty realised Elsie's breathing was now coming in ragged wheezes, each lungful clearly more painful than the last.

'Let go now, sweetheart,' Kitty whispered. 'I'll love your Joe enough for the both of us, it's time for yer to go and find peace and happiness with mine.'

Elsie nodded softly and closed her eyes. 'Find your own happiness, Kitty,' she rasped. 'Don't waste time . . . promise me.'

With that Elsie's fingers loosened their grip around Kitty's and her chest sank like a stone as she drew her last breath. Sensing her friend could hold on no longer, Kitty kissed her gently once more, and as her lips grazed Elsie's flesh she felt the life drain from her.

'She's gone,' Kitty whispered, raising her face to meet Nora and Arthur's gaze, 'she's really gone.'

The next thing Kitty felt was a pair of strong arms around her. 'I know, Kitty,' Arthur said, bending down to whisper in her ear. 'She's at peace now.'

The feel of Arthur's warm arms around her after the night she had endured caused Kitty to give in to the tears she had been holding back all night. Burrowing into Arthur's chest, she wept like a baby, sure her heart was about to break into thousands of tiny pieces, while Arthur remained solid and strong.

She pulled away and looked up into his eyes and saw they were red-rimmed and raw, but he was determined to put a brave face on his feelings for his mother, Kitty and baby Joe.

Shooting him a watery smile, Kitty saw Nora was now clutching the baby to her bosom.

'He's perfect,' Kitty said as she wiped the tears from her eyes and went to stand next to Nora and stroke Joe's cheek with her forefinger.

'He's that all right. Ten tiny fingers and ten tiny toes. He's the spitting image of our Elsie,' Nora cooed softly.

She looked at Nora and saw the older woman looked exhausted. Like Kitty her face was covered in grime, only the rivers of tears she had shed over her only daughter revealed the pale grey skin beneath.

Looking at the child in Nora's arms, Kitty felt a rush of love. 'Can I hold him?'

'Of course, sweetheart,' Nora said quietly, gently handing him to Kitty.

As the baby gazed up at her, his eyes full of innocence, Kitty found herself making a silent promise to make sure Joe felt loved every single day of his life. Rocking him gently in her arms, she felt all the chaos and destruction that stood outside of the shelter disappear. It was just her, the baby and a lifetime full of hopes and dreams. It was only when she heard the sound of a low cough from the entrance and saw Peter that she returned to the present.

'I'm sorry to interrupt, but there are some firemen outside who are here to help,' he said gently.

'Thanks, Peter,' she replied, handing Joe to Arthur.

'Who's that?' he whispered, holding the baby like a born father.

'He's baby Joe's uncle,' she smiled as Arthur exchanged looks of confusion with his mother. 'And my brother,' she said quietly, recognising him as the family she never knew she had.

Chapter Twenty-One

Once the firemen arrived, the night became something of a blur, with Kitty only briefly aware of being led towards the nearest public shelter, together with Nora and Joe. In that moment she was grateful not to see Elsie's cold, lifeless body being carried away. Her friend had always been so vivacious and full of life. To see her like that would have tainted the memory Kitty had of the woman who she considered a sister in every way that mattered.

The only small comfort she could find in that moment was that Hetty and George were safe and well. Word had reached her that Joe's parents had been on the other side of the city when the bombs hit and taken refuge in one of the underground shelters.

Kitty had wanted to join Peter and Arthur, who were working with the teams of volunteers helping free those trapped in the wreckage. Yet the boys had insisted she had gone through enough for one night, and ordered her to rest. Arthur told her he would be grateful if she would sit with his mother and comfort her.

And so Kitty and Nora, cuddling baby Joe, had sat side by side, drinking tea in silence, each wrapped in their own grief. Kitty had become so lost in her own world, she was unaware of the comings and goings around her and the tears that streamed down her face like rivers went unnoticed. So did the actions of the kindly volunteers who refilled her teacup, and the hordes of people who had been bombed out of their homes that sought refuge. Kitty also failed to notice the way Nora fed baby Joe with some warm milk a volunteer found, clasped her cold hand through the night or helped her blot her tears with a spare hanky. In fact it was not until Nora suddenly squeezed her fingers that Kitty slowly came to and realised where she was.

'I just wanted to say I'm sorry, Kitty,' Nora said quietly. 'I'm sorry about Billy.'

'Whatever have yer got to be sorry for?' Kitty replied in astonishment.

'He's me cousin. He's always been a bad lot, ever since he were a nipper,' Nora said quietly. 'Born with bad blood, that one. I was so worried when I heard he'd taken a shine to yer, I wrote to warn yer.'

'I know,' Kitty nodded sadly. 'I never got your note. Peter reckons Billy would've had someone up the postroom intercepting me letters like.'

Nora gasped in horror. 'I should've known. Evil pours out of Billy Miles like water from a leaking tap, always has done. But that's why I wrote to your sergeant, Kitty. When I didn't hear from yer I was so worried you'd been taken in by his lies, I had to do summat and he promised to sort it.'

Kitty's eyes softened as she patted Nora's knee. 'This is the last thing yer should be worrying about at a time like this. It's all right now, and all any of us should be thinking about is little Joe.'

At the mention of her first grandchild, Nora's face crumpled. 'Oh, my precious girl. She didn't deserve this.'

'No she didn't,' Kitty said, suddenly feeling overcome with emotion. 'But Joe needs us all now, Nora. We have to be strong for his sake. We have to keep the memories of his mother alive.'

As they both turned their gaze towards Elsie's boy, still sleeping contentedly in his grandmother's arms, Kitty reached for one of his feet that was sticking out of the blanket and marvelled at the warmth of it as she tucked it carefully back under the covers. Life really did carry on, she thought as the siren signalling the all clear sounded. As she and Nora were ushered outside into the cold, dark morning air she saw Arthur walk towards her, his hair matted with dust. The sight of him gave Kitty a surge of joy and she rushed towards him, not caring what anyone thought, and clung to him as if her life depended on it.

'You're still here,' she gasped.

'That I am,' he replied, stepping back to give Kitty a reassuring smile. 'I'm made of strong stuff.'

'How did yer and Peter get on helping the survivors?'

Arthur shrugged, suddenly looking more vulnerable and helpless than Kitty had ever seen before. Quietly she led him to a corner away from prying eyes and managed to find a cup of tea which she pressed into his cold, blue hands.

'I thought I'd seen everything, Kitty,' he said wearily as they sat down on a mound of household bricks. 'But the shock on some of them people's faces. I swear half of them had aged overnight, they couldn't believe what had happened to their homes, to their city. '

'Is it as bad as it looked last night?' she asked.

Arthur sighed heavily. 'Worse. There were so many dead, so many who didn't survive. So many who were hurrying to shelters like the ones under Noel's, but they were killed in the blasts, and were lying in the street just covered in plaster and dust. It's heart-breaking, Kitty.'

Arthur clutched his cup, looking tired and defeated, and her heart went out to her friend. Squatting next to him, she rested her head against his shoulder.

'What about the city?' she asked hesitantly, though a quick glance at the fires still burning on the streets told her all she needed to know.

'Everything's gone, the entire city's virtually flattened,' Arthur replied, his face darkening. 'But the cathedral, dear God . . . our blessed St Michael's. There's barely anything left. Teams of men, including me dad who was nearby when the fire took hold, are still trying to put out the fires. But it's clear the Germans destroyed it along with everything else. In one night they took our precious city and killed it, and for what? Survivors are going back to see what's left, packing up what little they've got and going elsewhere. Folk are convinced Hitler's going to strike again tonight and nobody wants to be here for round two.'

At the sound of a building crashing to the ground behind them, Kitty and Arthur jumped and covered their faces as more dust blew their way.

'I wonder sometimes how we'll ever get through another day.' Kitty coughed, her eyes watering from the soot. 'There's been so much heartache and loss, it seems never-ending.'

'After tonight, I can't say as I'm filled with a lot of hope just at the moment,' Arthur said, his voice thick with emotion. 'I want to believe we can win this war, but . . .' He trailed off and Kitty said nothing, just waited and let him carry on when he was ready. 'I just can't believe our Elsie's gone, I feel responsible, I'm her big brother, I was supposed to look out for her. I let her down.'

'Don't yer dare!' Kitty admonished. 'Yer always did right by Elsie. How were yer to know the door of the shelter would hit her and cause all those injuries.'

Arthur hung his head in sorrow. 'When I was told I could have seventy-two hours' leave, I couldn't wait to get back and be with me family. But I could tell summat were up the moment I walked through the door. Elsie seemed to hang on that fella Mike's every word. I couldn't understand it, till I realised she was upset Charlie never wrote. I was going to take her out for a proper talk in the park before I went back, find out what was what like, but then all this happened.'

Kitty nodded, aware there was nothing she could say that would make the events of the last few hours even remotely bearable.

Arthur lifted his head and gazed at her, his eyes full of concern. 'Peter told me everything about Billy and Elsie, and how he came to be your half-brother. I tell yer, Kitty, if I ever get me hands on that Billy Miles I'll make him pay.'

'I know how yer feel, but Peter said the authorities had Billy now. That they've got evidence of all his wrongdoing,' Kitty said, her voice even. 'They'll throw the book at him.'

'I know, but he's created hell, Kitty. And for what? A couple of quid to line his own pockets. It's down to him our Elsie's gone to the grave thinking her husband wasn't bothered, and that little boy is going to grow up without his mam. The hangman's noose is too good for him.'

Kitty couldn't help feeling responsible herself. 'I'm sorry for all of this, Arthur, if I'd never met Billy, none of this would have happened.'

Arthur clasped her hand. 'Oh Kitty, yer mustn't think like that. Peter told me about Billy, how he set his sights on yer and told yer he was a widower and feigned his gammy leg. How me mam had written to him, so ashamed her own flesh and blood could behave like that.'

'I know,' she said, nodding sadly. 'This war's doing terrible things to folk. What sort of a world is baby Joe going to grow up in?'

'One that's full of love,' he said simply. 'We'll all be there for him, he'll want for nothing.'

Kitty smiled up at Arthur, his kind words soothing her very core. 'And while this war's raging ... how do we cope till it ends?'

Arthur fixed his eyes on Kitty, his expression gentle. 'Yer think about the nice things in life. For me it's your letters. They mean the world to me, Kitty.'

A feeling of warmth and contentment spread through Kitty for the first time that night. She had lost her best friend and had no idea if she would ever get over so much loss in one year, but it was important to remember all she still had. 'I know what yer mean, Arthur, whenever I get a letter off yer I feel happier and more alive. Like I don't have to explain everything, or worry about upsetting yer. Yer just know me and yer always have,' Kitty said, smiling.

'We've always known what to say to each other.' He grinned sheepishly, squeezing her hand gently once more. 'We've been through a lot together, and all this,' he said, gesturing to the buildings crashing down around them, 'it makes yer want to hang on to anything good in life.'

Kitty nodded in understanding, words were unnecessary. She stared straight ahead as the dawn light began to break and the full devastation of what Hitler had done to her beloved hometown became even more apparent. It had been annihilated, as Arthur had said. There was hardly anything left, the skyline changed forever.

'So a brother then, eh, Kitty?' Arthur said, breaking the silence, his voice gruff.

'I know,' she laughed. 'The night's been full of surprises.'

'He seems a decent enough fella,' Arthur replied. 'And genuinely sorry he made your life so difficult when yer first arrived under his wing. I read him the riot act for that, by the way, but I reckon he'll do right by yer now.'

'We'll see,' she said. 'I can't think about that now.'

'Tonight's got me thinking, Kitty,' Arthur said, his voice suddenly quiet. 'I've been wanting to tell yer for a while, but couldn't find the right words in me letters. If I've realised one thing tonight, it's that there's no such thing as a right time. Truth is, Kitty, I've fallen for yer. You're kind, you're special, you're strong, and I love yer and I think yer feel the same.'

Arthur's words took Kitty by surprise, each one causing happiness and pain in equal measure. Arthur was her friend, her rock, how could he possibly say these things? He was ruining everything. Joe was barely a year dead, how could he even think she had fallen for another man? There was only one explanation – he was overwrought and overtired. It was best if she set him straight.

'Come on now, Arthur, yer don't mean it,' she stuttered. 'You're tired and upset. And after the night you've had, it's hardly surprising. Don't say summat you'll come to regret later.'

'That's just it, Kitty,' Arthur said, his eyes filled with love. 'I'll regret it if I don't tell yer how I feel. I've known for a long time now, I'd do anything for yer. Don't tell me yer don't feel the same way.'

Wrenching her fingers from Arthur's grasp, Kitty got to her feet. 'How dare yer,' she snapped, eyes blazing with fury. 'Let me put yer right, Arthur Higginson. I lost my Joe just a few months back, the man I thought I was going to make old bones with. How can yer even think I'm ready to consider another man? I'm sorry, Arthur, you've got hold of the wrong end of the stick. I don't think about yer like that and I never will.'

Kitty stared at him in despair, watching Arthur's expression change from one of hope to desolation as he looked firmly at the floor.

'Kitty, I'm sorry,' Arthur said quietly, 'I didn't mean to upset yer. I should never have said anything.'

'No, yer shouldn't,' Kitty sniffed, 'you've ruined everything now.'

Turning on her heel, she ran from Arthur, back along the city's deserted streets. It was all such a mess, Kitty realised as she took in the devastation around her. A heady mix of chaos and horror at every turn. Like her life, Kitty thought bitterly. She felt as if she were putting out one fire after another until like her beloved city, her foundations would soon be destroyed. Passing the cathedral, Kitty gasped in horror as she saw how little remained. There were just a couple of the old walls still standing. With a start, Kitty wondered if either she or her hometown could survive another attack.

Staring in horror at the ruins of the medieval cathedral, she heard the sound of footsteps behind her. Whirling around she saw it was Peter. Like Arthur, his hair was matted with dust. He was covered in soot, his uniform was torn, but he was alive.

'Kitty!' he exclaimed, walking towards her. 'I wondered how I would ever find you.'

'I'm sorry, I didn't think,' she replied. 'I just had to get away and found meself here.'

Peter held her gently by the arm and steered her up the lane. 'An awful lot has happened in the space of a few hours,' he said quietly, as they passed several families searching for possessions where their homes had once stood. 'It's heart-breaking to see all of this.'

Kitty nodded, a knot of fear tightening in her stomach. In the harsh light of the new day she had no idea what lay in store for her future. Things had never looked so bleak for her or her beloved city. Arthur's revelation had turned her world upside down and now all she wanted was to get back to Northampton, to a life of rules, routine and work.

'Shall we try and see if one of our vehicles is still in one piece?' she asked, turning to Peter. 'Or do I need to go to the police?'

Peter looked puzzled. 'Why would you need to go to the police?'

'To give a statement. To make sure Billy Miles gets what he deserves,' she said bitterly, the events of last night beginning to hit home.

'No, Kitty,' Peter replied as they turned the corner and walked past what had once been Owen Owen. 'I've already spoken to the police who have Billy and John in a cell as we speak. You'll need to give a statement when we get back, explaining he coerced you and how, but that's it, it's over.'

Kitty stopped and whirled around to face Peter, her eyes wide in astonishment. 'Are yer sure?'

'Of course.' Peter nodded. 'I told them about Nora, about how I had seen him trick other soldiers into working for him and how you were just another pawn in his pathetic little game. You may be called upon to give evidence in court, but the police were very sympathetic when I told them what had happened. You'll have to see them when we get back to Northampton, but that's a formality. You can live your life without fear, Kitty.'

The knot of worry she had felt just moments earlier evaporated and was replaced with a sense of relief as she took in the possibility of some kind of future after all. All she had to do now was make sense of what lay ahead for her, Arthur, Charlie, Nora and Ron and of course baby Joe.

Peter interrupted her train of thought. 'I know you've had a terrible time, Kitty. You lost your best friend last night but if you'll have me, you have also gained a brother. I know I behaved badly when we met, but I've become very fond of you and would very much like to make it up to you, if you'll let me.'

Looking at Peter's features properly, she saw there was something familiar about his smile. With a jolt she realised that it was the mirror image of her mother's. The one she used to reserve for Kitty when she had been especially good.

'I'd like that,' she said simply, standing on tiptoe to kiss Peter on the cheek.

At the unexpected gesture, Peter wrapped his arms around Kitty and hugged her tightly. She had missed having a family, and in that moment, an embrace with her newly found brother after such a long and dreadful night felt like the best medicine.

As they broke apart and walked in silence they realised that all the roads were closed: no traffic could pass, aside from emergency vehicles. Although the Luftwaffe had stopped their bombing campaign hours earlier, there was still a great deal of work to be done. Hosepipes lay criss-crossed throughout the streets, putting out the burning fires, while teams of police officers and firemen lay blankets over those that had been killed. Elsewhere, staff from the council tried to salvage important documents from the building that had been virtually destroyed, while an underground shelter that had taken a direct hit and caused mass damage to a neighbouring primary school was being evacuated.

Kitty and Peter rolled up their sleeves and continued their efforts tirelessly and without complaint. For hours they helped free those trapped under the wreckage, and distributed blankets and hot tea to those in need.

The damage to the city was undeniable – it had been virtually razed to the ground. Yet despite so much devastation Kitty noticed there was a determined spirit among those who had remained. Everyone working together to do their bit, to show Hitler he wouldn't win, only served to remind Kitty that a city wasn't about buildings, or people. In fact, she realised as she looked around her at townsfolk all united, Coventry was still very much alive.

By mid-afternoon, the city was a little more organised and the roads had at last been declared open. Needing to return to the barracks, Kitty and Peter walked through the debris-strewn streets towards Kitty's truck, delighted to see it was still in one piece. Aside from a crack in the windscreen from what Kitty guessed had been flying rubble, the truck was in perfect order. As Peter climbed into the passenger seat, Kitty started the engine and was overjoyed when it burst into life straight away.

She navigated her way carefully through the city streets and was soon out onto the open country lanes. After so much destruction, Kitty felt a pang of relief to see green fields and trees that positively burst with vitality. Both Peter and Kitty were spent, and so exhausted they barely spoke until they reached the outskirts of Northampton, with Peter eventually breaking the silence.

'Did you manage to say goodbye to Arthur and Nora?' he asked.

At the mention of Arthur's name, Kitty felt tears prick her eyes. 'Yes, I spent a couple of hours with Nora in the shelter and briefly said goodbye to Arthur,' she replied.

'How do you think they'll cope without Elsie?' he asked carefully.

'They'll be devastated, as you'd expect. We all are,' Kitty said quietly. 'After Joe it doesn't seem real. But Nora and Arthur are strong, Arthur'll make sure he's there for his mother and baby Joe of course.'

Peter paused before he spoke again. 'You and Arthur seem close,' he said.

Kitty said nothing, just fixed her eyes on the road.

'Did you hear me, Kitty?' Peter tried again.

'Yes,' she sighed, as she changed gear and indicated. 'Yes, we are close – well, used to be at any rate.'

'Used to be?'

Kitty blinked back her tears of frustration. She really did not want to discuss Arthur after the night she had endured. 'Yes, used to be,' she said. 'Arthur is me pal, always will be, but lately, well, lately I think he's got hold of the wrong end of the stick.'

'And what stick would that be?' Peter asked.

Rolling her eyes heavenwards, she gritted her teeth as she turned into the barracks. 'Yer don't give up, do yer, sir?' she said sarcastically, hoping to make Peter angry so the subject would be closed.

Peter refused to waver. 'I only want to help,' he said evenly. 'I know losing your best friend is heart-breaking, but I think there's more to it than that.'

'I don't know what yer mean,' Kitty muttered angrily as she turned into the road.

'You do, Kitty. It's Arthur, isn't it? Something's happened?'

Wearily Kitty let her eyes flicker to the dashboard. She had reached breaking point, and Peter may well think he had her best interests at heart, but he barely knew her or Arthur and she clenched her jaw in anger.

'Yes summat's happened,' she blurted. 'That silly sod Arthur says he's gone and fallen in love with me. That he wants to be with me. Well, I've told him it's not on, that he can think again. I'm not interested. Joe's barely cold in his grave and I've his work to carry on. How can he think I'm ready for summat like that? I thought he had more sense.'

Peter said nothing, gazing out of the window for so long, Kitty wondered if she had offended him until he let out a deep sigh.

'If there's one thing I've learned in this life, Kitty, it's that happiness is hard to find. With a war on it's another thing that appears to have been rationed, though you'd be hard pressed to find any coupons for an ounce of it. So when you get a chance at happiness, you should seize it with both hands.'

They drove through the leafy parkland, Kitty thinking she might burst with anger. 'Yer surely don't think I ought to start courting Arthur?' she spluttered.

Peter shrugged. 'Why not? You obviously love each other.'

'I certainly do not,' Kitty protested as she pulled the truck into the motor garage and turned off the engine.

'Well for someone who's not bothered you have rather a funny way of showing it. I saw the way you and Arthur were looking at each other in the shelter, and don't tell me it was because Elsie had just given birth to baby Joe. There was more to it than that, and you know it.'

'I know no such thing,' Kitty replied brusquely. 'I was engaged to Joe. He was my world; he's the reason I'm here, because he wanted to stop Hitler. I'll never love anyone the way I love Joe.'

It was now Kitty let the tears that had been building over the last few hours fall. She sobbed, great gut-wrenching sobs for all that she had lost, for her parents, for the chance to grow up with a sibling, for Joe and finally for her beloved Elsie. Kitty had never been someone who felt sorry for herself, but in that moment she couldn't help it and she wallowed in despair. Finally she felt a pair of large, cool hands clasp hers, and as Peter squeezed her fingers gently, she felt strangely comforted.

'Come on, Kitty. I know you've dealt with more than your fair share these last few months, but it's time for you to be honest with yourself and face facts. Joe has gone, he's not coming back, not for all the tea in China. It's not a crime to fall in love again, and surely your Joe wouldn't want you to be alone and unhappy for the rest of your life, would he?'

'No,' Kitty sobbed. 'No, it would be the last thing he'd want. Before he left he told me if summat ever happened to him then I was to find someone else, that I shouldn't mourn him forever. But it seems so wrong.'

Peter sighed, and scratched his head thoughtfully. 'The only thing that could be wrong is if you truly love Arthur – as I believe you do – and do nothing about it. Love is hard to find, trust me. I let a girl slip through my fingers when I was your age because I had some misguided sense of honour. I thought she deserved better than someone like me, who had grown up in care homes, and I told her I wasn't interested.'

'What happened?' Kitty asked tearfully. The November wind rattling through the car windows cooled her hot cheeks.

'She left me,' Peter said, staring straight ahead. 'I kept telling her to go and one day she listened to me and went. It was one of the stupidest things I've ever done and there isn't a day that goes by where I don't regret it. We never know when love will strike, Kitty. Don't turn your back on it because you think you're being disloyal to Joe, or because you're afraid.'

Resting her forehead on the steering wheel, Kitty tried to gather her thoughts. She had been too harsh with Arthur, she could see that now. He was clearly in shock and like her, had suffered a great loss. Perhaps Arthur had been confused when he confessed his feelings, maybe it had been the grief talking, but even if he had been serious, she ought to have been more sympathetic. She knew that it wasn't Arthur who had ruined everything, it was her.

'It's all too late anyway,' she said quietly, lifting her head from the steering wheel. 'Arthur won't want to hear from me now. I hurt him too badly.'

'We always destroy the ones we care most about,' Peter said sadly, 'but you can put things right. Tell him that you were upset. He'll understand.'

'D'yer think?'

'I know.' Peter smiled. 'But Kitty, do understand that even if you admit your feelings for Arthur nobody would expect you to walk down the aisle next week. You can take things slowly.'

She said nothing. Instead she stared straight ahead at the parkland and the grey clouds beyond. All her life she had been searching for a happy ending and there were times when she thought she had almost found it. But something she did know was that there was no possibility of a happy ending without Arthur in her world.

Chapter Twenty-Two

Three weeks after that fateful night in Coventry, Kitty found herself packing up her belongings and folding everything neatly into her kitbag. Reaching for Joe's watch in the drawer beside her bed, she gave the face a gentle polish and stored it in her bag. With a last look around and a quick check under the bed to make sure nothing had been missed, she was finally ready.

'You done?' Di asked, lolling on her bed waiting for Kitty to finish getting herself together.

'I think so,' she replied, tugging her cap firmly over her hair and picking up her bag.

'Come on then. You've a few minutes before the train just yet, but you'll want a seat all the way down to Bicester.'

Kitty smiled. As ever, Di was right, the journey to Oxfordshire would be a long one and the chance to sit down would be very welcome.

She followed Di across the quad, wrapping her greatcoat around her as the rain pelted down, and hurried through the parkland down to the garage. Inside, she saw Peter was waiting for them.

'Hello, sir,' Di said, saluting her superior officer as always.

'At ease, Volunteer Mills,' Peter laughed. 'I'm not here officially, I'm here to say goodbye to my sister.'

'Oh thank Christ for that,' Di sighed, dumping Kitty's bag on the ground and shoving her hands in her pocket. 'It's far too wet and miserable to 'ave you march me off to fix a leaking valve or summat.'

Peter's eyes twinkled with merriment at Di's cheek. 'I'll pretend I didn't hear that, Mills,' he chuckled.

Kitty glanced across at her brother and friend and couldn't help smiling at them. Since she and Peter had returned from Coventry after that fateful night, she had noticed how well Di and her brother were getting on. They both seemed to light up in one other's company and although she would never have seen it coming, now she couldn't help think they were quite a good match. Peter was serious and steady, yet had a wicked sense of humour as she had recently discovered. Di had a keen sense of adventure and a thirst for life. Kitty found she couldn't help but hope for a happy ending for each of them and chuckled to herself. If she was planning on playing Cupid, then it was perhaps a good job she was being posted elsewhere.

'Well yer didn't have to do that, but it's very nice that yer did,' Kitty smiled, craning her neck to kiss her brother on the cheek.

'Don't be silly,' he replied softly. 'I'll miss you.'

'Me 'n'all,' she nodded.

In fact, Kitty was going to miss lots of things about her life here in Northampton. She had enjoyed it far more than she had anticipated, but too much had happened and the chance of a fresh start in new barracks would be a welcome one. With Billy safely behind bars, and likely to stay there for quite some time, Kitty had the opportunity to find her feet again, and for that she was grateful.

Everything had gone just as Peter had promised, and when they returned to the barracks, the police were already waiting for her. Nervously, Kitty had told them exactly what had happened, sure they would be ready to arrest her when they found out what she had done. But the inspector who visited had been surprisingly sympathetic and Kitty had been let off with a warning about being too trusting. She also had to promise that when the case came to trial she would give evidence if necessary, but that Billy would more than likely hang for his crimes. As well as Kitty, they had managed to track down a string of others the butcher had blackmailed in the past and with the doctor who had falsified Billy's exemption certificate also under arrest, the police had an iron-clad case.

It had been the news Kitty longed for, and happiness had flooded through her, until Peter told her he was transferring her. Kitty was devastated to learn she was being posted to Oxfordshire to work as a staff driver. They had only just got to know each other, she protested, they were the only family the other had left. How could they build a relationship if they were miles apart?

But as Peter pointed out, now everyone knew they were brother and sister he could easily be accused of favouritism and he felt that was inappropriate. They would have to survive with letters, and the occasional visit, like every other brother and sister away serving their country.

Kitty had disliked his answer, but knew he was right and so she had packed up her belongings without question and focused on a new start. It was more than most of the people in her beloved home town would have the chance to do, and so for their sake as much as her own she was determined to make the most of it.

Although the Luftwaffe hadn't returned the following night as many feared, the Germans managed to drop more than a hundred tons of bombs on Coventry that night, killing 568 people and injuring well over a thousand. Tragically, so many had been killed that the city elected to hold public mass burials, something that had never been done before.

Many had been shocked by such a suggestion but quickly realised that with so many dead, it was the easiest way to honour their loved ones. And so Elsie had been laid to rest at the first of the burials, along with the 172 who were among the first to lose their lives.

She had been buried just under a week after the raid, and although Kitty had not been granted compassionate leave to attend the burial, she had silently offered a prayer when she knew her best friend would be committed to the ground. Shortly afterwards, Nora had written to Kitty and told her that it had been a beautiful ceremony at the London Road Cemetery with over 1,000 mourners and that Elsie would have been proud. Charlie had made it home for the funeral. Nora, with typical understatement, admitted it had been bittersweet watching her son-in-law meet his baby boy for the first time just as he said goodbye to his wife.

Kitty could still scarcely believe it had happened at all, and knew she would never forget how much she had lost that night. She had to find some way of moving forwards. Elsie of all people would want to see an end to this dreadful war, not just for her sake, but for the sake of her little boy, her husband and their future as father and son. It was the thought of baby Joe that had kept Kitty going. She was determined to do right by him and win him back the freedom Hitler was so keen to take away.

Swinging her kitbag into the back, she climbed into the passenger seat as Di started the engine and the Humber roared into life.

'I'll write to you soon.' Peter smiled, leaning into the window to say goodbye.

'I'll hold yer to that,' she grinned.

As Di pressed her foot on the accelerator and drove the car smoothly away, Kitty turned to wave goodbye out of the rear window until Peter had disappeared out of sight.

'You all right?' Di asked as she indicated left and turned out of the barracks.

Kitty nodded. 'I think so. I can't believe I'm saying goodbye again after I just found him. Come to that, I can't believe I'm saying goodbye to yer either, Di. I'll miss yer.'

'You daft apeth,' Di smiled. 'I'm down that way all the time making deliveries, you'll still see plenty of me, don't you worry about that.'

At this news Kitty brightened considerably. She knew Di travelled the country but had no idea Bicester was one of her friend's regular haunts.

'Well why didn't yer tell me that before?' Kitty scolded. 'If

I'd realised yer were always down that neck of the woods, I wouldn't have wasted me last good hankie sobbing into it over yer and Peter, would I?'

Di turned her gaze from the road and looked at Kitty affectionately before she answered. 'Don't give me that old flannel, Kitty Williams,' she said. 'You weren't wasting tears over me or Peter come to that. It's time you realised you can talk to me about anything. You should've spoken to me about Billy and told me what 'e was really up to. You know I'd 'ave 'elped any way I could.'

Feeling guilty, Kitty chewed her thumbnail. Di had been full of support and concern when she heard what Kitty had been through and made her promise to never again keep secrets from her.

'I know,' she said quietly. 'Ta, Di.'

Di shrugged. 'So are you ready to admit you're really upset about summat or someone else?'

'I dunno what yer mean,' Kitty said, her cheeks going crimson with embarrassment.

'Yes you do. You 'eard from Arthur at all?'

The windscreen wipers squeaked against the glass as the rain fell, and Kitty felt a stab of pain at the mention of his name. Since Arthur had confessed his feelings he had kept his distance, and strangely enough Nora had kept his name out of her letters as well. She dreaded to think what Arthur would have told his mother, and not for the first time found herself wishing she had dealt with the situation differently.

'You've got to stop tearing shreds off yourself over what 'appened, Kitty,' Di said, reading her mind. 'You written to 'im?'

Shaking her head, Kitty stared out of the window. 'I know Arthur. I know he wouldn't want to hear from me just yet.'

'I think you're wrong,' Di said as she manoeuvred the car through the busy streets of the town centre. 'Just tell 'im what you told me. That you're sorry, and don't want to lose 'is friendship.'

Kitty said nothing, not trusting herself to speak. Instead she fixed her gaze on the road ahead. She had thought long and hard about what Peter had said to her in the car when they arrived back at Northampton and something about it had troubled her. A couple of days later, while collecting a general from the station, Kitty had realised her brother was right: her feelings for Arthur did run deeper than friendship. The thought had rattled her until she understood that did not mean she had to do anything about it. She could never betray Joe like that, despite what he'd wanted for her, but at the same time, a piece of her heart now belonged to Arthur, of that she was sure. She missed his letters and the very action of writing to him. Kitty would do anything to put things right between them, to renew their friendship, but it was all still too raw. Perhaps at Christmas when she was home on leave there would be the opportunity to sort everything out and carry on just as they always had.

'Just don't leave things too long,' Di said, as she pulled the car into the station. 'You know 'ow folk can get hold of the wrong idea. Best to clear the air sooner rather than later.'

Kitty reached behind her for the kitbag containing all her worldly goods and climbed out of the car before hugging Di goodbye.

'See you soon, love,' Di said, wrapping her arms tightly around her.

'Yer better.' Kitty smiled as she gave her friend a gentle squeeze and reluctantly pulled away.

Lifting her hand to give Di a wave, Kitty walked down the path towards the station, ready to start the next chapter of her life, when she heard Di shout.

'Oh wait a minute, Kit, I forgot to give you summat.'

Turning around, she saw Di hurry towards her. 'I forgot to tell you with all the excitement this morning, but I picked up your mail earlier on when I got me own. Thought you might need these, if nothing else it's a bit of light entertainment on the train.'

Kitty took the two envelopes from Di's outstretched hand and glanced at the handwriting. The first she recognised as being from Nora and she felt a warm glow at the thought of Elsie's mother keeping her company as she began her new life.

Turning the second envelope, Kitty thought her heart would explode out of her chest as she took in the gentle slope of the handwriting outlining her name. It had been a while since she had seen it, but there was no mistake, this was a letter from Arthur.

Clutching the mail to her chest, she hugged Di gratefully before continuing her walk towards the station. She already had a rail warrant for her journey so there was no need to join the queuing hordes for a ticket. She found herself a window seat on board, then examined each envelope, wondering which one to read first. Steeling herself to read Arthur's she decided to open Nora's first. She needed the support and strength of the older woman.

5 December 1940

Dear Kitty,

I just wanted to write you a few lines and let you know we're all doing well. Baby Joe is thriving despite his entrance into the world and settling well. Charlie's here with us and all for a while and it does my heart good to see the two of them bonding in a way that'd make our Elsie proud. Mike is long gone, and I for one am glad to see the back of him. If I ever lay eyes on that lad again I'll string him up myself for what he did to our Elsie.

Anyway, I won't write much, I know you're busy but we'll see you at Christmas and are looking forward to it. No doubt it'll be a sad celebration of sorts but as baby Joe reminds me every day, we've a lot to be thankful for. Ron especially has promised to do us proud with his crop of potatoes he's grown especially for a winter harvest and given the time he's been up the allotment since Elsie's passing, I don't doubt that's true.

Lots of love,
Nora xx

Kitty smiled at the few lines on the paper and felt comforted to know Elsie's boy was doing so well. After everything that had happened, she wanted that little boy to never know the pain and devastation of what it was like to lose someone. Finally she could stand the suspense no longer and ripped into Arthur's note.

30 November 1940

Dearest Kitty,

Since I last saw you I've written to you every day, but never had the courage to send any of the letters. I kept reading and rereading what I'd written and none of them did justice to how I felt.

That said, I knew I had to get something to you, Kitty, that although I was trying to find the right words, that didn't matter. What really mattered was you knowing how sorry I was about what happened that day. You were right to walk away from me, what I said was very wrong and I only hope you can find it in your heart to forgive me.

If anyone knows how much you loved Joe it's me. The two of you were soulmates from the beginning, anyone could see that. What happened to him was a tragedy. I wish I could take back what I said to you, it was foolish and for that I'm sorry. The last thing I want to do is jeopardise our friendship, you mean far too much to me for that. The only thing I will say is that I did mean what I said. It wasn't just something that came out if thin air, or something I dreamed up because of what had just happened to our Elsie.

The truth is, Kitty, I fell for you a long time ago. I've loved you since we were nippers, long before you and Joe started courting. I've loved you that long our Elsie used to tease me rotten about how I followed you around like a puppy dog. Course, I always denied it but my feelings for you are the reason I've never found anyone else. I always thought you were the girl for me, even though you'd always been Joe's girl.

*Although I knew you never felt the same way about
me, I've always felt we were friends, and that has meant
the world. I've missed your letters these last few weeks,
especially after losing our Elsie like that. I've thought of you
every day, wondering how you're coping and to be honest I'd
give anything to go back to how things were before.*

*I'm so sorry for upsetting you, Kitty. I've kept my feelings
to myself for years and all I can say in my own clumsy way
is that I think the way Elsie died, and what with baby Joe
coming into the world, well I think it caught me off guard. I
should never have said anything, I have always known how
much you loved Joe and still do. I didn't mean to disrespect
his memory by telling you how I felt and implying you felt
the same.*

*I saw something that wasn't there, so I'm begging you, can
we please forget about what I said? I can't and don't want
to risk losing you as my pal and I'll do anything if you'll just
forgive me.*

Yours affectionately,
Arthur

Kitty scanned the letter once more, smiling at her friend's complete and utter honesty. How she had missed the warmth and
love that radiated from his letters. As the train rattled along the
track and through the countryside, Kitty hugged the letter to her
chest. Arthur had managed to say everything she needed to hear,
just as he always did.

Emotion stirred and she knew without question that of course
she could forgive him. Sliding the letter back into the envelope,
she resolved to write to Arthur as soon as she could.

Chapter Twenty-Three

It did not take long for Kitty to discover life in Bicester's barracks was much the same as it had been in Northampton. There was still the same early morning alarm at 6.30 a.m. precisely, still the same square bashing, albeit in a slightly larger quad, and still the same comforting cups of tea to be found in the mess. Although with Christmas around the corner, the barracks looked cheerier than usual. Some of the girls had hung paper chains over the doorways, and a small Christmas tree had even been found and placed in the corner of the mess to mark the time of year.

Work as a staff driver was just the same as it had been in Northampton, too, with Kitty largely ferrying officials to and from the station and of course fixing the odd mechanical failure in true spark girl tradition.

Even the recruits were similar, Kitty discovered. She met a girl named Jean who reminded her of Peggy and another named Clara who had more in common with Mary than just looks. Sadly, there was no Di, but just as her old friend had promised, they had seen plenty of one another as Di had been down to the Oxfordshire barracks twice already in the fortnight Kitty had been stationed in the town.

The only real change was the fact Kitty was no longer staying in the barracks themselves. Instead she had been billeted to stay with the local GP, Doctor Samuels, his wife and their two daughters, May and Chloe. Kitty had been given the attic room and each morning before Mrs Samuels served breakfast Kitty would look out over the rolling Oxfordshire hills admiring the view. The comfortable bed and soft sheets felt like heaven, she had thought on her first night and with a start wondered if this was how Mike, the Higginsons' lodger, had felt when he had been posted with them.

Just the thought of him sent a shiver down her spine and she was glad that the day after the raids in Coventry he had been ordered to a new posting. Kitty had no idea where he had gone and no intention of finding out either. She was just grateful that he, along with Billy, was out of the Higginsons' lives for good.

Peter had been very good about keeping her informed and written to her only last week to tell her a trial date had been set for the new year. It was almost certain she would need to give evidence. Kitty was delighted and practically champing at the bit to tell everyone just what Billy Miles was really like. Since learning of his arrest, she had come to despise him more and more. Not just for what he had done to Nora, and the web of lies and blackmail he had constructed just to get her to work for him, but because during this dreadful war, where it was important for everyone to pull together, he had chosen to make an easy penny and feather his own nest.

Just thinking of him made her blood boil, and so she did what she always did when she was anxious and stroked the face of Joe's watch that rested in her pocket. The very action of it calmed her, as she hoped it had done him when he had faced trouble.

All in all, Kitty thought, it was turning out to be an enjoyable posting. Peter had been right, the chance to put some distance between them as well as the chance of a fresh start had worked out well and she had appreciated getting to know her new brother through letters as they talked about their lives and their hopes for the future.

With so much misery and devastation, it was important to look forwards not back, Kitty realised. A fact that had been spelled out to her by Hetty, of all people, who had written to Kitty shortly after her move to Bicester.

Kitty had read and reread that letter so many times, she knew it off by heart, ready to recall whenever she needed an ounce of common sense drummed into her.

14th December 1940

Dear Kitty,

I'm sorry it's taken me such a long time to write. I've been meaning to get in touch with you for a while now, but the truth is every time I've put pen to paper, our Joe's face has come into my mind, and the pain of losing him hits me so sharply, I have to put my pad away.

But the time has come for me to be brave now Kitty, and I hope that's something you're doing too. I saw Nora in the town the other week. We had a nice cuppa and talked about how we'd lost our precious children. It's a tragedy that never gets any easier to bear, Kit, but we're doing our best to move forward. I told her George had planted a little cherry tree in the garden in the summer to honour our Joe. Nora thought that was a lovely idea, and wants to do something similar in the spring for Elsie. I told her I would help any way I could to honour the girl that thought to name her baby in memory of my son. Oh Kitty, none of us should have to endure so much loss, but facts are facts, Joe and Elsie have gone and we're still here, living, breathing and carrying on. Out of respect to them it seems only right to make the most of the time we have left.

I hope you won't think I'm speaking out of turn, but I want you to know you don't have to give up on your life just because Joe has gone. No amount of suffering will bring him back. I know you're hard at work in the Army, serving your country and your king, and I'm as proud of you as if I were your own mother. But Kitty, hear me when I tell you, don't forget to live life for yourself. Find happiness whenever and wherever you can because there's no sense in you living with one foot in the grave. So for me, for Joe, but mostly for yourself, make sure you do some living while you can.

Yours with love,
Hetty

The letter had surprised and shocked Kitty at first, but as she read and reread the note she could see the wisdom in Hetty's words. Kitty knew she was living a sort of half-life, too afraid and even guilty to do anything but work. There was no sense in it and she resolved in the New Year to try and find just a little fun, like her life-affirming friends Di and Mary. But for now, with a precious couple of days at home in time for Christmas, all she could think about was the chance to be with the Higginsons and rejoice at the little they had left.

Yet, walking through Coventry's streets, it was hard to retain her feelings of joy, as understandably there was very little Christmas cheer to be found in the city, despite the fact it was Christmas Eve. The salvation work was continuing in earnest as teams of people cleared wreckage, patched up houses and sold bread and cakes on makeshift stalls as there were barely any surviving shops.

In fact, it had taken several days for running water and electricity to be restored to the city, but the townsfolk had soldiered on and looked after their own. The homeless, of whom there were many, found temporary accommodation in the public underground shelters, while mobile catering vans descended on the city, distributing food and water to those in need. Elsewhere, knitters across the country had sent warm clothes by the thousand, and incredibly, news of Coventry's plight had even reached America with many posting warm shirts and goodies to help those with nothing left. But it had been the visit of the King and Queen, the Saturday following the raid that had really lifted the city's spirits. When pictures emerged of the royal couple walking through the cathedral's wreckage, the people of the city felt royalty was standing in their shoes, walking the same path as them.

Together, we would win this fight against the Germans, and a few bombs would never defeat the British spirit, Kitty thought.

It wasn't the city she remembered, she realised as she reached the Higginsons' front door, which she saw had been repaired with offcuts of wood. But the people, filled with courage and fire, were just the same. Hesitantly she knocked, feeling a stab of nervousness at seeing Arthur. Although they had exchanged several letters, this was the first time they would lay eyes on each other since that night.

The door swung open and Kitty gasped in surprise as she saw a tall, thin man with dark hair and big blue eyes. Clutching a baby with a smile a mile wide, Kitty wanted to cover them both in kisses.

'Charlie!' she squealed in delight, dropping her kitbag to the floor and kissing first baby Joe's cheek and then Charlie's.

'Hello, Kit.' He smiled. 'Come on in, tea's brewing.'

'I timed that well.'

As she followed him through the tiny passageway, Kitty marvelled at how homely Nora had managed to make the house again in just a few weeks. Despite the bomb damage, Nora had scrubbed, cleaned and repaired most of the furniture and bric-a-brac, to such a degree you would be hard pressed to know anything had happened at all. Incredibly all of Kitty's belongings had arrived, including the precious engagement ring she had been given by Joe.

Entering the kitchen, Kitty felt a surge of joy as she took in the familiar surroundings and saw with delight Nora had even found time to decorate a small Christmas tree which stood in the corner next to the range. Kitty had wondered whether it would still be appropriate for her to spend Christmas with the Higginsons after everything that had happened with Arthur, but Nora had refused to take no for an answer and insisted that she was family and it was only right she stayed with them.

'Kitty, love, you're here!' Nora smiled as Kitty set her bag down in the corner. 'Sit yer down, yer must be exhausted after that journey. How did yer manage? The trams are still out, yer know.'

Pulling out a chair and sinking into it, she smiled up at Nora as a cup of tea was placed on the gingham oilcloth before her.

'I'm fine, ta, Nora, I got a lift with one of the drivers who was passing this way,' she replied, sipping her tea gratefully. 'How are yer all?'

'We're fine.' Nora beamed as she took a seat next to Charlie and cooed adoringly at baby Joe, who was tightly swaddled in a muslin cloth in his father's arms. 'This little one's thriving, especially now his daddy's home.'

Kitty gazed at Joe: she couldn't believe how much he had grown in just a few weeks.

'He looks more like his mother with every passing day,' Charlie said adoringly, stroking his son's cheek. 'But he's blooming.'

'How long are yer back for?' Kitty asked as she took another sip of tea and removed her hat.

'I'm on compassionate leave so I'll be going back in the New Year. I've been here since the funeral,' he said.

At the mention of Elsie's burial, Kitty felt a lump form in her throat. Since arriving at the house, she had half expected Elsie to burst through the door full of life, demanding to know exactly what Kitty had been up to. With a jolt, she realised that was something that would never happen again, and a stab of pain pierced her heart. Turning to look at baby Joe and Charlie, she couldn't miss the look of love across his face, and felt a stab of hope that everything would be all right.

He may have lost Elsie, but at least Charlie would always be linked to his wife through their son, this symbol of hope, and living proof that out of the very worst of times, something good could come. How she would have loved to have had a link like that to Joe, Kitty thought, but there was nothing living to remind her of the man she had adored with all her heart. All she had was his precious watch and a lifetime's worth of memories to fill the void his death had left.

Looking again at Charlie as he gently kissed his son's forehead, Kitty understood just how fleeting happiness could be. Peter was right, life was short and if you were lucky enough to find the chance of joy, no matter how small, surely you should take it.

'You're looking well, Charlie,' she said and meant it. Her friend may have lost the love of his life, but the support of his family seemed to have given him strength.

Lifting his head from gazing at baby Joe, Charlie smiled. 'Yer have to carry on, don't yer?'

'That yer do.' Kitty smiled, an understanding forming between them, knowing they shared each other's pain. 'There's no other choice.'

Charlie's face darkened. 'No, there is no other choice, but I feel haunted, Kit. I'm haunted by the fact that it turned out Mike stole my letters. That Elsie may never have known how much I worshipped her. She was my world, and thanks to that man, she may have gone to her grave thinking I didn't love her.'

'Nonsense,' Kitty said firmly. 'She loved yer from the moment she laid eyes on yer. That never changed.'

'Even so, when I think of what Mike did, and Billy come to that,' Charlie continued, shaking his head sadly. 'I knew Mike was a wrong 'un. I'd never met him before we spent that weekend on leave together, but I knew the minute I saw him he was not to be trusted. He was poison.'

Kitty nodded, suddenly understanding why Charlie had looked so unhappy when she had last seen him. It had been because he saw Mike and smelled a rat, Kitty realised. If only she had done the same. But Kitty knew better than anyone there was no sense or pleasure to be found in looking back.

'What counts now is the future, Charlie,' she said gently. 'Don't torture yourself any more than yer have already. You've a beautiful baby boy, cherish him the way Elsie would want yer to.'

'It's all I want,' he replied, his voice thick with sorrow.

'Then concentrate on that.' She smiled, taking a sip of her tea.

As Kitty set her cup down, the kitchen door opened and in walked Ron, followed by Arthur, larger than life in his Navy uniform.

'Found this one loitering on the step,' Ron announced cheerily, dumping a bunch of muddy carrots and potatoes fresh from his allotment on the kitchen table. 'Kitty love, I'm so pleased to see yer. Are yer here for long?'

'Just till tomorrow night,' she replied as Ron squeezed her shoulder. 'I've only forty-eight hours' leave.'

'Me too,' Arthur said gently, shooting Kitty a shy smile as he stooped down to kiss baby Joe on the cheek.

Nora stood up and clapped her hands together. 'Well it's a pleasure to have yer all here for Christmas. I know our Elsie's gone from our table, but the only comfort I can take is that at least this rotten war makes yer grateful for who's still with us, doesn't it?'

Kitty glanced at Arthur from under her lashes, and felt a burst of emotion as she realised he was studying her intently. 'Yes,' she nodded. 'It does.'

'Well, I dunno about the rest of yer, but I've things to do,' Nora said, taking the baby from Charlie's arms. 'I need to put this little one down and then I need to get a start on tea.'

'And if yer don't mind, I might get me head down.' Charlie smiled, getting up from the table. 'Our Joe had me up all night and I'm exhausted.'

'Didn't realise yer were getting up with the baby, Charlie,' Arthur said admiringly, patting his brother-in-law on the back. 'Good on yer.'

Charlie shrugged good-naturedly. 'I couldn't let Nora do all the work, she'll be doing more than enough when I'm back on duty. Besides, your sister would no doubt give me rock all if I let your mam do the lot.'

Kitty chuckled. 'You're not wrong there, she was always very forthright was our Elsie.'

'She was,' Charlie said sadly.

As he walked out of the room, Kitty suddenly felt so very tired. Glancing across at Arthur, who was sipping his tea, she remembered Elsie's last words to her, how she had wanted her to promise she would find a happy future. And then there was Hetty, she too wanted Kitty to find some sort of happiness for herself. It was time, Kitty realised. She had the chance to make something of her life. For Elsie, for Joe, for her parents, for Hetty, George, as well as for herself, she would do this.

'D'yer fancy a stroll around the town? See what's what,' Kitty asked.

Arthur's head shot up in surprise. 'Yes, all right,' he agreed.

Together they rose from their chairs and walked out of the house and down the path. Since Kitty had arrived in Talbot Street light snow had begun to fall and she clutched the collar of her jacket to keep out the cold. Rounding the corner, they walked past the rubble of what had once been the bakery and Kitty suddenly felt tongue-tied. Nervously she glanced at Arthur and wondered if he felt as awkward as she did. They continued to walk in silence until they neared the site of the cathedral. The wreckage took Kitty's breath away. She knew there were plans to rebuild, but in this strange half-light, the ruined walls, with a hint of the hauntingly beautiful stained glass that had once risen so gloriously over the city, seemed even more damaged; a horrifying reminder of all Coventry had suffered.

'I didn't think it would hurt this much,' she gasped.

'Being back, yer mean?' Arthur asked gently.

'Being back, everything with us, losing Joe and Elsie,' Kitty replied despairingly.

Arthur fixed his eyes on Kitty and glanced at her warily. 'Us?'

'Yes, us, Arthur. Yer were right before that night, yer know, when yer said yer didn't think yer were the only one who had feelings like,' she wailed, closing her eyes and feeling butterflies flap their wings wildly in her stomach.

As Kitty opened her eyes she saw Arthur's gaze had turned from one of fear to shock and hope.

'Oh, Kitty, love,' he replied gently, taking a step towards her and clasping her hands in his. 'I never dared hope yer might feel the same after yer walked away from me like that. I thought I'd got it all wrong.'

Kitty nodded furiously. 'I thought yer had got it wrong, no I *knew*, but I *wanted* yer to have got it wrong. I didn't want to admit what I felt for yer. It felt so wrong after Joe. I still love him.'

Arthur raised one of Kitty's hands and gently brushed it against his lips. 'I've known yer almost all your life, Kitty Williams. I know yer still love Joe, and yer always will. You've so much love in your heart it's one of the many, many things I have always loved about yer.'

At the kindness of Arthur's words, Kitty felt the tears start to flow. She had finally found the courage to admit her real feelings for her best friend's brother, but was still terrified at what was to come.

'Let me be clear, Kit,' Arthur continued urgently, 'I don't want to replace Joe, I can only hope that one day yer might find room in your heart for me too. But I can wait. You've been through so much already, I only want yer to feel happiness when yer think of me, I don't want to add to your troubles.'

'You'd really wait for me?' Kitty spluttered. 'But why? Yer could have your pick of the girls, Arthur. I'm scared I'll never be ready, that I'll let yer down.'

Arthur let go of Kitty's hands and wrapped his arms around her, enveloping her in a hug. At the feel of his bodyweight against her, Kitty inhaled the scent of him and knew in the moment she was right where she needed to be.

'Yer could never let me down, Kit, and I don't want anyone else but yer, I never have,' he whispered in her ear. 'Kitty, I've never wanted yer to be anything or anyone else but yourself and if you'll only let me, I'll give yer the world. But I'm a patient man, and if I've hope, I can wait for an eternity. Just to know that yer feel the same way as I do, well, it's like Christmas.'

Despite the tears that had started to fall, Kitty laughed at the statement. 'I can't promise yer anything, Arthur, but I want to try, I want to give yer all of me heart, I just need a little time.'

'Then that's what we'll do, take our time.' Arthur smiled.

'I'd like that,' she whispered, slipping her arm through his as they faced the cathedral. 'Perhaps we can start with a trip to the pictures when we're next back on leave together. I hear *Gone with the Wind* is very popular.'

Arthur chuckled. 'I'm no Rhett Butler, Kitty, but to quote Scarlett O'Hara, I can assure yer tomorrow is another day.'

Kitty smiled tenderly into his eyes, and as Arthur pulled her into his arms Kitty caught the familiar scent of Lifebuoy soap and lemons. She shivered in delight; it was the smell of safety, peace and love. Quite simply, it was Arthur, and suddenly, she felt something unlock deep within her. As Arthur leaned down and gently brushed her lips with his, Kitty returned his kiss with a longing she didn't know she possessed. Her heart was soaring, her senses alive, and she knew she was exactly where she was meant to be.

'Tomorrow is another day,' she smiled as they parted, her eyes shining with hope, 'and I know you'll be a part of it, Arthur.'

'There's nothing I want more,' Arthur murmured, stroking her cheek with his forefinger.

Out of the corner of her eye Kitty could see the cathedral looming large above them as the darkness fell. Like Joe, the cathedral had always been such a constant presence in Kitty's life. She remembered attending services with her mother on a Sunday and the odd wedding and christening as an adult. It had always been such a grand and beautiful place, but the one thing she had always felt inside was a sense of peace. Looking at it now, a shell of its former self, Kitty saw it still possessed a stirring sense of beauty. Feeling the warmth of Arthur standing beside her she realised that although the Jerries had done their best to devastate the city she loved, they had been unable to destroy the one thing the cathedral had always given her and the rest of Coventry – hope. Like the cathedral, she too had hope, she would be reborn, and she would emerge stronger. Tomorrow really was another day, and it was Kitty's for the taking.

The End